Amanda Cinelli was born into a large Irish-Italian family and raised in the leafy green suburbs of County Dublin, Ireland. After dabbling in a few different careers, she finally found her calling as an author after winning an online writing competition with her first finished novel. With three small daughters at home, she usually spends her days doing school runs, changing nappies and writing romance. She still considers herself unbelievably lucky to be able to call it her day job.

Emmy Grayson wrote her first book at the age of seven, about a spooky ghost. Her passion for romance novels began a few years later, with the discovery of a worn copy of Kathleen E. Woodiwiss's *A Rose in Winter* buried on her mother's bookshelf. She lives in the US Midwest countryside with her husband—who's also her ex-husband!—their adventurous son, smiley daughter and two cuddly kitties.

PREGNANT IN THE ITALIAN'S PALAZZO

AMANDA CINELLI

CINDERELLA HIRED FOR HIS REVENGE

EMMY GRAYSON

MILLS & BOON

First published in Great Britain 2023
by Mills & Boon, an imprint of HarperCollins*Publishers* Ltd,
1 London Bridge Street, London, SE1 9GF

www.harpercollins.co.uk

HarperCollins*Publishers*
Macken House, 39/40 Mayor Street Upper,
Dublin 1, D01 C9W8, Ireland

ISBN: 978-0-263-30661-3

01/23

PREGNANT IN THE ITALIAN'S PALAZZO

AMANDA CINELLI

MILLS & BOON

This one is for the big girls

PROLOGUE

NYSIO BACCHETTI WAS rarely surprised.

He was the sole heir to an Italian dynasty that dated back to the Renaissance, and the majority of the milestones in his privileged life had been mapped out from the moment he was born. From his elite boarding-school tuition to the prestigious business degrees that hung upon the walls of his office where he ran their family's sizeable estate and holdings, his life always tended to follow a neatly predictable path.

Until today.

Nysio forced himself to breathe, his eyes blurring as he reread the first page of the last will and testament of a man he'd never met. A man who was apparently his biological father, according to accompanying DNA test results dating back twenty years. The neat black envelope had been hand-delivered at noon by a representative of Mytikas Holdings. The sensitive details within had been briefly explained, along with an invitation to come to New York to discuss matters further with Zeus Mytikas's oldest son, the new CEO.

His brother. He had a brother.

He had *two* brothers, he'd discovered upon voraciously reading through the remainder of the shocking documents and turning to the Internet for more information. There was the stern-faced business mogul Xander Mytikas, the oldest son, and the one whom Zeus had apparently chosen as his protégé. Then there was Eros Theodorou, a laid-back blond playboy with a scandalous reputation. Both of them had the same blue eyes and sharp cheekbones as his own. Features apparently given to them by the biological father they shared.

All three of their names had been listed in Zeus's last will and testament. Not an offering, but a competition. The first of them to marry and remain married for one year…would inherit the entirety of Zeus's estate. It appeared that iron-clad legal bindings had forbidden Zeus from revealing the Bacchetti secret—that Nysio was apparently not a Bacchetti by blood—or using it against them. Until now. It seemed the old tyrant had decided to throw up one last middle finger from beyond the grave.

He found himself pacing the length of his office, throwing open the nearest doors and stepping out onto the terrace like a drowning man. The lights of the city spread out below Palazzo Bacchetti like a glittering blanket, taunting him.

The people of Florence lauded the Bacchetti family as their own unofficial royalty, and Nysio had grown up as their raven-haired prince, trained to perform his part to perfection, no matter what was happening behind the closed doors of their mountaintop *palazzo*. They were more than just a wealthy family, his elderly father often reminded him whenever Nysio dared to complain. They were an institution. And institutions needed to maintain their image to project stability to the people who relied upon them.

But now he knew better than anyone that the people who seemed most perfect were simply the ones who possessed the most secrets.

He had no need of any paltry inheritance. He had amassed more wealth at his computer trading stocks than the Bacchetti name alone could have ever given him. It was public knowledge that he was a recluse who rarely left his palatial compound in the Florentine hills. But unlike some of his ancestors, he had never needed public adoration or intimidation to keep his business in perfect working order, not when his patience and instincts as a financial trader were world renowned. Even on the most tumultuous days in the global stock markets, he had remained calm and in control.

But as he stared down at the documents he still gripped in his hands, he felt the edges of his hard-won control begin to fray with every breath he forced into his lungs.

Arturo Bacchetti was a good man and the only father Nysio had ever known. He had been trained with the sole purpose of taking his father's place as a public figure, despite the social anxiety that made many of his duties almost unbearable. He had dropped all of his own plans and stepped into that duty much earlier than planned, when his father had become ill and his parents had retired to Sardinia.

He had given his whole life to this city, safe in the knowledge that it was his birthright. That it was his duty. But all along his parents had been hiding this from him. The temptation to lash out was strong, but he had never been one for outward displays of emotion. He preferred to wait, to analyse, to plan his actions. And that was exactly what he would do, he decided as he strode back into his office and grabbed the phone from his desk.

Gianluca, their family's most trusted employee answered promptly, used to playing the part of Nysio's assistant on occasion among countless other jobs he took charge of. The older man was stunned to hear him request a jet to be readied for immediate travel but he gave no details other than to say it was a business trip. There was no need to disclose any more than that. No need to alert his parents, or speak of any of this at all. Zeus Mytikas had broken a legal promise to keep this secret under wraps, dead or not, and Nysio intended to ensure that the current CEO of Mytikas Holdings knew exactly where the Bacchetti family stood on the matter. He would regain control of the situation, have his name struck from that damned will and walk away. One quick trip across the Atlantic and things would go back to the way they were.

He would make sure of it.

CHAPTER ONE

WHAT AN UTTERLY dismal location for a wedding. Nysio scowled as his car came to a stop amongst the growing crowd that had gathered outside the grey brick Manhattan courthouse. The groom stood in their midst, stony-faced and proud even as he watched his bride-to-be turn tail and run, disappearing into the busy city streets.

Cameras flashed immediately upon the scene, and Nysio felt his body tighten in sympathy at the familiar invasion of privacy, even though he was tucked safely behind tinted glass. He studied Xander Mytikas from afar, curiosity making him analyse the strong nose and harsh brow that were so eerily similar to his own. For much of his flight across the Atlantic he had wondered how it might feel to meet one of his two half-brothers in person. Wondered if he might feel a sense of kinship or connection.

The fact that he felt nothing should be a small relief.

So far, his team of private investigators had already uncovered no effort on either of his brothers' parts to sabotage his privacy. In fact, they had both seemed far too involved in their own private dispute to even consider that their surprise Italian counterpart might make an appearance. They both knew of his existence, they had all received the exact same document…and yet, other than having that copy of the will sent, they had not tried to contact him or acknowledge his existence at all.

Before he could think of his next step, Nysio could do nothing but watch as his brother cut through the crowd and disappeared into a limo down the street. Clearly, Xander Mytikas was not planning to sit around waiting to see if his runaway bride returned. The acting CEO needed to marry fast in order to keep control of his shares in Mytikas Holdings and, according to Nysio's investigators, he had no plans to reveal the previous terms of the NDA that protected the secrecy of Nysio's birth.

A flash of pink caught his attention, jolting his attention back to the street. A woman emerged out onto the courthouse steps, a shaft of sunlight illuminating her red hair into an amber glow against the dull grey stone of the building behind her. The chilly autumnal breeze blew her pink gown tighter against her, seemingly outlining her shape for his further perusal. She had flowers in her hands and shock on her beautiful face and Nysio was stunned to silence for a moment, thankful for the privacy windows so that he could look his fill.

From a distance, she reminded him of one of the ancient goddesses in the paintings in the gallery of his Florentine *palazzo*, as if she should have been in repose with cherubs feeding her grapes. And her *breasts*… He bit his lower lip, forcing down the jolt of arousal that shot through his solar plexus.

Stunned at the reaction her presence had evoked in him, he tracked her progress as she moved down the street, calling out for the runaway bride. She turned back, the expression on her face one of absolute confusion as the rain poured down and splashed up against her bare legs and the pale pink material of her dress.

Most of the press in the street had dispersed now, but

the woman in pink lingered. Such fierce emotion emanated from her, he found himself powerless to look away.

She approached the remaining security guards, her hands gesturing wildly as she spoke. The vague sound of a lyrical British accent reached his ears as he strained to make out the conversation. Her expression changed from pleading to furious as the men got into their car and drove away too, leaving her alone on the concrete steps in the rain.

Nysio watched as she dug around in a tiny purse hooked onto her wrist and heard the distinct sound of her guttural curse as she came up empty. Then, for the first time since she'd emerged onto the street, she went completely still. If he'd been struck speechless by the strength of emotion passing through her when she realised the bride was gone, this sudden deflation was even more provoking. She looked around the street for a moment, then ducked back under the portico for shelter from the rain.

Maybe it had been her clear distress moments before or maybe it was the delicate shiver that passed through her voluptuous frame as she tried to hug herself against the chill but, before he could rethink it, he stepped out from his car, opening his own umbrella against the downpour.

Aria Dane clutched the mud-covered skirt of her dusty pink bridesmaid gown and shivered, once again wishing that she'd had the foresight to design a matching coat to shield her from the October weather. The delicate satin and tulle gown had been a flamboyant last-minute choice, back when she'd assumed she would be standing and posing for pictures for the majority of the afternoon, not running through Manhattan in the pouring rain in pursuit of a runaway bride.

She checked her phone once again, waiting for a response from the recently departed billionaire groom's security team. They said that Priya had probably just got cold feet but she knew her friend. She knew that something was very, very wrong.

She looked up at the old stone courthouse with its windows glowing orange in the rapidly fading evening light. She had made a few calls to the places she thought Priya might have run to, only to come up empty. Now she was stuck at the scene of the crime, so to speak, with less than five dollars left in her tiny clutch bag and no way of getting home. The sense of abandonment was strong and deeply triggering, but she refused to let her mind wander back to the one other time she'd found herself discarded by someone she trusted in a strange place.

She banged on the tall oak door of the historic building, not surprised to find the venue had been closed up. It was Sunday evening and the space had only been booked exclusively for the wedding, after all. The rain still fell in a light shower, the streets glistening under the feet of pedestrians. She stood frozen in her spot under the portico, her mind whirring over her options. Her flight home to London was due to depart in a few hours and all of her possessions were locked inside Priya's apartment. Including her passport, her ticket and the tablet computer she used for work. She froze, feeling panic and worry break through the first rush of adrenaline.

She was stranded.

Aria had long ago accepted that she was a natural helper, the kind of person who saw a problem and jumped into action without a thought. And yet every time she was in trouble herself, she always found herself alone. Like right now.

She looked at her phone once again, feeling her stomach twirl. She was going to miss her flight and that meant missing her opportunity to give the presentation that she had been working on for the past month. The one constant in her life over the past ten years was her job as a fashion buyer in one of London's largest department stores. She'd walked through the doors as a college dropout and worked her way up to a place where she now actually had some creative input on what went out on the floor each season.

In fact, over the past few years they'd even supported her as she undertook an online textile degree at evenings and weekends and relentlessly pitched her ideas to expand their minuscule plus-size lingerie section. She swallowed past the knot that formed in her throat. With all of the downsizing that had swept through the departments lately, she *really* needed to get home.

She briefly considered calling her parents for help and fought the swift wave of discomfort that followed. Being an outspoken, spontaneous creative in a family full of very calm, very organised accountants was hard enough without the fact that, unlike her three older sisters, she didn't earn a six-figure income. She barely earned enough to pay the rent on her studio flat in Richmond as it was.

None of them would be surprised that she needed help, of course. It had been more than a decade since her own ill-fated elopement, but her parents still saw her as the foolish daughter who'd found herself abandoned on a Greek island by her spoilt, rich boyfriend.

She was the last person who could judge anyone for an impulsive jaunt into matrimony, but the moment Priya had asked her to travel to Manhattan to support her through a last-minute marriage of convenience with a stranger, her intuition had screamed at her. She'd felt a soul-deep sense of unsettlement about the arrangement, but put it down to knowing this marriage meant Priya had to leave London.

There were a great many things in life that she was not sure of, but the intention of never entering into matrimony with another person was one that she'd thought she and her best friend had shared.

A low tinny whistling noise made her jump and it took her a few moments to realise that the noise was coming from the phone she'd stuffed into the bodice of her dress.

She hissed a greeting, the past ninety minutes of adrenaline making her hands shake even as she fought to keep her voice civilised.

'Relax. I'm fine. I'm safe.' Priya's voice was strangely breathless, her words uncharacteristically quick and clipped. 'I… I found another way to solve my problem but I need to leave town for a few weeks.'

Aria pressed her lips together, silencing the instant exclamation of disbelief on the tip of her tongue. First her calm sensible friend had run away from a wedding that would have solved all of her problems, then she suddenly had to leave town for a few weeks…? Priya *never* made spontaneous plans, she hated breaking routine.

'Another way? Another groom, you mean?' Aria asked, her heartbeat pounding loudly in her ears as she tried to think of what she needed to ask Priya to ensure her safety. 'Where are you going? Where is he taking you?'

Priya's voice was hesitant as she explained, as if she couldn't speak freely, but she was adamant that she was safe. It was obvious that whomever she was accepting help from was with her, standing nearby. Definitely a man. Yet another out-of-character action for her best friend. They both had their own issues with trusting the opposite sex, it had been what drew them together in a college bar as they'd bonded over stories of their disastrous first attempts down the aisle. They trusted one another with the hard stuff, or at least they had.

Her fingers tightened on the phone's hard case. 'I don't like this. I don't like any of it.'

'I don't like it either, but it's what I need to do.' Priya's voice cut off for a moment, a strange tapping sound coming from the background. When she spoke again her voice was calmer. 'Look, it will all be fine. I'll explain everything once I'm back.'

Suspicion clouding her senses, Aria whispered into the phone. 'If you can't talk, just say yes or no. I heard Xander sent guards in pursuit of his brother…there was this one really intense, dark-haired man. Are you with him?'

The line went dead.

Aria chewed on her nail, feeling a pinch as she bit her skin. She had begun to pace at some point, a habit of hers when she felt restless, but when a throat cleared nearby, she realised she was no longer alone.

She fought to hold in the strange reaction that caught in her chest as she took in the man standing a respectable distance away from her. The same man she'd seen earlier, watching from a car across the street as the scandalous wedding unfolded. Working in the fashion industry, she was no stranger to beautiful men, but this man wasn't just handsome…he had the kind of magnetic presence and other-worldly good looks that made him stand out. His swarthy tan and silk pocket square made him look like a movie star from another time.

Was this the brother that Priya's erstwhile groom had seemed so frantic to find? He would fit the bill for the wealthy Mytikas family—everything about him seemed to scream wealth and privilege. Passers-by gave him a wide berth, some even stared as though they knew they were observing someone important…someone of power. And yet, when she gave herself a moment to look at him in detail, she could practically feel his discomfort as he barely tolerated the attention. He reminded her of a lion in captivity, one who had been tethered and seemingly tamed but…still vibrated with a fierce primal energy obvious to anyone who looked beyond the polished surface of his designer suit.

He was looking directly at her, his eyes scanning along the mud splatters that now painted her sheer stockings, as though the sight irritated him. He had stopped at the end of the steps and she was intensely aware that she was a woman standing alone on a quiet street…yet she strangely didn't feel any fear. In fact, she seemed to be waiting for him to speak, her breath held and her body leaning ever so slightly forward.

His gaze met hers for a split second and for a moment she stood frozen, her body enthralled under the laser focus of stormy blue eyes and long lashes. It was an assessing glance, barely lasting more than five seconds or so before he looked away, but Aria instantly felt her heart thundering in her chest.

'Do you require assistance?' he asked in heavily accented English.

'What gave me away?'

'I saw what happened with the wedding. You are a friend of the bride and groom?'

Aria paused, noticing the way this man was very deliberately trying to seem nonchalant in his questioning. He could be a reporter, trying to get a scoop. She paused to set him straight, but they were both startled by the sudden blinding flash of a camera exploding against the dull grey concrete around them.

Aria inwardly groaned. She had spent so much time

protecting her socialite best friend from the paparazzi and she had no wish to answer any invasive questions about the failed wedding. Especially since Priya was still missing.

But the photographer disregarded her completely, their focus solely upon the mysterious man at the end of the steps. 'Nysio Bacchetti, what are you doing in Manhattan?'

The man, clearly shocked at being addressed by name, began to walk away towards the side of the building, but the reporter was relentless, caging him with questions and snapping photo after photo.

'Hey, leave him alone,' Aria shouted, only to be thoroughly ignored. The rain fell down upon her as she stepped out from the portico and ran down the steps. 'I said leave the man alone, for goodness' sake.'

The paparazzo scowled, stopping only to press a few buttons on his camera then turning back to continue his photographic assault. A single wheezing breath sounded out loud over the soft patter of rain around them. The gorgeous man in the fancy suit had stopped retreating and was now frozen in place, half leaning against the thick branch of a tree as his breaths came hard and fast.

'What did you do to him?' Aria raised her voice, pushing past the paparazzo and using her body as a make-shift shield.

'Hey, I never got closer than six feet. Just trying to earn a living, lady. It's nothing personal. He's some fancy Italian billionaire, you'd think he'd be used to this.'

With a shrug, the pap turned and jogged away down the street, leaving Aria alone to deal with said fancy Italian billionaire, who was now really in difficulty. He pushed away from the tree, listing to one side as he tried and failed to gather himself. His eyes widened when she moved closer and grabbed his hand.

'Are you okay?' she asked, then instantly scolded herself. 'Sorry, that's a stupid question. You're clearly hyperventilating. Are you asthmatic?'

The man shook his head, somehow managing to look haughty and irritated by her babbling even as he fought to remain upright.

'Okay…maybe try to count out your breaths?' she urged him, using her hands to mimic the action of slow calm breaths in and out of her own chest. She felt rather helpless, her mind clutching at the few times she'd helped Priya through moments of anxiety. Assuming that was what this was. His breaths were coming sharp and shallow, even as he held her at arm's length, trying to get himself under control.

'Mr… Bacchetti, Nysio, was it? Let me help you.' She eyed him, wondering if he was too far gone to even register her words. But then his blue gaze met hers, the pleading look in them the first sign of vulnerability he'd shown. She was deeply relieved when he allowed her to take his hand, using his own fingers as tools to count out his breaths.

'Focus on your senses one at a time,' she said calmly. 'Look at my hand on yours, feel my touch, listen to my voice. Breathe.'

After a few minutes, his erratic breathing began to slow and Aria let out the breath she'd been holding herself, glad that he wasn't in danger of fainting on her. He was incredibly tall and even more broad and she wouldn't have had an easy time trying to break his fall. Now that he was out of danger, she should leave. Time was ticking and she still needed to track down Priya and figure out how on earth she was going to get home.

But when she made to take a step away, he surprised her by holding onto her hand. The heat of his skin seared into her, sending shivers up her wrist. She wanted to pull away, to keep some space between them, and yet she remained firmly in place.

'I'd just like some privacy for a moment. I have no wish to engage with any more of the New York press just yet.'

She frowned down at his hand, puzzled by something. 'Were you invited to the wedding today?'

'No. I'm here on business.'

'That paparazzo mentioned that you are someone important. A billionaire.' She narrowed her eyes on him. 'But I saw you watching all the drama from across the street. Then you waited around afterwards...why?'

She moved to step out of his embrace, but her dress had somehow got snagged on a low-hanging branch during their conversation and the resulting pull made her trip, falling sideways into him. He reached out to steady her, his hand coming in contact with her bare kneecap. The touch made her entire body jolt, as though a current of electricity had passed from his strong fingers and into her skin.

Their eyes met and she gulped. That same angry vulnerability still burned in his deep blue eyes but the pupils were now wider, his nostrils flared slightly and she was pretty sure that his chest was rising and falling a little faster than it had been seconds before. Was she imagining it or was he flexing his fingers ever so slightly, tightening that grip and watching her reaction?

He inhaled sharply, still not fully recovered. 'I told you, I'm here on business. I stopped to make a call...but then I saw everyone leave and you remained. I intended to come to your rescue. Not the other way around.'

Against her will, Aria found herself smiling, a shaky laugh escaping her chest at the utterly ridiculous turn this day had taken. 'Just your friendly neighbourhood superhero in a pink bridesmaid dress.'

'Bridesmaid?' He frowned.

'Did you not see the bride who just ran off down the street? My best friend. Well, possibly my ex-best friend now that she's abandoned me here.' She rolled her eyes. 'Quite inconvenient when I'm supposed to be on a flight back to London in less than three hours and all of my things are in her apartment.'

'So I was right, you *were* in need of assistance.'

'I suppose so.' She shrugged, tensing at just how uncomfortable it felt to admit that. To admit that she needed help. For so long now she had made a point of ensuring she got by just fine on her own, not relying on anyone else. Things were just easier that way. Safer.

He was quiet for a moment, his eyes assessing her with a shrewd intensity that made her squirm a little. Her chest flushed, her skin felt slightly fizzy and, well…it was quite embarrassing, the effect this man was having on her.

'I happen to be on my way to the airport. Let me help you.'

'You would offer to help a stranger, just like that?' She raised a brow, wondering if his hyperventilation had made him dizzy or something. He was clearly someone important. He would have far more pressing things to do.

'What's your name?' he asked, his posture rapidly straightening back to what it had been twenty minutes before. When he had stood below her, gazing up at her with such imperious purpose. 'You know mine, and you can do and internet search on me too if that helps. Once I know yours, surely that would make us acquaintances at the very least?'

'It's Aria,' she breathed, trying not to be distracted by the effect that this man's proximity seemed to be having on her. The sodden material of her dress was still warm from his body heat, but cold where the loose skirt blew against her thighs. She felt off balance and completely unsure of herself. Perhaps that was why she remained silent and actually considered his offer for a moment before shaking her head.

'I have no passport or ticket, and my luggage is all locked in my friend's apartment. Even if you could somehow help me resolve all of that and get me on a later flight, it would mean I wouldn't arrive in London until much later and I have to get to work.'

'I have never encountered a problem that I couldn't solve.'

His words almost made her laugh, but then she looked at his expression and realised he was completely serious. He had the power to get her on a flight, even without her documents. She had gone out of her way to fly to New York at the last minute, knowing that her friend was in a worrying situation and possibly in need of rescue. Maybe for once she could put her own situation first and accept when someone appeared to be doing the same for her.

'You came to my rescue here today, Aria. I'm simply asking for an opportunity to return the favour. I cannot restore your lost friend or your lost luggage, but I can get you home to London before dawn. That is a promise.'

CHAPTER TWO

FROM THE MOMENT she decided to throw caution to the wind and nod her agreement, things moved quickly. Aria felt butterflies fill her stomach as Nysio's car moved smoothly through the rain-soaked streets of Manhattan and then out of the city. Her mind raced, guilt mingling with anger as she tried to tell herself that she was doing the right thing, putting herself first for once. She had tried calling back the number Priya had contacted her on but had got no answer, not even a voicemail.

She was so deep in thought that she didn't realise that they were driving away from the main international airport until the car slowed down to enter a private airfield.

Security waved them through and her handsome rescuer brought the car to a stop alongside a sleek white jet. Aria felt her jaw sag. 'When you said you could get me on a flight… I was thinking you had contacts in one of the airlines.'

'Is this a problem?' He frowned.

'It's a private jet.' She stared out at the sleek unmarked aircraft, watching as a small crew descended the steps to greet them. 'Do you seriously own your own aeroplane?'

A weak laugh escaped her lips and for a moment she thought she might be on the verge of hysterics as he stepped out of the car and walked around to the passenger side.

Was she actually about to accept a ride from a billionaire on a private jet? Her original flight had been the cheapest seat she could afford on a standard jetliner, where the seats were cramped on her hips and she almost always ended up sitting next to someone falling asleep on her shoulder or loudly munching on cheesy snacks.

'I could try to get you on a standard flight if you prefer. I couldn't guarantee the same timeframe or ease, but if the thought of being contained with me for the next eight hours is an issue...'

'It's not you,' she said quickly. 'I don't usually accept help from anyone, never mind a complete stranger in the street.'

'A trait we share, it seems.' His jaw ticced. 'But your kindness today was...unexpectedly easy to accept. I'd very much like the chance to repay you.'

His low response surprised her with its honesty and the reminder of the intimacy of the moment they'd shared on the street. She had witnessed his private panic and seen how unsettled he was by needing assistance. Maybe it was that common ground that made her step out of the car and close the door behind her with finality, her decision made.

His hand gently gripped her elbow as she stood in the chilled evening air. The crew made quick work of bustling them on board and a grey-haired man appeared, introducing himself simply as Gianluca. Her details were taken in a calm, efficient manner that made her wonder if this kind of situation was a common occurrence. They would be waiting for a short time for travel documentation and other red tape to be dealt with, but she was assured it would be sorted with minimal fuss. Evidently, when stranded in a foreign country, it paid to have wealthy connections.

It was strange to hear her host addressed as Signor Bacchetti, and Aria watched as he was called to the head of the craft to speak privately with the pilot, leaving her sitting alone down the opposite end of the enormous aircraft. Now that they were on board, would he expect her to go and sit somewhere quietly? She could usually small-talk anyone's ears off but this guy…didn't seem like the chatty type. She fiddled with the small gold pendant she wore on a chain around her neck, an old birthday gift from Priya. Fidget jewellery, her friend had called it. Aptly named, the solid gold letter A spun within a series of circles and made for a helpful tool when she just needed something to do with her hands.

Nysio was intense and brooding in a way that made every nerve ending on her body tingle with awareness. For a moment earlier, she'd been sure he was about to kiss her and the thought had made her panic, pushing him away. But then he'd made it clear that it was only gratitude that had him holding onto her so tightly and she'd felt…disappointed. Ridiculous, really, she wasn't a teenager…so why couldn't she stop wondering about what it might have been like? She inhaled a deep breath, trying to shake off the shiver that instantly travelled down her spine.

As a child, Aria had often been told by her parents and older sisters to stop bouncing on the sofa. Or tapping her feet, or chatting non-stop about the various aspects of her school day that wouldn't seem to stop swirling around in her mind. One would think that as she grew up that kind of energy excess would have waned, but it had not. It had simply morphed into an internal restlessness that proved just as frustrating to manage. She'd been in her mid-twenties when a doctor had suggested ADHD as the root cause for her struggles.

Maybe it was simply the adrenaline of the day, but Nysio Bacchetti's presence seemed to reinvoke the echoes of the kind of heated, needy sensations she'd hoped never to feel again. She prided herself on always remaining in control during the pitiful amount of dating she'd done over the past decade. She was a social creature by nature and had always enjoyed the excitement of meeting new people. But when it came to romantic entanglements, she played it safe, never getting in over her head. She had given her own foolish romantic heart away to Theo as a naïve twenty-year-old, and that experience had left scars deeper than she could have ever imagined.

She was so focused on taming her own swirling thoughts that she hardly noticed Nysio's return. He lowered his tall frame easily into the seat directly opposite, his attention engrossed in a loose sheaf of papers that he'd spread out from a slim folder. He sighed and plucked a pair of sleek, black-framed eyeglasses from his inner pocket to begin reading, a fact that should not have made him look any sexier than he already did. But when he slowly licked one finger and flipped over a page with one strong hand... Aria's traitorous mouth let out an audible sound of appreciation.

He looked up instantly, because of course he'd heard it. He was sitting directly in front of her. One dark brow quirked in question and Aria felt as though the heat of a thousand spotlights had zoned in upon her.

'Was that a groan?' he asked, placing his papers down to give her his full attention.

'No...well, yes, but not for the reason you're thinking.'

'Oh? What reason might that be?' His lips quirked at the corners and she was pretty sure he found her awkwardness to be immensely amusing. She glanced away, silently praying that he would turn back to his papers as she felt a definite flush travel along her chest and up towards her cheeks. Her redhead's colouring was usually one of her favourite things about herself, but not today. Not when every X-rated thought she had around this man was so brutally obvious. If she had any doubt that he might not see the effect his presence had on her, he confirmed it when she looked back to find him still staring.

'You are even more beautiful when you're embarrassed,' he said softly. So softly she almost thought she'd misheard him for a moment. He hadn't given any indication of being attracted to her so far, had he?

But she couldn't deny that all of a sudden the air felt charged between them, just as it had on the street outside the courthouse. His eyes darkened, his gaze falling to where she could feel her embarrassment had now heated the skin on her neck and chest to a rosy hue.

'You are blushing, Aria,' he remarked, his voice a low murmur, his attention unwaveringly rapt upon her. 'Have I made you uncomfortable?'

'No, of course not,' she said quickly, shaking her head as she rose to her feet. Ever the gentleman, he stood too, his frame broad and looming above her now that she had removed her heels. Before she could embarrass herself any further she mumbled something nonsensical about needing to freshen up, but really she just needed to step away. To gather her composure and remind herself that accepting this man's offer of rescue was just a means to an end and not some wild beginning.

She walked further down towards the end of the cabin where she could see a large master bedroom through an open doorway. She debated going inside but chickened out at the last moment, turning into the doorway on her left instead. She gazed longingly at the full-sized water-fall shower inside the spacious bathroom; this place was more like a penthouse apartment in the sky and most certainly an upgrade from the commercial flight she'd been booked on. If only she had her luggage with her, she would have jumped straight into the shower to wash off the city mud and grime.

Longing overtook her as she stared in the mirror at her dirty reflection. Her dress was no longer damp from the rain, but it felt sticky on her skin. She took a wash-cloth and ran it under some cold water, dabbing it against the sides of her neck and along her chest. A sigh escaped her lips as the cool conditioned air hit her skin and she felt a little relief. Sadly there was absolutely nothing to be done to save her sheer stockings so she decided that disposing of them and going bare-legged was better than being covered in mud splatters.

She reached under her dress, unhooking the clip of her garter belt, and rolled off one ruined stocking with a sigh before changing to the other. She had just gripped the material at her thigh when she heard a gruff inhalation of breath behind her. When she looked up towards the doorway, she found she was no longer alone.

Nysio had simply intended to follow Aria to apologise for his forward behaviour, instead he'd ended up transfixed in the bathroom doorway, frozen in place as she slowly rolled her stocking down one leg.

Unaware of his presence, she'd pulled her skirt up higher, baring just a hint of the pink-and-black-printed lingerie she wore beneath, and he'd forgotten to breathe for a moment. The resulting gulp of air he'd taken in had alerted her to his presence, making her jump with fright.

Nysio instantly raised his hands and took a step backwards. The door had been ajar, but still...his reaction had not been one of innocence and the last thing he wanted was for her to fear him. As if he were a creep standing outside a window trying to catch a look at his obsession. He was *not* obsessed. He was perhaps a little more interested in her than he had been in any woman in a very long time...but he was not past the point of his own self-control.

'Apologies, I didn't mean to alarm you.'

'Top tip? Maybe don't stand silently in a doorway if you don't want to alarm the person inside. I could have been nude.'

He pushed away the instant image his mind tried to conjure at that statement and nodded, schooling his expression to one of remorse. 'I came in here to apologise for unsettling you and now it seems I have only succeeded in making things worse.'

He was seriously losing control of himself. First the impulsive trip across the Atlantic and now acquiring an unexpected detour and a guest on the journey home. He had already made the decision to leave New York immediately once he'd discovered his half-brothers were far too occupied in their own personal matrimonial race to bother threatening him. But for some reason leaving *her*, leaving Aria alone... It had felt wrong. Now here they were, having been alone on this jet less than half an hour, and he was already thinking of ways to get her even more undressed than she was right now.

'You didn't make me uncomfortable. It's just that... well, you keep looking at me like *that*.' She gestured towards him. 'The smouldering eyes and the unblinking stare. I'm honestly trying to figure out if you're planning to murder me once we're up in the air, or...'

He felt irritation break the surface of his control. Was

she truly this oblivious to the effect she was having on him? Did she not feel it too? 'I'm not planning to murder you.'

'Well, that's a relief, I suppose.' She let out a small laugh, but her mouth remained tight and her eyes lowered as though she couldn't quite look at him.

'Is this a game that you play?' Nysio took a step into the room, unable to resist the invisible thread that seemed to be pulling him towards her. 'The pale pink dress in the rain, the refusal to behave like a damsel in distress… now this *blushing*. Is it real?'

'It's my natural skin tone. Of course it's real.' She took a step towards him, her little dimpled chin tilting up stubbornly as she pressed a single pink-painted fingertip in the centre of his chest. 'How dare you? You are the one who insisted on helping me, remember? If anyone was a damsel in distress today, it was you.'

The reminder of his vulnerable moment was like a shock of cold water over his libido. He'd thought he'd got the anxiety attacks under control, but then again, he hadn't travelled this far from his home in an entire decade. As though she felt his shift in mood she took a step closer, her features softening.

'I'm sorry, I didn't mean for that to come out that way. I promise that I really don't see your moment earlier as weak. You just…seem to have got under my skin.'

He'd got under her skin? Nysio fought the urge to laugh. Good, that made two of them now, at least. He realised that if he'd been an honourable man he would have walked away. He would have removed himself to the furthest end of the jet and maintained maximum distance until she was safely deposited on English soil. He inhaled a breath then fought the urge to groan as her delicious scent filled his lungs, scrambling his senses all over again. Her sweet perfume was everywhere. He couldn't get away from it.

'I...don't wear perfume.'

Nysio looked up and met her questioning gaze, realising he must have spoken the words aloud. 'Your soap, maybe?'

'Maybe you should hold your nose, then. But don't forget to breathe.' She nibbled on her lower lip, the ghost of a smile playing upon her lips. She was trying not to laugh at him.

Rather than feeling affronted at her reaction, Nysio smiled, feeling his usual serious veneer slip completely as he realised the utter absurdity of their situation. He'd set out to play the chivalrous hero with this woman and she continued to surprise him at every turn. Was he truly annoyed at her for smelling good? He felt his own chest rumble with laughter and was shocked at the sensation of the mirth in his chest loosening the tightness there. Was his life really so devoid of humour that verbally sparring with this fireball of a woman could affect him so?

Lyrical laughter hummed from between her berry-coloured lips and Nysio found himself mesmerised by how the light made her lips shimmer. Would she taste as good as she smelled? Desire trickled along his spine, tracing down below his belt. He was suddenly very aware of their proximity and decided he needed to put some space between them pretty soon or she'd notice the thickly growing evidence of his sudden shift in mood.

Their eyes met and once again he found himself absolutely transfixed by their depth and gravity. By the time he realised he was moving closer to her, it was too late. Her balance swayed and all of a sudden she was in his arms, her lips seeking his. He allowed himself one maddening caress of his lips on hers, drinking her in like a drowning man before he forced himself to pull back for a moment.

'I didn't offer to take you on my jet for this purpose,' he said heavily, staring into her eyes and trying to ignore the fact that their bodies were still completely fused together. 'I don't want you to feel like this is what I expect from you...like some kind of twisted payment for your airfare. I can still arrange for you to get another flight.'

He waited a moment, studying the reaction on her face as it slowly changed from lust to disappointment. He wasn't lying, of course he would let her walk off this plane if that was what she wanted. He could be a gentleman, despite the teenager's libido that had seemed to overtake him ever since he'd set eyes on her. He would get her on the next flight home...

'But I don't want to do that,' he admitted, shocking himself with his own honesty.

'You don't?'

'Do you?' he asked, his eyes not leaving hers. She seemed to consider her options for a moment. He took in the stubborn set of her jaw and tried to ignore the sensation of something shifting into place within him like a car engine roaring to life when she finally looked him in the eyes and bit her lower lip softly.

'I want to stay here,' she confessed in a whisper. 'With you.'

He ran a finger along her lower lip, tracing his hands along her jaw before gripping the soft skin at the sides of her neck. Her pupils dilated just as he knew they would.

At the first subtle nod of her chin, he closed the space between them. He bent his head, following the line of her jaw with kisses, trying and failing not to groan a little as he inhaled some more of the warm scent she wore. It was sharper in the hollow where her neck met her shoulder and she shivered when he pressed his lips there, lingering for just a moment.

He leaned back against the wall and used the front of her gown to pull her to him, perching her side-saddle against his thigh. This position evened out their height difference a little, giving him much more freedom of movement.

'Do you feel this same energy, humming in your veins...demanding a release?' he growled.

He heard the arousal in her voice as she murmured yes, and he could sense her body telling him what he wanted to hear. But still, some part of him wanted her to leave, wanted her to run away from him and whatever madness this was between them. He didn't quite trust it, the seemingly effortless flow of mutual attraction that pulsated between them. Perhaps for her it was simply the aftermath of the adrenaline of the day and the chaos that came with it. He wanted to test it out, he wanted more time.

'I want to be the one to give you that release,' he said, inhaling her sweet berry scent and feeling it scorch his lungs. 'Do you want me to kiss you again, Aria?'

CHAPTER THREE

'YES.'

The word was the barest whisper on Aria's lips before Nysio's mouth was reclaiming hers and she felt him press her backwards, caging her in against the wall. They kissed for what felt like hours, his mouth devouring hers with expert precision, and she was lost…completely lost to whatever madness this was that had taken hold of them both.

She wanted it never to end. She wanted him to consume her whole and put out whatever needy fire he had ignited within her.

She'd never felt arousal quite like this, not even the handful of times she had actually enjoyed sex in her life. She had always been too self-aware, too inside her own head.

Why wasn't she overthinking everything right now? She had never felt this way before, as if she were in a freefall of pleasure, on the brink of madness. And madness was the only way she could accurately describe the feverish sensation taking over her body. It was reckless and heady and a part of her felt as if she needed to revel in every second, just in case it was all taken away again. Her throat was dry, her pulse racing as he began a hot trail of kisses from her ear down her neck. One strong hand cupped the side of her jaw while the other traced along the side of her breast and down the curves of her waist and hips before settling with a firm squeeze upon her behind.

'From the moment I first saw you, I wanted to do this,' he murmured against her skin, pulling back for a split second to stare into her eyes in the dim light. Searching...

She exhaled, a soft moan escaping her lips as she felt his grip tighten, his fingers pressing into her flesh through the fabric of her gown. His lips resumed their kisses and licks along her collarbone, his clever fingertips found and pinched her nipples through the flimsy pink material.

'You are so honest in your reactions...even when you hide, your face tells me what you're feeling.'

His sensuously accented words circled around her, increasing the impression that she had entered into some kind of trance. Perhaps this was not reality at all. The sensation of his touch and the soft gravelly whisper of his words seemed to melt into one, drawing her deeper and deeper into this intoxicating battle that she never ever wanted to leave. Everything melted away replaced only by him.

'What am I thinking right now?' she asked softly, splaying her hands through his long thick curls and feeling a strange comfort in the silky warmth she found there.

'You're wondering if I'm just a cocky bastard or if I'm actually going to make you come, right here.'

'Oh. Can you...do that?' she stuttered, hardly believing how brazen she felt.

'The question is not *if* I can give you pleasure,' he replied with a wicked tilt of an eyebrow. 'It's about where you'd like me to start.'

The look in his eyes made her pulse quicken and a

fine point of heat began to throb between her thighs. She thought of all the clever things she might say, to seem sophisticated and seductive, but came up short. She had never been good with silence, it made her twitchy, but this silence was heavy and laden with dark twirling tension. She smiled nervously, pressing her lips together. She should lay the ground rules, she thought. She should say...something.

But no sooner had she opened her mouth to speak than his head was descending for another punishing kiss.

Aria thought she had been kissed before. She had a vague recollection of how the act was supposed to feel... but this was something else entirely. Her body felt as if it had been plugged into a stream of vibrant electric energy, the kind that fuelled euphoric fever dreams. She felt his strong hands against the sides of her neck, anchoring her and angling her jaw upward as he took everything she offered.

This was a kiss of pure domination, something that should make her run a mile considering her track record with wealthy domineering males. Why wasn't she running? Why did the thought of this kiss ending make her want to dig her nails into this man's arms and refuse to let him go?

It seemed he had been holding back before. This kiss was brutal, a magnificent storm of perfectly aimed sensuality that utterly ruined her for any kiss that might come after. He was all hard male, brawn and beauty as he caged her against the marble-topped vanity until she leaned against the mirror. The cold glass dug into her back, the slight hit of pain only seeming to heighten the wicked pleasure of his mouth as he began to trail hot, suckling kisses down her neck.

'Do you realise how long I have been waiting to get

you alone?' he murmured against her skin, his hands greedily savouring the full weight of both of her breasts through her dress.

'We only met for the first time about an hour or so ago.'

'Believe me, I know,' was his only answer, as if that were explanation enough. Then he continued his ministrations, sliding the square neckline of her gown low enough to tease one breast free from her bra.

His fervent murmur of approval chased away the ever-present layer of anxiety that lay in wait, threatening to ruin the mood with the slightest hint of rejection. She wasn't insecure about her plus-size body, but her performance in bed…well, there were still some scars there that had never quite healed. A small voice in her mind told her to be careful, to slow down a bit.

Sex wasn't easy for her, not with the way her mind liked to wander and delve into everything. It was probably the reason why she had never reached orgasm in any way other than by herself, in the dark alone at night. Every time she'd got close to being assertive in the past, to asking for what she'd wanted, that voice in the back of her mind had chimed in. The one that spoke in Theo's voice and told her that she would never be good enough in bed, that she should be grateful for what she was given. But the thought of scaring Nysio into stopping made her clutch his shoulders tighter.

She gasped as Nysio leaned forward, pressing the evidence of his arousal against her stomach. The difference in their heights was probably close to a full foot, so he compensated by taking her hand and placing it right… there.

The action was so hot, and the evidence so undeniably large…she almost begged him to just take her right there on the floor. He clearly was thinking something similar as his eyes scanned the immediate area, his breath coming in harsh bursts. He swiped the surface of the vanity clear with one hand, sending small plastic bottles of soaps and lotions crashing to the floor. Aria eyed the surface incredulously, sure it looked pretty solid, but she was short. He couldn't actually expect her to hoist herself up there while he...no way.

'Let me help.' He didn't await an answer, gripping her hips with his big hands and lifting her with ease as though she were a dainty doll and not a fully grown woman. Who knew she had a strength kink? But wow... that was hot!

For a split second he simply looked at her, his expression so reverent and hungry it created a pulse of longing between her legs. But then he was standing right between her thighs and his mouth was everywhere. He really liked her breasts, that much was certain. But he also liked her neck...and her lips. She knew this because he growled it, in between kisses. He was quite vocal in his lust, a fact that made her relax more and more with each new touch and caress. But when he began to pull the hem of her skirt even further up her thighs, she stiffened.

'Wait,' she breathed. 'I don't know if I can...'

He stopped instantly, holding himself so that even though their bodies were still pressed together, the gap between their faces gave an illusion of space. A rough laugh escaped his lips and he shook his head, as though he too could feel the absurdity of the moment. At how quickly things were flying beyond their control. She braced herself, waiting for his regret. But instead of coming to his senses and pulling away, he tucked one errant strand of hair from her face and slid it behind her ear.

The air between them was silent and still for a moment

as they just stared at one another. She could still feel the press of his muscular abdomen holding her thighs open and the clear shape of an unmistakeable erection. All that separated them was the thin fabric of his clothes, her dress and bra, and the barest slip of her matching strawberry-printed high-waist thong. The urge to tilt her hips upwards, to move against that hard heat, was almost unbearable. He felt it too, she realised as he began to adjust his position then froze, a low hiss escaping his lips.

'I don't have any protection.'

'Oh.' She breathed, sheepish that she hadn't actually thought of that herself. 'I'm on birth control. I haven't been with anyone in a long time, but I know I'm safe in that regard too.'

'Me too.' He spoke the words against her skin, his hands stroking up and down her spread thighs. 'It's been years since I've even gone on a date.'

Aria paused, wondering if that kind of dry spell was enough to explain their complete loss of control. Was he using her simply as a convenient way to break his long drought? Did she care? Wasn't she using him too, in her own way? Maybe it was enough that they were both using each other in this moment. Maybe that was what made it even more magical.

'All I know is I can't seem to stop touching you. I don't want to,' he growled.

'Then don't,' she whispered, writhing in his arms as he continued his path of sensual destruction downwards, his tongue and hands invoking an equal amount of pleasure.

Madness indeed. Stunned laughter threatened to escape her lips as Aria met his gaze and realised that she was going to do it, she was actually going to make love with this handsome stranger on his private jet.

'I can feel your heart beating under my tongue,' he

said softly, lacing each word with such dark promise it made her skin prickle and her insides melt. 'Right here.'

She thought of all of the reasons why she shouldn't be doing this, why she should have run far away from such a scandalous proposition from a stranger. But she had spent so long holding in every impulse she had, playing the good girl, and look where it had got her.

Perhaps just once, instead of feeling guilty about her own life choices, she could simply do what she wanted to do. And right now…she knew exactly what she wanted.

She lowered the straps of her dress and bra down and pushed the garments down below her breasts.

'It's been a while for me,' he warned. 'I don't know if I can be gentle.'

'I won't break,' she promised, her skin sizzling with excitement at his words. But it was the truth. It was the one secret fantasy she'd always harboured but never managed to realise, to be taken fast and hard this way. No preamble, no time for her brain to overthink anything.

Her words only seemed to spur him on further and he pulled the gown up towards her waist in one rough tug. Thank goodness it was a stretch material or he might have ripped straight through it. Actually…that might have been kind of hot too.

She gasped and accidentally released a small giggle as his fingers slid along the sensitive skin of her hips and he moved her thong aside. Their eyes met and for a moment she worried she'd ruined the mood, but then he smiled and let out the sexiest husky male laugh before claiming her lips once more.

It was the kiss of a man on the edge of his control. Their eyes locked for a moment and it took her a couple of beats to understand that he was waiting for something from her. His eyes searched her face and for a moment she thought she caught a glimmer of the mere mortal underneath his all-powerful façade. But just as quickly, it was gone again and he was back in control.

At the first touch of his erection against her molten heat, Nysio almost lost his sanity entirely. Or what had remained of his sanity from the moment he'd met this beguiling woman. She'd exploded into his orderly life like a monsoon, hot and wet, just as she was right now. He moved, unable to stop himself from plunging fully inside her in one torturously slow slide.

She hissed just a little, her body initially resisting the intrusion and he searched her face, confusion and concern threatening to call a halt to his entry.

'I'm okay,' she murmured. 'You're just…big, that's all.'

Flattery was always welcome, but her discomfort was evident in the taut set of her mouth and the tightness around her eyes. He should have prepared her more—he had barely been in here two minutes before he'd plunged himself inside her like an impatient teenager.

'Just need you to…' She breathed out slowly, biting her lower lip as he slid back and forth the barest few millimetres. 'Yes…like that.'

'I should have gone slower,' he said regretfully, resisting the urge to speed up, to deepen their intimate contact.

'No, this is perfect. Everything is perfect.'

Their matching groans of pleasure were perfectly in sync, just as their bodies were as he kept a tight hold of one gloriously rounded thigh and increased his rhythm. Her skin was butter soft and begging to be licked, but he'd make time for that later. He'd make love to her slowly next time. He wouldn't let her out of his bed until she was crying with pleasure, exhausted and muttering his name like a curse. He wanted to ruin this woman for all others. He wanted to claim her.

The thought made him pause, his breath heaving in his chest like an approaching battle drum. And yet he was past the point of heeding his own intuition to walk far away from this beguiling beauty with her sharp tongue and vibrant spirit. He thrust again, taking her faster and harder, as she breathlessly urged him on. Far be it from him to deny a lady's demands. But the tempo crashed through what remained of his futile control, bringing his own release closer with a powerful sizzle of electricity downwards along his spine. He was close, too close.

He paused for a moment, closing his eyes in a frantic attempt to delay the powerful onslaught of his own pleasure. This feeling…this riotous lack of finesse…he hadn't felt so undone since his youth. Even then, he'd had the good manners to ensure his partner had reached their own pleasure before he dived into seeking his own. But he was already inside her and she was writhing against him, urging him to recommence the harsh rhythm of moments before. She met his eyes, vulnerable and unsure. He leaned down, taking her mouth deep and hard to reassure her that he was still very much okay, too okay truthfully. With one hand, he widened her thighs and pressed his thumb against her centre.

'Is this what you need?' he asked, cupping her jaw with his free hand as he continued to rub slow circles on her swollen bud.

Long lashes fluttered open, pinning him with vibrant green eyes that were dreamy and out of focus. She moved her hips, guiding him to increase the pace of his fingers against her flesh, and as she became more breathless he felt his own excitement build.

'Yes, that's it, come for me,' he demanded, trying to

hold himself still in an effort to slow down, but as she began to writhe against him he didn't stand a chance. Nysio let out a guttural curse, his body helpless not to move, to *take*. Two more thrusts were all it took before his release came crashing over him like a tidal wave he had no hope of holding off.

Reality descended swiftly, and he looked at her, searching her face. 'I didn't intend for that to happen. Not until you'd been satisfied.'

She avoided his eyes, sliding her hands down to cover where she was still spread open and bared to him. 'It's okay. I've never been able to…get there.'

'Not even from your own touch?'

Her cheeks bloomed an even deeper shade of pink. 'That's different.'

'It's not.' He saw her visibly shrink from him, her discomfort and unfamiliarity with his concern evident. She moved to straighten herself further but Nysio kept his weight right where it was, his hand centring gently on her chest.

Her eyes widened and for a moment he was fully sure she would push him away. She looked uncertain and deflated as she tried to relax back. Tension filled her shoulders and the lines of her mouth.

'You were close…weren't you?' he murmured, sliding his hand to cup her over the wet, strawberry-patterned silk. 'You were so close to losing it for me.'

'Really, you don't need to do this.' She gasped as his finger slid along the inside of her thigh.

He leaned down, resuming his torture of her breasts. He took his time, glorying in each light moan that escaped her lips as he savoured her with his tongue as though he wanted to devour her whole. In a way, he supposed that he did. He felt wild and untamed, so completely far apart from the beacon of control he had fought hard to become in the past ten years. He was ready to lose himself all over again in this woman, and to hell with the consequences.

He looked down at her, gripping one of her wrists and holding it high above her head to keep her where he wanted her. This was good, he reminded himself, control was good. With his other hand, he tested her wetness with his index finger, watching her face until her eyes darkened and he knew he'd found exactly the right spot. Her breathing deepened and her hips moved ever so slightly.

'I want to taste you while I make you come.' He breathed the words against her ear, punctuating the final syllable with a soft nip of his teeth against her skin.

'No.' She stiffened a little, still circling those delicious curves against him. 'No tongue. Just…just touch me, please.'

'Whatever you need,' he murmured again, shocking himself with how calm he sounded in light of the battle drum pounding within his chest as he got down to his knees before her.

A second digit joined the first and he kept up the same steady rhythm until she began thrusting back against him. He found his rhythm, spreading her even wider. When he hit a certain point inside her, what little control she had shown unravelled completely. Her hands gripped his hair as she writhed and let out the most delicious breathy moans he had ever heard. He felt her tightening around his knuckles and he remembered the force of his own release, remembered spilling himself inside her and claiming her as his own.

The thought made him pause. She was not his, she was just a stranger who had come crashing into his life. But then she looked at him, cheeks rosy in the afterglow of her pleasure, and he realised with a stunning bolt of clarity that he needed to make love to this woman again. More than he had ever needed anything before.

He was fully hard and ready to go again almost instantly and he cursed low in his throat. This didn't happen to him. This couldn't happen. This woman was a walking liability and he had done something with her that he never normally did. He had acted on impulse. But as he stared at her he felt something else coil tight within him. Something darker and needier than lust, and infinitely more dangerous. He wanted her, the kind of want he usually reserved for the things he kept out of public view. His hobbies and passions.

The things that were his very own.

He moved backwards as though burned, averting his eyes and doing up his trousers as she slid the skirt of her dress back down into place.

This was a problem.

CHAPTER FOUR

IT TOOK A few moments for Aria's soul to return to her body. But when it did, she realised with swift clarity that he was not feeling quite so relaxed as she was. Her arms were still clasped around his shoulders and she could feel that he was very much still engaged in the moment but…something felt off.

'You said you never come with someone else.'

'I usually don't,' she breathed, her heartbeat still loud in her ears.

'I've never been so turned on; just watching you lose it for me has me ready and wanting you all over again…and again…,' His voice was a gruff groan, his words more of an accusation than a lover's whisper. But the look in his eyes was what almost undid her completely. He looked… tortured. Over her? How on earth was this even possible?

Her thoughts jumbled over one another in an effort for first place and as a result she said nothing at all.

'We should take a moment,' he said. 'Slow down.'

'Of course.' The polite response escaped her lips on a reflex, followed by silence as she watched him put as much space between them as humanly possible. He stood with his back against the black tile wall on the opposite side of the opulent bathroom, his chest still heaving and his eyes pinning her in place. Like a man who had just

come to his senses, her inner voice, still sounding like
Theo, sneered.

She exhaled a slow shuddering breath and tried to get
her wobbling emotions under control. She had long ago
vowed never to shed a tear over anyone who could walk
away from her so easily.

No, whatever emotion this was had to be something
to do with the massive release her body had just experienced. The aftershocks of which had barely even sub-
sided and her body was throwing a tantrum, demanding
more of him. What on earth was she doing?

Mortified, she began to pull up her bra and the material of her dress to cover her still bare breasts. The silk
fabric had already been tight, but now that it was damp
from both the rain and the kisses he had dragged over
her skin it hiked her breasts up into a lurid cleavage. Her
nipples were still hard from where they had been practically devoured, and she inhaled sharply as the dress
caught on one jutting peak.

'What are you doing?'

Aria looked up, to find herself pinned by a dark gaze
as he watched her.

'Getting dressed, obviously.' She choked out the
words, praying she could hold herself together just long
enough to get far away from this too-small bathroom with
all of its mirrored surfaces. She turned away to face the
small vanity, but there he was reflected in the glass. Everywhere she looked, she saw him.

The realisation that they hadn't even taken off yet
made her stomach sink even further. They still had an
entire transatlantic flight ahead of them. As far as impulsive actions went, this one was pretty spectacular. 'I
didn't intend for this to happen.'

'I never said you did,' he said.

'Well, I just needed to clarify that. Considering you're looking at me like…like you regret everything we just did.'

He watched her for a moment, then he bridged the space between them, hooked one finger under her chin and tilted her face up until she met his gaze. 'You could not be further from the truth. Do you regret it?'

'We literally just met,' she muttered. 'It's all a bit over-whelming.'

'That's not what I asked.' His eyes darkened even further, impossible considering they were already glittering obsidian. 'I just had the best orgasm of my life and yet I immediately want to take you again.'

She was pretty sure she felt her jaw drop, her mind stunned to silence. But what else was a girl to think when a guy made her see stars and then tried to put as much space between them as humanly possible right after they had just…*you know*. She shivered, hearing the way he pronounced orgasm repeating over and over in her mind. The way he looked at her, the way he made her feel… She had always thought people simply lied when they said sex could be addictive. For her, it had always been a chore, a performance. But now…now she finally understood.

'I don't regret it, Nysio.' She reached out and touched her hand to his shoulder, still clad in his shirt. 'And actually that was the best orgasm I've ever had too.' She simply wanted to show him that she understood, that she could see this loss of control was affecting him just as much as it had affected her. But her words and her touch seemed to be the only spark needed to reignite the madness once more.

This time when his lips claimed hers, there was no restraint whatsoever. It was as though the man who had devoured her moments before had been a mere appetiser to this. His mouth was cruel, demanding and utterly sin-ful as his tongue tangled with her own. His hands gripped her waist tight, holding her in place as though he feared that she might try to leave.

Yet somehow she knew that if she did call a stop to this right now, he would. Whatever this was between them was not about either of them holding more power or manipulating one another or seeking a reward, this was pure primal lust as she had never dreamed of experiencing. It had been pretty easy not to date much when she had never really enjoyed things in the bedroom.

Strong fingers moved up her ribcage and his hips pressed harder against her, spreading her wide again, his eyes seeking hers, questioning…

'You said you want me again…then have me,' she said boldly, determined to wring out every last drop of pleasure from this night. Because she knew that tomorrow would come and she would be back to the cold, harsh reality of the life that awaited her in London. Was it really so bad to choose to live in a dream for a little while?

'The plane will take off soon. But first, I think you wanted to get freshened up?' He began taking off her dress and she let him, feeling it pool around her feet. He tried to unclasp her bra, but she had to help him.

'The clasp is quite tricky. I still haven't quite mastered that part of the sewing process.'

'You made this?' His brows rose. 'You're a fashion designer?'

'Well… I want to be.' She smiled, wondering why it felt more intimate to be having this conversation than any of the other interactions they'd had during this wild evening. But before she could stop herself, she was launching into telling this half naked stranger about her plan to pitch a boutique plus-size lingerie line at her team evaluation meeting tomorrow. How it was a long shot, but she had to try. She knew the fashion buying and marketing business like the back of her hand and now she had practical experience in the design and manufacturing processes too. She'd done all the numbers and she knew it would work, she just needed them to believe it too.

If he was surprised or bored by her enthusiasm, he didn't show it. He studied the strawberry-print silk bra in his hands, analysing the stitching and boning she'd agonised over during her final examinations, and placed it down carefully on the vanity as though it were something precious.

'If you are this passionate about everything you do, I expect them to jump at the chance to keep your vison and skill on their team. I know I would. Passionate people are few and far between in my world. It's mostly about routine and consistency…and money.'

'I'm ADHD, so excitement is fuel for me. Boredom and routine are rather painful.' He nodded with apparent understanding, a strange look entering his eyes for a moment. Why was she oversharing so much? She cursed herself, wishing he would just start kissing her again so she'd stop talking.

'We are very different people, aren't we? But perhaps that's why I can't get enough of you. You're like an injection of pure energy. I haven't felt this alive in a long time.'

His shirt joined her dress on the floor, then the rest of his clothing. He walked them backwards towards the rainfall shower, reaching out to touch a button that set hot water cascading down. His eyes met hers, his hips rocking that hardness against her for a moment. 'Once we're up in the air, I'm determined to get you into an actual bed and not let you back out for a very long time.'

Aria woke with a jolt, her sleep-fogged brain struggling to make sense of the current time and place. The bed was empty and the white sheets were a tangle around her body, a crude reminder of last night's erotic efforts. She held her breath, craning her neck to listen for any sounds of life beyond the bedroom door.

No Nysio, she registered, refusing to note her own disappointment at that fact.

They'd landed on the tarmac in London before dawn and what had been meant to be a goodbye kiss had ended up with both of them falling back into bed for yet another quick round of mutually explosive lovemaking. She must have fallen asleep again afterwards…and he'd left. She covered her face with her hands. She was trapped in here, naked, and whoever was outside the door was likely fully aware of that fact. The memory of her gown and underwear sliding over her body and abandoned on the bathroom floor was branded in her mind, sending a fresh wave of goosebumps along her sensitive skin.

She flopped back against the luxury mattress, as soft as air. She refused to feel ashamed of last night, when it had been so life-changing for her. She'd known what this was.

But had he really just left her without so much as a goodbye?

No, she was not going to lie here and feel even a tiny bit sorry for herself. With a deep fortifying breath, she stood up and wrapped the white sheet around her torso like a toga. The wall of mirrors in the luxurious master cabin mocked her with her own ridiculous reflection, showing panda eyes and the utterly destroyed remnants of her bridesmaid chignon.

Memories assailed her mind from the night before, tightening up every muscle in her body with a mixture of embarrassment and astonishment that it had all been real. She had truly been seduced and pleasured by a billionaire on his private jet while they flew across the Atlantic. She would not regret it, not when her body felt so deliciously satisfied and loose from pleasure. They were both adults, after all.

He had said he didn't make a habit of picking up women, but he'd admitted he was under pressure. Tensions were high and she had been a...convenient outlet.

He hadn't kidnapped her onto his jet, she'd walked on of her own free will. She'd given into temptation all over again. More than once. She closed her eyes, exhaling a shaky breath as she tried to get a handle on herself.

She hadn't known her body could work that way. She'd always known her previous experiences in the bedroom had been uniquely bad and unlucky, but wow. The flight had lasted eight hours and she was pretty sure he had made it his mission to make her lose count of the amount of times they'd made love before she fell asleep in an orgasm-drunk haze.

Was it even a one-night stand if they had crossed time zones?

Considering she had to slip back into her gown from the day before, she decided to forgo using the lavish shower again. Her pendant necklace had disappeared from her neck and she tried to keep calm as a quick search of the cabin came up empty. Another look in the mirror confirmed that she looked exactly like a woman who was about to make the walk of shame off a luxury jetliner. Not exactly a sentence she'd ever thought that she would use in her lifetime.

There was only one staff member still on board when she exited the bedroom and walked gingerly along the central cabin in her bare feet. A quick search along the floor produced her shoes and little clutch bag. But it was okay—a quick look at the time on one of the screens showed that it was still early enough for her to make it back to her basement apartment in Richmond and quickly change into something before her usual commute into the city.

But when she exited the jet, the morning light momentarily blinding her as she stepped out into the chilly English air, it was to find a dark car coming to a stop mere feet away on the tarmac with the object of her thoughts behind the wheel. She inwardly cringed at the situation, pasting on a much too bright smile as Nysio stepped out and turned up the collar of his tan jacket against the harsh breeze.

'I apologise for leaving without explanation, but you needed some sleep and my presence was needed to resolve a small dispute with the customs officer.' He moved to the rear of the luxury car and produced something from the back seat. 'I was hoping to return with this before you woke up.'

In his hands was a suitcase. But not just any suitcase. It was her very own neon-pink one, easily recognised by a large blue ink splash from where her pen had exploded mid-flight at some point during her last travelling spree. She felt her jaw go slack, a handful of questions crowding her mind all at once.

'How did you get it from Priya's apartment?'

'I have people.' He shrugged.

Aria took in his calm expression and admitted he didn't look quite like the rueful morning-after guy on the run she'd expected. But that didn't mean anything, did it? She didn't want it to mean anything, and she had told him exactly as much last night. So then why did it make her heart jump a little when he looked at her?

'I'll wait here while you shower and change.'

Aria took the bag, silently walking back towards the

bathroom, her heart beating fast in her throat. There had been absolutely no need for him to go to such lengths to retrieve her things. But as she opened up her suitcase and spied the black high-waisted trousers and baby-blue blouse she'd chosen specifically for her presentation she felt her throat tighten with emotion.

She was just tired, she told herself. Tired and nervous about work and still recovering from the whirlwind of the day before… And the night.

She took the quickest shower known to man, dried off and dressed, staring at her reflection in the mirror sternly. She would not keep thinking about the night. With a light slick of matte red lipstick, and a quick kiss blown in the bathroom mirror, where she absolutely did not gaze longingly at a certain countertop while her cheeks blushed, she was ready.

When she emerged once more, taking the steps slowly in her kitten heels, Nysio was still leaning against the bonnet of his car. He opened his mouth as though to speak, then closed it again and, for the first time since they'd laid eyes on one another the day before, an awkward silence fell between them.

Nysio had expected someone who worked in fashion to dress well, perhaps one of those businesswoman shift dresses with office-appropriate heels. Of course this woman would turn office fashion into something better suited to the pages of a risqué magazine. Or perhaps there was nothing risqué at all and he was simply looking at her through the new lens of knowing exactly what hid beneath the satin layer of her delicate blue blouse. He wondered if she still wore the strawberry bra beneath and his mouth quite literally watered. *Dannazione*, his thoughts had a mind of their own around this woman.

She looked unsure. He knew he should say something—he should tell her that last night had been wonderful, because it had. He should tell her that when he had awoken after losing count of how many times they'd made love he had been busy making plans to see if he could stay in London for a few days. He wondered how she might react to the proposition. But before he could say any of that, Aria was the first one to speak.

'Okay... This is the part I was dreading.' She avoided looking directly at him while shuffling through her purse.

'What part might that be?'

'The whole awkward morning-after part.' She finally looked at him, her smile a little too bright and not quite meeting her eyes. 'So I'm going to make it really easy, I've already asked the crew to call me a cab.'

'Easier for whom?' he heard himself say.

'For both of us, I suppose. This way, there are no empty promises or small talk. I get to my presentation on time and you get to go back to your fancy billionaire life after taking this...detour.'

'You think I see you as a detour?'

'No. I just mean that it was all very unexpected and neither of us was in the market for anything more than one night. Right?'

He allowed silence to follow her question, his mind stumbling over the threads of his own intentions. He remembered holding her in his arms, in between the copious rounds of sex they'd shared. They had laughed, they had spoken of trivial things, never getting too deep. But still, he'd got the impression that she had been hurt badly in the past. She'd told him that she didn't date much now as a result, that she was focused on her career. But if he asked to see her again, would she assume that he was offering her more than just a casual affair?

Once upon a time, he had been supremely sure that one day he would settle down and marry, continue the family line. But now...now that he knew his position, his very identity as the Bacchetti heir, was built upon nothing but lies...he knew that he would never put his own child in that position. The darkness of his thoughts must have shown on his face, he realised with chagrin as he looked up to find Aria still studiously avoiding his gaze.

'Well...' Aria shuffled awkwardly on one foot. 'Thank you for everything.'

'You're thanking me as though I have provided you with a service of some sort.'

'A very efficient service, if that helps?' Her laugh jarred his nerves with how false it sounded. Gone was the confident, honest siren from the night before and in her place was someone he had no idea how to read. Those walls he had had to work so hard to dismantle the night before had clearly sprung right back with extra reinforcements.

'I'm confused... Have I misread something?' she asked, just as a second chauffeur-driven car slid up beside his own. His over-efficient crew had been all too eager to help his guest, it seemed. The driver stepped out and called her by name, taking the suitcase from her hands and stowing it efficiently in the rear before holding open the passenger door.

'My presentation starts in less than an hour, so I asked the crew to call me a car. I assumed that you would have things to do.'

'You *assumed* that I make a habit of sleeping with women and disposing of them like trash. I promised to deliver you to your interview.' He gestured to the car behind him. 'And that's what I plan to do.'

'Oh... That's very kind of you. But completely unnecessary. I came to your aid back in Manhattan, and you felt obligated to repay me. Last night was amazing, but there's no need for either of us to make out that it was more than a pleasant distraction for us both.'

Her words should be giving him comfort, but instead he found himself holding back from lifting her back up onto the jet... He scowled, watching as she turned to him and for a moment he feared she might reach out and shake his hand. He had never experienced this before; any entanglements he'd had in the past had been ended by him. Was that why this felt so uncomfortable? Was he so privileged and entitled that he was balking at the idea of her being the one to walk away? Perhaps he needed to ensure that he was the one in control.

He took her hand, meeting her eyes in the golden morning light. 'What if I asked you to come and join me in Florence for another weekend of...pleasant distraction?'

'Why would you do that?'

'Why not?' He shrugged. 'It could be fun.'

She seemed to deflate at his answer. 'I could really like you, Nysio, if I let myself. But I've learned that when I like someone, I really like them and, well... It tends to just get me hurt. I don't think either of us is prepared for this to get any more complicated than it already is.'

With a final kiss on his cheek, she got into the car and was gone. Nysio scowled again, not quite pitiful enough to watch the car's departure across the tarmac. The jet's interior was a quiet welcome, Gianluca appearing predictably at his side to ask if he'd made a decision on their flight plans.

'Get us slotted in for the next departure time to Florence,' he said, aware that his tone was far surlier than necessary.

'Back to our usual routine this week, then?' the older man asked.

Nysio nodded, feeling far less satisfaction with the idea of returning to his old normal than he'd ever thought possible.

CHAPTER FIVE

ARIA'S PRESENTATION WENT without a hitch as she knew it would. Fake it till you make it was her motto and by the time she was walking out of the conference room full of executives she was filled with hope that this was actually going to happen for her. The strange aches and twinges in her body had lasted for a few days, a crude reminder of her wild night of passion every time her mind tried to convince her it had all been a mirage. She spent the rest of the next two weeks working extra hard on her usual projects as her team awaited the results of their evaluation.

Of all of the outcomes she'd expected, it wasn't to walk into work the following Monday morning to find that their entire clothing department had been made redundant. Moving to an online-only model had been one of the biggest terms thrown around. She'd cleared out her desk in a daze and found herself at home sitting on her couch by lunchtime after a tearful goodbye.

News of the shocking lay-offs had made global news and, one week later, flowers had appeared on her doorstep accompanied by a small box containing a golden necklace that almost exactly matched the one she had misplaced on the jet. It was not the same one, she could tell, because this one was clearly infinitely more expensive.

The note read:

*My offer still stands. If you find yourself with time
for another adventure, the city of Florence will
await you.*
    Just call.
    N

Aria ran a finger over the embossed gold lettering from
the boutique florist. There was no way he could have
known that she'd just been made redundant, was there?
No way he could have known how badly she'd needed
some kind of pick-me-up as she'd found herself sitting
around in her own self-pity. In the past three weeks, she
had thought of that mile-high night of passion more times
than she could count. She had wondered where he was,
wondered if he was thinking of her too. But she also remembered how Nysio had admired her underwear design and listened to her plans, how he'd seemed to truly
believe she had a chance at success. He'd called her passionate.

She didn't feel especially passionate now, in the face
of her defeat. But still she found herself digging out her
plans and projections, an entirely new and infinitely risk-
ier plan beginning to form in her mind. She was unem-
ployed for the first time in a decade, but she had her nest
egg from the redundancy pay-out, which had been generous in lieu of a long notice period, and she could get a
bank loan for the rest. Starting up a plus-size lingerie line
alone as an entrepreneur was a ridiculous idea…wasn't it?

She smiled, picking up another sample design and feeling her brain hum with plans and ideas. She had spent
so long trying to rein in her high-energy mind and not
make mistakes. She'd finished her textile degree against

the odds, she'd worked hard and advanced through her job all while sacrificing her love of travel and spontaneity. She had often dreamed of taking some time to wander, to fall back in love with the world and come up with a way to forge her own path on her own terms. Maybe it was time for her to stop hiding away her passion and let herself run wild with it?

As she stared at the vibrant flowers on her coffee table and opened up the envelope containing a number for a premier flight operator and details of a prepaid ticket, she felt tempted to be spontaneous once again.

Nysio cursed and slammed the lid of his computer down. His concentration had been atrocious over the past month and he'd just made yet another careless error in his projections, resulting in an unprecedented loss of capital that would have brought most investment firms to their knees. Luckily for him, he was not most investment firms and his unusual business practices meant that his reserves ran deep. Of course, this was now the third day this week that he'd made a mistake and his accountant had even called to ask what on earth was happening.

And what exactly *was* happening? he asked himself, pushing his chair back from the antique mahogany desk in an effort to not give in to the impulse to hurl something against the wall. He had not been himself ever since that impulsive trip across the Atlantic. It was the only possible explanation. The return journey, specifically…

An image of flame-coloured hair and strawberry-scented skin filled his mind as though it had been waiting for the right moment to assault his senses. His stomach clenched, his fists tightening against the rush of arousal that always accompanied thoughts of her.

Her.

That single pronoun was how he'd been subconsciously referring to the woman who had occupied a space in his mind for almost a month now, as though the use of her name might cement his obsession any further.

Not an obsession, he corrected himself. He was not under some kind of thrall. Their night of passion on the jet had just knocked him off kilter, that was all. It had been far too long since he'd been with a woman, it was only natural that he wouldn't be satisfied from just the scant few hours he'd had her. Especially when she had walked away from his offer so easily.

He had returned to Florence and thrown himself right back into his usual punishing work routine of eighteen-hour days spread across the various global stock markets. He'd got used to keeping odd hours, filling any downtime by working up a sweat in his gym or swimming length after length in the heated pool in the solarium. When he was physically and mentally exhausted enough, he eventually slept. But never for long enough and never quite as deeply as he had on that jet...

He stared out at the view from his window, wondering why memories of that one night felt like a drug. Other than that, the only time he broke his rigid routine was the bi-monthly weekend he set aside to spend visiting his parents in Sardinia. A visit he had postponed in the aftermath of last month's revelations about the identity of his biological father. His mother had called numerous times and he was pretty sure they knew he was avoiding them. But the alternative was actually facing the reality that his father was not his father and his parents had lied to him for his whole life.

He had always adored the blissful silence and solitude of the *palazzo* in the evenings after all the staff had returned to their homes in the city, but these past weeks he'd found it made him feel tense and on edge, as though he were waiting for something. Since his return, he had struggled to fall back into the few leisurely pursuits he allowed himself like reading or cataloguing his vast wine collection. He had tried, countless times, but his eyes would blur along the lines of text, his mind wandering to other, more X-rated thoughts.

As a result, the insomnia that he'd thought he had fully cured himself of with his exercise regime had now returned with a force that left him restless and wandering the halls.

One night in particular, he'd found himself in the pantry of the kitchens searching the shelves for jars of preserved sweet berries and jams, opening each one and inhaling deep, only to curse and move on to the next, furiously seeking the one particular scent that his memory was unable to fully recall.

Nysio hadn't even realised he had left his office and begun pacing the halls until he found himself staring up at the vaulted ceiling of the ancient family gallery that ran the length of the ground floor along the vast east wing. He scowled up at the painted cherubs and imperious gods and goddesses, feeling their judgemental gazes bear down upon him. This had always been Arturo Bacchetti's favourite place in the *palazzo*, before his parents had retired to the vineyard in Sardinia. The gallery was a place that Nysio actively avoided, now that the more historic parts of the estate were occasionally opened to the public.

Their family's status was one that was earned, not only by their vast fortune and collections of priceless art, but by their position as the city's most prolific charitable benefactors. Their presence at their historic Florentine *palazzo* provided year-round tourism for the locale.

They provided patronage for local artists and funded most community efforts. Many of the other noble family names had died out, but the Bacchettis had remained. And perhaps that had been a cushy position a hundred years ago and more, when the Bacchetti family had been far more numerous and able to widely delegate.

Now, there was only Nysio.

He ran a finger along a glass case that housed a four-hundred-year-old golden throne, wondering if smashing some priceless and irreplaceable Bacchetti heirloom might jolt him out of this wretched stagnation he'd fallen into.

As if on cue, Gianluca appeared in the entryway, as though he had sensed Nysio's temptation to destroy a part of his beloved estate.

'You're not normally out of your office at this time,' the other man said, dropping a box full of freshly printed tourist guides onto the floor beside the door before surveying him with concern.

'I may as well be here.' Nysio sighed, looking at his watch to find it was only early afternoon. 'The markets are not my friend today. I decided it was best for all of us if I took a step away.'

Gianluca frowned. 'That's not like you. Are you ill?'

'I'm fine,' Nysio snapped. He was fine, he would be fine. Eventually... This feeling, it reminded him of the first few months after his father's Parkinson's diagnosis, after he had vowed to fully accept his role as Arturo's heir. To perform his birth-given duty, even if it suffocated him. He had been restless, fresh out of a short-lived post-university period of debauchery and rebellion. But what was his excuse now?

Surely spending less than twelve hours with the most alluring woman he had ever encountered was not enough to completely change his personality? It was ridiculous and infuriating and he would not tolerate it. He made a few enquiries about the day-to-day running of the estate, happy to distract himself with Gianluca's entertaining tales from the city before he turned to head back to work. As he moved through the *palazzo*, he internally readied himself to prove to himself that he was above such distractions, only to have the other man appear behind him in his office, jolting him from his thoughts.

'Nysio, I wasn't going to say anything…but, do you remember your *guest* that we deposited in London a month ago?'

Nysio froze, his body turning around in slow motion as though pulled by an invisible string. 'What of her?'

'She's in Florence.' The older man met his eyes. 'She called at the estate foundation office in town yesterday, and made a donation for the exact same price of her flight.'

Nysio felt frozen in place. 'She's still here?'

Gianluca nodded. 'At least, she was when I checked earlier today. But her return flight is tomorrow.'

Nysio fought the urge to roar with frustration. She had been here for a whole day already without him knowing. He had been within walking distance of the object of his frustrations… But what did it mean? Surely if she had come to accept his proposition, she'd have travelled here to the *palazzo*. She would have come to him. He felt his chest tighten even more, some uncontrollable vibration of energy that seemed to rise from his stomach upwards, but he somehow kept his body completely still.

'Thank you for telling me, Gianluca.'

The other man's eyes widened. 'That's it?'

'Was there anything else you needed to discuss? I have work to do.' Nysio sat down behind his desk with barely constrained energy humming through his veins, the computer screen blurring in front of his eyes as his mind turned this new information over and over. On impulse, he pulled a small object from his pocket, turning the small golden letter A over and over in its miniature circle. The pendant had been broken from being crushed under someone's foot before he'd found it under the bed on his flight home from London.

He'd repaired it, but decided to send her a new one once he'd seen the news of her company's harsh lay-offs. He hadn't banked on the fact that every time he held it, he remembered seeing it dangling from Aria's neck as she straddled him, leaning over so he could suckle on her...

Gianluca's voice intruded on his thoughts. 'All I'm saying is, perhaps the lady wished for you to know that she was here. If she didn't, she wouldn't have left this note.'

Nysio's gaze snapped back up. 'What note?'

Gianluca smiled knowingly. 'It must be at least five years since I've seen you showing any kind of interest in a woman.'

Nysio narrowed his eyes, his look clearly conveying his inability to take a joke on the subject because the other man quickly pulled up a screen on his tablet computer and laid it on the desk. 'It was only given to me today.'

Nysio only half listened, his attention fully taken up by the few lines of communication thanking him for the ticket. She had not contacted him immediately after he had sent the necklace, the flowers and plane ticket. So he had accepted that she was serious about not continuing their entanglement any further. He had never been the type of guy to force his attentions on anyone, most especially on someone who had been clear that they were not interested in more. At least, she had *seemed* sure she was not interested in more…but the fact that her note was clearly headed with the name of the hotel she was staying in said quite a different story. He smiled broadly, inhaling a deep breath, and felt something loosen within his chest.

'Clear my meetings for tomorrow, Gianluca. Actually, clear them for the whole weekend.'

'Where are you going?'

'To be spontaneous,' he called back over his shoulder, striding out of his office and in search of the nearest car as fast as his legs would take him.

Aria was thoroughly enchanted by Florence.

For two glorious days, she had ambled along narrow cobbled streets flanked by elegant Renaissance palaces, marble basilicas and world-class art museums brimming with iconic paintings and sculptures. It was quite a culture shock, travelling from her traffic-clogged London suburb to this small city with its extraordinary art and architectural masterpieces at every turn. It was quite possibly the most beautiful city she had ever visited.

But all the while she had found herself looking over her shoulder, hyperaware of her surroundings and wondering if she would turn to find a familiar pair of sensual dark blue eyes watching her.

There had been no need for her to leave the note at Nysio's foundation along with her donation, and yet she had not been able to stop herself. She'd told herself that she just needed to let Nysio know that she had used his ticket, and only because the flight had been the best option available at the last minute.

Perhaps she had also come here with a small hope that he might seek her out. But the idea of outright contacting him and accepting his arrogant offer to fly over to him, like a paid and packaged gift for his entertainment...she just couldn't bring herself to do it.

Still, she now knew by the disappointment churning in her gut that she had very obviously hoped to see him again. It was her last night in the city and her small suitcase was packed and ready to leave for the airport back to London tomorrow. She was excited to get started on her plans. Her parents had been less than happy with her news when she'd shared her plans to start up her own line of plus-size lingerie. They'd sermonised on job security and the risks of start-ups. Her mother had made the predictable comment that she was *thirty-one*, as though that was a reason in itself to avoid following her dreams.

All of these thoughts seemed to compound into one giant splitting headache as her eyes fell upon the single cocktail dress she'd left hanging in the wardrobe. The midnight-blue mini was a custom piece from an exciting plus-size designer that she'd acquired for the store more than a year ago but never found the occasion to wear. With its full-length sleeves and deep plunging neckline, it was the kind of outfit that one wore out on a hot date, not down for dinner at her table for one before taking an early night alone...but then again, Aria had never been the type of girl to follow the rules, had she?

Feeling a spurt of energy, she showered and took some time to dry her hair in soft waves around her face, adding red lipstick and some smoky eye make-up. Simple black lingerie and stockings ensured she felt smoothed and supported and as she gazed upon the final result in the bathroom mirror, she smiled. The fabric of the dress sparkled like a night sky, the material clinging to her curves like a dream.

It might be overkill for a night dining alone, but if there was one thing that could be said about Aria Dane it was that she bounced back, every time. This weekend had been exactly what she needed to clear her head before she had a meeting with her bank next week to discuss her business plans. Her redundancy money was enough to get started, but not enough if things took off as she really expected them to. She wanted to be prepared.

By the time she was seated in the hotel's extravagant fine dining restaurant, she was feeling quite elated. The waiter had just delivered her drink order and she was perusing the menu when she felt the hairs on the back of her neck tingle.

With her wine glass halfway to her lips, she looked up to find the grey-haired maître d' hovering by her side with an unusually flustered air. 'Is everything okay?' she asked the man, noticing the slight sheen of sweat on his brow.

'Signora Dane, I have been asked to extend an invitation to you from a most important patron of the hotel… to a private dinner in the penthouse.'

'An invitation from whom?' she asked, thinking he must have approached the wrong guest, but then she looked behind her and felt her breath catch.

The important patron in question leaned against the archway of the restaurant entrance, his brooding gaze and broad silhouette unmistakeable in the golden light. Nysio was here…he had come to seek her out. Blood pounded in her ears and she could have sworn that every nerve ending on her body jumped to attention.

But his invitation to a *private* dinner made her pause. She might have come here with the intention of seeing him again but she had not been lying when she'd made it clear that she was not in the market for any further secret rendezvous. She had made a promise to herself that she would not be another wealthy man's secret lover, ever again. Even if said lover had given her the most pleasure she had ever known in her life.

The maître d' still awaited her response and Aria straightened her shoulders, determined not to lose her composure. 'You can tell Signor Bacchetti that I am flattered by his offer to dine privately, but I am going to have to politely decline. He is quite welcome to join me here at *my* table, however.'

'Signor Bacchetti does not dine with the other guests,' the man replied, clearly stunned at the audacity of her response.

'Well, it will be a novel experience for us both, then.' She took a tiny sip of wine, trying not to react at the sudden nausea it caused as it mixed with her swirling nerves.

The man disappeared from view and it took all of Aria's control not to crane her neck to look back. After a couple of minutes she gave in and felt her entire body react at the sight of Nysio making his way across the restaurant floor, his gaze filled with intent. He had told her that he shied away from the attention his name got him here in Florence, but she hadn't truly understood what he'd meant until now. The waitstaff around him bowed their heads in deference, a shocked hush carrying across the restaurant as though he were a celebrity or royalty...or both.

Frantically trying to get her erratic heartbeat under control, Aria remained frozen in her seat until he was but a few steps away, then realised she should probably stand up to greet him. The restaurant was full and it seemed as though every eye was upon them when he finally reached her.

'*Buonasera*, Aria.' His lips curved up ever so slightly on one side and she suddenly had another flashback to that night on the jet.

'I thought you didn't dine with other guests,' she said breathlessly, powerless against the shiver that coursed through her when he leaned in and laid a customary kiss on each of her cheeks. He lingered on the second cheek, his breath fanning over her ear as he paused there for the briefest moment.

'I usually prefer to dine away from prying eyes, yes. But I think I can tolerate it…in the right company.' His voice was smooth as silk as he let his eyes wander down over her body for the briefest moment, but it was enough to set her pulse racing all over again. This man was a menace to her composure, an absolute menace.

'Has no one ever told you it is considered rude to refuse a dinner invitation from the owner of the establishment?' he said silkily as he helped her back into her chair before sliding into the seat across from her.

'You…*own* this place?' She whistled low, looking round at the ornate vaulted ceilings and priceless art that lined the walls. 'I knew you were wealthy, but clearly you undersold it. I planned to buy you dinner, to thank you for rescuing me in Manhattan, but now I'm wondering if we should split the bill.' She laughed.

'You are now here as my guest. There will be no splitting the bill.' He uttered the phrase with distaste, as though she had deeply offended him, gesturing to the waitstaff nearby to come and take their order. 'If I had known you were planning to accept my offer, I would have ensured no expense was spared. For now, an upgrade to the penthouse will suffice.'

'Okay, hold on.' Aria sat up straight, feeling her irritation rise. 'You're rich, I get it. But I didn't come here to be given a free ride on the luxury billionaire train.'

'Why did you come, then?'

'I came to see Florence and I can pay for my own room, Nysio.'

'You can. But I'd like to show you my Florence, if you'll let me?'

If she'd thought his accent while speaking English was sexy, his voice as he spoke rapid-fire Italian almost set her aflame. She could do little more than sit and stare as he conversed personally with the chef, gesturing with his hands and pausing to translate and enquire in English about her individual preferences for food. When she explained that she didn't eat a lot of meat, he ensured that an array of tasting platters was brought out, each dish gourmet and more utterly divine than the last.

Occasionally, he seemed uncomfortable when other diners stared or spoke in hushed whispers, but mostly the meal passed in pleasant conversation as she talked about her recent entrance into unemployment. She attempted to sound relaxed, but he still frowned at her words.

'I'm sorry.'

'Thanks. I'm okay, though. I actually took some of your advice.'

'My advice?'

'I've always dreamed of starting up my own lingerie line, but I was comfortable in my job and I told myself I could never do it. But then you told me about how you incorporated your talents into your family business and made it your own...well, I found that quite inspiring.'

As the last of their desserts were cleared away, the air between them had become tense and fraught with countless words it seemed neither of them were quite brave enough to say first. He surprised her by taking her arm and guiding her through the lobby of the hotel where it opened out onto a private courtyard. The sky was rapidly darkening to dusk, making the building glow amber, and tiny golden lamps accented the sprawling fountain in the centre.

'I think Florence has ruined me for all other cities.' She sighed with pleasure.

'Sometimes it feels like that,' he murmured, seemingly mulling over something in his mind as he paced away from her to inspect a statue in their periphery. When he spoke again, his eyes were more focused. 'The necklace suits you.'

Trying not to raise a brow at his odd manner, she smiled, her hand instantly moving to the golden pendant resting on her collarbone. 'It was very kind of you to send it. You didn't have to replace it.'

'I felt it was only fair, considering it was my fault the last one was lost.'

Aria's breath caught as she took in the heat in his eyes and knew that he too was remembering the events from that night. His eyes did not waver from hers. His hand dropped to his side in a clenched fist as though he was trying not to touch her again. Or was she imagining that?

'I didn't see the note you sent until this evening. You didn't respond to my gifts, you told me to stay away. I told you that I would not pursue you and I am a man of my word. But if I had known you were here...'

'You would have rushed straight to me?' She laughed, then paused, realising he was completely serious.

'Without a second thought. Still, it was not soon enough.' The last word escaped his mouth on a breath and again his hand rose, this time making contact with her skin as he gently grazed the side of her elbow. 'Aria, I am going to ask you one question and one question only before I do something that I've wanted to do from the moment I walked through that door this evening.'

Aria's chest tightened, her skin tingling with awareness as she saw the dark promise in his eyes. 'What question?'

'Did you really come here to explore the city...' he moved closer, his voice a low purr near her ear '...or did you come to me?'

Breath exited her chest on a shudder as she fought to contain the visceral reaction that she was beginning to realise always came from having him near. He was a magnetic force, determined to pull her off course every time their paths crossed.

'Because if you came to me... I have already been robbed of the forty-eight hours you've been wandering this city alone, when you could have spent them in my bed.'

'I realised once I was here that I came because I wanted more. But only on my terms. I want you to be *my* entertainment for the weekend, Signor Bacchetti,' she said with a wicked smile. 'I had planned to fly back tomorrow, but I might be persuaded to extend my trip a day or two for the right reasons.'

'What reasons might they be?'

His words were whispered huskily against her ear, while his hands finally gripped her waist, warming her skin through the thin material of her dress. She swallowed hard, planning to respond with something clever and sensual, something to let him know that she was the one calling the shots here...but then his lips touched the sensitive skin of her neck and she instantly seemed to lose the ability to form a coherent sentence.

'You want me to act as your personal tour guide?' he murmured against her skin. 'I will show you everything this city has to offer... You want to be wined and dined in the best restaurants and bought gifts from the finest boutiques? Tell me and I'll make it happen.'

She paused, pulling back to look into his eyes. 'Nysio… I told you already, I don't want you to buy me things. You're all the entertainment I need…that is, if you wanted to…'

Understanding dawned and his eyes darkened even further, his lips finally claiming hers in a scorching kiss. His hands fisted into her hair, his lips and tongue laying claim to her with a passion she had only ever felt in his arms. But if she'd thought that the kisses they had shared on the jet had been illicit and hungry, this one took her breath away.

CHAPTER SIX

HE HAD HOPED his mind had exaggerated the memory of having this woman in his arms, but now he knew that the opposite was true. She seemed to not be aware of the connection between him and her friend's new husband, Eros Theodorou, and for a moment a part of him almost wished that she did. That she had stumbled upon his secret and he was forced to keep her here, to ensure that there hadn't been any more leaks. Maybe then he could explain why he felt such possessiveness over her.

She moaned under his kisses, pressing her gorgeous breasts up against him, and he realised that if he didn't get them somewhere private soon, he would be powerless not to take her on the nearest flat surface.

Reason and propriety won out and he guided her through the hotel lobby towards the private elevator that led up to the most exclusive suite in the hotel, the penthouse. Of course, the three minutes it took to get to the top provided him with just enough time to release one ample breast from the neckline of her dress and give it one thorough suck before he tucked it safely back from view of wandering eyes.

Did she know how much power she had over him? He should slow down, regain control and tell her his rules. The problem was…he had pretty much broken every rule he had from the moment he'd laid eyes on Aria Dane. He'd pursued her, he'd changed his plans, he'd ignored his work. He tried to stir some sense of remorse in himself, but found himself smiling instead.

This woman was like a single bright spark in the darkness. He couldn't look away. She caught his eye, an answering smile crossing her lips as she extended her arms to him, drawing him in closer. Holding him to her as though she feared he was about to disappear too.

Weakness overrode his common sense and he went with her easily, moulding his body against hers on the large four-poster bed that dominated the Royal Bacchetti suite. There would be rumours in the papers by tomorrow, no doubt. He hadn't dined with a beautiful woman in public since his days as a young man on the party scene. Back then, he'd always needed to be a few drinks in before he could loosen up enough to not feel the effect of others watching him. He was very careful what he drank now, for good reason. He had always found difficulty in moderating his use of anything that provided him with relief from his anxiety, from the burden of being a Bacchetti.

Joy, relaxation, happiness, these were all emotions that were in short supply in his world and yet one look on Aria's face and he saw all three. During dinner she had conversed with wild abandon, her emotions open, her face unguarded and absolutely fascinating. He could study her for hours, just as he had once studied ancient tomes from his favourite poets or his favourite classic paintings. He had always been a lover of the arts and she was like a newly discovered fresco, rare and filled with untold meaning and fascination.

When she moved against him he didn't make any move to disguise his attraction, just as she didn't try to hide her own. Such honesty…it was as heady as any drug. She licked her lower lip and gazed up at him through hooded lashes, her cheeks pink as she moved against him. Her eyes widened when she came into contact with the unmistakeable hard ridge of his erection, but she made no move to retreat.

He sucked in a breath through his teeth and tightened his grip on her arm. The urge to pull her into the nearest bed was strong. He wondered how she might respond if he told her how he wanted to have his way with her… He felt unhinged, like some kind of depraved primal beast. He wanted her spread out like a sacrificial offering at an altar, laid bare for him.

But this was not the Middle Ages, he reminded himself as he fought to control his body's complete disregard for propriety. She was a person, not an item for him to take and ravish.

Accepting her proposition felt like the prelude to possibility. The possibility of something more. Suddenly the things that had felt so urgent no longer seemed so important. Not when she looked at him like *that*. As he undressed her and finally sank into her molten heat, he wondered if it would ever be enough.

Aria took her time showering after a second night spent in Nysio's arms. They had hardly left the ornate four-poster bed of the hotel's penthouse suite. The experience was only slightly marred by the steadily tightening knot of nausea and nerves that was building in her stomach as the afternoon progressed. She could only assume that such nerves had something to do with her handsome date for the evening, which was silly considering this wasn't a date at all but a peace offering.

One of the maids had brought up a glass of champagne and a bowl of strawberries for her to enjoy as she readied herself for a surprise date Nysio had organised for her last night in Florence. Fresh flowers had also been arranged on her dressing table, pink roses today rather than the usual simple arrangement of magnolias that were placed strategically throughout the hotel. All in all, it was a lovely way to spend the afternoon, she thought absent-mindedly as she dabbed blush onto her paler than usual cheeks. She took a moment, stepping out onto the balcony for a few deep breaths and willing the bubbling nausea to settle.

By the time Nysio returned from a quick trip to his office she thought she'd got it under control but one look at his face said otherwise.

'Are you feeling well?' he asked, his eyes roving up and down as he assessed her closely.

'Thank you, you look lovely too.' She quirked one brow, nerves making her spin in a silly little twirl. 'My dress? Oh, it's just something I dug out of the wardrobe.'

'You look pale.'

'I'm fine. Just some cramps.'

His brows rose slightly, but he seemed unperturbed. 'Do you need something? Aspirin, perhaps?'

Aria inwardly prayed for the ground to open and swallow her up. The man looked like a god in his designer suit and she was talking about *cramps*?

He touched her hand, stilling her thoughts as he waited for her eyes to meet his. 'You look beautiful, by the way. I probably should have said that first.'

'Thank you.' She felt the butterflies swoop and dance in her tummy all over again as he leaned down to lay a featherlight kiss upon her lips. 'I'm going to stop talking now, lest I start rambling about other bodily functions.'

'Let's not aim for the impossible.' He smirked, leading her outside where a sleek silver sports car lay in wait.

He wore a full tuxedo for the occasion, and she hadn't quite been ready for the visual onslaught of seeing him in formal dress. His hair, usually curled and unruly in its natural state, had been slicked back from his forehead in an effortlessly elegant style.

She found it hard to continue being annoyed with him when he was so obviously trying for her. She just wished she knew why. He had made it quite clear on the jet that night that he was comfortable in his workaholic bachelor lifestyle and she'd thought she had made her peace with that. They were polar opposites in most ways other than the bedroom, so really it was best not to get too attached. She could only assume that tonight was a peace offering of some sort before they parted ways. Her flight had been rebooked for tomorrow morning, her suitcase was neatly packed and her room already put to rights.

It was all very civilised really, she thought as she wiped what was most definitely *not* a tiny tear from the corner of her eye.

As they were served a five-course meal in Nysio's stunning town house in Florence by a world-class chef, she wrestled with the steadily rising discomfort in her gut. She hadn't felt any nerves on their first night together, or their second, so why was she feeling such unease now? Such was her digestive discomfort, she could barely manage a drop of wine and the sight of the pink-centred venison main course made her stomach heave a little.

'Is everything okay?' Nysio asked. His brow furrowed with concern when she stood abruptly from the table and walked to the open patio doors for some fresh air.

'I'm fine,' she assured him. 'Just a little warm.'

She was warm; she had been feeling overheated all week, in fact. But just as she moved to suggest that perhaps Nysio should take her home, the bell rang from the foyer and the butler came in to announce that the evening's surprise entertainment had arrived.

The surprise turned out to be a private performance from a world-renowned opera singer and her accompanying Grammy-winning pianist husband. Nysio's town house was far from small considering it had its very own ballroom in which to enjoy this auditory extravaganza.

The lights had been dimmed, and candelabra lit, making the room seem to glow with atmosphere as the first strains of music floated through the air.

The private show was short, but breathtakingly beautiful, and Aria was stunned as she learned of the many countries in which the duo had performed together, and the names of the numerous members of royalty and governments and celebrities they had performed for made her eyebrows rise into her forehead.

Even though she had dressed the part, wearing a knee-length fifties-style black gown and elbow-length gloves, she still felt the pressure of having to appear cultured in the way that these people clearly were. She had not been raised in this world, a fact that she had no reason to hide but, hearing Nysio discuss the elite university he had apparently attended alongside the beautiful opera singer, she prayed that the conversation would not move onto her.

He left to see them outside and she found herself feeling a little dizzy so she located the nearest place to sit, which just so happened to be at the beautiful piano at the edge of the dance floor. It was an antique Steinway, the black enamel so beautifully preserved and polished that she could see her own reflection in the case. She sat down, dancing her fingers playfully across the keys with a flash of memory.

The song was one she'd learned by heart years before, but it seemed her fingers needed no further notice. She played the simple piece in full, a smile filling her lips as she finished on a perfect chord. She didn't notice she had an audience until she heard the slow clap from behind her.

'When did you learn how to play?' Nysio walked slowly into the room from where he'd perched against the doorway.

'My father refused to pay for lessons because he said I would only quit and it would be a waste of money, so I bought a keyboard and taught myself a few pieces when I was a teenager just to annoy him. I haven't played in years. I don't read music or anything fancy like that. I'm not actually trained.'

'You are full of surprises, Aria Dane.'

'I like to think so.' She gave a delicate curtsy, standing up from the instrument and swaying a little before she corrected herself. She still looked too pale, he thought as he moved to take her elbow and guide her out onto the terrace. She had barely eaten at dinner and there was something just a little off…

She moved to stand beside the stone balustrade, gazing out at their perfect view of the Duomo lit up in all its glory. He wondered if she liked it, if she was enjoying the evening. He'd thought that perhaps the champagne and flowers had been too much, but she hadn't said anything to the contrary.

'It's so beautiful,' she whispered.

'Yes,' Nysio agreed, watching the glitter of the skyline dance in her eyes. How fitting that this woman would be named for both the life force that filled his lungs and the most striking and poignant moment in any opera. As though she could be named anything less.

'How come you don't live here?' she asked, turning to look at him and startling a little to find his eyes already trained upon her.

'This place was a remnant of my old life. I have no need for it any more since I moved to the *palazzo*. I have rarely left the palace grounds in the past decade, ever since...'

'Since what?'

'My father became suddenly unwell soon after my graduation from university, and my mother was struggling to care for him and keep him from becoming prey for the media. He has Parkinson's and it is a difficult condition to live with, very unpredictable. He is a proud man, quite old school, and he wished to keep his illness private. I stepped in to take his place as the head of our family. So I don't have much need for a party house any more.'

'I beg to differ. This place is a wonderful space to entertain in. There is always a need to dance. To have fun. To enjoy occasions with friends.'

'I have no time for any of those things. Once I stepped into my father's place, I discovered issues with the finances and set about resolving them.'

'You suddenly became allergic to fun?'

'I suddenly realised how empty the party scene was. I decided to dedicate my energy to better things.'

'Like crashing stock markets and increasing profit flow? That kind of thing?'

Nysio smiled, against his will. Something that she was beginning to make him do with increasing frequency. 'You don't have any idea what my job is, do you?'

'How could I? You are a man of mystery. I know that

you're pretty rich. That you're descended from some kind of blue-blooded Italian royalty.'

He steeled himself against the sting her words gave him and forced himself to smile. 'Hard to hide that with the whole palace situation though.'

'Then… Tell me something new about yourself. Share a secret.'

He looked away, busying himself by clearing away their glasses to a nearby side table. She couldn't know that so much of his world was built around secrets. Maybe it was the lack of stress in the past two days or maybe he'd uncharacteristically drunk too much wine with dinner after all, but Nysio felt something within him stir at her innocent request. A yearning that begged him to do just as she asked…to share his darkest secret. To lean on someone.

'Have I…said something wrong?'

She was frowning and he realised he hadn't spoken in a couple of minutes. He shook it off, closing the distance between them and claiming her lips in a soft exploratory kiss. Using the easy attraction between them to soothe away the prickly feelings this conversation had unearthed. She relaxed into him, giving back as good as she got, but when the kiss finished her eyes still held echoes of confusion. Nysio rubbed his thumb along the soft curve of her shoulder and felt an ache throb from somewhere deep in his chest.

'I like poetry,' he said finally.

Aria blinked, her mouth forming a small o for a split second until she grasped that he was in fact answering her earlier request. 'Are we talking limericks and haikus?'

'The dirtier the better.' He smirked, feeling his chest ease slightly at the smile that lit up her face. 'No, I actually took a few classes in university. I read every poem

I could get my hands on. It consumed me for a semester or two.'

'Did you ever write any of your own?' She narrowed her gaze upon him, a Cheshire-cat smile taking over her face. 'Oh, my God, you did, didn't you? Can I hear one?'

'I may have written some terrible, brooding sonnets, yes. Ones which will never, ever see the light of day to avoid offending the art itself.'

'Please?'

He let out a wry laugh, remembering his youth and how he had once dreamed of joining the ranks of the writers and poets he admired. Without thinking, he began reciting the first refrain of the only one he could remember. On the surface it was a simple collection of words about a drunken man having an argument with the night sky, but to him it was filled with frustration and a longing for change.

When he'd finished, he cleared his throat, not quite able to look at her for fear of what emotions might be visible on her far too honest face. 'Have my literary talents rendered you speechless?' He laid his glass down on the nearby side table, leaning back and crossing his ankles to survey her. She had one hand on the balustrade, the other splayed across her chest as her eyes drifted open slowly.

'That was…hauntingly beautiful.'

'My professors certainly thought so; it was my one and only claim to fame as a creative writing student before my father made me switch to an economics major.' Nysio remembered how embarrassed he'd felt when his father had discovered his new hobby and had begun reminding him of his responsibilities. He'd felt ridiculous for even considering his brief dream of forging his own path when he'd been raised to perform his duty to the family name.

Being a Bacchetti was a privilege, that was what he had been taught from the moment he'd been old enough to speak. He enjoyed his work now and he was good at it, and that was more than most people ever got in their lifetimes.

He turned back to the woman before him, reaching out to touch her once again, remembering the words he'd planned to speak tonight before they had become side-tracked. But really, this kind of ease and intimacy was only more evidence that his instincts were right. That he was not ready to say goodbye to Aria Dane just yet.

Aria met his gaze so openly and he felt as if he could see every needy part of her, every salacious thought that she was entertaining about him. How could one woman affect him this way? How could one look ignite passion in him that he had never felt before?

She had been hurt by a wealthy man in the past, she had told him that much. It had made her hide away much the same way that Nysio had been hiding at the *palazzo*. Perhaps that was what he had seen in her? Perhaps that was why whatever this was between them felt like more than simple chemistry. There was nothing simple about it.

He couldn't offer her anything more than pleasure... he would never marry, never have children, that much he would not be swayed upon. But they didn't need to put a label on things. She had told him she believed in spontaneity, so maybe it was time that they acted a little spontaneous.

Aria could hardly believe how wonderful this trip to Florence had been. And Nysio...he was a dream. 'So...you live in a palace, you write poetry in your spare time, when you're not breaking the stock market, of course. What *can't* you do?'

'I'm just a man.'

'That word seems so utterly banal to describe someone who does the things that you do. And yet you hide yourself away in your stone fortress. Hiding your talents from the world, keeping it all to yourself. Why do you do that?'

He shrugged. 'Maybe I simply dislike people.'

'No… That's not it.' She took a step towards him, analysing the furrow between his brows. 'There's something you're not telling me, isn't there?'

'Perhaps.'

'These things… You don't have to tell me about them if you're not comfortable. I won't dig, if you're worried.'

'Did I say I was worried?'

'There it is, that fragile ego.' She smiled good-naturedly. 'I just feel like someone needed to remind you of what the world actually sees. What your talents are, your value,' she said softly.

His eyes met hers and she inhaled a breath at the sudden intensity she saw there. He took her hands, stepping closer so that they almost stood chest to chest.

'Aria… I know that tonight is your last night here. But I brought you here…to this property to show you what might be if you reconsidered my offer from London.'

'Isn't that what we've been doing these past couple of days?'

'Yes, but I was thinking of a more regular set-up.'

She felt her stomach drop instantly. 'Please tell me you're not about to suggest that I become some kind of kept mistress.'

'That's a very outdated phrase. I was thinking more of two consenting adults who live separate lives but regularly enjoy each other's company.'

'You want to…date me?'

'I don't *date*.' He practically growled the word. 'I want

to continue getting to know you, but I don't want to give you the wrong idea.'

'Oh, heaven forbid.' She laughed, moving away from him.

He held onto her wrist. 'I don't think this has run its course yet, do you?'

For a moment, Aria thought she'd heard him wrong. That she was simply grasping onto a wishful hope that he might actually want her, truly want her. But then she heard that word again: yet. Meaning that he thought this would run its course eventually. That even if she stayed for a while, it was inevitable that he would eventually tire of her.

'Do you feel fully satisfied?' he asked, his low rumble coming from just behind her right shoulder. Soft lips touched against the side of her neck and she felt her heart throb a little. She couldn't tell him the true reason why she needed to leave…not without risking something far more delicate than just her pride, something she didn't want to examine too closely.

She turned her head to find him standing directly behind her, his brow furrowed as he tried to read her face. He struggled with that sometimes, she realised. She recognised that often he needed to hear the exact words from her, plain and simple rather than relying on guessing games. She loved how plain and honest he was. She loved being here with him, talking with him…

If she gave more of herself to him on his terms, he had all but written down in ink that he would take it. Passion, sex… But nothing more. She knew with heartbreaking clarity that something more, a deeper connection, was what she truly wanted. Yes, the sex had been amazing, but the man she had come to know over the past forty-eight hours was infinitely more attractive to her. And infinitely more unattainable.

But was she really prepared to walk away from him completely? Would this be the single moment she looked back on in her old age and wished that she had done differently?

She had promised herself that she would never again be made to feel disposable by a man. Prolonging this affair was only prolonging the inevitable moment that he would break her heart, a heart that, if she was honest, was already falling headlong in love with him. The longer she stayed here, the more it would hurt when he walked away.

Her tortured thoughts seemed to be having an effect on the rest of her body as she felt another violent surge of nausea sweep over her like a wave. Determined not to show how unsettled she was by his offer, she turned from him and leaned on the balustrade to try to compose herself. When she seemed to sway forward slightly, Nysio was right there beside her in a flash.

'Be careful you don't hurt yourself,' he chided, placing his strong hands on her upper arms and drawing her towards him.

The world spun even more, and her sensitive stomach followed suit. 'Nysio… I think I'm going to be sick.'

That was the only warning she managed to give him before she pitched forward and was violently ill all over his designer shoes.

CHAPTER SEVEN

THE ROOM WAS bathed in darkness when Aria awoke. Even with the lack of light, she could tell that this wasn't the same sofa she'd fallen asleep on earlier once she had stopped being sick. Alarm swept through her, followed swiftly by nausea when she tried to shimmy herself across the vast mattress to reach the edge of the massive bed.

The low rumbling sound of someone's breathing made her freeze and alarm had her reaching out to the bedside table for any source of light. A dim reading lamp flickered to life above the bed, casting the room with a soft golden hue. A broad male frame loomed large in the shadows, taking up all of the space upon one of the silk-covered wingback chairs in the corner. It only took her a moment to realise it was Nysio.

He lay reclined with one arm thrown haphazardly above his head, an action that had evidently spread the edges of his robe wide open, revealing a tanned, toned torso. The chair was likely another priceless family heirloom passed down for hundreds of years, a chair she would bet was made for decorative rather than practical use and yet he was using it as a bed while she had apparently stolen his.

Aria shimmied the last few feet across the bed with

as much dignity as she could muster until her feet finally dangled over the edge. The drop to the floor was ridiculously high, yet still she managed it and made her way slowly through to the en-suite bathroom. A light flickered on automatically above her head, momentarily blinding her, and she braced her hands on the cold marble cabinets for a moment in case any more of that strange dizziness returned. It didn't.

In fact, she felt mostly fine, other than the noise of her stomach growling after the lack of food she'd consumed at dinner. But still, the thought of eating anything made her want to gag. Aria leaned back against the cool tiled wall and frowned.

It had been a little over four weeks since the night she'd spent with Nysio on the jet. She hadn't had a regular period since going on birth control, so missing her cycle this month hadn't even made her think twice. She pushed away the niggling concern of what else might be causing her symptoms and instead distracted herself with the memories of the previous night when Nysio had held her hair back while she was ill. Not exactly the romantic last night together that she'd hoped for.

'Smooth moves, Dane.' She covered her face, hardly believing she had blown their final night together so spectacularly. And now she was being even more ridiculous by worrying when she had a flight to prepare for. She shook her head, staring at her reflection in the gilded mirror above the vanity. She was still paler that usual, which was saying something considering she had been born with the world's palest complexion. Her eyes were glassy and her hair was…completely beyond salvation. She settled for a quick swish of mouthwash she found in a cabinet and a bracing splash of water on her face before trying to finger-comb her frizz.

Giving up on trying to look presentable, she inhaled a deep breath and opened the bathroom door only to walk face first into Nysio's very warm, very naked chest. The intoxicating scent of him enveloped her with its drugging warmth and she just barely resisted the urge to bury her face in further before sanity intervened.

If this man had still been harbouring any illicit fantasies about her, she was pretty sure she'd done a top-notch job of obliterating any chance she had after last night's embarrassing performance.

He had most definitely seen her at her worst, and when she took a hasty step backwards and reluctantly met his gaze she was met with a strange look on his face that she was pretty sure was pure pity.

'You still look unwell,' he drawled, his voice a husky rasp from sleep.

'You're such a flatterer,' she mumbled, squirming a little under the intensity of his assessing gaze. He seemed to scan her for a moment before moving aside, allowing her space to awkwardly shuffle past him in the doorway. Likely he was keeping his distance, in case whatever she had was contagious. She realised he was still wearing a fancy robe, briefly taking in the dark hair on his chest and realised that he in fact was wearing matching silk lounge pants. It was so quintessentially posh that she would most definitely have smirked and made a joke under normal circumstances. Of course, nothing about their situation was normal, nor had it ever been really.

He stepped back, pulling the front of his robe closed in a way that made Aria wonder if he'd actually heard her thoughts. Or perhaps he thought she was ogling him, which she most definitely was not. Well…it was hard not to look at a body like his, especially when he was flaunting it mere inches from her face.

Realising she had begun to blush again, she folded her arms and tried to ignore how the movement made her chest ache uncomfortably. 'I'm sorry about last night. You didn't have to…mind me.'

'You needed minding.' He reached out and touched her cheek, scanning her face once more. He was looking at her in much the same way she'd seen him analyse his computer screen on the handful of occasions she'd spied him working. As if she were a puzzle he needed to solve and he would get his answers through sheer force of will.

'Well…thank you. I'm fine now. I promise.' She stepped around him, her chest accidentally brushing his forearm. She winced at the pain in the tender peaks. She glanced up to find concern lacing his brow.

'Are you feverish? Can I check?'

She didn't answer, her vacant silence apparently acting as consent for Nysio to step closer to continue playing amateur doctor, his cool hands touching her cheeks and forehead.

'You seem fine, but the doctor will know better.'

'You called a doctor?' She looked up at him, anxiety making her voice sound small and fragile. She only half listened as Nysio wondered aloud if she was experiencing food poisoning…or a viral infection…or maybe even both at once. He continued to talk, listing off the doctor's qualifications as he washed his hands at the small sink, then paused in the doorway of the bathroom to survey her in silence.

Exhausted, she moved to sit on the edge of the bed, only to feel a cool hand upon her elbow, guiding her away from the soft heavenly mattress and into a nearby chair.

He produced a tray, one that she was pretty sure hadn't been there when she'd awoken. Upon it were some paracetamol, some still water and one of those sachets of electrolytes claiming to be berry flavoured but that just tasted like dirty water.

She was silent as he handed her the pills to take while he set about preparing the drink. Then he sat and watched while she swallowed and sipped, his brow furrowed as he appeared deep in thought.

'Is there anything that I can do?' he asked, eventually breaking the silence.

Aria felt her mouth move but no sound escaped. Even as something within her snapped to attention, she shook her head on the pure reflex of not wanting to be a burden. Of not wanting to ask this man for help even though he'd made it quite clear time and time again that he quite liked being of practical assistance. She liked being minded by him too.

He went to get dressed, blessedly leaving her alone for a moment to gather her feelings back into her chest where they were safer and far less likely to make a mess. She closed her eyes, hoping that the doctor would arrive quickly and give her a clean bill of health. Then there would be no more delaying the inevitable. It was past time to get back to normal life.

'Miss Dane…is there a chance that you may be pregnant?'

Aria stared at the pretty blonde doctor who sat perched on the opposite end of the low coffee table in the suite's living area where the dawn light had just begun to filter in through the windows. She blinked, half thinking she'd misheard the question. It was absurd. She was vaguely aware of Nysio's swift intake of breath nearby but couldn't muster the courage to look at him.

'No. *No*... Definitely not. I'm on birth control. I have an implant in my arm.'

'Birth control is not always effective, and you wrote down here that your last cycle was more than six weeks ago. Is it a possibility?'

But as she sat in choked silence, her subconscious continued to analyse the past week and how *different* she'd been feeling. The food aversions, the vague nausea she'd thought was anxiety, the tender breasts, even feeling more exhausted than usual.

'It might be a possibility,' she said hoarsely, the last word coming out as a whisper.

'Cosa?' Nysio frowned at her with confusion, then straightened abruptly. 'You think...you might be...'

'No,' she said quickly. 'Well... I shouldn't be.'

'But you might be.' He stared at her, his gaze unflinching, the sharp tilt of his brows utterly unreadable.

She forced herself to meet that gaze, to straighten her shoulders and accept that this was one situation she couldn't currently run from. 'Yeah. I might be.'

Nysio was utterly silent as the doctor listened to her symptoms and gently asked if she'd like to do a quick test to rule it out. She hummed to herself, her feet bouncing of their own accord as she waited and studiously avoided where Nysio sat silently observing.

'But I have a contraceptive implant,' she repeated. 'So this test is just a precaution, isn't it?'

'No form of protection is fully effective against pregnancy,' the doctor said again patiently. 'Other than never having sex, of course.' She chuckled, clearly finding humour in her own words. Meanwhile Aria was horrified. The other woman smiled softly, her head tilting to one side as she surveyed the small plastic rectangle in her hands.

'Well, it appears we have a very clear result.' She moved closer, placing the test on the surface of the low coffee table between them. 'You are most definitely pregnant.'

Nysio could do nothing but watch as Aria shook her head wildly for a moment before swiftly excusing herself to use the bathroom as if the hounds of hell were at her feet. The unmistakeable sound of retching ensued.

Nysio studied the pregnancy test. It was barely the length of a credit card and only a third of the width with one small plastic screen at the centre. A screen that currently showed two pink lines, side by side.

He paled, composing the rapid thrum of his own heartbeat under his fine silk suit jacket and placing the small test back down onto the table as though it were a bomb, set to erupt any moment. In a way, he supposed it might be, considering the doctor was now studiously avoiding looking at him. He knew that she was a medical professional, but as a man who had lived decades now with people using even the most ridiculous information against him, he felt the swift instinct to protect this delicate new development.

'I'll give you both some time to talk,' the doctor said gently. 'But I'll need to return to remove the birth control. It's a simple procedure. I'll talk you both through some more of the details of what to expect then too.'

'Thank you, Doctor. You will receive an additional payment for your discretion,' he said quickly, grateful when the woman shook his hand and disappeared without any prompting. Nysio wandered back to the bathroom door, knocking once and noting the stark silence coming from within.

'Just let me know you are still conscious in there.'

A small sound, suspiciously like a muffled sob, came from the other side of the locked door and Nysio felt his chest tighten in response.

'I just…need a moment.' Aria spoke between deep breaths.

Something tightened in his chest at the forced strength in her words. Even now, she was putting on her brave face. The urge to force his way into the bathroom to see that she was okay consumed him, but alongside that was an equally strong urge to run far from this apartment and the momentous life-changing revelations that had taken place.

He took a seat in the living area directly across from the bathroom, feeling the weight of reality pressing in upon him. Before finding out the truth of his birth, he had assumed that once the reserves for their foundations and investments were restored he would settle down and have a family of his own. It was the Bacchetti way, after all, to ensure the bloodline continued no matter what it took. But, of course, he was assuming that this pregnancy was a result of their night on the jet. That might not be the case. That realisation stopped him in his tracks, his gut tightening. Was it even his baby?

He sat frozen for a while longer, until the silence was broken by the sound of the bathroom lock sliding open. Aria emerged, her face wan and flushed and her shoulders sagging with clear exhaustion. Nysio stood, stalking across the open expanse of the living room, and took her gently by the elbow, guiding her to a cushioned armchair with a footstool. Once she was adequately seated, he busied himself with pouring a glass of water and placing it within her reach.

To his surprise she didn't fight him off for fussing, instead she seemed to deflate before his eyes. Her muttering of a limp 'thank you' under her breath was almost enough to have him calling the doctor back.

The question of their situation lay between them in the form of the positive pregnancy test on the coffee table, a gauntlet of sorts, and Nysio tensed as he anticipated her next move. The woman he had come to know over the short time they'd spent together had been a refreshing force of brutal honesty. But this pale-faced version looked weak and cagey, as if she was poised to run from him at any moment. He felt his fingers tighten on the arms of his chair with the effort not to reach out to ensure she stayed put.

Her eyes dropped and she spied the test still lying in the centre of the table behind him. She paused, her lower lip quivering as she averted her gaze, trying to hide her expression from him. The look of vulnerability on it shocked him.

He waited until she finally met his gaze. 'So, you're pregnant.'

'Yes.'

He waited a moment, waited for her to elaborate on that monosyllabic response but no more came. 'Do you have any idea how far along you are?' he asked delicately, watching as she sipped the water slowly.

She closed her eyes for a moment. 'No more than six weeks for sure.'

His own knowledge of reproductive biology was pretty basic but he knew that if she was six weeks along, that put conception right around the time they had first met. He had no idea how many times they had made love that night but he knew it had been…a lot.

One night of abandon.

Was that really all that it had taken for his carefully laid plans to be so thoroughly changed? His recent decision to remain a bachelor was a deliberate one, born of the knowledge that his very existence was a lie and he would never want to inflict that upon another generation.

He kept his voice neutral, seeing the tension in the fine lines around her mouth. He needed to tread carefully, to be tactful. 'That night on the jet you said you had not been with anyone for a long time. Is that still the truth?'

She met his gaze instantly. 'Yes. I…there has only been you for years now.'

He felt her hushed words pierce the breath he hadn't realised he'd been holding. And they stayed there in the air, vibrating through him for a moment with quiet finality. He nodded once. Even though he'd suspected as much, he'd needed to give her the space to confirm it. To acknowledge that there were two of them in this.

A movement jolted him out of his thoughts and he looked up as Aria put her glass down with a heavy *thunk* and dropped her face softly into her hands.

'I know it's not what either of us had planned.' She spoke from between her clenched fingers. 'I know that I have options. But my first thought was that I hope it's okay. I want it to be okay, I want it to be healthy. I know that's probably crazy.'

'It's not crazy. I hope it's okay too,' he said, feeling the truth of his own words.

'It's probably barely the size of a seed. How can something so tiny have such an instant impact on everything?' She looked down at her stomach and he found himself following her gaze. They sat in silence for a moment, the weight of their situation bearing down upon them in equal measure. But then Aria placed her hand unconsciously over her stomach and Nysio felt something raw and primal roar to life within him.

This woman was going to carry his child. They were

going to become parents. As progressive as he claimed to be, he felt the urge within him to bundle her close and demand she remain nestled in his bed for the next few months for her own safety. The memory of the night before didn't do much to relax his mood. She had been about to fly back to London this morning, despite his offer for her to stay. She had made her feelings on the matter clear.

Something of the intensity of his thoughts must have shown upon his face because when she looked up at him, she immediately sat up straight and frowned.

'You're not about to demand that we get married or something, are you?' she said, in the same tone that one might ask, 'You're not about to murder me, are you?'

Nysio remained silent, not having considered *demanding* it, as such.

'Is this reverse psychology?' he asked, running his thumb across her knuckles and feeling his eyes drift to the bare skin of her third finger. 'Do you want me to demand marriage, Aria?'

'Of course not!' She stiffened, pulling her hand back and cradling it as though he'd burned her. 'I just thought that's what stereotypical brooding Italian guys usually do in these situations.'

'I've never been in this situation before, have you?'

'No.' She relaxed slightly, but still gave him another sidelong glance for good measure. 'I suppose there's no rush to think about logistics yet. I can still return home today as planned and we can…keep in touch. Make plans on how we can make this work together when the time comes.'

He stood up suddenly, feeling adrenaline fill his veins at her mention of her boarding that damned passenger plane she'd insisted on booking with her own money.

'Do you intend to discuss our child's future via text messages?'

'Don't be cross. It's very early still. We can carry on with our lives as normal, for a while at least.'

'Normal,' Nysio repeated, feeling his pulse quicken as she stood up and walked towards the windows. 'What is normal about the fact that you are carrying *my* child and you're already planning to leave the country before we've even properly discussed it?'

Aria inhaled on a gasp, her fists tightening by her sides as she stared at him for a long moment. 'You sound like a caveman.' She gritted the words, her clenched teeth becoming visible for a moment before she walked away into the bedroom.

He followed her. 'Aria…you cannot claim to want to be together on this while simultaneously walking away from me at every chance.'

'I didn't say I wanted to be together, I said we could *work* together.' She stared at him as though he were the one being completely irrational. 'I have a bank appointment next week about the backing for my lingerie line… I haven't even thought of what effect this is going to have on all of that yet. I just lost a pretty steady job so it's not ideal timing for me to be pregnant… I—I just need some time to think. Can you just give us both that?'

Nysio reached out and placed a hand on her arm. '*Calmate.* Relax. Deep breaths, remember? You need me to count your fingers?'

She let out a weak laugh at the reminder of their first meeting and Nysio decided that questioning her any further in this frame of mind was simply going to make her spiral further.

He folded his arms and watched as she moved past him to gather the things into the case he'd had couriered over from the hotel while they awaited the doctor. With every folded garment she placed in the case, he felt his own resolve tighten. She wanted time, she'd said. Well, he would be the one to give it to her. As much time as she needed to understand why a long-distance co-parenting plan was simply not possible in his world.

Like it or not, Aria Dane had just become a more permanent fixture in his life than he'd ever imagined. A fact that he felt strangely at ease about, for someone who'd been so hell-bent on remaining a bachelor for the rest of his days. Having a family might not have been in his plans recently, but now that it was happening, he knew what he wanted.

As he guided her out into his waiting car, he knew that she was not going to be happy with what came next, but if the alternative was letting her leave…he'd risk her anger.

CHAPTER EIGHT

ARIA KNEW THAT she was being too quiet on the drive, that they should be communicating with one another before her flight left, but it had seemed that the reality of their situation was sinking in more and more with every mile, making her hyperaware that there was actually a tiny life growing inside her.

It should be positively illegal for a man to look as cool, polished, and collected as he did in his open-collared black shirt and charcoal trousers combo. His shoes today were a deep tan, embroidered with delicate symbols upon the sides that looked almost like hearts.

His hair was still slightly damp from his shower, and her enhanced sense of smell meant that she could make out every different note of his shampoo. Or maybe she was just imagining that? It was far too early for her to be feeling anything like that, surely.

She closed her eyes, praying that she could hold herself together long enough to get through this goodbye, even as every muscle in her body screamed at her to cancel her flight and stay in Italy for longer. But she couldn't do that. Not when she could tell that Nysio was harbouring some archaic sense of chivalry.

She startled, feeling warmth covering her hands where

she had been twiddling her thumbs and picking at her cuticles.

'Calmate, tesoro.' Nysio spoke quietly from beside her as he put his hand back on the wheel. 'You will wear your fingers away.'

She looked across at him, suddenly realising that she now carried the heir to an empire that had stretched back for centuries. She had no idea if he had ever planned to have children of his own, if he was as panicked as she was.

'Aria, I can hear your thoughts speeding along. Everything is going to be fine.'

'How could you know that? I've been taking antacids for my nausea all week. I drank a little wine with dinner. I haven't been taking any prenatal vitamins.'

He frowned, nodding once. 'My mother told me she didn't know that she was pregnant with me till she was four months along. She was just eighteen and quite the wild child. I'm sure she did much worse before she found out.'

The admission was effective in stopping her overloaded mind, making her turn her stunned focus on him. 'Were you both okay? Was the pregnancy uneventful?'

'She was an unmarried teenager from an upper-class Sardinian family. Although she married my father pretty quickly, I doubt anything about that time in her life could be considered uneventful.' He let out a harsh laugh that didn't quite meet his eyes. Then he reached out again, taking her hand and waiting until she met his eyes fully. 'She was fine and I was born healthy. And look at me now, a perfect strapping man in his prime.' He let her go and gestured to himself with false bravado, the expression on his face so stern it made her laugh involuntarily. She let out a sigh of relief, nodding once.

Without words, his expression seemed to convey the multitude of emotions passing through her in that moment and she felt the stranglehold of control she'd been clinging to begin to slip.

Aria exhaled a long slow breath and covered her face with her hands, peeking out at him through her fingers. 'I can't even keep a houseplant alive, let alone a baby. Do you know how many ferns I've killed through sheer negligence?'

'Aria, I promise you will not be doing this alone. We will be figuring this out together.'

She looked up at him, feeling a wave of gratitude for the fact that, despite their lack of communication regarding how they would be proceeding, not once had he wavered in his support for her about their unnamed bean. She closed her eyes, thinking she might nap for a bit, but startled when she felt the car jostle off the motorway and onto a narrow mountain road.

'This isn't the way to the airport.'

'We're not going to the airport. We need some time to discuss how things will be, going forward.'

How things will be.

The phrase made her sit up straight in her seat, her throat convulsing slightly as she strained to get words past her fury. 'Turn this car around, *now*.'

He remained stubbornly focused on the road, ignoring her. By the time the car slowed and passed through wrought-iron gates, her muscles were sore from the anxious tension. A large stone wall spanned for miles and she read the words *Palazzo Bacchetti* engraved deep in the stone. Tall cypress trees lined the long avenue in perfect formation, interspersed with tall golden lamps and sculptures. But when they passed through a second set of gates and she was presented with the enormous sprawling palace she stopped breathing for a few seconds.

Nysio Bacchetti lived in a palace. An actual, real-life Renaissance palace.

Her momentary awe didn't last for long though, and when the car came to a stop in the beautiful courtyard, she immediately threw off her belt and stepped out, slamming the door behind her pointedly.

'Aria,' Nysio warned. '*Calmate, per favore.* Stress is not good for you or the baby.'

'Well, then, stop doing things that you know will stress me out!' she snapped. 'I'm not suddenly made of porcelain, simply because I'm pregnant. I will not be ordered around and ferreted away somewhere for safekeeping until I give birth to your heir.'

'You expected me to just allow you to return to England this morning without even discussing our situation properly?'

'You are not in a position to decide what I am *allowed* to do simply because I'm pregnant.'

'Pregnant with *my* child.' His eyes were twin pools of cold obsidian, dark and unwavering. 'I've tried hard to be patient and rational here, so as not to overwhelm you. But I am a very wealthy and powerful man, Aria. There are measures that people in my position need to take to ensure *safety* for their families. To ensure that my vulnerabilities are not exploited or used. Like it or not, you and our baby have just become my biggest vulnerabilities and I have to protect you.'

'So that's it? I don't even have a choice?' She stared at him, feeling her jaw clench.

'You said you needed time. Well, I'm asking for the same. We both want the same thing...space to figure this all out. I'm just asking that we do it here, together, so that I can keep you safe. Both of you.'

She felt caged in, as if she were a bad mother already if she didn't take this time to process and decide upon their child's future. She knew he was right, that there were so many things to decide upon.

Aria stared up at the stone building, the sprawling land surrounding them. Sprawling land that seemed to be surrounded by a very high brick wall as far as the eye could see. She wasn't even sure if they were in the city any more, to be honest, it was so quiet, peaceful and beautiful. A beautiful prison.

Was this really happening?

'I told you I have plans in motion back in London and a meeting with the bank to get to. I can maybe push things out by a week, but that's as much as I'm willing to do.'

'Most people wouldn't see an unexpected stay in this *palazzo* as such a tedious endeavour.' He pushed agitated fingers through his dark curls, his expression shifting. 'All I'm asking for is a little time.'

It felt ridiculous to keep having the same argument over and over again, and so she did something she almost never did. She gave in.

'One week.' She looked up at the façade of the *palazzo*, feeling a shiver course down her spine.

Aria stared around her at gold gilded furniture, luxury marble flooring and priceless portraits lining the walls. For goodness' sake, even the chandelier that hung from the vaulted double-height hall ceiling of the entryway was probably worth more than she had earned in her entire lifetime.

A man arrived at the bottom of the stairs looking rather harangued, but still perfectly coiffed in a spotless three-piece suit. Aria inwardly groaned, recognising him as the same man from the jet on that first night. He recognised her too, his eyes lighting up as he greeted them, and Nysio announced that Aria was to be their guest for the week.

If Gianluca found any of his employer's behaviour to be absurd, he didn't show it. They gave her a short tour of the public areas of the grounds and Aria was glad for the distraction as she cooled off from her heated exchange with Nysio. She fought the urge to swoon at every new room and piece of history she was met with, realising that the father of her unborn child lived in a home that came complete with its own art gallery and staff.

Nysio disappeared for a while, returning when she had just begun settling into one of the many bedrooms in his suite. But not his bedroom, she realised quickly. A fact she should probably be relieved about, now that they were trying to build a co-parenting relationship. Sex would definitely only complicate matters further and that was not the kind of world she wanted to bring a baby into. They needed stability, communication, respect. And she was fast beginning to realise that he was right, they needed time to get to know one another so that they could be a better team.

He stepped into her bedroom, his eyes strangely guarded as he took in her half-unpacked case upon the floor. 'If you have need for more clothing, I can arrange to have a selection sent up from your preferred store.'

'I can drive, you know.'

'I'd prefer if you remain within the grounds. Besides,

I have a relationship with most boutiques in Florence and Milan.'

'So…ordering women's clothing is a service that you avail yourself of often?' His brow instantly rose at the snarky question and she felt a little chagrined. 'It's none of my business of course. I know I'm just here as a *guest*, after all.'

'I assumed you wouldn't want me to announce the private details of our situation to my entire staff…but if you prefer, I can call them all back to clarify the exact nature of our relationship.'

She crossed her arms. 'We don't have a relationship, Nysio.'

He gritted his jaw and for a moment she thought he might lean down to close the gap between them. When had they even moved so close to one another? He was so close, she could feel the heat of his breath fanning her cheeks. She felt her pulse quicken, her body instantly betraying her the way it always did when he was near.

She knew that he could feel it too, the sudden shift in the air between them. She reflexively licked her dry lips and saw his eyes darken as he homed in on the movement. But instead of moving closer, he remained stubbornly frozen in place.

He stared down at her, his chest rising and falling with each breath. 'If I wasn't so sure you'd run away at the first chance, I'd have laid claim to you in front of them all. I'm not like that bastard who used you before. I'm not playing games here, Aria…when I said we will be discussing all of our options while you are here, I mean *all* of them. Including the one that involves you wearing my ring on your finger and remaining here as my wife.'

He enunciated the last word with a rough silky promise that sent a shiver coursing down her spine. 'If you think that you can force me into some kind of...old-fashioned marriage of convenience—'

He raised one brow. 'I don't plan to force you into anything. You gave me one week, Aria. I plan to use that time to explore all of our options quite thoroughly.'

CHAPTER NINE

ARIA FOUND HERSELF seated at one end of an opulent ten-foot-long dining table the next morning, being asked how she would like her eggs. Her cup was filled with the richest, most delicious decaf coffee she had ever smelled in her life, and when she tasted it she had to close her eyes for a moment to tackle the onslaught of sheer perfection.

She was alone in the breakfast room, a fact that she was quite grateful for considering how aggravated her esteemed host had seemed the night before when she had declined eating dinner together. She'd needed time alone to think and thought it better to have a simple meal brought to her room so that she could deal with the phone calls she'd needed to make. A quick voicemail to her parents was all she could muster the courage for, just saying that she'd met a friend and decided to explore Italy a bit more.

She'd also bitten the bullet and sent a long rambling series of voice texts to Priya, outlining her new business idea. She knew the plus-size fashion market like the back of her hand, she knew plenty of vendors and production factories. She knew her own designs were good and she had personal experience of having a more voluptuous body and wanting to dress it with the same level of elegance that could be found in high-end boutiques.

She inhaled softly, letting the breath hiss from her chest on a slow pulse. The relaxation technique had been a helpful online suggestion to combat anxiety. After barely two minutes, she stood up, her fists tight with what was decidedly even more restless energy than she'd begun with.

Of all the brooding Italians she had to meet, how on earth had she wound up with the one guy who practically owned a mausoleum? A mausoleum that she was expressly prohibited from leaving. The hallway outside the dining room was thankfully deserted, as was every other long corridor in the sprawling wings of the ridiculously gigantic palace.

She had never been as calm and carefree as when she'd spent time city-hopping and wandering and learning new things about each new place by walking through it and drinking it in with all her senses. Some people described wanderlust as a hobby, or avoiding reality, as her older sisters often laughed. No one back home had probably even batted an eyelid when she'd told them she was staying in Italy with a stranger for an extended break. For a time Priya had been her companion on her travels when they could book time off work, and that had been the happiest, most peaceful she had felt. They had seen so much of the world together, and she had held her friend's hand as she healed from her own past.

Of course, according to her friend's last call to her, now Priya was a newly-wed herself, and busy with starting up her new business venture. In order to access her inheritance, she'd eloped with her former groom's hot blond billionaire brother and now apparently, they were madly in love. She hadn't even mentioned trying to see each other, nor had she apologised for abandoning her in New York...though it sounded as though it had been pretty unavoidable. Aria told herself that was why she hadn't mentioned Nysio or the pregnancy in her voice-mail. She could be mysterious too.

Over the past year, maybe even the past few years, she and Priya had drifted apart. Their jobs had become more time-consuming, especially when Aria had been finishing her online degree in every bit of spare time she'd had. She had finally become open about her ADHD diagnosis to her employers and received some modest accommodations to her working schedule. She'd tried a few things to help herself. Medication hadn't suited her at all but taking scheduled walk breaks and using visual timers to complete tasks seemed to help a little. Simply accepting her different neurology had been a huge step in itself, one that had given her the confidence to go back and get her degree and open herself up to her dreams again.

But still, she missed her best friend.

She let her thoughts continue to wander as she walked through the impressive galleries filled with countless historical paintings and sculptures. It was a sin to keep things like this locked away from the public, unable to be appreciated and admired as they'd been created to be. She wondered if Nysio had always kept this obvious slice of history locked up like a fortress, and himself along with it.

She didn't buy his workaholic line; surely a man with his kind of wealth had no need to work full-time hours? Surely he'd feel the urge to spend his money, to own multiple homes, yachts, islands even? Thoughts of her mysterious host held her attention more effectively than anything else she'd tried, so she let her mind turn him over and over like a puzzle. She almost didn't realise she had reached a completely new part of the house, one that seemed more modern and quieter than the rest, overlooking the beautiful ornamental gardens to the rear of the property.

Without a thought, she slid off her shoes and stepped out onto the cool grass. Rows of vibrant flowers lined a flagstone pathway leading up to a large fountain and, beyond, she could see what looked like a giant maze. She wandered for a while, happy to let her thoughts run at full tilt while her body exerted some energy. It helped sometimes, moving her body to calm her mind. By the time she walked back towards the *palazzo*, she felt a little more clarity in her situation.

Through open patio doors, she spied walls upon walls of books and in front of them was Nysio, sitting at an ornate black marble desk. His hair was dishevelled and falling over his forehead, but she could just make out a pair of stylish reading glasses on the bridge of his nose.

She moved closer, but he didn't hear her footsteps. She debated clearing her throat to announce her arrival, but what would she even say? He had made it quite clear that she was there so that they could take time to discuss the baby, but just barging into his office and demanding they get to it was possibly a little too much for day one? Then again, he had been *so* eager to get her here. Irritation warred with uncertainty as she hovered in the doorway, her bare feet getting cold on the stone.

'My office has an open-door policy, Aria. There is no need to hover.'

His voice startled her; he hadn't once looked up from his work but evidently she hadn't been quite as stealthy as she thought. Slowly, he slid the glasses from his face and placed them down on the desk beside what she could now see was not a live screen of stock markets or accounts but a book with a pregnant woman on the cover.

The title read, *What To Expect*... He quickly pushed it out of sight, clearing his throat.

'You look well rested.' His gaze slid down to take in her simple jeans and T-shirt.

She knew he had to be able to see her dark under-eye circles, her hair tied up in a messy bun, and her appearance was infinitely more casual than his sleek white shirt and tailored trousers. 'I'm as well rested as a captive can be, I suppose. Who knew prison cells had four-poster beds?'

The corner of his mouth quirked. 'Your sense of humour has recovered, I see.' He stepped around the desk, lazily propping his lean lengthy frame against the front edge. 'I had thought we might engage in some banal pleasantries before we jumped at one another's throats today, but then I'm reminded that this is infinitely more entertaining.'

'Glad to be of service,' she said dryly, entering the office and feeling his gaze lower to her bare feet. His eyes darkened for a moment on her red-painted toes and she felt a hint of self-consciousness creep in. Being in his fancy home and seeing him in his polished suit, aware of how he very much belonged here...it only seemed to cement the fact that she didn't. She was just the quirky stranger that had entertained him for a while. Even when he'd said he wanted her to stay, he'd wanted to hide her away in his town house; he had never meant to bring her here, into his inner circle.

He'd wanted to discuss all of their options for the baby...but he had already moved them to separate bedrooms without even a conversation and had not once tried to touch her romantically since the night they'd found out she was pregnant. And despite her anger at his heavy-handedness in getting her here...she missed him.

She shook off that vulnerable thought, reminding herself that she had logistics to sort through with this man. Plans to decide upon and details to iron out. This was essentially a negotiation and she needed to be on her guard. 'I decided that I may as well make the most of my time here. Explore the grounds, clear my head.'

'You should have come to me. I'm happy to give you a longer tour.'

'I'm okay exploring alone,' she answered quickly. 'I needed the time to get my thoughts in order. I was already stressed about my business plans, before we found out about…our situation.'

'Is that what we're calling it?' His mouth tipped up at one corner but he remained thoughtful as he watched her. She wandered along one bookshelf, touching the few leather-bound tomes and classics she could recognise by title. She'd never enjoyed reading as a child—it had always felt too slow. Now, she'd found that audiobooks were a little easier to process and she could actually enjoy reading that way. But there was something so romantic to her about a shelf of dusty old books.

'My career problems probably seem a bit trivial when you're managing millions…or billions.'

'Success is a relative concept, in my experience. Even the most outwardly successful people can still be unsatisfied.'

She looked up, seeing a hint of something vulnerable in his gaze. He was the kind of man that gave his full attention to every conversation, a fact that was fast becoming quite disconcerting. He was so observant and so effortlessly polished and articulate. She cleared her throat, taking another few steps into the room, and spotted a large marble chess set that sat propped on a table in the corner.

'Do you play?' he asked.

'My older sisters taught me.' She laughed softly. 'They quickly regretted their decision when I started to beat them every time. My parents had to give away our chessboard to stop the arguments.'

'You have a temper, then?'

'I'm a redhead, most people simply assume that I have a temper.'

'I am not most people.'

Aria blinked, a pithy retort dissolving on the tip of her tongue. She stared around at the rows of thick books that lined the shelves of his study, books that were clearly not just for aesthetic purposes judging by the stack in disarray on the floor beside a tall wing-backed chair near the windows.

'Well, I definitely had a temper as a child.' She sat down at the chessboard, running a hand over the pieces. 'Too little patience and far too much energy. Once I learned that my brain works differently, that part of my life made a lot more sense.'

Nysio frowned, taking a seat on the opposite side. 'Did no one mention ADHD when you were a child?'

'No. My parents are very calm, academically driven people. They didn't understand me and I didn't really want to be understood.' It was hard enough not being able to understand or cope with the challenges without the added pressure of trying to explain her challenges to others. Her three older sisters had been such high achievers growing up, busy with piano concerts and dance recitals and sports tournaments. She frowned, not knowing how she had got onto this topic and why she was oversharing so much. 'Things were very different back then. I don't blame them. Our family has drifted apart a lot, we're not close.'

'It's hard when you don't fit the plan of who your parents want you to be.'

She studied his face, seeing another hint of that restlessness she'd noticed the first time they'd met. 'Is that how yours made you feel?'

'My anxiety attacks have always been a part of me. My father never accepted that I struggled with large events, just told me to be a man. He's old-school that way, he doesn't really believe in talking about feelings or emotions…' A dark look came over his face and he was silent for a long moment.

'It must be hard, with your father's illness and them moving so far away.'

'I had a very privileged life.' He shrugged. 'I was taught to appreciate the position I was born into. I was trained to take over all of this from the moment I could talk so even though I struggled to begin with, I eventually fitted their plan. I am who they needed me to be.'

She remembered his story of the poetry and wondered if he had ever wanted to be something different. If his entire life had always been centred around being this intense Florentine prince…if he had ever been allowed to just be him. It seemed impossibly sad to think of a little boy being *trained* to play a role.

She didn't remember accepting his offer to play, but suddenly they were both moving pieces on the chessboard. He didn't let her win, and he was clearly an expert player, but she managed to get a few moves in before he hammered her with a quick checkmate.

'One more?' He quirked one dark brow in her direction.

She nodded, feeling the tension in her shoulders ease. And she kept talking, realising that she didn't feel self-conscious at all. Nysio was a great listener, asking questions and letting her interrupt him in her usual way. It was always strangely effortless to talk to him, so much so that she found it hard not to overshare. When he asked again about the reason why she had sworn off relationships so adamantly...she paused for a split second, then decided to tell him the whole story.

She explained about meeting a wealthy older guy named Theo in her first year of uni and the shadowy nature of their relationship. How he'd taken her away on holidays and breaks but never actually been happy to go public about their relationship. How he'd claimed to love her curvy body so much that his occasional sharp comments and criticisms about her size had felt like love. It wasn't until the end that she'd realised how many parts of herself she had bent and broken to try to fit into his expectations both inside the bedroom and out.

She told him about Theo's wild ideas and impulsive traits, how he'd used her and discarded her at will. How she'd always gone back when he apologised...every time. By the time she got to the part where Theo had proposed and booked a wedding in Greece before abandoning her there...she felt that soft wounded part within begin to shake with memory.

She reached down to busy herself with clearing the pieces, accidentally brushing Nysio's hands as he moved to do the same. She had felt the tension in him, but when she looked up, his eyes were stark with anger.

'I'm not a violent man...but if I met this Theo in the street, I'm pretty sure I'd struggle not to dislocate his jaw.'

'A kind gesture, but he got his comeuppance when his trust fund ran out and all of his so-called friends deserted him. Priya was such a great support.' Aria smiled. 'Strange to think my runaway-bride best friend is the only reason you and I met one another. She actually went and married the groom's brother. Can you believe that?'

A strange look crossed Nysio's features, and she realised she hadn't really mentioned Priya or that scandalous wedding since the first night they'd met. She'd got far too swept up in all of the magnificent sex they'd been having, to be fair. Was he uncomfortable at the reminder of his panic attack in the street?

She hadn't spoken to her friend again since the last call they'd had in London, the one where she'd dropped the bomb that she was in fact married. Her husband was a wealthy Greek tycoon named Eros Theodorou, their marriage initially brought on by a ridiculous term in a will and a race to the altar between Eros and Priya's former groom, Xander. A thought occurred to her, one she was amazed she hadn't questioned until now.

'You know that day on the street, I heard Xander send his men in pursuit of his brother.' She waited a moment, noticing the flare of Nysio's nostrils and the slight widening of his eyes. Feeling her gut tighten with foreboding. 'When I saw you first... I wondered if that brother was you. But you said you were only there on business, so I presumed you didn't even know Xander. Was that the truth?'

'No.' Nysio spoke carefully. 'It was not the truth. But I think you've figured that out already. The truth is that Xander and Eros are my half-brothers. We're all Zeus Mytikas's illegitimate sons.'

She gasped. 'You lied to me?' Aria whispered, shaking her head. 'Is that why you offered me a flight home? To ensure that I hadn't uncovered your secret?'

'That wasn't the reason, but it was a consideration that occurred to me only briefly. It soon became pretty clear you didn't know and then…things developed between us. It's not something I've spoken about with anyone, it's not just you.' Nysio felt his chest turn cold, his mind warring with him to walk away from this conversation he didn't want to have. But still, seeing the hurt clearly evident in her eyes made him feel like the worst kind of scumbag.

'Did you know that Priya had married your brother?'

Nysio winced at the word. He'd largely avoided thinking about Eros or Xander at all since leaving New York. Even when he'd received an invitation to attend a meeting with them both to discuss alternative options for that damned will, he'd ignored it. He'd been in the dark about their existence for over three decades; he had no need to play happy families now.

'Yes, I've been made aware that both of my half-siblings have recently got married in a bid to win an inheritance from Zeus.'

A pained expression passed over Aria's face, marring her soft brow. 'Is that why you want to get married to me? To compete with them for the terms of the will?'

'No,' Nysio growled. 'And I can't believe you even have to ask that.'

'I don't know what to believe.' She let out a low curse under her breath and covered her face with her hands. 'My best friend's husband is your *brother*. Our child's future aunt and uncle. God, I haven't even told Priya that I'm pregnant yet. I… I need to go and lie down for a bit.'

Nysio was silent, allowing her to walk away. Silence was easier than explaining to her the fact that he himself hadn't known about Zeus or his brothers until just before he'd met her on that rainy Manhattan street. He'd been in shock these past weeks, he realised. He'd been like the man in his poem, drunk and grasping around in the dark, determined to make the night sky change back to day. It wasn't going to change the facts, and he'd been foolish to ignore the truth for as long as he had, but everyone processed things in their own way. His way had apparently been furiously clutching to his old reality and completely refusing to acknowledge the fact that so much of his life had been a lie.

Aria had been like a brightly shining star, keeping him from falling further into the darkness. But that was not a burden he could continue to put on her. She was about to have his child, and he had asked her to trust him…and yet he had not shown her that same trust.

The day he had found out the secret behind his birth, he'd lost a part of himself he hadn't even realised he'd treasured. As a young man the burden of being Arturo Bacchetti's only heir had made him restless, but he'd poured his all into reaching his father's incredibly high standards and doing their family proud. Now it felt as if he was just a hair's breadth away from bringing scandal upon the Bacchetti name.

He had barely left this palace in years, and the first time he'd given in to the impulsive temper that always bubbled below the surface of his control it had brought him to Aria. The first woman to tempt him in years. The first woman who had ever come close to making him want to break his own carefully laid-down rules.

Now look where he was.

He had refused to offer her more than a casual affair, then, once he knew she was carrying his child, he had essentially taken her prisoner in his palace so that he could convince her to marry him. He growled under his breath, moving to slam the door closed only to find Gianluca staring back at him from across the threshold.

'Someone is in great spirits, I see.'

Nysio ignored the other man, stalking across the room and sitting down heavily behind his great black desk.

'Your mother called.'

'I don't care,' Nysio growled.

Gianluca grimaced, standing up to place his hands on the desk, forcing Nysio to look up at him. 'Cora knows about the will, Nysio. She knows that you know about Zeus.'

Nysio froze, looking at his father's oldest friend and seeing in his eyes that the other man also knew about Zeus. Of course it would be impossible to hide such a secret from the man who had helped keep the Bacchetti family in check for almost five decades. Gianluca was their most trusted employee, their curator, the man who kept the entire *palazzo* running...he'd seen everything.

'Sit down,' Gianluca urged, a long sigh escaping his lips. 'Let's talk.'

He had assumed that his mother had tricked his father somehow into thinking Nysio was his baby, that his father had found out the truth and been forced to litigate to protect the family name. He wondered if his father had ever seen him as a disappointment, a cuckoo in his polished nest.

But through Gianluca's eyes, he heard the story of how his parents had been very much in love. But one foolish mistake while they'd been briefly broken up had led Cora to Zeus. Shortly afterwards, she'd reconnected with Arturo and they'd become engaged. She'd been four months pregnant when she found out about the baby, the week before their wedding. She'd told Arturo straight away and handed him back his ring but Arturo had chosen to claim Nysio as his own. And that, according to Gianluca, was where it was always supposed to have ended.

Zeus was a notoriously powerful and cruel man, so

the best way to protect Nysio and Cora was to pretend the baby was Arturo's. That had worked, until Zeus had stumbled upon Cora Bacchetti's handsome blue-eyed sixteen-year-old son at an event and secretly had a DNA test performed. The legal proceedings to protect their family had been gruelling and Cora had begged Arturo to tell their son the truth. But he'd refused, not wanting his relationship with his son to be changed. Not wanting Nysio to have to face such a long-buried truth…risking losing their son's trust for ever. They'd been in too deep.

Nysio sat, reluctantly. And he listened to every word, not bothering to hide the tears that gathered in his eyes. By the time an hour had passed and Gianluca finally left him alone with his thoughts, he had an entirely different perspective on the sordid Bacchetti secret that he'd been avoiding thinking about and haunted by for weeks. He'd seen it for what it was, two parents doing what they thought was best to raise their child.

To protect him.

CHAPTER TEN

ARIA AIMED HER knife in a downward arc, feeling a sliver of satisfaction when it sliced the courgette cleanly in two. Offering to help in the kitchen had been a necessary outlet for the hurt she'd stewed over since yesterday's revelations. The only respite from her thoughts had been when the doctor had come back to remove the implant in her arm and explained that Aria would need a scan at the twelve-week stage.

The kitchen was full with staff preparing for a meal-delivery service that she discovered Nysio had delivered daily to a couple of homeless shelters in the city. The scent of bubbling marinara sauce and freshly chopped parsley assailed her nostrils and made her stomach grumble. She had already decided that she would not be dining with Nysio this evening again. He'd sent a note to her room, handwritten with an apology and a request for her to talk to him when she was ready. But she wasn't ready, not when she felt so misled. The memory of how honest she had been, how she'd told him everything about her. Even told him about Theo.

Whether he had meant to lie to her or not, the secrecy was something that cut through the veneer of her confidence more effectively than any knife could.

She shook her head, popping another grape in her

mouth and closing her eyes at the utter divinity of flavour that exploded there. She would really need to bring some of these with her when she went home. Food like this just wasn't the same in England. She hadn't had a bad meal since landing here.

She finished chopping the vegetables, chatting away to the chef until the woman went on her break and the other staff went back to their work and once again she was left alone with her thoughts.

An unexpected wave of emotion rose within her and it took everything she had to tamp it back down. Damn Nysio. Damn his suave Italian accent and whatever magical thrall it had held her under. She set her jaw and tried to calm the strange roiling sea within her chest.

The stairs at the rear of the kitchen led down to a basement corridor of sorts, the kind that you might see in a fantasy movie leading down to the dungeons. Did palaces even have dungeons? she wondered, feeling a little trepidation trickle down her spine as her steps echoed on the stone. A large doorway at the end opened up into a cavernous hall. Automatic lighting flickered on at her movement, and for a moment she stood frozen in absolute disbelief at what she saw.

It was some kind of huge underground lair. Well, that was her first thought until the lights along the vaulted stone ceiling began to brighten illuminating rows upon rows of giant barrels.

She walked along the cold stone floor that ran down the centre, looking at the labels upon each vessel, her eyes widening at the years listed upon them. Whatever was inside these things, some of them seemed to be over one hundred years old.

She moved through another archway and into an even smaller stone cellar. The temperature was not cold down here but not truly ambient either. Modern vents were visible in the walls, and small digital thermometers displayed the temperature and time.

A third area revealed itself even further down the impossibly long space. This room was lined with gleaming glass cases rather than wooden barrels. The wine here had already been bottled and labelled, the same brand name that she had seen that first night on the jet and on their dinner table the night before. Viti Di Cora.

Hard footsteps sounded from behind her and she turned just as Nysio's broad-shouldered figure appeared in the archway behind her.

'I saw you wandering down here. I wanted to talk to you...'

Aria looked down at the floor, her feelings still a little sensitive from the revelations the day before. But still, she wanted to talk too. She realised she hadn't given him any time to share the details surrounding his secret. She had no idea how he actually felt about it. So she nodded, accepting his hand on her arm as he guided her further into the belly of the giant mountaintop *palazzo*. 'What is this place?'

'It used to be an armoury, but now it's a wine cellar. One of the most prestigious collections in the country.'

She looked back along the line of vintage caskets of wine from many other labels. 'This is all yours?'

'It is.'

'I will admit, I have absolutely no idea why anyone needs this much wine.' She made an attempt at laughter. 'But far be it from me to judge.'

Nysio opened up one of the sliding glass doors by pressing a series of buttons that revealed a small pad on which he pressed his thumb. Aria felt her brows rise a little higher. 'Who needs a bionic lock for his drinks cabinet?'

'To call these caskets mere drinks would be akin to calling the *Mona Lisa* a doodle.'

'Well, well. I've always wondered what fancy old wine tasted like.'

He looked adorably aghast. 'These are not for consumption.'

'Seriously?' She frowned. 'That's like buying cupcakes only to display them for a hundred years on your mantelpiece. That's torturous. Surely a good wine exists in order to be consumed?'

'I don't disagree. However, this particular collection is more of a museum and about preservation than simply owning something expensive in order to possess it.'

'Ah.' She nodded. 'Books, chess sets, wine…you do like collecting things, don't you?'

'Wine has long been a passion of mine.'

'Really, I'd never have guessed, what with the seventy million barrels of it lining the bowels of your palace.' She laughed, stopping when she saw he hadn't joined her. Was she imagining it or was he just a little sheepish at his own passionate admission?

'Clearly you have a favourite brand.' She gestured to the opposite wall.

'Viti Di Cora is certainly my favourite, but mostly for vanity reasons.' He pulled a bottle from the top shelf. 'I'm probably biased, considering it's mine.'

'When you say yours, you mean…'

'I make it. Well, it's a collaborative effort, of course. But the grapes are grown on our vineyard in Sardinia where my parents reside. The land there has belonged to my mother's family for more than a hundred years. The grapes are a very specific variety, one that produces quite a unique…' He paused. 'Ah… I apologise. I'm probably oversharing.'

'No, I'm fascinated, to be honest. I know absolutely nothing about wine other than which colour to order for fish or meat. Even then, I always forget.'

'I know far too much about it, as evidenced by our present surroundings.' He looked uncertain for a moment, running a hand through his hair, his eyes suddenly very focused on the stone-patterned ceiling above them.

'Nysio, is something wrong?' she asked.

'Yes.' He exhaled. 'Well, no. I simply came down here to speak to you…about yesterday. To apologise. I know how closed I am about the topic of my birth…the truth is, I'm still processing it. I only found out that Zeus Mytikas was my biological father after his death, when I received a copy of his will.'

He needed to walk as he spoke, a feeling she knew all too well and so she took his hand and allowed him to lead the way back through the cellar and out onto the terrace at the rear of the kitchen. The evening light was dim, so it was hard to make out his expression as he told her the full story from start to finish. How he'd been raised to carry on his father's name, how he'd always suspected he was a bit different but had never questioned it. He'd known his parents had married because of an accidental pregnancy, but he hadn't known that his mother had been carrying another man's child.

'My mother knows that I received the will…she will likely descend upon the *palazzo* if I don't go to Sardinia to address the matter. But… I'd already been avoiding visiting too often, as seeing my father grow more and more ill with every visit is devastating. Now, how am I supposed to interact with him…knowing he was never truly my father?'

'Sounds to me like he was your father in every way that matters,' she offered helpfully. 'I'm pretty sure that I'm both of my parents' biological child and I've never felt like I belonged amongst my siblings. It seems like maybe you were smothered with belonging…a little bit. But it was done with love.'

He nodded, his jaw tight as he stared out at the setting sun.

'You can't hide from your parents for ever,' she said softly.

'I don't want to waste any of the time you have left here.'

'I could come with you. Your parents will need to know the news of the baby eventually. It's their grand-child, after all. Why not now, while I'm here?' She shrugged. 'It could help me to understand this family better…or worse. I'm not sure. I just know that I don't want to let you go through something so difficult alone.'

'I'd like for you to see the vineyard,' he mused, still lost in his thoughts. 'And we still have a lot to discuss.'

When he walked her back to her room, it was to lay a single kiss upon her cheek and wish her a goodnight before disappearing into his own room. She stood fro-zen in the hallway, feeling foolish that she had expected him to come inside. That she had hoped he would. The thought of spending another night alone with him nearby was torturous to her overheated libido.

Was he trying a new tactic to get her to agree to what he wanted? Using their chemistry as a bargaining chip? Of course, she hadn't expected him to do something so ridiculous as fall in love. Men like him were probably used to using and discarding women at will. Having one of those women fall pregnant was probably his worst nightmare. She should be grateful for his honesty. But as she walked back into her room alone, she felt the urge to give in to his demands pulling at her stronger than ever. Would it truly be so terrible to become his wife?

The Bacchetti family's Sardinian *castello* was an expansive property built into the edge of a cliff overlooking the sea surrounded by acres upon acres of farmland and vineyards. Cora and Arturo Bacchetti greeted them at the bottom of the steps, hand in hand. The beautiful brunette was much younger than her husband but seemed very much in love as she ensured he was strong enough to walk the few steps across the courtyard to greet them.

Aria stood awkwardly to one side, unable to understand the flurry of Italian that flowed as Nysio leaned in to offer his mother a stiff hug. The tension was palpable and Cora made a visible attempt at holding in her emotional reaction to her son's arrival but the small woman eventually crumbled when Nysio hesitated, then carefully leaned in to place the customary kisses upon his elderly father's cheeks.

Nysio seemed frozen for a moment, he and Arturo standing side by side, as loud sobs filled the courtyard. Aria cleared her throat, urging him with her eyes to do something, to offer his mother comfort. He took the hint, swooping in to embrace the tiny woman with his broad frame. Hushed words in Italian followed between the three and Aria realised that there was to be no preamble, no polite British cup of tea or beating around the bush. These Italians were just diving into their family trauma right here in the driveway. After a long while, the crying stopped and Aria felt the spotlight turn back to her.

The stranger in their midst.

But instead of introducing her politely, Nysio murmured something in Italian, gesturing towards her and making an unmistakeable motion towards her stomach.

'*Diventi* Papa?' Cora cried, moving to swing her arms around Aria's shoulders before switching into broken English. 'I am so happy I cry again. Welcome to the family, *bellissima*.'

Aria barely had a moment to process *that* comment as they were bustled inside and immediately presented with a table full of food and cold drinks, including a strong red wine.

'Little bit is good for the baby,' Nysio's father assured her, his hands shaking slightly as he filled the glass to the brim. They weren't at all what she expected, considering the *palazzo* she'd just come from. But it seemed the quiet island life suited them. Arturo's nurse arrived a short while later and she heard Nysio ask if the staff had sent their things to his master suite.

'Wait just a minute.' She hurried after him. 'I understand that this big family reunion is all about you and I'm totally here to support you in that. But since when are we sharing a room again?'

Nysio had the decency to look chagrined. 'My father presumed that we're engaged and had the master suite made up for us.'

Aria paused and stared up at him, feeling her chest flutter with discomfort. His father assumed she was his fiancée. And he hadn't corrected it? *'Welcome to the family,'* his mother had said to her. *Oh, my God.* Once they got safely behind a closed door and away from prying ears she was going to kill this man.

He conveniently climbed the sprawling stone staircase two at a time, leaving her to huff and puff her way up in his wake as she fumed. Aria looked out of a narrow medieval-style window on the stairway and saw colourful market stalls being erected along the winding streets in the distance.

But that bubble of excitement was quickly popped when Nysio took one look at her lightly fanning herself in the pleasant breeze and growled. Literally growled.

'*Merda.* You're too hot.'

'Thank you, I try.' She stepped around his glowering form and moved to inspect a giant painting on the wall. Her view was torn away as Nysio turned her to face him, placing his hand on her forehead.

'None of your jokes. I read in one of the books that getting overheated can be bad for you and the baby.'

'I'm not in danger of getting overheated. It's late autumn.' Aria pushed his hand away gently, feeling her chest flutter a little at his concern. 'So you're…reading pregnancy books?'

'Of course,' he said simply. 'I now know what to expect now that we are expecting. At least, up as far as the second trimester. I haven't quite braved the birthing chapter yet.'

Aria realised she had been completely avoiding looking into the details of what lay ahead of her. Maybe she should download some of those books on audio…was she already being a bad parent by not doing her homework? She brooded, her mood taking even more of a downturn as she trundled along in his wake. If he noticed, he said nothing but the moment they had entered his wing he set about opening doors and producing a glass of cool lemonade from somewhere.

His eyes, however, remained steadily focused upon her. But as he watched her, she felt his gaze shift momentarily from practical and assessing to something else that she found infinitely harder to compose herself before. She was relieved when he disappeared to talk to his head of staff so she took her time testing out the gigantic four-poster bed in the centre of the room. Her feet ached and her body felt heavy, the beginnings of a headache forming in her temples.

She looked down, realising she had once again been cradling her gently curved but not yet especially different abdomen. She was barely even seven weeks pregnant, after all, she wouldn't be seeing any rounded bumps for months yet. But this time she didn't correct herself and allowed her hand to rest there, closing her eyes as she imagined what lay ahead. She opened her eyes to find Nysio in the doorway, his eyes trained on the spot where her hand rested.

She straightened instantly, embarrassed at being caught in her private moment. But his gaze trailed over her with a look that seemed perilously close to tender and she felt a lump form in her throat. Suddenly, the thought of growing huge with his child while he possibly paraded other women around his huge palace just seemed a little cruel. Maybe she should tell him that. She should *definitely* tell him that.

Boundaries were important in this situation, after all. For the baby, when they came to visit, she corrected herself. She looked up and for a split second she saw nothing but raw sensual hunger, filled with echoes of moments she'd tried to forget. They had only spent a few stolen nights together and yet she felt this undercurrent of need crackling to the surface with each moment they spent alone.

Something hot and needy thrummed to life within her but she tamped it back down with a brisk clearing of her throat. She could have sworn that Nysio smiled for a split second, a small sigh escaping his firm lips.

'So...your parents think that we're engaged.' She

pinned him with her most serious gaze, refusing to be distracted by her own body's reaction to him.

'My father has enough to deal with without being upset by our untraditional situation. My mother has already been told that you rejected my proposal.'

'You didn't propose, Nysio. You…demanded. There is a difference.'

He shook his head, a low laugh escaping his lips. 'If you thought that was a demand…you have a lot to learn about me.'

'You're only proving my point. We know so little about one another.' She moved towards the windows, staring out at the sea crashing into waves in the distance below. 'Coming here won't change anything, not when we are both so different.'

She felt him move behind her, felt his presence inches from her back, begging her to sink into his strength and rest.

'You see our differences as an obstacle, whereas I see them as the very fire that drew us together. We could have a wonderful marriage, *dolcezza*.'

'Marriage is about more than sex, Nysio.'

'You seem to have a great many opinions on the institution. Is your resistance truly about us, Aria, or is it about that spoilt man-child who broke your heart?'

'I don't want to talk about him again,' she said swiftly, turning from him to stare out at the waves as they crashed into the cliffs directly below her window. 'I'm here to support you, to spend time with you until my week here is up.'

'You think it's fair that I'm being held accountable for the wrongs of someone else and now our child—'

'Our child doesn't need their parents to be married. *You* need it. As you made evidently clear today when you didn't challenge the assumption that I was your fiancée just to avoid an uncomfortable conversation.'

'What matters to me is that my child is born into a home with both of their parents. Yes, it's also about tradition and image, but marriage is the most clear-cut way to obtain that.'

When she didn't answer him, she felt him sigh heavily, his breath tickling the back of her neck. How could she feel so furious at someone, and still want them this much? It was absurd and unhealthy. She closed her eyes, deciding distance was the only way she would survive this man.

She kept her voice calm, turning to face him fully. 'Don't you have vineyard duties to attend to?'

'I was hoping to take you out with me, to show you the groves.'

'I'm tired, Nysio.' She sighed. 'I'll see you at dinner.'

He nodded once, moving towards the door. He paused under the archway for a long moment, one hand braced on the frame so tightly his knuckles glowed white. 'I'm sorry I didn't tell my father the truth about us. I already regretted forcing your hand to get you to stay in Italy with me...but once I had you here, Aria... I didn't want to let you go. If you believe nothing else, believe that.'

Then he was gone.

CHAPTER ELEVEN

Aria was falling apart.

It was their second day in Sardinia and, true to his word, Nysio had given her space. He'd had the sofa bed made up in their adjoining living room and slept there. She'd listened to the sounds of him tossing and turning in discomfort all night, but he hadn't complained once. When she'd awoken this morning, he was already up and walking the grounds slowly, his elderly father by his side deep in conversation. She couldn't help getting emotional at the sight.

She'd also taken the opportunity to get some work done, checking her emails and voicemail and finding that Priya had been trying to contact her for days. She and Eros were taking a trip to Europe and she wanted to meet up. She could tell by her friend's tone that she was checking up on her. Her finger hovered over the button to return the call, her shoulders sagging with the effort of having to speak. Of having to explain the details of why she didn't really want to meet up. It was too much right now, everything felt like too much.

Feeling the onset of her anxiety reaching a peak, she threw on her sneakers and set about wandering through the groves of olive trees, feeling strangely disconnected from such beautiful surroundings. She didn't know how long she'd wandered alone, until she turned and found herself faced with another wall of fresh green olives rather than the exit she'd expected. At her height, the house wasn't visible over the branches, and neither was the sound of the sea particularly loud enough to guide her.

She was lost.

Panic threatened to overwhelm her completely until the sound of footsteps crunched from behind her. She turned to find Nysio striding towards her, his hair windswept and so long it reached the collar of his sleek riding jacket. Breath sagged from her lungs as she ran to him, burying her face into his chest. He and his mother had gone out horse-riding on the beach after lunch, an activity Cora had informed her quietly that they hadn't done in years.

Remembering the look in the older woman's eyes as she'd quietly thanked her for bringing her son back to life…it had tightened something painfully in Aria's chest that had refused to loosen since. As she looked up at Nysio's handsome face, another fresh wave of tears filled her eyes.

His strong arms enveloped her so tightly, soothing away the raw edges of her panic from moments before.

'Did you get lost? This place is like a maze,' he murmured, holding her even tighter.

'I did. But I'm not crying over that… I don't think. I can't stop crying today. Stupid hormones,' she sobbed, feeling the moisture flow from her eyes, dampening the front of his soft jacket.

This was mortifying, being so wildly out of control of her own body. She was used to feeling her emotions more than others seemed to feel them, but since she'd been pregnant everything seemed so much more intense.

But right there, in the midst of it all, was Nysio, his eyes filled with that steady, ironclad warmth.

'I'm right here, *dolcezza*. Just let go,' he said softly, running one hand along the length of her hair from crown to shoulder. It wasn't a sexual touch, it was comforting. It was understanding. He did understand how she felt, she realised. He always had. Her breath exited her lungs in a gust and she let her body sag against him, her softness welcomed against the safety of his hard, broad chest.

She didn't think, she just did what he said, she let go. She let go of all the pent-up emotion inside her, feeling it cascade outwards on a wave. Her chest heaved with it, with the raw break of everything she'd held inside. The obsessive pull towards this infuriating man and the confusing world of his that she'd walked into. The panic for the tiny life growing steadily within her. An innocent being that she had no idea if she would be enough for.

When she finally became aware of her surroundings again, it was to find that Nysio had guided her under the cover of a gazebo in the centre of the olive grove, and produced a handkerchief from his coat pocket. It was so old-fashioned for him to carry such an item it made her smile softly through the sobs that still racked her chest.

She sat still as he wiped under her eyes gently, overcome with tenderness at the realisation that he was caring for her in such a simple and beautiful way. The handkerchief came away black with mascara and she knew she must look like a sight but she didn't care. She was looking at him, truly *seeing* him, and she couldn't look away.

'This pregnancy has just opened up every wound I thought I'd healed. The worry…it hasn't stopped. I never worry. I'm the queen of laid-back.'

'You expect to still hold that title after that tidal wave of anxiety?'

She laughed, feeling something lift within her, leaving a lightness that felt dangerously close to hope. He had a way about him that made her want to relax and trust someone else for the first time in her adult life. She thought of his proposal again, only this time she didn't feel a cold sweat coming on. Was she actually tempted to consider it?

Could they try to make things work together or was it just her hormones talking? In her mind's eye she imagined a life she'd only dared to dream of, a family of her own. A home filled with laughter and joy. But she needed to know that he wanted to marry her for her and not just for the baby or to keep his traditional parents happy. While she knew that she would be fine if she chose to go down the single-parent route...choosing Nysio was infinitely more of a risk to her heart. Was she being selfish by holding back from the possibility of being hurt?

Could she truly trust her own judgement again?

'I cried a little when I saw you walking with your father this morning, how you care for him. Your love for your family...it's beautiful.'

'Do you include yourself in that yet?' he asked.

'I'm not foolish enough to include myself in your family, Nysio.' She swallowed over the sudden lump in her throat, laying a hand over her lower stomach. 'But I trust you to care for your child. To love them.'

'You weren't carrying our child on the first night we met.'

'That was different. You were still...honourable.'

'Not that honourable, considering I couldn't keep my hands off you.'

'Well...yes. But we both felt that madness that night.'

'It's not madness. And it wasn't just that night, Aria. I've wanted you from the moment I saw you on that rain-soaked street and I have not stopped wanting you since. Not once.'

'Nysio.' She shook her head, knowing she felt the exact same way but still telling herself to wait, to be cautious. She was afraid to take that risk again, especially as this time there was more than her heart at stake. There were her child's feelings to consider too. 'I didn't think you wanted me any more.'

'I know I forced you to walk away from your plans in London so that I had more time to ensure that I could keep our child safe. But I haven't stopped fantasising about having you again, not once. I've been half mad with lust, having you so close. You've haunted my dreams...my days...every moment I'm not touching you is torture.'

She remembered his words in the car, when she'd thought he was driving her to the airport. She'd thought him arrogant and high-handed, expecting her to be grateful that he was protecting her when she'd thought he was acting purely in his own best interests. She'd thought she had misread all of the signs that there had been something good between them, something real.

'Put me out of my misery, *bellezza*. Kiss me.'

Nothing could stop her from doing that in that moment. Aria leaned forward, her lips touching his with the softest reverence as she felt his arms slide around her waist and pull her close.

Of all the kisses they had shared in the short time they had known one another, this one was quite possibly her favourite. Not because it was becoming increasingly steamy and frantic in a public place, or because things had been so fraught between them for the past week as they navigated their new situation. But as Nysio's tongue slid over hers, his teeth nipping her bottom lip and his hands caging in either side of her neck, she felt all the feelings that she had tried to deny build up within her to a fever pitch. Not just the raw sensuality that he brought out in her, but the emotion too. It choked her throat, bringing moisture to her eyes and stealing the breath from her chest.

But before she could examine it too closely, he pulled a thick blanket from a chair onto the floor of the gazebo and laid her down on it, and began to draw the skirt of her dress upwards.

'We can't do this here,' she chastised with a little moan as he began to slide her underwear to the side, his intent clear as he licked his lips and stared down at where she was swollen and ready for him.

'They know not to disturb us,' he growled. But instead of stopping what he had just begun, he simply switched up the method, sliding a finger between her sex and swirling in gentle circles that made her sigh in delight.

'Just let me give you this,' he murmured against her lips, his hands still working their magic between her thighs. 'Just let me remind you why we're so good together. To think that you could ever believe me to have lost interest in you…is madness. If you knew how much you consume my thoughts on a daily basis you'd never accuse me of such a thing.'

'Is this a punishment?' She gasped as the first wave began to build deep within her and he showed no sign of stopping.

'Perhaps,' he murmured, 'or maybe it's just a reminder. One that I am only too happy to give you every single time that you doubt my attraction to you.'

His words struck a chord within her, alarm bells sounding. But they were swiftly drowned out as her orgasm began to build and melted all coherent thought from her mind.

Then he paused and she nearly screamed with frustration.

Nysio was delicate with her, but firm as he pinned her hands and pulled her down gently onto their blanket once more. She was flushed and gorgeous, her newly swollen breasts and darkened nipples peeking out from the top of her bra.

'I want nothing between us.' He leaned down, licking the barely visible little bud once before taking hold of the front clasp. 'I want to see you, *cara*. All of you.'

He waited for her to tense up, to mention any one of the numerous reasons why he probably shouldn't be making love to her at this very moment, in this place. But she simply smiled, a shy smile filled with a raw vulnerability that took his breath away. Then she reached up and replaced his hands with her own, unclipping the clasp and baring herself to him, then shimmying the rest of her dress down and away.

Nysio swore his erection suddenly gained a heartbeat all of its own as he gazed down at the visual feast laid out before him, making him heat up to self-combustion point with lust. Perhaps she couldn't see the changes that pregnancy had brought to her body yet, but he could.

Her breasts had already been full, but now they barely fitted in his hands. Their tips were the colour of his favourite sweet pink grapes, begging to be tasted. In fact... he reached over and put action to the thought. He swore they tasted better than vintage wine.

He realised he must have spoken his thought aloud when she gasped and said, 'You...really are obsessed with wine.' She made an attempt at laughter, but her breath caught, her hips undulating as his tongue darted out to flick one hardened peak, her breath hissing through her teeth.

'Obsession is not enough to describe what I feel,' he growled, his eyes pinning hers as he bent to kiss each sweet pink bud again. 'I…adore it. I worship it. I fear that I'll never get enough.'

Her eyes held his and he knew by the slight flicker of uncertainty there that she understood. A part of him whispered that he should slow down, that he should continue to show her that she could trust him. But another, much darker part of him just wanted to know that she felt the same.

She still had her eyes half closed, her hips undulating with barely restrained need. She was so responsive, so effortlessly sensual, he could read her without a word spoken. It had been this way that first night, he remembered. He kissed her, fighting the urge within him to push her once again, to demand that she agree to his terms. That she stay in Italy by his side as his wife, in his *palazzo*, in his bed… He fought against the tightness in his chest, the need to possess her completely.

He took his time, whispering his adoration against the skin of her thighs as he made his way to the silk covering of underwear she wore. The intricately embroidered red silk was dark with her moisture and he couldn't resist laying the first of his kisses against the fabric.

'Wait,' she whispered, her eyes wild with pleasure as she reached down to unbutton his jeans. 'It's always about me. Let me give you pleasure for once.'

He lay back on his side, his fingers still idly stroking her even as she withdrew his hard length and held him in her hands. She stared at him, her tongue darting out to lick her lips for a split second before she shyly leaned forward to press a kiss against him.

From their position lying side by side, top to tail…it seemed only natural for him to mirror her movements, pressing an answering kiss against her centre. She smiled, getting braver by the minute, and took him deeper, almost making him lose control completely.

'*Amore mio*, if we continue this I won't last.' He groaned. 'And I want to be able to feel you around me.'

'I want that too, but right now I want you to lose control like this…from me.'

Nysio needed no further convincing and spread her wide for deeper access. They continued their erotic game of mirrors until he felt her body tighten and tasted her shuddering climax, his own body thrusting wildly as he found his release at the same moment between her lips. Her answering sigh of pleasure vibrated through him, connecting him to her. Joining them together just as they were meant to be and he knew he would never let her go.

CHAPTER TWELVE

EACH DAY THEY spent in Sardinia seemed to challenge so many of Aria's reasons behind not wanting to accept Nysio's proposal. He showed her his sensitive side, showed her his love for his family and his passion for the vineyards and produce that came from Viti Di Cora. She met his extended family on his mother's side, who all lived close by in the small town and worked in the vineyard. She watched while Nysio rolled up his sleeves and got his hands dirty during the harvest. It was like living in a different world and he seemed a completely different man now that he was away from all the duty and pressure from the *palazzo*. He'd even reached out and contacted his half-brothers, at her urging, and a tentative connection was being formed.

When he asked her to stay a little longer...to try to move her bank appointment out another week or two... she accepted without question. Suddenly the thought of leaving him and returning to London felt completely wrong. So instead, they returned to Florence, as Nysio had commitments he had to honour.

Aria rationalised that Italy was a much better place for her to be while planning out the manufacturing process for her lingerie line. It was the heart of the fashion world, after all! But when she suggested that maybe she could take a trip out to some factories to learn more, Nysio seemed less than enthused. He was a busy man, she understood that. She'd quickly seen just how busy he was between the curation of the Bacchetti collections of art and jewellery that required his signature. Then there was the property arm of their company, not to mention the numerous charities, scholarships and community projects. He worked long hours too, with the stock markets opening and closing at odd times. But still, once he eventually slid into bed beside her, their lovemaking was as passionate and exciting as ever. She could hardly remember why she'd had hang-ups about things like oral pleasure because, well…it turned out that Nysio was an expert in that arena. Her happiness would be complete if he'd even hinted he felt more for her than desire.

Aria stepped in front of the mirror in the *palazzo*'s master suite and took a final look at her reflection. The long red gown fitted her curves to perfection, the material like a second skin over her breasts and waist before flowing out from her hips to the floor. For all of her insistence that agreeing to stay here for the past week was not her agreeing to become the lady of the palace…she felt surprisingly regal.

The Bacchetti annual charity event was in full swing as she descended the stairs alone. Nysio had said he had a surprise for her to attend to. Nerves jittered in her stomach as she wondered what that could be. But before her foot had left the last step she found out as a familiar silhouette with long black hair came barrelling across the hallway through the crowd.

'Priya?' she squeaked, the only sound she managed to get out before she was embraced in a tight hug and cloud of perfume. They stood like that for far too long, their frantic voices only half intelligible as they apologised to one another for the past couple of months of silence. When they finally pulled away there were tears in both of their eyes.

'Damn it, I'm going to ruin my make-up.' Aria took a deep breath. 'I wish this party wasn't going on now, we've got so much to catch up on.'

'We'll talk properly later. Xander is here too, with his new wife Pandora. It seems we both wound up madly in love with gorgeous men, so I guess things worked out.' Priya raised one brow. 'So...you're dating a guy who lives in an actual palace. Let's at least mention that?'

Nothing got past this woman, she saw everything and far too much. As was evidenced by the way her eyes instantly narrowed when Aria smiled and refused a glass of champagne from a passing waiter. The headache that had been plaguing her all week had held off a bit today so she felt mostly fine, once she kept eating and didn't try to stand up too quickly. But when another waiter appeared with a tray of fresh seafood hors d'oeuvres, she felt her entire body threaten to revolt.

'Are you sure you're not ill?' Priya asked quietly, her brow furrowing.

'I'm fine.' Aria scowled, but inside her heart warmed at the obvious concern in her best friend's face. She inhaled a calming breath; now was not the time to tell Priya about the baby. She would need more time and privacy for that conversation. 'Look at us, standing at the sidelines of a party while you play mother hen...it almost feels like we're back in college.'

Priya laughed and Aria felt her body relax at the sound. The whole runaway-bride incident had put pressure on their usually easy relationship. But her friend was happy, as was evidenced by the soppy grin that slowly transformed her face at the sight of the tall blond man crossing the room towards them.

'Your husband is looking quite god-like,' Aria murmured dutifully. 'Now, allow me to go mingle before you two start making besotted eyes at one another again.'

'It better be more than eyes, with all the effort I put into this outfit.' Priya winked, pasting on a bright smile just as her husband reached her side and drew her into his arms for a kiss that bordered on scandalous.

When had her friend become so sultry? Aria forced herself to look away from the easy display of wedded bliss, feeling something shamefully akin to jealousy burn in her gut. Or was it just another bout of nausea? She honestly didn't know which might feel worse in her present state of exhaustion.

She wandered through the crowd of well-dressed guests, taking in designer shoes and tailored trouser cuffs as she followed the mosaic path towards the bar for some water. She didn't know what made her pause and redirect her gaze towards the opposite end of the room.

Nysio stood alone under an open archway at the entrance, his eyes sharply assessing the crowd around him until he spotted her. He was by her side in an instant, taking her by the hand and drawing her away from the mass of people that stood around, admiring the Bacchetti art collection and impressing one another with their knowledge.

'Where are we going?' She laughed as he continued to be mysterious, guiding her along the flagstone path, past the fountain until they were walking deep into the maze she had admired so many times from their bedroom window. The late November breeze was cool on her skin but not unpleasant as they pressed deeper, only coming to a stop when they reached the centre where a small gazebo lay surrounded by illuminated water features and statues.

'Every good maze needs a monster at the centre,' she mused, idly running her hand over one polished marble beast.

'This palace has more than enough of those,' Nysio said.

Something in his voice made her pause.

'You're not a monster, Nysio,' she said, putting as much steel in her tone as she could manage.

'You're sure about that?' His voice echoed around her, that same haunted darkness in his eyes.

'You're not a monster,' she repeated, needing to say this to him, needing him to know how wrong he was to see himself as the product of a tyrant's seed and his father's desire to keep a scandal quiet. 'The monsters are the ones who seek to hurt people. Being overprotective and making decisions out of fear doesn't make you a bad person. But refusing to change your behaviour when you learn that it's hurting someone is.' She raised one brow, leaning down to press a gentle kiss against his forehead.

She moved to walk away but he grabbed her hand at the last minute, holding tight and pulling her into the circle of his arms. 'I brought you here to ask you something.'

The words were murmured against her hair, and for a long moment there was nothing but silence between them, nothing but the strength of their embrace and the beating of her heart.

'I've waited for the right moment to give you this, waited to be sure that you felt happy here. That you could see our future as clearly as I can. These past few weeks have shown us both just how right we can be together when we're working as a team...' He pulled a ring out from his pocket, a beautiful gold band with a giant ruby at the centre. Aria felt her chest hammer, the headache intensifying in her temples as she panicked.

'Aria…will you marry me?'

Nysio knew he had misjudged the situation even before Aria shook her head sadly. He tried to hold in his anger, his confusion, tried to wait for her to explain. Because he fully expected an explanation.

'Nysio… I'm sorry but I can't marry you.'

'Can't or won't?' he growled. 'You would just so easily refuse to be my wife, when you could have access to everything that you need?'

'Everything?' she asked, tilting her head. 'So if I decide I want us to move back to London to open up my own fashion label there like I'd planned?'

His eyes narrowed. 'You're being deliberately obtuse.'

'If I wanted to take our child out for a walk in the park without any security guards? If I wanted to show them how to ride a train, or just take a spontaneous trip to the beach?'

'I admit that our security protocol is heavy, but it is necessary as you know in order to ensure—'

'Safety,' Aria finished for him. 'Yes, I know. You have talked of nothing else from the moment we first met. I can't resign myself to living a life of imprisonment.'

'You still believe me to be keeping you prisoner?' He raised his voice, gesturing at the opulent grounds around them. 'If this is a prison, then I'm right here with you. You believe me to be some poor soul trapped in a life of luxury?'

'Do you feel free?' she asked quietly. 'You seemed free for a moment back there, in Sardinia on your vineyard…

For a moment, I thought that perhaps things might actually work out for us. But then we came back here, to this place, to this world and this way of life that you refuse to see is not making you happy. I know you made a promise to your father, and I understand that loyalty is deeply important to you. But it's just not who I am. And it's not the kind of life that I want for our child, being raised to carry on the Bacchetti name without a care for who they are inside. When you jumped straight to wanting marriage for the baby's sake it was easy for me to say no. Because I was terrified of how you made me feel. I was terrified of how much you made me hope and want for more. I do want more… But I cannot be your wife. Not when I know that the only reason you're asking me is to ensure that I stay here, at the *palazzo*, with our child. I'm sorry. You deserved that choice as a boy and our child deserves that now.'

'You will not take my child from me, Aria.'

'Never. I would never do that to you. I promise you that I won't run away, I won't hide from you. Because I know that, despite the bounds of loyalty that you have to the Bacchetti history, you're going to be a good father and you want the best for your child. So, I'm prepared to compromise and find a way to raise this baby with love even if we're not together.'

'So that's it? We're done? I don't have any further say in it?'

She lowered her eyes. 'I… I'm sorry.'

As Aria walked out of the maze and back towards the *palazzo*, she thought she heard a loud curse erupt from the depths of the maze behind her, but then there was nothing but the echo of her own footsteps on the stone steps that sounded like just how she felt inside.

An overwhelming sense of anxiety rose within her, and she found herself unable to speak as she entered the front door of the *palazzo*. Gianluca walked towards her, his eyes crinkled at the sides with concern, his hand reaching for her even as she pulled away. She was vaguely aware of her own voice muttering an apology, excusing herself on the pretence of using the bathroom.

Once she was in the hallway, she quickened her pace, walking hard and fast in no particular direction at all. Her chest burned and inhaling each breath took a sudden effort as she had never experienced before. It felt as though she were underwater and fighting not to breathe in. She needed fresh air before her lungs burst open. The migraine that had been threatening all morning erupted with impressive force in her temples, bringing with it a wave of nausea that almost brought her to her knees. She stopped in an open doorway that led out onto the back gardens. The cool breeze in her face did nothing to abate the awful sense that her legs were about to completely give out from underneath her. She needed to calm down, she needed to...

Unable to stand a moment longer, she felt her body slide parallel to the door until she was suddenly sitting down on cold, hard tiles. The blue of the sky seemed to blend into the green of the grass, colours jumping and mixing with one another to form a kind of Impressionist painting rather than reality. A shadow in the distance moved closer, and a rough shout sounded very close by. She was vaguely aware of strong arms lifting her, pulling her against a familiar hard, warm chest.

She shook her head, hearing a guttural demand for

an ambulance seemingly coming from far away, though, when she looked up, Nysio held her tightly in his arms.

'Tell me what is happening, *tesoro*,' he pleaded, his face pale under his swarthy tan.

'Nysio,' she murmured, shocked at how weak and thready her own voice sounded. 'There's something very wrong.'

CHAPTER THIRTEEN

NYSIO WAITED PATIENTLY. His eyes completely focused on the door that a team of doctors had disappeared through along with Aria. He was vaguely aware of Eros and Priya seated across from him, worry evident on their faces. Xander and Pandora had stayed at the *palazzo* to tend to their guests, which he was immensely grateful for. He felt like a caged animal, unable to stop pacing the length of the waiting area. He had practically growled when the doctors said they all needed to leave the room in order for them to properly examine the patient. His chest went painfully tight as he remembered the sight of Aria hooked up to tubes on the hospital bed. She had been unconscious for barely a minute, but still…

A man in a white coat exited the room and Nysio stood straight, aware of the others moving to attention as well.

'Is one of you the next of kin?' the doctor asked.

Both Nysio and Priya stepped forward, answering yes simultaneously.

'I meant the baby's father?' the doctor said, unaware of the sudden tension.

'That would be me,' Nysio said.

'The…baby? Aria is having a baby?' Priya eyed him in shock.

Nysio ignored her. 'Is Aria okay?'

'Ms Dane is suffering from acute anaemia and low blood pressure, not uncommon in the first trimester. Her iron levels are incredibly low so we will be admitting her overnight for observation. She lost consciousness for a short time, as you witnessed today. She's going to need an iron infusion, but I believe that, once she's had it, she'll be fine as long as she's careful.'

Nysio felt relief flood him, his fists loosening by his sides. 'And the baby...'

The doctor removed a sonogram from his clip chart, holding out the blurry black and white image. 'It's still early, but from what I can tell, the pregnancy is at about nine weeks gestation and both babies are developing nicely according to the dates.'

'Both...babies?' Nysio froze, his hand seeming to reach out of its own volition, grabbing the sonogram from the doctor's hands. He absorbed the news, relief flooding him that Aria was going to be all right. But there were two babies. Two.

The doctor had him sign a few forms before saying they could go in and see Aria once the nurses had finished the infusion. Nysio still stood there, staring down at the two barely visible white shadows on the small sonogram in his hands. He traced one finger across each blob, amazed at the fierce urge to protect them with all of his might. He would protect their mother too, he silently vowed. Even from himself.

After a couple of minutes of tense silence, the nurse emerged and ushered them into the private room. Aria lay propped up on pillows in the large white bed, tubes in her arms connecting her to various medical devices that surrounded her. Nysio felt a lump in his throat, as Priya rushed forward and gently embraced her friend.

After a moment of inaudible sobbing, the women separated and Priya shook her head sharply. 'I can't believe you kept this big a secret from me.'

Eros stepped forward from where he had been hovering in the doorway, and Nysio felt enormous gratitude towards his brother as he gently suggested to his wife that they leave Aria to rest. Nysio simply nodded once, a silent thanks to the family member he'd never believed he would have. The family member that Aria had given him really, through her encouragement to reconnect with both his brothers ever since she'd found out about them.

And then they were gone, and the room was finally silent except for the soft beeping of the machines she was hooked into. He looked at her then, really looked at her. She looked so pale and exhausted in the hospital bed, her hands clutching the blankets as though she held on for dear life.

'I'm sorry about all of the drama,' she said, twisting the hospital bracelet on her wrist. 'You heard the doctor, the babies are fine, there's two of them… And I just need some extra iron… Probably because there's two of them, did I mention that there's two?'

Nysio tried to smile, but felt an uncomfortable lump growing in his throat as he took a seat on the edge of the bed. 'I guess that answers my next question, if you were surprised.'

'I was so scared.' Her voice cracked. 'I'd been working too hard on my plans for the line, forgetting to take my vitamins and then there was all the sex… I was so sure that there was something terribly wrong.'

'Time has never moved slower than that half-hour today as I tried to get you here.' He shook his head. 'I thought…'

'I know,' Aria whispered. 'I thought the worst too. I had been getting the migraines and dizzy spells all week.

I should have got checked sooner. I'm just not quite used to being cared for quite so much.'

'Well, you should be,' he said soberly. 'You have two babies to grow now, which means you need to be watched more closely. You're going to need to take it easy for a while.'

Aria sat upon the bed, twisting the cover in one hand. 'I know. I realise now that I hadn't fully accepted the pregnancy. I was distracting myself with all the wrong kind of worries. Rather than worrying about myself and the physical challenge of growing a child inside me.'

'Two children,' Nysio said pointedly.

'Yeah…' Aria shook her head. 'I think I'm still processing that part, to be honest. Are you as terrified as I am?'

Nysio was quiet. He stood up, walking over to the large window and bracing his hands on the ledge. 'I think today has made it more real for me too. Of the plans we need to make and decide upon. Now that we know the pregnancy will need extra care.'

'Yes… I know.'

'Right now, you need to rest.' Nysio placed his hand over hers and felt his heart squeeze when she gripped onto him so tightly. He wanted nothing more than to hold her tight enough that she could never get free again. He wanted to wrap her in luxury and care and attention, and stand in front of anyone who intended her harm. He wanted to give her everything. But she didn't want it from him.

'They said that you can leave by tomorrow, but I called Priya to see if you could stay with her.' He removed his hand, shoving his fists into his pockets to force himself not to reach out again. 'I assumed you'd want your space to make your plans.'

Nysio hardly noticed his surroundings as he walked out of the hospital room and left three quarters of his heart behind him. The terrible reality had already begun to dawn on him that the most selfish thing that he could possibly do would be to keep her and their children by his side. Aria was not built to live in his cage. She was too vibrant, too full of life and love to be imprisoned in the world into which he had been born. All along he had told himself he needed to keep her, to convince her to parent their children together and do the best for the Bacchetti legacy.

The thought of letting her go killed him, but he would do it if it meant seeing her smiling and happy. He could be selfless for her. He could show her his love that way... because he knew with certainty that he must be in love. Nothing else could possibly hurt this much. He sat in his car, feeling the silence cocoon him, but it gave him no comfort as it usually did. He had grown to adore all the noise and movement and unpredictability that came with loving Aria Dane.

CHAPTER FOURTEEN

THE NEXT TWENTY-FOUR hours passed quickly as the hospital staff performed numerous checks to make sure that it was okay for Aria to be discharged from their care.

Aria sat up in the bed, as she took in the two identical blobs for the thousandth time. Those blobs were inside her, she thought with a sense of awe. Until now, this pregnancy hadn't seemed real yet. Obviously, she knew she was pregnant and would eventually give birth. But she hadn't really given thought to the fact that there was an actual life forming and growing inside her. There had seemed too much else to consider. But when the doctor had placed the ultrasound wand on her stomach and she had heard those two little hearts beating slightly out of time with one another… Nothing else had seemed more important.

She leaned back on the pillows, placing both of her hands on her slightly rounded stomach and closed her eyes. 'I know you guys are probably much too small to hear me,' she said softly. 'I'm sorry if things got a little crazy in there lately. I've been making myself far too busy. But you're going to be my priority now.'

Priya was surprisingly patient when Aria arrived at her hotel. She listened as Aria talked about what had occurred in the weeks since her friend's failed wedding and her reappearance, and Priya shared her own story.

It surprised Aria deeply to learn that Priya had trusted Eros so blindly, but then she realised that she was not so different herself. She had done exactly the same thing, had she not? She had taken one look at Nysio and wanted him badly, so she'd jumped into bed with him the first chance that she could. Or jumped onto a bathroom vanity counter, whatever! Priya's eyes widened when Aria shared that particular story. She wasn't ashamed of her actions. She'd always shared everything with Priya, after all. But things were different now, Priya was in love and somebody's wife. She had plans for the future. Aria was still adrift.

'You could set up your business wherever you are; why don't you come back to New York with me?'

Aria thought about it, thought about taking Priya's offer and going ahead with her plan to start up a small lingerie label. But the thought of embarking upon the pipe dream that she had rolled over for so long suddenly had absolutely no pleasure in it.

'No… The time isn't right, I think,' she said, lowering her hand to her stomach where her two little beans were safely nestled. 'I got a scare, thinking something was wrong with the babies. I think I want to stay here, in Florence, for a bit. Here is where I'm going to live. I want the babies to be near their father…and I want to be near him too.'

She hadn't realised that was how she felt until the words left her lips. When she said them aloud, she knew it was true, she knew it was what she wanted. Stay here with Nysio, to raise their children near their grandmother and grandfather who had already shown more love and excitement at the babies' existence than even she had.

'Have you told Nysio that?' Priya asked, a strange look in her eyes.

'I haven't seen him since yesterday; I think he's been avoiding me. We had a fight. He asked me to marry him and I said no.'

Priya's face stiffened with surprise. 'Oh. That probably didn't help you to relax.'

'But now I've thought about it, I think I've been an absolute fool. He's amazing, Priya, and I think I've been completely unfair to him and allowed my own wounds to still dictate my life. I think... I think I at least owe it to myself and my babies to try.'

'I should tell you that Eros had a meeting with Nysio and Xander this morning. He told me that your baby daddy was planning to do something big with them. Something about getting balance?'

Aria sat up straight. 'What does he mean?'

'I'm not sure... I only know that he said that it was for his family, so I didn't question it. But Eros seemed stunned on the call, and he asked Nysio if he was sure he could part with so much history.'

His history. His place as legitimate heir. Aria felt her stomach drop. What had he done?

'I actually can't believe he would do something like that for me without talking to me first. I have to go.' She stood up and moved, grabbing her bags and hastily throwing in her belongings.

'Slow down, you've just got out of the hospital,' Priya begged.

'I'm not on bed rest, I'm quite able to go downstairs and get into a cab.' She closed her eyes, placing a hand on her chest as she felt a panicked sob pass through her. 'I've made so many mistakes; I need to go to him. I need to make this right or I'll never forgive myself.'

'Okay, but at least take my car. Being lovesick makes you crazy apparently,' Priya said, smiling. 'But I can see why you love him. I see the way he looks at you too, the way he cared for you in the hospital. I think you know what you want now, so go and get him.'

Aria still couldn't believe what Nysio was telling her, as they stood once more in the centre of the maze at the *palazzo*, where she'd found him.

'I realised that I don't want my children to be raised under the same weight of expectation that I was,' he was saying. 'I don't want them to have that life.'

He moved away from her and she felt something tense within, urging her to move closer, to hold him to her, but she held back.

'So you just…gave it all away? The Bacchetti part of your wealth?'

'I've given it back to the people who treasure it most: the people of Florence. I've set up a charity for the benefit of our community and all funds will go to those in need. They can also open the *palazzo* to the public; you were right that the treasures inside should be seen and admired.'

'It's a wonderful thing to do,' she said approvingly.

'For decades I hid myself within these walls, working myself to exhaustion just to try to prove that I was worthy of the Bacchetti name I had been born with. But then I met you…' He smiled at the memory. 'You made me remember what it felt like to feel free. Then I brought you here and you made me see it for what it was. A prison of my own making. I believed I had no choice but to continue clinging to the reputation that my father had guarded so fiercely. I believed that I owed it to him and to my mother. You made me see that what I wanted mattered too.'

She smiled tremulously back at him.

'Once upon a time, being a Bacchetti was everything that I was. I was raised to be the heir to a dynasty that spanned generations. It was a duty that I performed happily, because it made my father proud. I idolised him. But I know now that love doesn't always mean having to live up to other people's expectations.'

'Oh, Nysio…'

'I'm not trying to change your mind about marrying me. You've made it very clear why you don't want to. I did this for me. I did this because you made me realise where my true passion lies. I never actually wanted to be the man that my father raised me to be. I never cared all that much about being a Bacchetti. You made me remember the person I had once wanted to be until my guilt forced me back into a role I felt duty-bound to accept. I don't think I truly knew who I was for a very long time.'

'I know who you are,' she said gently.

'When you came to my rescue on that street in Manhattan, I thought at first it was just attraction, lust. It was easy to disregard the raw need within me that refused to let you go, easy to brush it off as amazing chemistry but nothing more.'

'To be honest, I felt the same thing.'

'I thought I was rescuing you, the day we met. You were abandoned, alone and afraid and yet…you wound up being the one to rescue me. You brought something back to life in me the moment you commanded me to look in your eyes and breathe. That was the moment I felt that shift within me from simply existing to wanting more. That was the moment I fell in love with you, Aria Dane. I think a part of me has felt it all along and it terrified me. I brought you to my palace like a prize that I feared someone would come along and take away. I have made so many mistakes with you, *tesoro*. I cannot undo the things that I've said that have made you feel trapped. I never want you to feel trapped, Aria, never. I love you too much.'

Aria felt a burst of emotion choke her, the weight of his revelations pressing down upon her as her hand instinctively dropped to cradle her stomach and the precious cargo that nestled within. While she had been lying in her hospital bed feeling slightly sorry for herself, he had been busy acknowledging the cracks in his foundations and setting about doing the work to make himself whole again.

She remembered what he had told her of his life, the man he'd been raised to be. She knew that he'd never truly wanted it, had seen how much it took from him every time he played the part that had been assigned to him. She had witnessed his passion when they were in Sardinia, his love for the wine and the people who made it, but she had never truly believed that he would listen to her. That he would finally choose balance for himself.

'I haven't done any of this in order to convince you to marry me. You helped me to see that our children would be more affected by me remaining here…in this palace, than by being born in or out of wedlock. I don't know how else to explain it, I'm just…'

'You're choosing the path that will make you the best version of you,' she finished for him.

'Yes…that's exactly it.' He blinked, then a smile transformed his face. If the smile he'd given her that night when she'd played the piano for him had been like fireworks…this one was a full-on explosion. His eyes shone and gone were the shadows that she'd grown so used to trying to coax away. He didn't need her to coax them away, he was shining through his own darkness just fine. The realisation made a little part of her ache. But the thought of him living that life to the fullest without her being the woman standing by his side was suddenly utterly ridiculous.

She closed her eyes, fear and uncertainty clogging her throat as emotion finally won the battle and put an end to her composure. Tears filled her eyes and she shook her head, turning away from him, trying to hide her own weakness.

He moved towards her in an instant, as she knew he would, strong hands encircling her shoulders and pulling her back tightly against his chest.

'Damn hormones,' she gasped, grateful that he was still behind her and that he couldn't see her ugly cry.

'Why do you insist on hiding your vulnerability from me? Do you fear that I can't take it? Because I assure you I can. I will be here to support you over these next months, no matter how hard it gets. That was never an option. You may have refused my proposal, but I never intended to walk away from you. Never, *tesoro*. I only want your happiness, whether that is being with me as my wife, or simply as the two primary caregivers for these two incredibly lucky children that are growing inside you.' His hand drifted down, covering hers gently, reverently.

'I know I hurt you when I refused your proposal,' Aria said. 'And once I'd realised what a mistake I had made, I was worried it was too late. I knew I'd messed up but had absolutely no idea how to put it right.' She felt his breath on the crown of her head and could hear the steady thump of his heartbeat directly behind hers. He was holding her so tightly, but not inappropriately so, she could feel him holding back from crossing that line. A line that seemed so utterly ridiculous to her now that she could see what she needed to say and do so clearly.

Honesty. Trust. A leap of faith.

She turned around in the circle of his arms, realising that she had run from her own feelings long enough and her children deserved for her to be brave. To believe that he loved her. To fight for their family, the one that she truly wanted for them.

Aria met his gaze, her voice shaky. 'There is more I need to say, so much more that I want to say... I just can never seem to get the words out the right way when it's important. When I have you looking at me, all the words pile together and I...'

'How about if I close my eyes?'

She gasped, stunned once again at how easily this man took care of her. How ridiculous it had been for her to run away from his natural protective nature when it lit her up inside like this. His eyes fluttered closed and it took all of her strength not to just rush past the words that needed to be said and simply kiss him until neither of them could breathe. But kissing had never been something they needed to work on together.

Communication first, she reminded herself. Kissing later.

'Nysio, I think I've deliberately kept you at arm's length because I was afraid of my own feelings after what Theo did to me. I also thought that what I needed to gain self-respect was to push myself as hard as I could to succeed at a career. I wanted to feel capable and worthy of the life growing inside me. Both of them.'

She stopped for a moment and he smiled encouragingly at her, still with his eyes shut.

'The past few days have just become a haze of brain

fog. The scare that we had, worrying that something terrible had happened to the babies… It made me realise that I was running in entirely the wrong direction.' Once again she placed a hand over her stomach where the tiny lives within her were growing steadily and healthily. 'I don't think that I truly processed what was actually happening until I thought it had been taken away from me. I've always been different from the rest of my family, and I've felt ashamed that I've struggled so much. I've always judged myself far more harshly than anyone else ever has. And when you proposed to me…when I said no to you, and it felt like my heart was breaking in two… I knew I was in way deeper than I'd thought I ever could be.'

'I know Theo destroyed your trust,' he said gently.

She winced. 'I didn't think I'd ever be able to trust anyone again enough to marry them.' She forced the words out past the lump in her throat. 'I figured I'd only be setting myself up for failure and abandonment. That I was better off alone. But then you came into my life and for the first time I found myself actually wanting more…and it terrified me. So when we found out about the pregnancy, it was the easiest thing in the world to put on my armour again. It's so much harder for me to be vulnerable…to allow myself to hope. But the more I thought about it, the more I realised that I wanted nothing more than to be married to you. To wake up in your arms every morning and be surrounded by our beautiful children, wherever that may be.'

He opened his eyes and smiled down at her.

'I love you too,' she said, meeting his gaze and not letting go. 'I want everything that you have to offer me, Nysio. I really don't care where we are living, or what life looks like, so long as we're together.'

'*Dannazione*, I don't have the ring on me.' He looked

flustered, a small blush appearing on the tops of his cheeks, something that made her smile wide and soft and lean even further into him. She wanted to draw pictures of this man and take photos of him and just stare at him all day. Hardly believing that he was truly hers, that he truly loved her as deeply and unconditionally as she loved him. Because she could no longer deny that that was the truth. He had given up more than anyone she had ever known; he had walked away from a fortune and a status that had given him a riches and power beyond most people's dreams.

'I don't need a ring,' she said, emotion forcing the words out in an unsteady cadence. 'So long as I have you in my heart and in my arms, I need nothing more.'

'I know you don't need a ring, but I'll still be giving it to you. Consider it an echo of my archaic caveman. I want everyone to know that you are mine, just as I am yours.'

'You know... I really do like the sound of that,' she said huskily, 'but if you get to show everyone that I'm yours, perhaps I should brand you in return?'

'What exactly did you have in mind?'

'A tattoo perhaps.' Her voice was a soft murmur as she trailed a finger up his sternum, his throat and then up past his lips and nose to point at his head. 'Right in the centre of your forehead.'

He laughed, a sound she'd once thought she might never hear again and now it came from him so easily. She silently vowed to make him laugh like this every day for the rest of their lives.

'Will you brand me with your name?' he asked, stroking a hand down her ribcage. *'Property of Aria. Do Not Touch*?'

'Property is a word just so devoid of passion. I was

thinking more along the lines of *Taken by Aria... Possessed by Aria... Beloved by Aria.*'

'I really like the sound of that last one.' The hint of humour had left his voice, and he suddenly sounded hoarse with desire. In one rapid movement he was gathering her deeper into the circle of his arms so that every inch of their bodies touched from chin to knee and suddenly Aria's mind was only focused on getting as much of his delicious body under her palms as she could manage. Their kisses were slow and sensuous, filled with the whispered promises of their future and even a few tears on her part.

'So if you've given this place away to your charity now, to open up to the public...does that mean that you're essentially homeless?'

He raised a wicked eyebrow. 'I'm still in possession of a rather sizeable fortune, an entire stockbroking company, not to mention a billion-euro wine label.'

'Oh, you poor man. Just the one wine label?' She tutted. 'Sounds like you're in need of rescue.'

'Miss Dane... Are you wondering about the fastest way to get your fiancé into bed?'

Her fiancé. She had once thought that word would hold nothing but bad memories for her for ever, but now, looking at this man, she felt only excitement for the future, and the absolute certainty that it would be wonderful.

'My fiancé should know by now that I am utterly insatiable when it comes to celebrating moments. And this definitely feels like something we should be celebrating. In an aeroplane bed, on a bathroom sink, in a gazebo... I don't particularly have a preference for the location. But I'm pretty sure that if we don't get all of our clothes off in the next five minutes, I won't be held accountable for my actions.'

'I suppose I should take you seriously…'

'Always.'

EPILOGUE

ARIA SIGHED AND tilted her head up to let the Greek sun warm her face for a moment. The small beach was a quiet respite from the noisy house party up above while Nysio chased around after their twin boys, Emilio and Mauro. They had been guests on Eros and Priya's private island paradise for the past two days and it had been just what they'd all needed. Her decision, backed by Nysio, to go ahead and take the leap and start up her own line of lingerie while pregnant had seemed utterly ridiculous at the time, and even more so when the orders had begun flooding in and they'd had to increase their warehouse size three times. But they still prioritised family time above all else.

'There you are.' A familiar voice spoke from the wooden stairway above, and she looked up to see Priya making her way down, her four-month-old baby daughter, Amara, in her arms.

'I swear, if one more person asks me where my husband is, I'll scream.'

Aria smiled as her best friend came to sit beside her on the loveseat, her tiny daughter kicking and cooing in her arms. Aria instantly put her arms out to take her goddaughter, grinning when the baby gave her a gummy smile in response.

'Amara, tell your mama it's time for her to come and live in Italy,' she said.

'Amara, tell your godmother that if she wants to hold a baby more often, she has a very handsome husband who is more than willing to oblige her,' Priya teased.

'I'm so going to tell Nysio you called him handsome.'

'You seem to forget that time you asked my husband if he would be interested in modelling for one of your ad campaigns.'

'She asked Xander too.' A quiet voice came from behind them and they both turned to see the familiar smile of Xander's wife, Pandora, as she came into view.

'Okay, this is beginning to feel like a pile-on,' Aria grumbled good-naturedly, shifting over to make room. 'And yes, when it comes to business, I admit I'm a little bit shameless.'

A little bit? ' Both women laughed aloud, making the baby jump with surprise in her arms. Aria shushed them, rocking the small bundle in her arms with ease.

Aria stared down into her goddaughter's big brown eyes and almost felt a momentary pang of longing strike her.

'I know that look.' Priya smirked. 'Changed your mind on having more babies?'

'Not a chance.' Aria laughed and stood up, swaying from side to side, and hummed a little bit of one of the Italian nursery rhymes her mother-in-law had taught her. Her muscles remembered doing this, night after night when both of the twins had developed colic at the same time.

Nysio had held one and she'd held the other and some nights they'd both fallen into bed exhausted, only to be pulled awake again a short time later. She had no shame in admitting that the first year of parenting had brought her to the brink of her own limits. But that wasn't the reason why they'd decided they were content with their little family as it was. It was simply something they'd both discussed and unanimously agreed upon. Two was their number.

Their boys would turn four soon and they adored being parents and couldn't wait to see what wild times lay ahead. She had loved watching Nysio find his way as a new father and had felt his support as she did the same. They had a beautiful balance in life that meant they could do things like sail off to Greece for this past week. They had also taken a long-overdue honeymoon last year when Nysio had sailed them on a romantic week exploring the Mediterranean for their second wedding anniversary.

She still laughed every time she remembered how long she'd made him wait before finally getting married. It had been a running joke amongst him and their new extended family that Nysio had been the only brother not to marry in a rush after that fateful jilted wedding, despite being the first to become a father. So when the time finally came, Aria had suggested they play a trick on their loved ones, inviting them all to a party where they joined the brothers' anniversary club as a surprise.

Their wedding had taken place exactly two years after the mile-high night that had bound them for ever, in the centre of the maze where he had first told her he loved her.

'I'm actually pregnant.' Pandora blurted.

Priya and Aria both froze and looked down at the third sister of their slightly unconventional extended family set.

'Oh, my God, did I just say that out loud?' Pandora clapped a hand over her mouth. 'Oh, no, I promised Xander that I wouldn't tell anyone yet. It's really early.'

'My lips are sealed.' Priya beamed, reaching out to give her a one-armed hug. 'But now you get the honour of minding Amara for practice while I go meet Eros at the dock.'

'No funny business!' Aria shouted at the rapidly shrinking silhouette of her best friend as she practically ran down the beach towards the opposite end of the island where the small dock resided. Aria looked down to find Amara's head lolling slightly as Pandora tried to get a handle on the active infant. Aria smiled, carefully helping to readjust the baby's head.

'I don't even know how to hold a baby.' Pandora groaned, shifting the little girl's weight awkwardly into her elbow. 'I have absolutely no idea what I'm doing.'

'Neither did I, back when Emilio and Mauro were born,' Aria confessed to the woman who had joined her life as a sister-in-law but had quickly become one of her best friends. 'You must remember the day of their christening when I almost dropped one of my sons in the font?'

Pandora laughed at the memory. 'Oh, yes… I'd almost forgotten that.'

'I was so nervous, having so many family members watching me. I was a wreck as a parent most of the time at the start, but I found my way.'

'I wouldn't mind skipping ahead to this stage.' Pandora gestured to the party above.

Aria looked up at the party, spying the familiar broad silhouette of the man she loved up on the deck above them. Two tiny heads bobbed on either side of him as the boys jumped and called for her and Pandora to come and join them. She waved, feeling her heart thump painfully with so much love.

'The hard times are made easier with the right person by your side. I promise.'

Nysio sneaked a look at the two little boys resting peacefully in their bunk beds on the yacht and sighed with relief. Asleep at long last. The impromptu football game with Zio Eros and Zio Xander had been the perfect way to end their weekend, but the excitement had made the boys even more difficult to get to sleep than usual. Still, he'd never tire of the sight of seeing his wealthy and powerful half-brothers felled by the boundless energy of the Bacchetti twins.

He smiled and wondered what the all-powerful Zeus would think, knowing that his attempt to pit his sons against one another in a race to inherit had only succeeded in bringing them together. Their joint charity efforts were now numerous and they met regularly for family gatherings. A shadow in the doorway made him pause, and he looked to see his wife watching him as he gently tucked the duvet around both boys and tiptoed backwards from the room.

'That was a long day,' he said, once the door was safely closed behind them. 'I never thought I'd say this, but I think this age might be the hardest yet.'

Aria's brows rose in disbelief. 'Harder than the potty-training stage?'

'They couldn't run quite so fast back then.'

The medium-sized yacht had been one of his best purchases in the four years since Aria Dane had walked into his life. Dinner was a beautiful cheeseboard with a side of home-made crusty bread gifted to them by Eros and made with all local ingredients. They ate in companionable silence out on the top deck, accompanied by nothing other than the sound of the waves and the small flickering light of the baby monitor.

Nysio was content. An emotion he'd never thought he might claim for himself. Gone were the constant stomach aches and the need for rigid routine and control. It hadn't disappeared fully, of course, he was still a creature of habit and ferociously dedicated to the three-day working week he'd adopted for himself. A life of balance suited him beautifully, he'd soon discovered. Travelling the world had never been a part of his plans but every time he watched his wife's eyes light up exploring a new city, he felt a peace as he'd never known before.

She'd given this to him, this powerful, beautiful warrior of a woman who had come bursting into his life like a comet, changing everything for evermore.

'You're looking strangely at me again,' Aria said. 'What are you thinking?'

'I'm not thinking, I'm living,' he answered honestly.

'Ah yes, living in the moment. Glad you thought of that one, babe.' She rolled her eyes, then squealed when she seen his brows raise in dark challenge.

Nysio pounced, gripping her around the waist and pinning her between him and the yacht's galley-kitchen counter. Aria made a weak attempt at wriggling away before relaxing into his hold, smacking him lightly on the shoulder for good measure.

The scent of her wild-summer-berry shampoo filled his nose and he groaned, taking a single playful nibble of her earlobe before whispering softly, '*Bellezza*...must you take credit for everything?'

'Yes, I must when I am the one responsible for the vast majority of wonderfulness that we experience every day. Case in point, the two little hellions currently asleep next door.'

'I agree on that point.' He smirked. 'Considering they both clearly take most of their fiery temperament from their mother.'

She lunged for him, but he turned her playful attack into a passionate embrace that quickly escalated until they were both suddenly tearing each other's clothes off and he was laying her out on the galley floor.

'You know how I feel about these wrap dresses,' he groaned, pulling at the tie sash at her waist. One pull and the material fell open, revealing her signature strawberry-printed silk lingerie. 'You are like a prize I've been waiting to unwrap all day, *dolcezza*.'

'Spoken like a true ship's captain.' She laughed, then writhed as his hands traced the outline of her breasts. 'Sometimes I wonder if you love these gifts more than you love me.'

'You're jealous?' He growled playfully, nipping at the soft supple skin along the edge of the delicate fabric. 'You need me to show you how much I adore all of you?'

'Perhaps. Can you do that for me, *amore mio*?' She smiled, knowing full well how much it affected him to hear her speak his native language.

'*Sì, tesoro.*' Because that was what she was: his greatest treasure.

Only when she was fully bared to him did he fulfil his promise, showing her exactly how much he appreciated every one of her gifts. Each touch an unspoken promise that he would never stop ensuring that she felt the full extent of his love for her, for ever and always.

* * * * *

CINDERELLA
HIRED FOR
HIS REVENGE

EMMY GRAYSON

MILLS & BOON

To my husband and my children with love,
with a special note of thanks to my new baby girl,
who got me up at one a.m., three a.m. and five a.m.
for two weeks, to make sure I had time to finish this book.

CHAPTER ONE

ALEXANDRA MOSS GAZED out over Central Park, her eyes drinking in the welcome signs that spring had finally arrived: bright green grass, rosy-pink blossoms on the cherry trees, sidewalks crowded with joggers, bikers and families. Winter had held on to New York City with a vicious, icy grip through the end of March. But finally, the sun had started to beat back the gray clouds, and spring had arrived in all her beautiful, colorful glory last week.

Alexandra's fingers tightened on the black leather sport folio clutched in her hands. Just in time for the final nail to be hammered into her coffin. Her landlord had raised the rent on her little shop in SoHo the same day her biggest client, a bride with a soap opera star for a mother, decided to elope and canceled her entire floral order. It was enough of a financial setback that she'd had to let her part-time employee, Sylvia, go, leaving her working sunup to sundown to make the arrangements, monitor online orders, manage social media and oversee everything else that came with running a floral store in New York City.

Ten thousand dollars, minus a one-thousand-dollar deposit, gone in the blink of an eye. That and a chance to show The Flower Bell was capable of handling the exclusive, high-priced events that would keep her store running.

She turned away from the floor-to-ceiling windows and faced down the empty mahogany conference table. No chairs yet, or any other furniture. The up-and-coming Pearson Group had just moved into the forty-sixth floor of the Carlson, an exclusive building that hosted the offices of public relations firms, ad agencies and financial organizations like Pearson.

When her friend Pamela, a manager with a luxury catering company, had suggested trying to land a corporate contract, Alexandra had hesitated. She'd done some work for businesses in her college internship, but she'd always imagined weddings, baby showers and anniversary parties when she'd thought of the types of events The Flower Bell would service. But the more she'd thought about it, the challenge and the change of pace, she'd decided to go for it. Pamela had snuck her a list of companies with upcoming events.

The first thing Alexandra had done was scour it for any familiar names. It had been seven years since her father, David Waldsworth, had landed in prison after his pyramid scheme had collapsed. The majority of the victims had been blue-collar workers and middle-class families. A point the media had used to hammer her family into the ground, with phrases like, "There's no way they could have not known," plaguing her throughout the trial wherever she went. She'd started buying clothes at thrift stores the week after the trial, unable to bear the thought that her silk blouses and sheath dresses had been purchased with a military veteran's savings or a grandmother's meager retirement fund. Most of her and the family's belongings, including the penthouse, the private plane, the house in the Hamptons and the seaside home on Martha's Vineyard, had been sold to cover her father's debts and start a victims' compensation fund. A fund that even now was several hundred million short of the amount her father had stolen.

Her stepmother had cried but Alexandra had breathed a sigh of relief, grateful to have the reminders of what David's perfidy had bought gone.

Now, after nine years of rebuilding herself, she was once again on the verge of losing everything.

But you won't, she told herself firmly as she breathed in deeply. *You're going to land another contract and The Flower Bell will be a success.*

She'd been nervous about approaching the Pearson Group. It sounded exactly like the kind of firm David had been trying to build his company into, except he'd built it on the backs of hardworking people who had trusted him. All to keep the family name among the elite of New York society after he'd squandered the Waldsworth fortune.

Plenty of people in those upper circles remembered the scandal. However, Pamela had mentioned that the new CEO had recently moved to New York from Los Angeles and so she needed to take the risk. The worst that could happen was that she could get escorted out by security. The best was that she could land a contract large enough to save her business while showing the people of New York what she was capable of before they found out who her father was and wrote her off.

Something that had happened one too many times, including when she'd first tried to find space for The Flower Bell. Her favorite spot, a corner shop close to her future sister-in-law's bookstore, had been her dream, one she'd scrimped and saved and kept her fingers crossed for, hoping it would come available around the time she was ready to launch.

By some miracle, it had been available. Until the leasing agent had found out who her father was and shared that her own father had lost his life savings investing in the Waldsworth Fund.

Alexandra brushed aside the hot rush of shame that pooled in her belly every time she remembered the agent's look of utter revulsion as she'd pointed to the door. She focused on the arrangement she'd brought with her and ran a critical eye over the flowers. Pamela's list of upcoming events for the Pearson Group included a brunch at the New York Public Library, a series of meals at a private address in the Hamptons and a formal reception at the Metropolitan Museum of Art.

"They're wining and dining prospective investors," Pamela had shared when they'd grabbed coffee last week, a tradition they'd carried on since they'd met in a community college class. "From what I hear, the client targets are the kind you'd see in Forbes. Whoever they are, the company's not holding back. They've gone with a mystery approach, only revealing a couple key contacts before they officially launch. Cloak and dagger, but it's working. Everyone's talking about them. The invitations they've sent out for their upcoming events are the most coveted in the city right now."

She'd decided to make a sample arrangement for the first event, the brunch. The low-lying design she'd created featured white roses and anise hyssop, tube-shaped clusters of lavender flowers, combined elegance with the soft color palettes of spring. Not too over-the-top that it would distract from the important business being conducted, but unique enough to generate conversation and show that Pearson could be both traditional and innovative.

She reached out and ran a finger over the velvet petal

of a rose. The delicate, silky texture stirred a memory, one filled with the scents of violets and cedar entwined with amber. When she'd opened her eyes, nervous butterflies fluttering through her veins even as her body grew heavy with desire, it had been to see his face inches away, his full lips hovering over hers.

"Do you want this?" he'd asked, the growl in his voice betraying his desire. But still he'd held back, not wanting to hurt her, not wanting to push her.

And she'd loved him for that. She hadn't thought it possible to love him any more than she already did, but she'd fallen so deep in that moment that she'd given in to the sudden burst of confidence, leaned up and kissed him, her fingers tangling in his thick hair as she'd arched her naked hips against his.

She jerked her hand away from the rose. Eight and a half years. Nine in September. She usually did a better job keeping his memory at bay.

Maybe the roses were a bad idea.

Before she could do something foolish, like try to rearrange the flowers and toss the roses in the trash, the door to the conference room opened. The willow-thin woman in the black pencil skirt and red silk blouse, who had led her into the conference room, stood in the doorway. Silvery blond hair hung down her back, straightened and cut perfectly to frame her face. Alexandra nervously tucked a stray brown curl behind her ear. When the Waldsworths had been the Waldsworths of Lower Manhattan, her father and his third wife, Susan, had pressured her to get her "plain brown hair" touched up with golden highlights to bring out her hazel eyes. Nowadays, getting anything more than a trim was beyond her budget.

But she should have splurged on a little more self-care before coming unannounced to a building like the

Carlson and asking to speak with the events manager of the newly-formed Pearson Group. The company website had listed an official launch date two weeks from now, with interested parties encouraged to contact the CEO's executive assistant, Jessica Elliott. Fortunately, Pamela had been working with the Pearson Group's events manager, Laura Jones. It was easy to find Laura Jones, corporate event planner to the wealthiest companies in the Big Apple. Her feature in *Fortune* magazine and glossy images from past events she'd organized for other high-profile companies had shown an impeccably dressed woman with a stylish red bob, a brilliant white smile and a closet full of the latest couture.

Alexandra's throat tightened. She should have put more effort into her wardrobe, splurged on a name-brand outfit.

"The CEO will see you now."

Her heart skipped a beat. She swallowed past the baseball-size lump that suddenly rose in her throat.

"CEO?"

"Yes."

"What about Ms. Jones?"

Jessica's eyes narrowed slightly. "Have you spoken directly with Ms. Jones?"

No. After her emails, phone calls and attempts at booking in-person appointments with the other companies on Pamela's list, she'd decided to go all in on the Pearson Group and show up with an arrangement that would show Ms. Laura Jones what she was capable of. Better to make one final attempt and close her shop knowing she'd given it her all than to always wonder what if.

She just hadn't anticipated having to make her pitch to the mysterious CEO.

"I assumed with her being the events manager—"

"The majority of our staff are at a corporate training seminar in Shanghai this week."

Okay. She could handle this. Though why the CEO would have any interest in meeting with a struggling florist was beyond her. But instead of questioning her good fortune, she needed to grab the opportunity with both hands.

"All right. It's kind of him to make time for me."

A perfectly-tweezed eyebrow arched upward as something akin to amusement crossed Jessica's face. "It's not kindness. You piqued his interest."

"Hopefully in a good way."

A pale shoulder moved up and down in an elegant shrug. "That remains to be seen. He has five minutes." She glanced at her watch, silver and trimmed in diamonds judging by the way it glinted in the light. Probably Cartier. "Starting now, not a second more. Follow me, Miss Moss."

Steeling her spine, Alexandra tucked the portfolio under one arm, picked up the arrangement and followed the secretary out the door.

This is further than you've made it all week. Don't give up now.

The inner pep talk did little for the sudden light-headedness plaguing her as she tried to keep up with Jessica's rapid pace down a hall enclosed by glass, empty offices on one side and views of New York's impressive skyline on the other. How the woman managed to walk so quickly when she was sporting four-inch stilettos was beyond Alexandra. She could barely keep up in her plain black ballet flats.

Her nervousness reached a fever pitch as the secretary turned a corner and stopped in front of double mahogany doors polished to perfection. Was it possible for one's heart to beat so fast without passing out? The entire future of her company was riding on how she conducted herself in this meeting.

No pressure. None at all.

"He's waiting."

"Okay. Thank you. And his name?"

"He'll tell you."

Alexandra blinked. "What…"

Jessica gave her another look, one that was almost pitying, before she brushed past Alexandra and walked back down the hall, her heels clicking ominously against the floor as she disappeared around the corner.

Slowly, Alexandra turned back to the double doors. She'd met plenty of eccentric and egotistical millionaires in the twenty years she'd been known as Alexandra Waldsworth. The man waiting for her behind the double doors probably just enjoyed being the one in power.

The rational excuse didn't dispel the tension that tightened around her spine with a vise-like grip as she knocked on the doors.

"Enter."

The muffled voice, deep with the faintest of accents, wrapped around her. It almost sounded like…

Focus.

She pulled up the memory that had pushed her to succeed all these years: her father in his orange prison uniform glaring balefully at her from behind the glass of the visitor's booth. A moment later she'd stood and walked away as he'd hurled one final insult at her:

You'll never succeed. Not without me!

He'd thought to shred her confidence, to make her turn around and come crawling back. But it had done the opposite. It had released the shackles around her spirit, set her free as she'd walked away with the resolution to prove him wrong thundering in her veins.

That she had come to that realization a little over a year after she'd hurt the man she'd loved had come with its own pain, one that had faded over time but still kicked up every now and then.

Focus on the future. Focus on now.

She squared her shoulders and raised her chin. No matter what happened in the next five minutes, she could walk out with her head held high, knowing she'd tried.

She opened the door, a welcoming smile on her face.

"Good morning. Thank you for seeing me…"

Her voice trailed off as her steps faltered. She blinked several times, hoping against hope that she was just imagining things.

But the image stayed firm. A tall, broad-shouldered man dressed to perfection in a black Armani suit and red tie was seated behind one of the largest desks she'd ever seen. His face had hardened over the years, the lack of beard emphasizing the angular cut of his chin and the long, elegant line of his nose. His hair had been cut short on the sides and left longer on the top, swept to the side and styled so perfectly that not even a wisp dared to be out of place. He leaned back in his chair, his amber eyes sharp and focused on her with a cold intensity that made her feel like she was being examined under a microscope.

"Alexandra Waldsworth."

The rich timbre of his voice washed over her, sank beneath her skin and ignited a simmering warmth deep in her veins even though each syllable of her name was coated in icy disdain.

She glanced down, saw her business card sitting in the middle of the perfectly organized black walnut desk trimmed with glass edging. He must have looked her up, she realized as she tried to tamp down the nausea rising in the pit of her stomach.

Her eyes snapped back up to his and she barely kept her composure as she met his condescending stare. Why had he agreed to meet with her instead of having Jessica kick her out? Or even call the police to have her removed? Perhaps he had wanted to tell her to her face to never walk into the gleaming halls of the Pearson Group again.

"It's Moss now," she replied, proud that she managed to keep her voice steady.

He arched a brow. "Marry one of your rich beaus?"

"No. My mother's maiden name. I stopped going by Waldsworth years ago."

"Last I knew, you were dating some oil tycoon's son from Princeton." His lips curled into a sneer that nearly made her flinch. "Named after a car?"

"Royce."

She didn't elaborate. What was the point in explaining that her father had basically forced her to spend time in Royce's company in a bid to bring his parents on as investors in the Waldsworth Fund? That the one time Royce had attempted to kiss her, he'd reminded her more of an overexcited puppy than a potential lover?

"Didn't work out?"

"No." She gestured to the incredible view of the city's skyline. "You've done well for yourself, Grant. Congratulations."

"Mr. Santos," he corrected. "Chairman, CEO and founder of the Pearson Group." His eyes moved from her face to the flowers clutched in her hands. He raised one thick brow. "And you're now using a false name and selling flowers." One corner of his mouth flicked up. "My, my, how times have changed."

Guilt rooted her feet to the floor as the simmering

warmth disappeared under a flush of hot shame. She deserved every bit of his contempt. He'd done nothing but love her, support her, encourage her. And when push had come to shove, she'd fallen beneath the force of her father's wrath instead of standing up for the man she loved.

The man who had obviously continued on to bigger and better things. Floor-to-ceiling windows to one side of the room gave yet another impressive view of Central Park and the cityscape. Behind Grant's desk black bookcases lined the walls, the shelves playing host to books on finance, politics and history, along with artfully-placed sculptures, awards and the occasional picture of Grant with people who looked very important. Leather chairs were arranged just so around a glass coffee table by the windows. Not what she would have pictured for Grant— too austere and cold—but that was based off the Grant Santos she'd known nine years ago.

"I apologize, Mr. Santos." How she managed to sound collected, she had no idea, but the sound of her own voice, quiet yet confident, gave her enough strength to meet his stare. "Had I known you were the head of the Pearson Group, I wouldn't have bothered you." She walked forward, acutely conscious of the material of her secondhand pants brushing against her legs as she moved to his desk and set the flower arrangement down, glass clinking on glass with a soft *tink* that sounded like a gunshot in the cavernous room. "Please accept this with my compliments and my apologies for taking your time. I'll see myself out."

She turned and walked away, as she'd done when she'd last seen him. Both times hot tears had burned at the backs of her eyes. Both times her heart felt like it was cracking in two. But this time she didn't want to turn around and throw herself into his arms. No, she just wanted to get as far away from him as possible.

Her hand was on the door handle when his voice rang out.

"You still have two minutes."

Her fingers tightened on the silver handle. It took every ounce of willpower to force herself to turn around and face him again.

"Excuse me?"

He gestured to the flower arrangement. "I told Miss Elliott you had five minutes. You still have two minutes to sell me on whatever it is you came here to pitch." Disdain flashed in his eyes as he glanced at the hyssop. "Perhaps you're looking for investment in a wildflower farm?"

Irritation steadied her feelings. The one constant in her life had been flowers. In the precious few years she'd had with her mother before she'd passed from cancer, Amelia Waldsworth had instilled a deep and abiding love of flowers in her daughter. From the native plants that grew in the woods around her mother's family home in upstate New York to creating bouquets filled with not just colorful blooms but also meaning, Alexandra's early life had been filled with flowers.

It had been one of the silver linings in the mess her father had created with his fraudulent dealings. A chance to start over, to move away from the corporate event-planning degree he'd bullied her into and instead pursue her true passion.

"You have a good eye, Mr. Santos. Those are lavender giant hyssop, a native wildflower found here in New York."

"And why have you brought me wildflowers?"

She steadied herself with a deep breath as she opened

the leather portfolio, pulled out her proposal and laid it on his desk, resisting the temptation to take a giant step back. His tan fingers rested on the top page, but he didn't read it. His gaze stayed fixed on her face.

"You're courting new clients to sign on with the Pearson Group."

Not a flicker of emotion, not a single facial tic. The frozen expression, handsome as it was, made her unexpectedly sad. There had been a time when his face had shown her his every thought, from a joyful smile as he'd savored the simple pleasure of a glass of lemonade on a scorching summer's day to soul-wrenching heartbreak as she'd turned her back on him.

"What led you to that conclusion?"

"Rumor has it that you're hosting several events in two weeks' time, events to impress potential clients." She tapped the paper, making sure their fingers didn't touch. "I can help you do that."

"Aside from my curiosity about who would be so indiscreet as to share details of my private affairs, how will your collection of weeds help me convince clients with millions to billions of dollars to invest with the Pearson Group?"

"Flower arrangements at corporate events have been proven to increase guest perception of a space, the event they're attending and even the host themselves," she said, her voice firming as she warmed to the topic she'd pursued professionally. "Having fresh flowers can increase attendance, the attention span of your guests and demonstrate that you're investing in your prospective clients." She laid a gentle touch on a cluster of pale purple blossoms. "Given that you've recently moved here from Los Angeles, including a unique native flower along with the state flower of New York is a subtle but explicit gesture that you care about the small details, that you're not just moving here to make a quick buck before jetting off to your next destination."

"And you think the wealthiest of New York's residents will know the difference between a hyssop and a daffodil?"

"They will with the customized cards I include for events such as these that explain the meaning of the flowers in the arrangements."

Or they will, if you hire me, she added as she mentally crossed her fingers.

No one had yet given her the chance to make her grandest ideas come to life.

His eyes shifted to where her hand rested, his lips thinning. Her fingers trembled slightly as she removed her hand and let her arms fall to her sides, resisting the urge to cross them over her stomach.

"How long has your shop been open?"

"Six months."

He snorted. "What can you do that a more established shop can't?"

She pulled the proposal from beneath his fingers, taking care not to touch him, flipped the page and set it back in front of him. "I offer very competitive rates. I have five years of training with some of the top florists on the East Coast. And, most of all, I don't do the usual arrangements."

"Yes, I can see that."

Whether the words were meant as a compliment or an insult, she had no idea. And she didn't care, she realized with surprise and a small degree of pride. The arrangement was one of her best ones to date.

"The Flower Bell would be pleased to provide arrangements for your upcoming events, Mr. Santos. My phone number is on the card your secretary provided to you if you have any further questions."

Grant looked down at the paper and she took the opportunity to turn once more and head for the door. She'd tried and now her five minutes were more than up. He hadn't called security, hadn't yelled at her or called her names. Really, she consoled herself, it had gone better than she could have hoped for. At least she'd gotten good practice for the next time she made a pitch to a prospective client.

"Why should I hire you, Miss Waldsworth, after the way our last association ended?"

She nearly tripped over her own feet as her heartbeat stuttered. The question, she had no doubt, had been crafted to inflict as much pain as possible. But it was a fair one. She'd ruined his life once. Not that she had a snowball's chance in hell of him hiring her regardless, but she couldn't bear to hurt him again.

She turned and faced him the way she should have all those years ago.

"I'm good at my job, Mr. Santos. My business has excellent reviews. But I understand your concerns given the way things ended between us. If our previous history would impede what you're trying to accomplish, then I'm not the best choice. Thank you for your time."

She made it out the door and let it close behind her before he could say anything else. Her feet guided her down the hall, around the corner and to the elevator. Jessica was seated at a black desk, looking up to give a brief nod before resuming a phone call, allowing Alexandra to escape into the elevator.

The doors closed. The car whooshed down. Alexandra collapsed against the wall, keeping her gaze averted from the mirrors surrounding her and the chandelier gently swinging overhead. She bit down on her lower lip, the tiny burst of pain enabling her to keep her sorrow locked in her chest.

Of all the people to agree to hear her pitch, it had to be Grant Santos. The first, and only, man she'd ever given herself to. The one man she'd loved, and who had loved her in turn, until she'd been so weak and allowed her father to ruin their chances at a happily-ever-after.

The man who had fathered her child, a child she'd found out about and lost just weeks after she'd cut Grant from her life.

She scrunched her eyes shut, willed herself to stand straight as the elevator neared the first floor. If she'd entertained any possibilities of Grant booking The Flower Bell, those hopes had been dashed by his razor-sharp query.

As she walked out of the Carlson and halfheartedly raised an arm to flag down a taxi, she wondered not for the first time if she'd made a mistake pursuing her career in New York. Perhaps she should have moved out of the city, or even to a new state.

It seemed no matter how fast she ran, her past would always be one step behind her.

CHAPTER TWO

GRANT SANTOS WATCHED Alexandra Waldsworth, or Moss or whatever the hell she was calling herself these days, walk through the reception area on the security screen. She returned Jessica's nod before stepping into the elevator. As the doors swished shut, Alexandra stared straight ahead, her hands clenched around the leather portfolio in her hands as if it was a lifeline.

How was it possible for him to feel anything approaching sympathy for the woman who'd broken his heart and orchestrated his firing all those years ago? Yet, it was most definitely sympathy that tugged at his chest as he looked down at the proposal in front of him.

She'd come down quite a bit in the world since he'd last seen her nine years ago. She'd looked good—*too good*— in an ivory tie-neck blouse and emerald green pants that followed the long curve of her legs. But he hadn't missed the subtle signs that Alexandra was no longer shopping at Chanel or Saint Laurent: the scuff marks on her shoes, the slight fraying at the end of one of the ties on her blouse and the lack of highlights in her dark brown hair. A far cry from the polished socialite he'd fallen in love with.

She'd looked like a sun-kissed mermaid when he'd first laid eyes on her all those years ago, white teeth brilliant against perfectly tanned skin as she'd laughed up at him when he'd asked if she was one of the gardeners. A reasonable assumption, she'd assured him as he'd helped her to her feet, since she'd been sitting on the grass pulling weeds. It had been two days of walks in the gardens and long, intimate conversations before she'd revealed her name and that her father was the one who'd hired him as a seasonal landscaper. By then, it was too late. He was entranced.

Perhaps if she'd told him who she was that first day, he never would have allowed himself to fall for her. Never would have been duped by the illusion she'd created.

He pressed a button beneath his desk.

"Is the report ready, Jessica?"

"Yes, sir. Emailing it now."

"Give me five minutes, then report to my office."

"Yes, sir."

As he waited for the email from his preferred security company to arrive, he clicked on the website he'd minimized when he'd heard the clicking of Jessica's absurdly tall stilettos outside his office, signaling the arrival of his unexpected guest. The *About Us* page of The Flower Bell's website featured a photo of Alexandra in a plain yellow shirt and blue jeans, her face lit up as if the photographer had captured her midlaugh. She was holding up a terra-cotta pot overflowing with some bushy white flower.

When Jessica had walked in and handed him a business card for The Flower Bell, he'd noted the name of the proprietor. He'd been annoyed at the interruption to his carefully planned day. Still, he'd typed in the website address, intrigued as to who would have the guts to show up without an appointment.

Even though his office was on the forty-sixth floor, he'd initially chalked up the dull roaring in his ears to the sounds of New York traffic when Alexandra's smile had filled his computer screen. It had taken a moment for him to realize it was the pounding of blood rushing through his body as his heart sped up at the sight of his former lover. After that last photo of her with her new beau, he hadn't seen her in years. And it wasn't just being confronted with her image. No, it was that she looked so happy. Not the false smile he'd seen her paste on her face when she'd made the rounds at one of her father's summer parties, but the kind of wide grin that made her hazel eyes crinkle at the corners.

He'd once been the source of that smile. But, he'd reminded himself bitterly as he'd scrolled through the website, it had been an act. Alexandra was an excellent actress. What game was she playing now by suddenly showing up at his office after all these years? She'd finagled not only the name of his events manager, but also the list of exclusive events Laura had put together to entice his executive team's most-wanted prospective clients. Whatever she was up to, she had already shown herself to still be cunning and manipulative. Never in his wildest dreams would he have guessed that Alexandra Moss, owner of a little floral shop on the outskirts of SoHo, had any connection to his past.

Although, if he'd been linked to a man as sadistic and greedy as her father, he probably would have changed his name, too. David Waldsworth had been convicted of multiple crimes, including witness intimidation, during his trial. Grant had known the bare basics. It had been impossible to avoid the twenty-four-seven news coverage. It had been a wonderful spring day as he'd watched the verdict delivered: guilty on all accounts, with a prison sentence that ensured David Waldsworth would die in jail.

Grant had toasted the jury with a beer in a café on

the Santa Monica pier and then turned from the TV to order another round before the camera could pan over the people seated in the courtroom. Whether Alexandra had been there or not, he didn't care to see her face, see whether she cried fat crocodile tears for the man she'd let witness his humiliation. Instead, he'd focused on the deep satisfaction of watching a man known for his cruelties finally get his comeuppance.

But he hadn't completely been able to disconnect from the Waldsworth name or legacy. It had been a frequent topic in many of his early graduate courses. Fortunately, the coverage had focused on David, his firm, the victims of his crimes and the new laws that had been enacted in the wake of the trial. Very little was mentioned of David's family. Anytime Grant had even the tiniest bit of temptation to look Alexandra up, he squashed it with a ruthlessness he'd developed in the months after their breakup.

She was a part of his past. Never to be a part of his present or future again.

Until she'd literally walked back into his life with her fake, wide-eyed innocence and her carefully-curated appearance of a down-on-her-luck businesswoman.

His lips curled into a scowl as he scanned The Flower Bell's website. Once he'd realized who Alexandra Moss truly was, he'd had Jessica place her in the conference room as he'd conducted a quick review online while tasking his security company with digging into the past nine years of her life. Her business appeared legitimate and, given that she had started it a month before he'd decided to move back to New York, hadn't been created for the sake of trapping him into some scheme.

Unfortunately, he'd found precious little beyond her website, an Instagram page for the shop and old news articles about the Waldsworth Fund scandal. Still, satisfaction had settled deep into his bones as he'd consumed several of the articles on the fall of the high and mighty David Waldsworth. All of his homes, including the Hamptons beach house, had been sold by the U.S. Marshals to compensate his victims. David's wife, Susan, had filed for divorce and been allowed to keep half a million dollars. A fortune to many but, from what Grant remembered of Susan and her preference for all things name brand, probably not enough to keep her lifestyle funded for even a year.

As to David's daughter and stepson, Finley—a spoiled brat who had made Alexandra's life hell—there was hardly any mention of them. The majority of the news coverage had focused on David and his unapologetic interviews from prison.

Alexandra.

The first month after she'd looked at him, her lip curled in disgust, and denounced him in front of her father, he'd dreamed of her every night. He'd replayed their every encounter, from the first time he'd seen her in the gardens of the Waldsworth mansion in the Hamptons to the night they'd first kissed atop the Ferris wheel at a carnival, the roar of the ocean a background to the thundering of his heart as he'd tasted honey on her lips and surrendered himself to the fact that he'd fallen in love. None of it had made sense. He knew without a doubt he'd been Alexandra's first lover. What had happened between the night they'd made love on the beach and the very next day when she'd broken things off?

Even though it had been so long ago, humiliation still burned a slow, painful trail in his gut. He loathed admitting that he'd hoped something would change, that she would reach out and tell him it had all been a horrible mistake. It hadn't been until he'd seen a picture of Alexandra circulating on Instagram, smiling up at some blond Ivy League-looking trust fund brat, with the date showing it had been taken at her family's weekend party the day after she'd broken his heart, that he'd fully accepted he had been exactly what she'd told him—a summer fling, nothing more.

You're just a gardener, Grant. I'm a Waldsworth. It's been fun, but it was never going to last.

Since that photo had been published—and he'd barely resisted the urge to track down the man who dared to have his arm around Alexandra's waist and threaten him within an inch of his life—he'd purged everything that reminded him of her. He'd thrown himself into his studies and, been accepted into Stanford University's graduate business program for the spring semester. Since the day the plane had taken off from the airport and carried him to the Golden Coast the week before Christmas, he'd allowed himself to think about Alexandra exactly once a year, on Labor Day weekend when he raised a glass of scotch to her and her father. As painful as it had been, he had them to thank for his current success.

Her betrayal had also allowed him to focus on other more important goals. Goals like achieving a level of wealth that would ensure he and his mother never experienced poverty again. Goals like avenging his father and opening the door for a return to his country.

And now the goal of becoming what David and Alexandra Waldsworth hadn't believed him capable of—one of the denizens of New York's elite.

His computer beeped. With a couple taps on the keyboard, the initial background review of one Alexandra Moss, née Waldsworth, was pulled up on his screen. Wayne Security had demonstrated once again why they deserved the outrageous retainer he paid them every year with an initial detailed ten-page report and a guarantee from its president, Joseph, that a full write-up would be delivered by midnight. The Flower Bell was indeed a licensed and insured business, although one that was barely scraping by. Alexandra was financially stretched to the breaking point, and that was with a business address in a rundown part of town and her personal address listed as a one-room flat behind a bookstore nearby. The rest of the report carried meager but telling details: her spotty employment history with various florists while working gig jobs like waitressing or walking dogs, her graduation from a community college instead of Princeton.

Yes, Alexandra was definitely in trouble.

He looked down at the cream-colored papers in his hand, complete with a silver bell wrapped in flowers at the top. None of the possibilities of why Alexandra had chosen now to reenter his life had included her pitching her business for his upcoming Pearson Group client recruitment events.

Crawling back after discovering his wealth and status, maybe. Or some other nefarious scheme. But running a small business that was on the verge of collapsing? That possibility hadn't been anywhere on his radar.

Anger stiffened the muscles in his neck. Did she really think he'd bail her out? It also brought up the question of how she'd found out what he and his executives were planning. He'd have to find out who talked. The mystery approach of generating interest in the Pearson Group had not been his first choice. But he had to give credit to the team he'd so meticulously put together. The enigmatic tactics, from select potential clients being sent invitations and a fifty-page packet on the investment options, corporate backgrounds of Pearson's team and plans for the future, had netted him nearly one hundred of New

York's wealthiest residents for the brunch at the New York Public Library, with the five richest families also joining him for a week at his Hamptons house.

A house he had purchased partially for the incredible ocean view and private beach, and partially because it rivaled the home just a couple miles away where he had experienced the most intense pleasure and pain he'd ever known.

He dropped Alexandra's proposal on his desk and glanced around the office with a critical eye. Three of the walls had been painted a grayish navy, sedate and refined, a pleasing backdrop for the mix of modern, geometric silver light fixtures and brown leather chairs seated in front of his desk.

His entire body had tightened when Alexandra had approached his desk, shoulders thrown back with confidence, hazel eyes glinting with determination. She'd had every reason to appear guilty, embarrassed, humiliated. Instead, she'd stood in front of him and delivered a surprisingly articulate and convincing argument for doing the flowers for his events.

He'd need to look into who had been so indiscreet as to let the details of those events slip. But, he acknowledged as he picked up the proposal again, Alexandra had certainly done her homework. Her prices were competitive, even cheap, her knowledge of flowers and the floral industry evident in the details she'd included in her write-up.

Not surprising, he thought with a reluctant twinge of admiration. He could still remember the first time he'd seen her: golden brown hair tucked under a straw hat; the curves of her young body clad in a bright yellow tank top and jean shorts as she'd pulled weeds from the base of a rose plant along one of the winding paths in the gardens.

When she'd glanced at him over her shoulder with that sunny, sweet smile, he'd been lost.

But not anymore, he sternly reminded himself as he tossed the paper on his desk and stood, hardening his heart to the happy memories.

Memories and fairy tales, he thought as he moved to the glass wall of his office with purposeful strides and gazed down at the bustling streets of New York City. *Aside from the incredible sex, none of it was real.*

No, he'd made real progress after he'd accepted that Alexandra had used and discarded him. He'd graduated with his master's degree in business, accrued his first million before he was thirty and now stood on the cusp of becoming a billionaire before he was thirty-five. If he played his cards right, the Pearson Group would become one of the premier investment firms on the East Coast.

He turned back toward his desk, the unique arrangement catching his eye. It was striking, and despite the person behind the proposal, she'd made a good pitch.

That he had the upper hand this time certainly didn't hurt. In fact, he thought as he turned the possibility around in his mind, hiring Alexandra would serve two purposes. Adding a little extra class to the upcoming events, yes, but also showing her exactly what she had thrown away. He smiled as the plan formed, solidified in his mind. It would be even more satisfying to have the once high and mighty Alexandra Waldsworth working for him, following his every order as he wined and dined the kind of people she'd once shared dinners with. She had the gall to come to him for help after what she'd done to him—used him as her personal toy while whispering false words of love in response to his sharing a piece of his soul—so turnabout was fair play. While she struggled to maintain employment and make a go of what seemed like a rich girl's fantasy, he would show her up close and personally everything he had achieved, from his multimillion-dollar firm to the numerous luxuries his money could now buy.

Not bad for *just a gardener.*

He hit the button for Jessica's line.

"Yes, Mr. Santos?"

"Reach out to Laura Jones and ask her to get three proposals for flowers for the upcoming events. Something similar to the proposal Miss Waldsworth left us."

"Waldsworth, sir?"

"Miss Moss," Grant corrected with gritted teeth. "I want the proposals by five p.m."

"Yes, sir."

He tapped a finger against the papers on his desk, his lips tilting up. This time he wouldn't give Alexandra a single chance to hurt him again. From here on out, he would be in control.

CHAPTER THREE

ALEXANDRA STARED MOROSELY into her glass of red wine. The relaxing strains of jazz played against a backdrop of clinking glasses and hushed voices as customers milled around the shelves of The Story Keeper. A gentle spring rain tapped against the window. New Yorkers rushed by outside, umbrellas shielding their faces from the prying eyes of shoppers and diners ensconced in the warm interiors of the stores and restaurants lining one of Greenwich Village's popular streets.

"What's eating you?"

Alexandra took a long sip of wine as her stepbrother, Finn, dropped into the seat across from her. Hard to imagine the boy who ignored her existence as a teenager, unless he was mercilessly teasing her or ordering her about, had become her closest friend. Or that he would fall in love with a bookshop manager instead of a wealthy socialite.

Normally, she loved savoring a glass of red and flipping through a mystery book at her future sister-in-law's bookstore. That it was a darkening, rainy evening should have made it perfect.

But instead of vivid images of a plucky heroine tracking a potential murderer through the streets of London filling her mind, all she saw was Grant. Grant's eyes, so cold as he stared at her with disdain. Grant's lips, twisted into that menacing smirk. Grant's shoulders, broader and more muscular than the last time he'd held her against him and whispered romantic sentiments in Portuguese.

Had she really believed she'd placed all that behind her? Because right now it hurt just as much, if not more, than the day she'd laughed in his face and told him she'd never date a common gardener, much less fall in love with one.

Yup, she thought as she took another, longer, sip. *I deserve every bit of his contempt. Didn't mean a single word, but how was he supposed to know that?*

"Nothing."

Finn reached across the table and placed his hand over the top of her glass.

"If your goal is to get drunk, Amanda just got a port in. I hate wine, but even I drink that stuff."

An unwilling smile tugged at her lips. It was hard to picture the man sitting across from her, dressed in jeans and a black T-shirt with a little white book stitched on the pocket, as the former Finley Waldsworth, Princeton graduate, womanizer, rising star at Waldsworth Financial and favored by her father so much that he'd formally adopted his stepson so that he would "have a son with the Waldsworth name."

Now he was just plain Finn Davids, an economics teacher at a local high school, and engaged to the manager of a bookstore and adjoining coffee shop.

Finn's teasing smile disappeared as his hand shifted off her glass and settled on her wrist.

"Amanda and I can loan you some money, Alex."

Alexandra shook her head.

"Absolutely not. You have a wedding coming up, a

house to buy and I expect by this time next year a nurs-ery to fill."

Did it make her a rotten sister that her heart twisted with a slight pang of envy as Finn's eyes automatically warmed and slid to the blonde woman behind the cash register? Amanda caught his appreciative gaze and blew him a kiss before throwing Alexandra a wink. Alexandra raised her wineglass toward the woman who had brought her stepbrother to his knees two years ago.

"What about your plan to pitch The Flower Bell's ser-vices to some of Pamela's clients?"

"I actually made it into the office of one of them today."

Finn perked up. "Oh?"

Amanda walked up to their table and set a small-bowled glass filled with a dark ruby liquid in front of Finn and a fruit and cheese plate in front of Alexandra.

"Did you get a contract?" Amanda asked excitedly as she slid into the chair next to Finn. Finn looped an arm around his fiancée's shoulders.

"Not exactly." She swirled the remaining wine in her glass and tossed back the rest of it. "It was Grant Santos."

Finn choked on his port and Amanda reached over and plucked the glass from his hand before he spilled the rest on the table.

"Grant?" Finn managed to finally gasp. "What's he doing in New York?"

"Who's Grant?" Amanda asked.

Alexandra shot her stepbrother a pleading look. She loved Amanda and considered her a good friend, but just the thought of explaining her tumultuous history with Grant made her want to crawl under the covers of her bed and sleep for a week.

"Grant was Alexandra's…boyfriend," Finn finally

said. "My stepfather made them split up after a summer romance when she was nineteen."

Amanda's usually sunny expression darkened. She despised David Waldsworth. David had been fixated on Finn's success. Even though Finn had been Susan's son from her first marriage, he had become the son he'd never had. He hadn't accepted Finn's change of heart, his preference for a simpler life. He had written to his stepson numerous times encouraging Finn to dump Amanda and hold out for a woman who could return him to the lifestyle he'd been raised in. That Finn and Amanda were genuinely happy made no difference.

"Bastard."

"Agreed."

Alexandra stared glumly at her empty wineglass.

"I'll get you another," Amanda said, standing before Alexandra could protest. She leaned down, gave Alexandra a sisterly hug and disappeared into the back.

"You're really lucky, Finn."

"I am," her stepbrother agreed, "but don't try to change the subject. What happened?"

"He's doing well for himself." *Very well.* "Starting a new investment firm here in New York City. The Pearson Group."

Finn let out a low whistle. "I've heard about them. Grant's heading it?"

"Yeah. CEO and a couple other titles." She smiled slightly. "He's achieved a lot."

"Apparently. Did he book The Flower Bell? Was he nice to you?"

"No, and…coldly polite would be a better way to describe it."

Finn frowned. "If he knew what you went through—"

"He doesn't, and he's not going to," Alexandra said

firmly. "There's no point in rehashing the past. I made my choice and I have to live with it. I let Father tell me what to do. I said horrible, awful things and I got him fired."

"He threatened to deport Grant and his mother if you kept seeing him," Finn retorted. "And then you got preg—"

"Finn!"

Finn stopped midsentence, eyes narrowed, a vein ticking in his forehead. Finn was the only one besides the doctor and nurses in the emergency room who knew what had happened that awful October night. He'd been the one to rush her to the hospital when, after a few weeks of feeling exhausted, she'd suddenly started to bleed as a sharp pain stabbed her abdomen. He'd held her hand as the doctor had delivered the horrifying news; that she was pregnant with Grant's baby and was in the middle of miscarrying. He'd stayed with her at the hospital, cared for her at home and covered for her when she'd been bedridden the following week when David and Susan had come back from one of their frequent luxury vacations.

It had been the second of the two worst moments of her life. But if there were silver linings to be found, she could identify her tragedy as the turning point in her relationship with her stepbrother. They'd grown closer. Finn had matured almost overnight. When their worlds came crashing down just a couple months later, they'd had each other.

"I didn't know Grant well," Finn finally said. "But he seemed like a rational guy. And I do think he really cared for you, Alex." He reached out again and squeezed her hand. "You could still tell him what happened."

Not what I need to hear right now.

"No, Finn. Chances are I'll never see Grant Santos again."

"Good evening, Miss Waldsworth."

The dark voice cut through the pleasant din of the bookshop. Alexandra closed her eyes, willing the deep, rich tones that wrapped around her with the familiarity of a lover's caress to be a figment of her imagination.

"My apologies for interrupting your date."

Her eyes flew open at the whiplike lash of words. She turned in her chair to see Grant Santos in all his handsome glory standing just a couple feet behind her chair. He'd changed out of the custom-tailored suit. Even in a more casual outfit of dark blue jeans and a cream-colored sweater stretched perfectly over his large shoulders, sleeves rolled up to his elbows, he exuded wealth and sophistication from the silver Rolex glinting on his wrist to the dark gray Barbour raincoat draped over one arm.

"Grant." She mentally kicked herself. "Mr. Santos. What are you doing here?"

Grant's brown eyes flicked from her face down to where Finn's hand still rested on top of hers.

"I'm following up on your business proposal. It seems I've come at a bad time."

Finn stood and held out his hand.

"Long time, no see, Grant."

Grant's thick eyebrows drew together before recognition dawned on his face. Alexandra bit back a smile as his lips parted, the only sign of surprise. Grant glanced down at Finn's outstretched hand and let it hang in the air for a moment before shaking it.

"I didn't recognize you, Finley."

"Not having a stick shoved so far up where the sun doesn't shine probably helps."

Grant didn't even crack a smile.

"Yes."

Finn chuckled. "Still a straight shooter."

An elderly woman with fluffy white hair and hunched shoulders walked up to them.

"Excuse me, young man, do you work here? I saw your shirt, and I need your help looking for a romance book."

"Happy to help." Finn nodded to Grant. "Be nice to my sister."

Grant didn't respond, merely watched as Finn offered the customer his arm and escorted her toward a group of floor-to-ceiling shelves near the back. Alexandra took advantage of his moment of distraction to take in the details she'd missed earlier: the threads of silver in his thick black hair; the slight shadowing of whiskers along his sculpted jaw; the confidence he'd grown into since she'd last seen him, no longer cocky but self-assured in who he was and what he had accomplished.

Her heart twisted and she wrenched her gaze away. Where would they be if she'd trusted him with the truth? If she hadn't let her own fears overcome her love for him? If she'd stood up to her father?

That last thought sent a fresh wave of shame washing over her and she looked down at her replenished wine-glass. Losing Grant had been the highest price she'd paid for her own weakness. But she'd let her father order her about for pretty much her whole life, from her clothes to her college degree. Even when she'd heard the first murmurings of something not being right at Waldsworth Investments, of dollars not adding up, she'd cowered before her father's anger when she'd summoned enough nerve to confront him. And then she'd let it go until the police had arrested him at a company holiday party the Christmas after she'd broken things off with Grant.

Most days she felt like she'd paid her dues, living paycheck to paycheck, making donations to several charities she knew had supported her father's victims, forgoing luxuries like dinner at a Michelin-starred restaurant.

Yet, on days like today, she wondered if she'd ever pay the price for the people she'd hurt.

Awareness danced across her skin. Steeling herself, she looked up and met Grant's amber gaze. Her breath caught in her chest. Once he'd looked at her as if he couldn't believe she was real, as if she was the most precious thing in the world to him. For a moment she thought she saw a flicker of that old heat.

But no, she must have imagined it, because the coldness in his eyes could have frozen fire.

"This doesn't seem like your kind of place," she finally said.

"Yours, either. And certainly not your stepbrother's," Grant replied as he sat in Finn's vacant seat, his gaze roaming over the worn but colorful armchairs and sofas scattered among the towering bookshelves, then toward the back of the shop where two double glass doors led out to the little patio Finn had renovated for Amanda. Café lights lit up the wet paving stones. It was empty for now, but Finn would soon move the mismatched wrought-iron tables and chairs out of storage for the warmer seasons. Amanda and Alexandra would plant flowers, and the space would be transformed into an outdoor eating space and small venue for local musicians.

Definitely not the luxury shops and high-end restaurants she had frequented with David and his wives and girlfriends over the years. She could only imagine how many experiences she'd missed out on by falling in line with her father's snobbery.

"How did you find me?"

"I went to your shop. It was closed, so my security firm looked up your home address. I saw you through the window when my limo pulled up." He cast another dubious look toward the shelves where Finn had disappeared. "How did Finn come to own a bookstore?"

"His fiancée's family owns it and she's the manager. Finn helps out when he's not teaching."

"I never would have imagined Finley Waldsworth engaged to a retail manager. Or teaching," Grant added dryly.

"It's Finn Davids now. He went back to his birth father's name. And he and Amanda are very happy."

Grant watched her for a long moment.

"Are you happy, Alexandra?"

She covered her surprise by reaching for her wineglass, all too conscious of his opaque gaze focused squarely on her.

"I am," she finally replied.

The cynical twist of his lips told her he saw right through her bold-faced lie.

"Disappointed with your new station in life?"

She frowned and set her glass down a little more forcefully than she intended, the wine nearly sloshing over the rim.

"Do you think I'm that big of a snob?"

"'I would rather die than be seen in public with a gardener.'"

Her stomach dropped as the words she'd fired at him all those years ago hit her in the chest. She'd said terrible, cruel things as she'd watched her father out of the corner of her eye. The more pleased he'd looked, the nastier she'd become, hoping that she was putting on enough of the performance he wanted that he would leave Grant and his mother alone.

Whether David would have gone after Grant and his

mother later out of sheer spite would never be known, as just four months later he'd been arrested.

"I was a different person back then."

"Clearly."

She closed her eyes for a moment, trying to summon what little strength she had before giving up. What did it matter if Grant saw her as she was feeling tonight—defeated, lonely and on the verge of giving up? He loathed her. She didn't need to try and impress him. She would never get back in his good graces.

"I'm sorry, Grant. I hurt you."

He stared at her for a long moment.

"You did."

Not a hint of inflection in his deep, accented voice.

"I know." *I did it because I loved you.* "It might be hard to believe, but I am happy for you. I'm struggling right now with my business, but—" she waved a hand around at the shelves stacked with books "—personally, I'm the happiest I've ever been. That's more than a lot of people have." She forced a small smile. "Eventually, my head will catch up to my heart and I'll focus more on the blessings I do have." She started to stand. "But right now, unless you have something else to say, I'm going to say good-night. I have a busy day tomorrow and—"

"The Pearson Group would like to hire The Flower Bell."

CHAPTER FOUR

GRANT WATCHED AS Alexandra slowly sat back in her chair, her eyes wide with shock. He silently cursed. He'd planned on going about things very differently tonight, coming in more aggressively. But when she'd started to leave, unwanted sympathy and a hint of apprehension had pushed the words out of his mouth.

He'd spent the past nine years singularly focused on his career. Emotions like anger and jealousy had no place in his life. The two relationships he'd had over the years had been pleasant enough. He'd ended his time with Michelle, an accountant for a film production firm, when she'd started hinting at her favorite cut of diamond. Lindsay, a wildlife photographer, had texted him from Madagascar to apologize. She'd met someone and she hadn't seen him in three months anyway, so hopefully he wasn't too put out.

He'd written a brief text that had gone beyond his initial thoughts of *not put out at all*.

So when he'd walked into the bookstore and seen a dark-haired man with his hand covering Alexandra's, the jealousy that had unfurled in his chest and roared with a primal howl had been unexpected.

Unexpected and very much unwanted.

Even if he had wanted to rekindle his romance with

Alexandra—which he reminded himself very sternly he did not—he would never be able to trust her. Not after the abrupt about-face, the vile words she'd hurled at him, getting him fired and to top it all off, dating Mr. Named-After-a-Car the day after their breakup.

But when he'd seen her there, looking so sad and being comforted by another man, he'd wanted to toss her over his shoulder, stalk out in the rain to the nearest cab, throw her in and take her back to his place to demand all the answers he'd never received before kissing her senseless.

Suspicion whispered across the back of his neck. Despite the red haze of fury coating his gaze when he'd seen the photos on Instagram of her and Royce, there had been something about her posture, a strain in her smile, that had seemed off.

He gave himself a mental shake. All these years and he was still searching for answers when the truth was right in front of him. Alexandra had been a rich, spoiled brat who had used him for a fling, and with the summer drawing to a close, had chosen to return to her life of luxury.

"You want to hire me?"

He scowled. He'd expected a little more gratitude, even a relieved smile, not misgivings. He'd had his driver go by her shop first, then her home address when they'd passed by the dark windows of The Flower Bell. He'd wanted to deliver the news in person, savor her gratefulness in her rundown store or her tiny little apartment situated behind a string of shops, let her meager environment punctuate the generosity of his offer.

And instead, he'd nearly lost his iron grip on his emotions and was now prodding her to accept.

"Yes."

"Why?"

He tamped down his irritation so he didn't overplay his hand.

"Your proposal was strong and your arrangement unique. Our event planner, Laura Jones, reached out to three of her florist contacts for competitive bids. One didn't deliver by the deadline, one submitted ideas I could find in a grocery store and the third, while unique, listed a price triple that of yours. Ms. Jones was impressed by your work, as was I."

A sentiment he meant, even if his offer of employment came with ulterior motives. He wouldn't make a job offer if she didn't have something to offer him in return. Revenge alone was not worth risking everything he had poured into his company.

Alexandra's lips parted. His eyes darted down, then swept back up to meet her gaze.

"I can't believe Ms. Jones picked me."

The awed innocence in her voice made his blood boil. The woman belonged on Broadway. She'd seduced him with the same wide-eyed, naive act. Not only would he not be fooled again, but this time when their association came to an end, she would be the one left with regrets.

He tamped down his anger and smoothed his face into a cold mask as he started to stand.

"If you're not confident in your own abilities, Miss Moss, then perhaps this wasn't a good idea."

"Wait!"

He suppressed a smile that his bluff had worked so quickly. Slowly, he sat back down.

"I'm just… You have to admit, given our history, it's not unreasonable to wonder why you'd want to work with me."

"You and your father taught me a valuable lesson all those years ago. I've become adept at removing emotion from business." He ignored her flinch, even as something shifted in his chest at the low blow. "You presented a detailed proposal with very competitive rates. My events manager conducted additional research and agreed with my initial impression. You were the best choice."

She blew out a slow breath.

"Okay."

"Okay?"

She shook her head slightly, dark brown hair tumbling down over one shoulder. Once upon a time he'd run his hands through her hair, savoring the feeling of silk gliding over his skin as he'd kissed every inch of her.

He threaded his fingers together on top of the table. It had been nearly a year since he'd seen Lindsay, the last time he'd had sex. He and Alexandra had a history. It was only natural for his body to respond to pleasant memories.

Pleasant? a vicious inner voice cackled. *What about the most intense, physically and emotionally satisfying lovemaking you've ever—*

"I'm sorry, Gra— Mr. Santos." She smiled, and damn his heart if it didn't lift a little at seeing the genuine hope on her face. "It's been a trying few weeks. I think I'm in shock, but I appreciate you accepting my proposal and am looking forward to working for the Pearson Group."

She held out her hand. He eyed it for a moment before steeling himself and returning the gesture. If he was going to live up to what he had said, that he could keep business separate from their tumultuous past, he needed to not be afraid of something as simple as a handshake.

Except there was nothing simple about feeling her warm skin against his again as his hand grasped hers. The hint of callouses on her palms from working with the plants; the warmth emanating from her skin made more potent after coming in from the cool spring storm; the softness in her smile. All of it melded together into a siren's song that lured him back into the past.

No.

He released her hand and pulled his phone out, focusing his attention on the screen and off the quickened tempo of his heartbeat.

"I'm notifying Jessica to schedule an appointment with you to go over the events, their locations and what we're looking for. Even though your mole provided some detail, I would prefer you get any further details from me."

He shot her a look he'd perfected at Stanford, one he'd learned from a grizzly finance professor who had made undergraduates to corporate financiers quake. But if Alexandra felt intimidated or pressured into revealing her source, she certainly didn't show it as she calmly returned his stare.

At least she had loyalty to someone. He would pursue that line of inquiry later, use it as leverage if needed.

"Aren't you the CEO and some other fancy titles?"

"Yes."

"So why won't I be working with Ms. Jones?"

"You will some. But with the team in Shanghai until two days before the first event, your primary contacts will be myself and my executive assistant, Jessica."

Something dark and sad flashed in Alexandra's eyes.

"And you don't trust me."

The words were uttered so softly they were nearly buried beneath the murmured conversations, music and clinks of glasses and cups. If he hadn't experienced firsthand how she could make love as if her soul had been on fire for him and less than twenty-four hours later deliver the cruelest, most vicious insults as she sent him packing, he would almost believe her act.

"No. I don't trust you."

To her credit, she didn't tear up, didn't make excuses. She simply nodded.

"Okay."

It would have been easier, less painful, if she had protested, if she'd descended into hysterics. But both of them simply acknowledging the truth stole some of his determination and replaced it with an ache for what had been.

Or at least what he thought had been.

"Now that we understand each other, I'll be adding a fifty percent completion bonus to the contract if everything is done satisfactorily."

He'd intended the offer as a demonstration that at this point in his life money truly didn't matter. He would achieve his first billion before the year was out with his own personal investments, and that wasn't including whether or not the Pearson Group took off the way he wanted. But when her eyes lit up with gratitude, his initial flare of smug satisfaction flamed out as quickly as it had appeared, replaced by something almost like guilt.

Mercilessly, he pushed that feeling aside. She was getting paid, and generously. If she delivered, she would have more than enough business to keep her little shop from going under. And, he reminded himself again, when it came to emotions, she was manipulative and heartless. Giving her a taste of her own medicine as he helped save her business was nothing to feel guilty over. He had more than earned the right to enjoy this feeling of power.

"That's not necessary."

"It's not," he agreed, "but Jessica wrote it into the contract."

Her smile grew. "I can't thank you enough, Mr. Santos." She pulled out her own phone and started tapping away. "Do you have time for a couple questions?"

"Jessica will provide you with all the information you need."

A frown furrowed her brow. "Which is great. But these are clients you're courting, right? It would be helpful to hear what you're thinking firsthand."

A professional answer, and one that made sense. So why was he resisting? Why did he suddenly feel the need to put as much distance between himself and Alexandra Moss as possible?

"I have ten minutes."

The quick flash of another smile pricked his skin.

"Ten minutes. All right, first question..."

He answered her inquiries deftly, savored the surprise in her eyes as he listed some of the guests who would be in attendance at the brunch, the house party and the final gala. Big names and even bigger wallets.

"I can't believe you got Theodore Craig to come," she said. "He's notoriously private. In all the summers we visited the Hamptons, I think I saw him once."

"I worked for him after you fired me."

The color disappeared from her face. "Oh."

"Started off as just mowing lawns. He invited me to have coffee with him one morning. When he learned I was studying finance, we started talking." The memory warmed him, steadied him. It hadn't just been his heart that had taken a fatal blow that Labor Day weekend. His confidence had been ripped asunder, too. Had he been deluding himself that he could achieve the goals he'd set for himself?

It had been Theodore who had looked at him not just with interest but respect, who had listened to his opinions on current events and economics and guided him toward applying for Stanford's graduate program. Who, Grant had found out when he'd graduated, had paid for it.

Theodore, a millionaire several hundred times over, had treated him like an equal. Unlike David, who had treated him like scum, and Alexandra, who had used him for her own amusement.

Alexandra glanced at her watch and grimaced.

"Sorry. I took twelve minutes."

"You had good questions."

Ridiculous that such a simple compliment warmed her.

"Thank you. And I got your invite to meet with Jessica tomorrow to tour the library and see the space the first luncheon is being held at."

Even though working with her ex-lover was not her first choice, she couldn't deny the excitement and sense of purpose that had taken her from despondent to energized and determined. She enjoyed filling the small orders, a bouquet for a proposal or an arrangement to congratulate someone on a new career. But jobs like these, ones that presented a challenge while giving her creative freedom with her flowers and plants, were her favorite.

She tucked her phone into her pocket and stood, grabbing her wineglass.

"Have a good night."

"Are you staying here?"

A slight blush stained her cheeks as she followed his gaze to the empty glass in her hand.

"I'm not driving anywhere, if that's what you're asking. My place is just across the courtyard."

He looked at the double glass doors.

"Above the bookshop, I'm guessing."

"There's an apartment across the courtyard. Finn and Amanda live there, and I live in the studio above."

Another way her stepbrother and his fiancée had saved her. They could have easily rented the studio for a good price. Instead, they'd offered it to her for a song, enabling her to pour even more of her own money into The Flower Bell.

Grant stood, towering over her.

"I'll walk you to your door."

"It's literally across the courtyard."

"It's still New York City. The courtyard is dark, your stepbrother is busy and you've had at least two glasses of wine to drink." He crossed his arms. "It's non-negotiable."

She resisted rolling her eyes. Some things, at least, didn't change. Even all those years ago, he'd been steadfast in walking her home, opening the door for her, little things that back then had made her feel cared for.

Now it grated on her. She'd been so willing to let everyone take care of her in the past. But she'd grown up a lot. She'd lived in a couple of rundown apartments with nothing but a dead bolt between her and some nasty residents in the early years after her father's conviction.

Grant wouldn't care that she'd held her own against mean drunks and lecherous louts. He'd argue with her until she was blue in the face, and she didn't have the energy for any more drama tonight.

"Fine. Thanks," she added grudgingly.

She dropped the glass off in the kitchen and waved good-night to Amanda, who was still behind the register. Amanda glanced at Grant and then arched a brow. Alexandra gave her a reassuring smile in return and a thumbs-up as she and Grant stepped out into the quiet darkness of the courtyard.

The glass doors closed behind them, shutting out the music and conversation. Rain had turned to a light mist as she crossed the courtyard, Grant two steps behind her. She tried to ignore the uptick in her heartbeat, the quickening of her breathing, the awareness dancing through her veins. It didn't help that, with the noise of the bookshop gone and the only sound the distant hum of New York traffic, the courtyard was suddenly a very intimate space.

They were halfway across when thunder cracked across the sky. A second later rain poured down in sheets. Alexandra yelped in surprise as the icy-cold downpour drenched her. Grant grabbed her hand and dragged her across the cobblestones onto the tiny covered porch outside Finn and Amanda's apartment.

Alexandra stared out at the rain before glancing at Grant. She couldn't have held back her laughter if she'd tried. His perfectly styled hair was soaked, plastered to his forehead as he glowered at the rain.

"Something funny?"

His growl only made her laugh harder.

"I'm sorry," she gasped as she leaned against the brick wall. "It's just…you looked so perfect back there and now…"

"Now I look like a drowned cat?"

Just like that, her mirth disappeared as his lips curved into a ghost of the smile she'd fallen in love with all those years ago. It was a smile that had set her body on fire and made her heart soar.

He's your boss now, she sternly reminded herself. *Not your lover. Not anymore.*

"Something like that." She nodded to the pouring rain. "Finn has an umbrella inside his hall closet. I'll grab it for you."

"I don't need an umbrella."

"I didn't need to be walked across the courtyard, but here we are," she replied cheerfully as she pulled her key out of her back pocket. "Give me just a moment."

She hurried inside and pulled Finn's umbrella out of the hall closet. She started to smooth her wet hair off her face but stopped herself. What difference did it make what she looked like?

She stepped back out onto the porch. Heat scorched her cheeks as her eyes traveled from the state of his formerly styled hair to his body. His wet sweater had adhered to his chest, outlining every curve of muscle in lurid detail. Her lips parted as she remembered how he'd cradled her against his body after they'd first made love, her fingers curling in the dark hair on his chest as he'd traced his fingers across her shoulder, up and down her arm, over her belly. Each featherlight caress had simultaneously soothed the thundering of her heart while stoking the little flames left burning in the aftermath of their passion.

"Um, here."

She handed him the umbrella, keeping her eyes focused on the falling rain and off his perfectly toned abs.

Until his fingers brushed hers.

Sparks ignited and spread up her arm like wildfire. Her sharp intake of breath at the unexpected contact was surprisingly loud and echoed off the brick walls of the little porch. Her head jerked up. Grant's gaze was fixated on her, his body rigid. It was as if he'd turned to stone.

Whereas she felt horrifyingly, thrillingly alive for the first time in years. As if every nerve in her body had been brought back to life and was yet again responding to the man who had once brought her to heights of pleasure she hadn't imagined possible.

In the bookstore she'd mentally prepared herself before offering her hand in a gesture of professionalism. She'd also accepted her body's tingling response. Only natural when she was experiencing physical contact with her first, and only, lover after so many years. Her excitement over getting the contract, of finally having the possibility of saving her business, had been easy to focus on while dismissing the rest.

But now, with nothing between them but the coolness of a rainy spring evening, she couldn't have stopped her body's response if she'd tried.

Grant yanked his hand back, the umbrella clenched so tightly in his grasp it was a wonder it didn't snap.

"Good night, Miss Waldsworth."

His frigid farewell immediately doused the fire ignited by that unexpected spark. She didn't respond as he opened the umbrella and walked across the courtyard without a backward glance. She waited until she saw him disappear within the bookstore before going inside.

The stairs up to her little studio seemed steeper that evening, creaking under the heavy weight of each step. The pale yellow walls of her apartment and the iron-framed bookcase overflowing with plants by the front door usually elicited a feeling of comfort when she'd return home. Tonight, however, they failed to induce even the smallest bit of joy as she walked in, tugged off her wet shirt and tossed it onto the tile by the washing machine.

She focused on the mundane tasks of getting ready for the night: watering her plants, washing her face, checking her email one last time for any orders.

It wasn't until she was curled up in her bed with a cup of steaming tea that she allowed herself to fully accept how much of a fool she'd made of herself. If there was anything more pathetic than showing a man how much she was affected by him, it was showing her former lover how much she was affected by him after he'd just literally rescued her business.

She hung her head. She'd pushed Grant out of her

mind and out of her heart those first few years. Easy to do when just the thought of him had brought on a pain so sharp it made her feel like her heart was cracking in two. With time, when little things like the scent of roses or the music of a Ferris wheel reminded her of happier days, she'd allowed herself a brief moment of nostalgia before turning her attention to other things.

And when she'd seen Grant this morning, she hadn't had time to examine how she felt about him. Every time he'd crept back into her thoughts over the course of the day, she'd banished him by focusing on her work.

Unfortunately, she now had all the time in the world and a serious case of insomnia.

The dried violet petals she'd added to her tea drifted in lazy circles in the cup. She didn't know how long she stared at them, focusing on anything but the problem she needed to confront, but by the time she finally took a sip, the tea had turned cool and some of the petals had sunk to the bottom.

Obviously, the physical attraction to Grant was still there. *And why wouldn't it be?* she asked herself defensively. He'd matured into an even more handsome man. They had a history. She'd attempted dating a few times, but nothing had gone beyond kissing. It was only natural that her body would respond.

Slowly, cautiously, she examined her emotions, then breathed a sigh of relief. She'd been mortified and regretful, sad and resigned, even grateful, when Grant had done the unthinkable and offered the contract. But the rush of electricity and heat had been rooted in nothing but sexual attraction. There was no lingering hint of love. How could there be when the Grant she'd seen today was the complete opposite of the smiling young man who had lit up every room he'd walked into?

Did I turn him into that?

She pushed that thought away as she turned off her light and burrowed under the covers. The rain had abated but still fell steadily outside her window, a pleasant backdrop of noise as her eyes drifted shut.

Easier to focus on the shushing melody of rain and let herself drift into sleep than give voice to the lingering doubt that Grant had become so cold and reserved for one reason.

Her.

CHAPTER FIVE

GRANT PAUSED OUTSIDE the door of The Flower Bell. He'd been focused on his laptop and missed the details last night when his driver had taken him by, looking up only to see that her store was dark. The arrangements in the window were stunning, the logo crisp and neat. The door beckoned passersby to come in, a welcoming green with a white frame and a doorknob that looked as if it had been freshly polished.

A stark contrast to the rest of the shops lining the street. Most of the storefronts were empty with cracked windows and doors left ajar, as if their owners had fled so hastily one night they hadn't bothered to lock up. Hard to imagine that just a few blocks away the streets gave way to the more fashionable Greenwich Village district.

Rent in New York City was notoriously high. But was this truly the best Alexandra could do?

A siren screamed not too far away, followed by shouting. Grant frowned. He'd wanted to flaunt his success, yes. But this…this was far worse than he had imagined.

He opened the door and walked inside. The walls had been painted a misty gray that made the framed pictures of flowers on the walls jump out. A small chandelier hung over a round white end table flanked by two emerald wingback chairs. The album on the table was open to photos of various arrangements. Two refrigerators with glass doors took up most of the far wall, the bottom shelves filled with buckets of blooms and the top shelves with completed arrangements.

She'd done the best with what she had. But it would take more than a coat of paint and artsy photography to cover up the cracks in the walls, the signs of mildew in one corner and the harsh humming of the refrigerators.

Alexandra's back was to the door, her phone pressed to her ear as she scrolled through something on a laptop. She'd pulled her thick brown hair into a braid that nearly touched her waist and sported another T-shirt and jeans. A far cry from the brand-name clothes she used to wear. Yet, she wore it well, shoulders thrown back and her spine straight with a confidence she'd lacked when he'd first met her.

"I understand, but you're charging me almost what I'd pay in Greenwich."

Her voice whipped out, fierce and angry.

"I know most people wouldn't have given me the space, but—"

Her shoulders crept up toward her ears. Soft music drowned out most of the loud voice on the other end.

"But you told me the electricity would be fixed! I can't come in every morning wondering if my refrigerators are going to be out and all my flowers dead."

Curiosity morphed into quiet anger. He'd dealt with plenty of disreputable landlords in his time.

"I can't afford another thousand dollars!" A note of desperation crept into her voice. "Please, there must be something you can do. I have a big job that just came in, and I'm getting the first payment Friday."

The pleading in her tone catapulted him back into the past, to the night before Alexandra had turned on a dime and revealed her true colors. They'd been lying on the beach, sand and waves and her naked body bathed in silver moonlight, tangled up in each other after he'd made love to her on a silky blanket.

Let's run away.

He'd chuckled, one hand drifting lazily over her belly, the other cupping her breast. He'd asked where. She'd responded anywhere, as long as they could be together. At first, he'd thought she'd just been teasing. They hadn't discussed what would happen when the summer ended. But somehow, he would find a way to keep seeing her. He had another semester of school. He'd keep his search for graduate programs to New York City. He'd do anything to keep her in his life.

But she had turned to him, fingers fluttering against his face with an almost frantic energy as she'd suggested Paris, the Caribbean, South Africa, anywhere but the United States. Her questions had grown desperate, pleading, as she'd begged him to make a plan with her to escape so they could be together.

Except when he'd pressed her as to why, she'd shaken her head, bitten her lip and said she was being silly, that the thought of summer ending was making her melancholy.

And then she'd pushed him back onto the blanket, straddled him and eased herself down onto his hard length, chasing away his questions and destroying all rational thought.

The memory unsettled him. When she'd banished him the next day in her father's library, he'd chalked up the incident on the beach as a spoiled heiress's melodramatic antics. That and his own unease that had lurked in the back of his mind ever since he'd met Alexandra, that he wasn't good enough for her.

Alexandra's voice broke through his thoughts.

"Look, I'm getting paid Friday. Either schedule the electrician to come in and start work or I walk." There was a burst of noise on the other end of the line, but Alexandra cut them off with an impatient jab of her hand. "I can walk because it's in my contract that you'll take care of associated utility repairs within fourteen days of my request. It's been eighteen days. This place sat empty for twelve months before I moved in. It's your choice if you want to lose a paying tenant."

Alexandra hung up the phone and swore under her breath. She turned around, her face paling when she saw Grant standing in the doorway.

"How long have you been standing there?"

"Long enough to know your landlord is a bastard."

His answer startled a small laugh from her.

"He is. A greedy one, too."

Grant cast an eye over the water stains on the ceiling and the peeling linoleum in the corner by the refrigerators. When his gaze landed back on Alexandra, she was watching him with pink cheeks, arms crossed defensively over her chest.

"I know. Location, location, location."

"Why here?"

The shrug she gave him failed to mask her embarrassment.

"Cheap. Available."

"You said most people wouldn't have given you the space."

The pink deepened into a fierce red as her eyes skittered away.

"You were standing there quite a while."

"Tell me what that meant."

Her head snapped back around, her eyes narrowing as she frowned at him.

"When did you get so bossy?"

"Answer the question, Alexandra."

She huffed.

"I tried renting a space near Finn and Amanda. The leasing agent was the daughter of one of my father's victims." Her voice dropped so low he could barely hear her. "Her father killed himself when he lost almost all of his retirement."

Damn it.

"That wasn't your fault."

The laugh that escaped her lips this time was bitter and thick with regret.

"Wasn't it, though, in some way? I knew firsthand what he was capable of. I overheard some of his business deals. I had my suspicions and I did nothing about it but wear my pretty clothes and take his money."

Self-loathing dripped from each word like poison. Grant stared at her, searching for any hint of deception. How many times had he challenged her on the way her father treated her? His employees? She'd acknowledged it but practically quaked at the possibility of confronting him.

Before he could question her further, she shook her head and frowned again.

"What are you doing here? I thought Jessica was supposed to take me out to the Hamptons house."

"She had other work today. I'm taking you."

Satisfaction threaded its way through his veins at the flicker of panic in Alexandra's eyes. After his nearly disastrous moment in the courtyard the other night, he'd needed to remind himself of why he'd booked her services in the first place. Which is why he'd opted to escort Alexandra out to the Hamptons house personally. It presented the perfect opportunity to not only give her a glimpse of the world he now lived in, but also a chance to remind her of her place in it.

"Oh."

"Is there a problem?"

"No, just…ah…no. Let me grab my bag and lock up."

As she turned off the lights, he cast one more critical glance over the shop. He'd wondered if his wealth would have any effect on the woman who had once spent her spring breaks in an overwater bungalow in the Maldives on a private island.

Judging by how far Alexandra had come down in the world, it wouldn't be hard at all to show her just what she'd given up.

CHAPTER SIX

ALEXANDRA STARED AT the house perched majestically above the deep blue waves of the Atlantic as the helicopter began its descent to the helipad in the corner of the estate. The architect had done an incredible job combining luxury with a homey feel. Pale gray shingles covered the exterior of the house. White shutters glinted in the sun. The darker gray roof topped three stories of what Grant had casually mentioned was a six-thousand-square-foot house, complete with twelve bedrooms, pool terrace, numerous decks and balconies in the same glimmering white as the shutters, and a private expanse of beach. All topped off by six acres of perfectly manicured grounds.

It came close to rivaling the Waldsworth Hamptons house, which had sat at the opposite end of the so-called Billionaires' Lane.

Just a few miles away. She kept her eyes trained on the grass rushing up to meet them and resisted the temptation to glance in the direction of her former house.

A house that, despite its grandeur and castle-like appearance, had felt like a prison until Grant had stumbled upon her in the gardens. That summer had been the happiest she'd ever been. She hadn't returned to the Hamptons since, the memories of what might have been too painful.

She should have made an excuse when she'd realized it was Grant and not Jessica she would be traveling with today. The tour would take less than an hour. It'd be enough time for him to show her where the various house party events would take place, and for her to take photos and notes and make sure the arrangement ideas she had would fit the space, lighting and atmosphere Grant wanted to create for his guests.

The sensation that someone was watching her penetrated through her melancholy. She looked up, but Grant's attention was focused on a tablet in his lap, a phone pressed to his ear. Almost the same position he'd been in since they'd walked out of her desolate little shop. The black limo that had awaited them at the curb had been modest in length but luxurious inside, a stark contrast to the worn-down appearance of The Flower Bell. She'd been well aware of the abrupt change in her surroundings, from the buttery leather seats to the granite and hardwood inlays that put the scarred countertops of the little kitchenette in her studio to shame.

Not to mention that she was in jeans, sandals and a blue T-shirt with The Flower Bell's logo on the front. Compared to Grant's three-piece dark teal suit and a gold tie that matched the Rolex on his wrist, she looked like...

Well, like Grant had when they'd first met. Although even in his white T-shirt and ripped blue jean shorts, he'd looked so handsome it had made her heart hurt. He hadn't leered or fawned or acted like a macho jerk. No, he'd just smiled down at her and stolen her heart on the spot.

She'd been so focused on how he'd made her feel, on how she felt about him, that she hadn't even wondered what he'd thought about the differences between them. Had he felt as uncomfortable as she did now when she'd taken him for a ride in her convertible along the shore?

Or when she'd taken him to the beach party with her former boarding school friends who had name-dropped brands, exotic vacation locales and obscure food names in an attempt to shame "the gardener" she'd brought along?

Although, she remembered as she risked another subtle glance at Grant, he hadn't been fazed one bit. When she had paused, unsure how to handle their not so subtle snobbery without causing a scene, Grant had merely tightened his hold on her waist and calmly replied that he had preferred Cairo over Paris and that if they thought oysters Rockefeller to be a treat, they might want to broaden their horizons with Moqueca de Camarão stew with prawns. He'd said it all with a wide smile and steel in his eyes that had communicated he didn't give a damn how much money they had; he thought they were idiots.

And now, as he picked up the phone and rattled off a series of numbers to someone who sounded like a financial adviser, he had become one of them. Part of her was proud of him. He'd told her about growing up on the crowded streets of Fortaleza. His trips to exotic locations had been work trips with his father, overseeing the delivery of construction equipment to major worksites in Egypt, Morocco and Japan. Not the vacations her friends were used to going on, but Grant's father had made the most of the precious few hours of free time he'd gotten to share the world with his son.

"Hard work," he'd told her once. "But my father loved it. I think he took me along to show me what possibilities were out there, what I could do if I worked hard enough. And to make sure I didn't get pulled into the drug trade."

He'd spoken so matter-of-factly about it, told her the night of the bonfire about how he and his mother had fled Brazil after his father had resisted pressure from a local drug cartel to use construction equipment from the company he worked for to smuggle drugs into Europe, and paid for it with his life. His mother hadn't wasted any time in escaping to the US with her son before the cartel could come after them, too.

A fact her own father had held over her head days later when he'd told her that someone from the bonfire had told their parents, who had informed him that his daughter was "whoring herself to a common gardener."

"I'll be damned if the money I spent on your Ivy League education gets thrown down the drain so you can get pregnant by some opportunistic crook," David had said in that cold voice he used when he'd been trying to keep a hold on his temper.

"He loves me!" Alexandra had retorted in her first display of independence. "And I love him!"

Her father had laughed in her face.

"He doesn't love you, Alexandra. He loves your money and whatever you've been doing with him this summer that he could find with any other woman."

Still reeling from the harsh cruelty of his insults, she had scrambled backward when he'd stood and advanced on her, backing her into the shelves of the library.

"Break it off with him tomorrow or I will make sure he and his mother are sent back to Brazil before the end of the weekend."

"He could be killed!"

Even now, the memory of her father's merciless smile made her shiver.

"That's the idea."

She and Finn had barely been talking at that point. She'd also realized, as she'd scrolled through her phone trying to think of someone who could help her, that she didn't have anyone other than Grant she could depend on.

A realization that had left her numb as she'd sat on

her bed, surrounded by silk sheets, handcrafted Italian furniture and a balcony that overlooked the Atlantic. A princess trapped in a beautiful prison.

She'd stayed up late scouring websites, blogs, even contacted an immigration advocate organization the next morning. But she'd known the whole time that she was throwing pebbles against a giant stone wall. David Waldsworth had the money and contacts to make anything happen, including sending Grant and his mother back to face danger and possibly even their own deaths.

So she'd done it. She'd broken Grant's heart, and her own, to keep him safe.

Yet, she reflected as the helicopter touched down, had she really tried? She could make the argument that Grant's and his mother's lives had been at stake. But her whole life she'd been a doormat. Like at the bonfire, letting her former schoolmates say such hurtful things to the man she'd claimed to love. She hadn't been able to fully stand up to David until he'd been behind bars in an orange jumpsuit, cut off from the world and most of his resources that he could have used to retaliate.

She thought she'd grown stronger over the years. Standing up to her landlord and threatening to move out was not something the old her would have done.

But she'd still given in by moving in in the first place.

By the time the pilot circled around to open the door, she was thoroughly immersed in a pool of self-pity.

Great way to start off your first big job.

"Are you all right?"

She looked up to see Grant watching her with an eagle-eyed stare. She mustered a smile that probably looked as fake as it felt.

"Of course. Just thinking."

He knew she was lying. She could tell by the slight

tightening of his lips, the deepening of the crinkles by his eyes. But he didn't pursue it. Instead, he hopped out and turned back, extending his hand to her.

She accepted his offer of help as she alighted from the helicopter…and nearly yanked her hand back at the sensual electricity that crackled between them. If she'd thought their accidental brushing the other night had been intense, it was nothing compared to the heat that swept through her body as his fingers closed over hers. Slowly, she looked up to see his gaze fixed on hers, fire burning so hot she could barely breathe. Was it anger making his eyes glimmer like molten amber? Or something else, something far more dangerous and intoxicating?

Somehow, she managed not to fall out of the helicopter, to place one foot in front of the other and step down to the helipad. Grant kept her hand in his until they reached the grass. He dropped her hand and turned to the pilot, conversing with him as if the world hadn't just trembled.

She turned away and faced the ocean. Maybe she should have gone on dates with some of the men Finn and Amanda had offered to set her up with. Maybe she should have tried to get out more. Because then she wouldn't be acting like she was still a nineteen-year-old college co-ed who couldn't get her first love out of her system.

Grant strode toward the house. She followed, widening her steps to keep up with his fast pace as they crossed the cobblestone driveway and walked up onto a stunning front porch, complete with thick pillars, white rocking chairs and fans that whirred lazily overhead.

"This is beautiful."

Grant looked over at her sharply before he nodded once. "Yes, it is."

He opened the door and gestured for her to step inside. Her mouth dropped open as she took in the soaring entryway, complete with dark hardwood and a white staircase that curled up to a loft lined with bookshelves. Unlike the home she'd spent countless summers in, this one combined elegance with a homey feel. The art on the walls blended shots of New York City and the Hamptons with pictures of Brazil.

Alexandra walked up to one photo of a footbridge painted a vivid red made all the more eye-catching by the brilliant blue sky behind it.

"That's the bridge at the Dragão do Mar, isn't it?"

Silence followed her question before Grant cautiously answered.

"Yes. My cousin sent me that photo."

Alexandra glanced over her shoulder, barely catching the flash of pain in his eyes before his billionaire's mask dropped back into place. An ache built in her chest. She had never had any emotional attachment to the places she'd lived. Even the Hamptons home, one that had been in the family for centuries, had been redone so many times by David and the women parading through his life that all of its charm had been smothered by tasteless renovations.

What would it be like to have a home she missed so acutely? A loss made worse by the knowledge that she would most likely never be able to return without risking her life?

"It looks like an amazing place."

"It is." The ghost of a smile flickered about Grant's lips. "My father took me to the planetarium when it first opened. I'd never seen anything like it."

Before she could ask more, he stepped away and headed down the hall.

"We have thirty minutes before we have to fly back."

The moment of camaraderie evaporated as Grant

walked briskly throughout the house. She focused on taking photos of the breakfast room, formal dining room, library, beach deck and the pool deck. She asked questions, took notes and showed Grant pictures of what she'd envisioned. His replies were direct and professional, with no hint of the fire she'd glimpsed out on the helipad. Whatever had been there had been brief. Perhaps he'd felt some of the sexual tension, or maybe he'd seen her wide-eyed reaction to his touch and been irritated by it.

They moved upstairs.

"There will be five couples, including one who is bringing their adult daughter, and another couple with teenagers. Laura Jones and several other executives will also be present off and on throughout the week. The four-person catering crew will be staying in the guesthouse."

Alexandra walked past the open doors of the guest rooms. It had been a long time since she had been surrounded by such luxury. Each one had been decorated individually, from pale blues to soft lavenders. All were welcoming and full of light from the numerous windows. Every suite had its own balcony and full bathroom, complete with marble jetted tubs. It would be easy to do arrangements for each room, with little tweaks for each morning so that guests would be greeted as they returned from breakfast with pleasant displays that matched the themes and colors of each room.

"The rooms are beautiful."

"They should be. Each cost a quarter of a million to renovate between the bathrooms, furnishings and balconies."

The facts were stated plainly. But even after all this time, she knew Grant and heard the faintest hint of smugness beneath the words. She glanced sharply at him. She'd been pleased when he'd offered her a tour of the house. It was much easier to design flowers for a space she'd experienced herself. Yet, ever since he'd had walked into The Story Keeper and offered to hire her, she'd wondered why. Why had he hired someone he obviously still loathed? Sure, she'd saved him a few thousand dollars, but he had millions at his fingertips.

As he pointed out several other customized features, including imported Italian marble in the shower, a nasty voice whispered that perhaps Grant had hired her for another reason entirely—to rub his success in her face.

No. Even though he wasn't bothering to hide his dislike of her, she couldn't imagine Grant hiring her just out of spite.

"You've accomplished a lot."

"I have."

"Is it enough?"

The question slipped out before she could stop it. *Too personal*, she thought frantically, but it was too late to take it back.

He blinked, then frowned. "Is what enough?"

She decided to go all in and gestured to the opulent wealth surrounding them. "All of this? The Pearson Group?"

"Of course. Aside from achieving my first billion, I've accomplished all of my goals."

She should be happy for him. But something in his words rang hollow.

"That's great."

His eyes narrowed. "What are you not saying?"

"It's none of my business."

"Spit it out, Alexandra."

His haughty tone made her throw caution to the wind.

"It just doesn't seem like you."

The thundercloud that gathered on his handsome face

nearly made her take a step back. Foreboding washed over her.

"What doesn't seem like me?" His voice was deceptively soft, silky and menacing. "The success? The wealth? That people want to work with someone who started off as a mere gardener?"

Her heart clenched. The old Grant had been proud of his roots, uncaring about what others thought of him as long as he did his best. When had he started to care what others thought?

"No. I just remember you talking about starting scholarship programs for immigrant students, things like that."

"I've made millions in donations."

"And that's great." She put a hand to her forehead as a headache started to pound away at her temples. "You just seem more...removed. Like other things have become more important."

"I changed, Alexandra. You, more than anyone else, should know the reason why."

With that harsh parting shot ringing in the air, he turned and continued the tour. Alexandra stared at his back for a long moment. Her entire body ached for him, for everything he had given up on, the emptiness of his victories and, most of all, that he now saw his past and everything he'd overcome as weaknesses instead of incredible strengths.

"And your room will be around the corner in the other guest wing where the rest of the Pearson Group employees are staying."

She shook her head. She must have heard him wrong.

"My room?"

He turned to face her, a slight wrinkle between his thick brows.

"Your room," he repeated slowly. "Is there a problem?"

"I just… I thought…"

That I wouldn't be staying under the same roof as you. That I would barely have to see you.

"Did you think you would commute from New York every day?"

"No. But I can get a room at a hotel—"

"All of my employees are staying at the house."

"Okay, but I'm not a regular employee."

Could he hear her panic? She didn't want to shell out the money for a hotel, but anything was preferable to being just steps away from where Grant slept, showered, dressed…

"This is non-negotiable."

The finality in his voice signaled she had two choices: accept the inevitable and suck it up for a week or kiss the contract goodbye. She blew out a harsh breath. Okay, so they would be staying in the same house. A house full of other people. And it wasn't like her room was next to his, or that he even liked her. No, his icy contempt was on full display.

"Fine." She managed to force a smile that probably looked more like a baring of her teeth. "Thank you."

Did she imagine the flash of triumph in his eyes? Whether she had or not, she certainly didn't imagine the nauseating feeling in the pit of her stomach. While this was different from her father, she didn't like submitting to someone else's power, feeling helpless and like her life was being arranged for her.

As she passed by the last room toward the back, she stopped, her queasiness disappearing as she stared in awe.

"Oh."

Whereas the other rooms would have fit perfectly under the definition of "relaxing" in the dictionary, this room combined quiet grandeur with a masculine touch. The walls were painted a light gray, except for the accent wall behind the bed that was comprised of dark wood. An industrialized black light fixture hung over the bed, which was a gargantuan piece of furniture covered in a slate-colored blanket. Six pillows, the cases smoothed to perfection, were lined up against the headboard.

But it was the pictures that caught her eyes, three above the headboard. She stepped into the room, her eyes soaking in the colorful photographs. In one, a man wearing an orange feathered headdress with a bright red band of paint covering his face stared into the camera, his eyes piercing through the picture. The one next to it featured a woman twirling in a blue dress with a giant silver bow on her chest, her smile still visible despite the white fringe that cascaded from her matching headdress over her face. The third portrayed a man in a green robe with a birdlike mask obscuring his face, a jeweled beak jutting out over his jaw and emerald feathers standing proudly up from the top of the mask as he held a matching scepter out to the photographer.

"Grant, these…these are incredible," she breathed.

The colors, the energy, all of it drew her in as she neared the photos, soaking in every detail. Her florist's mind matched the vivid hues to different flowers, creating arrangements in her head that would mirror what she saw.

"You won't need to do flowers for this room."

She turned, not bothering to hide her disappointment. "Why not?"

"It's my room."

The room shrank around them as she realized she was standing just a foot away from Grant's bed. She felt like an idiot. Of course it was his room. All of the other rooms were beautiful but lacked that personal touch of having someone who lived in them. Whereas this room… She glanced over her shoulder once more at the picture of the woman swirling in a circle, so carefree and happy in the midst of what looked like a very joyful celebration.

"I don't mind doing flowers for your room, too. In fact, I'd like to." She gestured at the photographs. "These would—"

"No."

Her head whipped around, blinking in shock at the amount of coldness in that one word.

"Why?"

"I'm your employer, not your friend. Not your lover," he added with punishing precision. "I don't need a reason."

No, he didn't, she acknowledged as she did her best to ignore the bite of his words. But something was going on. Could it be that he hadn't wanted her to see his private room? Or was it something to do with his home country, the pain she'd glimpsed in his eyes downstairs?

Once upon a time she would have gently pressed him, laid a comforting hand on his shoulder as he shared bits and pieces of himself. Once, he had told her the horrors of coming home to find his mother bent over his father's body, cradling him to her chest and sobbing like she would never know happiness again. Grant hadn't cried as he'd told the story in a monotone voice, but he had leaned into her embrace, buried his face in her hair and breathed in deeply. It had been the first time she'd felt strong for someone else, been their rock.

No more, she reminded herself as she glanced once again at the photos and then turned her back.

"No, Mr. Santos, you don't need a reason." She looked

down at her tablet, focused on the screen as she typed in a note. "No flowers for this room."

Silence settled, thick and heavy. She tucked her tablet into her bag and started for the door, keeping her gaze averted. She was embarrassed, yes, but also sad. The room reminded her of the man Grant had become: professional, cool and aloof. Yet, somewhere beneath that suave exterior she suspected still beat the heart of the man she had fallen for that summer; someone with a big grin who would have given anyone the shirt off his back.

She was so focused on her melancholy thoughts that she didn't notice Grant was still standing in the door, blocking her exit. She walked straight into his chest, stumbling backward when she hit six feet three inches of immovable billionaire. Grant grabbed her elbow to steady her, but the quick motion just made her tip forward as she tried to keep a hold on her bag.

She fell against him and his arm snaked around her waist. Awareness crashed over her like the waves smashing onto the beach, leaving her breathless as she stared at the tan skin visible at the base of his throat.

"I'm sorry," she squeaked. "I wasn't looking."

"I noticed."

She started to pull back, but his arm was like a band of iron. She swallowed hard and finally forced herself to look up. The gesture had the unfortunate result of bringing her mouth within a few inches of Grant's. Her eyes dropped down to his lips, firm and full. What would kissing him be like now? Would he still tease the seam of her mouth with his tongue, nibble on her lower lip until she gasped and granted him access, laughing as he kissed her senseless?

His head lowered, just a fraction, but enough to startle her and make her pull back. Her eyes jerked back up to his.

"You should be more careful, Miss Waldsworth."

This time she couldn't stop the hurt that swept through her at the use of her old name. If he hadn't made it abundantly clear that he thought of her as nothing but an employee, his continued use of her father's surname was the nail in the coffin. There would be no kisses, no moments of intimacy, no lovers' confessions. That was in the past.

Focus on your job.

"I will, Mr. Santos." She shook his hand off and stepped back, squaring her shoulders as she met his gaze head-on. "If you'll excuse me, I have more pictures to take."

He stared at her with that unflinching glower. But this time she didn't back down. He had put her in her place. She would stay there. But she would do a damned good job as the florist for the Pearson Group and show Grant and all of his wealthy guests what she was capable of.

At last, Grant stood to the side. She walked past him and continued down the hall without a backward glance. The flight back to New York would be awkward. But after that, she had no need to see him again until the brunch at the New York Public Library on Monday. After the brunch it would be the weeklong house party here, and then the gala at the Met the week after that. A busy schedule, but one that would keep her attention focused on her work and off the man she had once loved.

CHAPTER SEVEN

ALEXANDRA GLANCED DOWN at her watch as she walked out of the Metropolitan Museum of Art. Her tour with Jessica and Laura Jones had taken nearly two hours, including an hour at the New York Public Library and an hour at the Met, but it had been worth it. Unlike with Grant's tour of the Hamptons house the day before, Alexandra had felt confident and in control. It had only taken Laura two minutes to put Alexandra at ease, and both women had responded to Alexandra's questions with detailed answers instead of Grant's short, clipped replies.

She'd liked Laura almost immediately. But she also liked Grant's executive assistant, she'd realized somewhere between the Met's Great Hall, where the guests would be welcomed, and the Cantor Roof Garden where, weather permitting, the cocktail hour would be held. What she had initially perceived as Jessica's cold exterior had masked a dry, witty humor and an intelligent mind. Jessica's feedback on the prospective clients in attendance and the whisperings she'd heard about what people were already thinking of the Pearson Group had been invaluable.

Such as the concern that Grant hadn't come from money. When Jessica had shared that bit, it had sparked a fierce defense inside Alexandra's chest. After everything he'd accomplished, after earning a graduate degree from Stanford and working for one of the most respected financial firms on the West Coast, people still looked down on him the same way her father had.

Her anger, fortunately, had also led to an idea for the breakfast at the New York Public Library that would kick off next week's schedule. The roses and hyssop were still a good fit for the centerpieces. But she wanted something even more impressive for the table where Jessica would be stationed at, something respectable and professional but also luxurious. Something people would take one look at and not only feel like Grant paid attention to the kind of details that would keep them swimming in their own money, but also that he could afford the kind of lifestyle he currently kept with or without them.

It probably wouldn't do much, she acknowledged. But doing something was better than doing nothing.

Being six o'clock on a Friday night, and with the first event taking place on Monday, that didn't leave her a lot of time to put something together. Hailing a cab proved difficult and by the time she reached her shop, it was after seven. She hurried inside and powered up her laptop. As it booted, she walked over to the small closet and opened it, eyes scouring the various vases she kept for displays and special occasions.

The bell dinged over the front door. Alexandra turned, her smile fading as she took in the stringy hair, torn clothing and shaky hands of the young man standing in the doorway.

"Are you okay?"

She froze midstep as the man reached into his jacket and pulled out a knife.

"Cash," he bit out in a grating voice.

"Sure. I have some in the register."

She raised her hands so that he could see she wasn't reaching for a phone or a weapon of her own. With slow, measured steps, she moved to the register, her eyes never wavering from the grimy knife clenched in his hand like a lifeline. She slid behind the counter, her fingers grasping for the key she foolishly kept in the lock of the register drawer. One twist and the drawer sprang open. She risked a glance down to scoop the meager pile of bills into her hands.

"Here."

She set the money on the counter. The thief darted forward, the knife still pointed in her direction, and used one hand to spread the bills across the counter. Her heart pounded, but she managed to keep her breathing even as his cracked lips moved, counting up the total.

He looked up, eyes narrowing in anger.

"More. I need more."

"That's all I have. Most people pay online."

"Then your laptop."

She paused. Logically, she knew she should hand it over. The computer wasn't worth her life. But in some ways, it was. The Flower Bell existed in that laptop, from her website and social media to client records and notes for all of her jobs. Because, like an idiot, no matter how many times Finn had reminded her, she hadn't backed up her files.

"Could I give you something else? There's some—"

"Laptop!" the man barked.

Before she could reply, he raised his hand over his head and then swung it down.

Grant instructed his limo driver to drop him off at the end of the block as he tucked the coat Alexandra had left at the Met over his arm. He wanted the element of surprise when he walked in the door. Petty, but he needed something to go his way. His ego still smarted over how yesterday had gone. Not only had showing off his wealth felt like a hollow victory, but they'd once again come so close to kissing and *she'd* been the one to pull away.

But yesterday, standing so close together in his bedroom, he'd been an inch away from scooping her into his arms and carrying her to bed. His body had throbbed with desire, a need to hold her in his arms once more and reacquaint himself with everything he'd missed the past nine years. The dip at the base of her spine that had always made her sigh when he'd kissed it. The smattering of freckles on her shoulders from all of the time she'd spent in the sun. The way she'd laughed when he'd kissed and nibbled his way up her legs, her chuckles turning to sighs as he'd trailed his lips higher toward the apex of her thighs.

Damn it.

What had seemed like her genuine reaction to the photos of Carnival had unsettled him. The couple of women he had brought to the Hamptons house since he'd purchased it had merely glanced at them before oohing and ahhing over the views, the pool, the caviar and the champagne enjoyed on the balcony. Symbols of who they thought he was, or at least the parts of him they were interested in: his money, his reputation, his connections.

That the first thing that had seemed to truly impress Alexandra had been his most prized possession in the house had unbalanced him. For those few minutes he'd been thrust back into the past, to a woman whom he felt had seen him, truly seen him, and loved all of him.

He inwardly swore. In the cold light of day, it had been easy to see that Alexandra had just been acting. He'd confided a lot to her years ago. It would make sense that, whether she was trying to save her business or worm her way back into his life, she would use what knowledge she had to wiggle past his defenses.

Next week was the biggest week of his life. And all he could think about was the past and what might have been. Which is why he was now spending his evening in a not great part of town so he could reestablish the boundaries that had nearly been undone instead of enjoying a glass of bourbon on the rooftop balcony of his penthouse. He determined the nature of their relationship, not she. Her reaction to the photos had thrown him off. He wouldn't be caught unawares again.

He'd arrived at the Met after she'd just left. His disappointment, he reassured himself, was because he'd wanted an opportunity to see her again in a professional setting, remind her that he was the one in control. When Jessica had handed him the threadbare raincoat Alexandra had left behind during her tour and told him Alexandra had mentioned running back to the shop to get some work done, he found the perfect excuse to see her before Monday.

His eyes moved back and forth over the darkening street as he neared The Flower Bell. Several streetlights were out, the bulbs most likely broken by vandals. The empty storefronts looked sad, paint worn by weather, time and neglect. It reminded him of some of the more downtrodden parts of Fortaleza.

Even though Fortaleza had its problems, the city had been good to him for most of his childhood. How many summers had he spent on the beaches to the south, hiking among the red cliffs that bordered the ocean with his father or snacking on *crème de papaya* under the palm trees with his mother? As his father's role in the construction company he'd worked for had grown, he'd taken Grant with him overseas when he oversaw the delivery of major orders. The locales had been incredible. But nothing had compared to coming home to Fortaleza.

Homesickness pricked him. It had been over twenty years since he and his mother had fled after their father had done the unthinkable and said no to a drug cartel that had wanted to use his construction equipment to smuggle cocaine to Belgium. The cartel had responded with a bullet and a notice that Grant and his mother would be next unless they helped. Jordana Santos had lived up to the meaning of her name—daring—and smuggled a twelve-year-old Grant out of the house under the cover of darkness. He had never learned how she'd done it, but less than a week later they'd arrived in New York City, where Jordana had channeled her grief at losing her husband into re-creating a life for her and her son. She lived a couple hours north of the city now, in a rambling Victorian with a garden out back where she drank tea, the occasional glass of wine and entertained her weekly book club.

A slow-paced, pleasant life. One she had more than earned. She turned down his offers of more—more trips, more clothes, more gadgets—with a soft smile. She told him the only thing that mattered to her was seeing him happy. A statement that, more and more, seemed to end on a question, as if she knew that his numerous successes hadn't yet delivered the happiness he sought.

But then she wasn't being completely honest with him, either. Yes, he knew he was the most important thing in her life. But returning to Brazil, seeing her family and friends, was a close second.

He would tell her in the fall that the head of the cartel that had ordered his father's execution had been killed, his organization taken over by a rival gang and moved to Natal. However, he wouldn't tell her the role he had played, that his interference time and time again in the cartel's operations had led to another organization moving in and taking care of someone they considered a weak link. He wanted to verify for himself that it was safe, take a trip before going with her again in the spring. He would not risk losing someone else. Losing his father, then Alexandra—or at least whom he thought Alexandra had been—had been painful enough. He would not risk heartbreak a third time by placing his mother in danger.

Oddly, the victory of his father's murderer being killed had felt unexpectedly hollow. Yes, one less drug dealer was on the streets. But it hadn't brought his father back. It had also left him restless, adrift, with nothing to focus his time, efforts, or money on. That restlessness had led to his next goals, of starting his own investment firm and achieving his first billion. Goals he was on the verge of realizing.

And Alexandra, damn her, had seen right through him yesterday. His hands tightened around her coat. How had she known that the harder he pushed himself to succeed, the closer he got, the emptier he felt? As if he would always be pursuing something just out of reach?

Up ahead, a figure in a trench coat rushed out of The Flower Bell. The door slammed against the wall. Glass shattered and rained down on the pavement. The figure glanced back into the shop before running down the street, arms pumping, something flat and metallic clutched in one hand.

His body roared to life. He stepped in front of the person and dropped into a crouch, his years of high school wrestling coming back as he surged forward, grabbed the runner around the waist and stopped him cold. Whatever the man had clutched in his hands dropped to the pavement as Grant swung him around and pinned him against the wall.

"Let go of me, man!"

Sweat and an all too familiar bleach-like scent stung his nostrils. Older boys in his neighborhood in Fortaleza had started to carry that smell on them when they started working for the cartels.

"What were you doing in The Flower Bell?"

The man finally lifted his head. Bloodshot eyes sat deep in a face with skin stretched so tight Grant could see the outline of his bones. The man smiled, revealing chipped, yellowed teeth.

"Just getting some flowers."

Grant glanced down, his blood turning cold as he realized what lay on the ground between them.

"Where did you get that laptop?"

The man wasn't high enough to miss the danger in Grant's voice. He shrank back against the wall. "Look, man, I don't want any trouble—"

A high-pitched siren cut off whatever the junkie had been about to say. Grant's head whipped around, his heart tripling in speed as a police car stopped in front of The Flower Bell and two officers got out.

"Officer!" he shouted.

They glanced at him, then did a double take as they took in the scene. Another siren sounded in the distance.

"Go help him," the female officer ordered her partner before she entered The Flower Bell.

It took every ounce of self-control Grant possessed not to toss the struggling addict at the officer approaching and rush inside. Once the officer handcuffed the thief, Grant scooped the laptop off the pavement with one hand and ran to the store just as an ambulance pulled around the corner.

No.

Past met present as the sirens and flashing lights sparked a cascade of memories: walking up to his house, seeing his mother cradling his father's body in her arms, the shriek of the sirens as the ambulance had arrived far too late to do anything but take him away covered by a sheet.

Por favor, não.

He burst into the shop, his chest so tight he could barely breathe.

Alexandra sat on a stool next to the counter, wincing as the officer placed a cool rag against a red gash on her forehead. Fury pounded in his ears with a roar that blocked out all sound.

She could have been killed.

Dimly, he heard his name.

"Grant?" She blinked, shook her head and then winced. "Sorry. Mr. Santos. What are you doing here?"

"You were just attacked and robbed, Alexandra. Screw the Mr. Santos."

The roll of her eyes reduced some of the tension in his shoulders.

"Okay, Grant, what are you doing here?"

"You forgot your coat at the Met."

She frowned and looked down. When she saw the laptop in his hands, her eyes brightened.

"You got my computer back!"

She started to get up, but the officer laid a hand on her arm.

"Ma'am, you need to get checked out by the paramedics first."

"I'm fine," she protested. "He whacked me on the head, but it's okay."

"It's not okay."

Both the officer and Alexandra looked up as Grant's words whipped out with ferocious intensity.

"It's not okay that he hit me, no, but my head just hurts a little. I'll be fine—"

"You're going to the hospital," Grant cut in.

The officer frowned. "Ma'am, while I think someone could use a lesson on manners, I agree with him. A head injury is nothing to mess with. Once the shock wears off, the pain might be more than you expect."

Alexandra's eyes found Grant's again and she sighed. "Fine."

It was after midnight when Grant's limo pulled up outside the bookstore. He took one look at Alexandra curled up in her seat, eyes barely open and skin so pale it looked like snow, and made a split-second decision.

"Ralph, go home. I'm going to take Miss Moss up to her apartment and stay with her tonight."

Ralph didn't even blink an eye.

"Yes, sir."

"You are not staying the night," Alexandra protested feebly as she moved to unbuckle her seat belt. "I'm fine."

"You look like hell," Grant replied bluntly before he got out and circled around the limo. He opened the door, reached in and hauled Alexandra into his arms. She gasped as she grabbed on to the lapels of his coat.

"What are you doing?"

"Carrying you."

"I can walk, you know. I got hit in the head, not the legs."

"You're also on strong painkillers after going through a hellish experience. Your stepbrother and his fiancée are out of town, and you told me yourself there's no one else to call." A point that had relieved him when the doctor had asked if there was anyone she could contact. Not that Alexandra's romantic life was any of his concern. They weren't together. But the thought of her being with anyone had sent jealousy slithering through his veins.

"Either I carry you up to your apartment or you're fired."

She huffed but didn't call his bluff. As he walked through the little alley next to the bookstore that led to the courtyard, her head drooped onto his shoulder. The heaviness of her head against the crook of his neck made his arms tighten around her as the reality of what he was doing fully sank in.

He was holding Alexandra in his arms once more. Her head lay where it so often had after they'd made love, as her fingers had traced soft patterns on his chest or she'd stretched up to plant a gentle kiss on his jaw. He'd had lovers before her, and two lovers in the years after he'd left New York. Pleasurable experiences, but none had come even close to the kind of emotional intimacy he and Alexandra had shared. That he had been her first, too, had brought out a fiercely protective side of him that hadn't existed with any of his other paramours.

A protective side she had adored. But tonight, until now at least, she hadn't seemed to need him. She'd stood up to her attacker, dialed 911 and, instead of breaking down in tears and turning to him for comfort like she would have in the past, she'd stayed strong and independent.

Her show of strength had ensnared him. Alexandra had been beautiful and sweet and kind that summer so long ago. But she'd also struggled with standing up for herself, preferring to withdraw or smile and nod instead of creating a scene. He couldn't picture Alexandra Waldsworth keeping calm during an attempted robbery, nor handling the aftermath with such aplomb.

But Alexandra Moss had done just that. She'd answered the doctor's questions, submitted to the CT and MRI scans Grant had insisted on to verify that she didn't have a concussion and argued with him when he'd provided his billing information.

"That's ridiculous!" she'd snapped as the charge nurse's head had swung back and forth between them like she was watching a tennis match. "I can pay for myself."

"Except you can't," Grant had fired back. "And you went back to the shop to do something for the job I hired you to do, making you my responsibility."

"I can take care of myself, *Grant*."

He'd gotten his way. But it had taken much more of a fight than he'd expected.

At first, it had been a relief to see that, aside from the nasty bruise developing on her forehead, she was okay. Then it had irritated him. He hadn't been terrified in a long time. Not since that first year he and his mother had barely scraped by in a crappy apartment on the Lower West Side and every knock on the door had made him reach for a baseball bat, convinced the cartels had arrived to finish what they'd started.

But it hadn't just been the initial fear when he'd realized something bad had happened inside The Flower Bell that still troubled him. Now it was the fear that he was worrying about Alexandra, admiring her strength, caring about her recovery. No matter what way he examined the issue, his feelings were undeniable.

Undeniable, but certainly not part of his plan.

Alexandra's head drooped, then snapped back up as they entered the courtyard. There would be time for him to dissect this new development later. Now his first priority was getting Alexandra up to her bed so she could rest and heal.

"My key…"

"Where is it?"

She fumbled in her pocket and produced a silver key on a chain. He leaned down enough for her to insert the key in the lock and turn the knob, then kicked the door shut behind them and started up the stairs.

"You can put me down now."

Judging by the slur in her words, the pain medication mixed with the sleeping pill the doctor had prescribed was having the desired effect.

"You'd probably fall down the stairs."

"Would not," she mumbled back as she burrowed closer to him, her face nuzzling his chest.

Querido Deus. He hardened at her touch, his arms tightening around her slender body as they neared the landing. He belonged in hell for even contemplating anything remotely sensual after the evening she'd experienced. But he couldn't stop the rush of possessiveness that flooded his body with an old yet all too familiar heat.

The door to her apartment was unlocked. A good thing, too, because judging by the heaviness of her breathing and the limpness of her body, she had fallen asleep. He walked inside, noting details like the frayed furniture and worn rug along with the unexpected homey touches. The Alexandra he'd pictured these past few years—the too many times he'd thought of her—would have found some way to live in luxury, whether that was living off whatever the government had left her after exhausting her family's finances to pay back her father's victims, or finding herself a new beau with the income to keep her in her preferred lifestyle. He'd never imagined an apartment like this, much less the care that had gone into making it a home, evident from the plants lined up on the windowsill to the cozy egg chair arranged next to a shelf crowded with what looked like used books. Not the untouched rare editions that had crowded the mahogany shelves of David Waldsworth's library in the Hamptons where Alexandra had broken up with him, but books with cracked spines and worn pages. Books that had been read and loved.

He walked over to the bed, his head spinning with a question that had been haunting him ever since Alexandra had walked back into his life last week: Who was she? Every time he thought he had an impression of who she had been and who she'd become, she turned around and surprised him.

He eased her down onto the lavender sheets with infinite care. The bed sagged slightly beneath her weight, a sign of its age. He frowned as she shivered and glanced at the thermostat. It was set fairly low for a chilly New York spring. He grabbed a blanket off the egg chair and covered her. There had been plenty of winters when his mother had kept the heat low, or opened windows in the sweltering heat of summer instead of turning on the air-conditioning, to save money. As soon as he'd banked his first major profit from his investments, he'd bought her the Victorian house in New York's wine country equipped with the luxuries people dreamed of, like a private pool, and the luxuries they took for granted, like a working furnace and a refrigerator that never gave out.

Yes, he knew the realities of living without all too well. But seeing Alexandra skimping on basic necessities like a comfy bed and heat bothered him. Just like her shop. She'd obviously done what she could to make it look as presentable and professional as possible. Unfortunately, it would take more than her meager attempts at decorating to erase the reality of its location, or for her to continue to draw in business from the kind of clients she was trying to attract.

Not your problem.

He had to keep perspective. Just because they'd shared something once, just because Alexandra might have changed and grown during their time apart, meant nothing. He had a company to launch and a fortune to make. Alexandra had a business of her own to save. Even if she had changed, even if he could begin to understand why she'd done what she had all those years ago, how could he ever let himself trust her again?

He started to stand up as Alexandra rolled over and let out a soft sigh.

"Grant."

Temptation reared and threatened to pull him under as the devil on his shoulder coyly whispered in his ear, encouraging him to lie down next to her for just a moment.

He stood up and stalked across the room, throwing himself into the chair by the bookshelf. He would stay until dawn in case she needed him during the night.

It was a hell of his own making, he realized ten minutes later as she sighed in her sleep and rolled over again, leaving a tempting empty space next to her. He had been the one to insist on accompanying her home, to carry her upstairs, to put himself in the role of hero when it was becoming clear that the last thing Alexandra needed was someone to take care of her. She had grown into an independent, determined young woman.

Or, he wondered as he dropped his head back against the chair frame, had she always been this way? She'd certainly appeared strong the night she'd broken his heart. Had this thread of steel always existed beneath her beauty and he'd just been so intoxicated with their summer romance that he'd missed who she really was?

The never-ending question rotated around and around in his mind as sleep finally overtook him. His last image was of Alexandra curled up in her bed, her face peaceful and a small smile playing about her lips.

CHAPTER EIGHT

ALEXANDRA PLACED THE last bouquet in the refrigerator and surveyed the white cymbidium orchids framed by red roses with a critical eye. Tomorrow Grant's exclusive guests would arrive between noon and five to fresh flowers in their rooms, followed by a cocktail reception and a dinner on the patio. It would be a nonstop whirlwind, but a welcome one. The hectic schedule meant less time to think about everything that had transpired the past few days.

Saturday morning she'd woken to a splitting headache, pain pills on her nightstand and a glass of water. Grant had left no sign that he'd even been in her apartment, save for the lingering scents of cedar and amber that clung to her body no matter how hard she'd scrubbed in the shower. She'd been torn between embarrassment that she'd been so far gone after her trip to the hospital that she'd allowed him to care for her like that, and savoring the brief flashes of memory she had of him carrying her in his arms and laying her on the bed.

She'd somehow hauled herself to the shop Saturday afternoon. She'd managed the few orders that had trickled in for dates, graduations and nearly forgotten anniversaries as she had worked on the arrangements for the Monday morning brunch. Sunday had been busy, too,

with finalizing everything for the week ahead and post-
ing two part-time positions made possible by her initial
payment from the Pearson Group. She would have loved
to have Sylvia back, but her former employee had already
found a new role. The wholesaler who provided her bi-
weekly flower order for the shop had set her up with a
floral company in East Hampton that would make daily
deliveries to Grant's mansion for her week away. It was
a lot of details flying around at once, more than she'd
ever had to coordinate in her six months of operating
The Flower Bell.

But it had been worth it. She'd arrived at sunrise to
the library, a staff member's grumpy face softening into
a smile when she'd handed her a small bouquet of daisies. She'd learned over the years that having extra arrangements, even something as simple as daisies, could
make all the difference when working with the often
overlooked employees who made magic happen behind
the scenes of events like weddings and graduations. The
employee had clutched the daisies in her hand as she'd
escorted Alexandra to Astor Hall, a white marble hall
with soaring archways and a grand staircase that swept
up to the second floor. The tables and chairs had already
been arranged, leaving it to Alexandra to adorn the tables with the hyssop and rose design she'd first showed
Grant in his office two weeks ago.

As she'd left, she'd deposited one last arrangement
on the welcome table at the base of the stairs: burgundy
roses, violet-hued dahlias, seeded eucalyptus and purple cymbidium in a silver vase she'd picked up at an estate sale last summer. Lush, vibrant but still elegant. It
also drew the eye to the table Jessica had set out with
materials on the Pearson Group's offerings, as well as

framed biographies of Grant and the other executives he'd brought on board.

Alexandra had glanced around the hall to make sure she was alone before she'd peeked at Grant's biography. Jessica had asked her opinion on Friday about three different photos. Two had been professional headshots, both featuring an unsmiling Grant. In one he'd looked directly at the camera, eyes slightly narrowed, lips set in a firm line. The other had him looking at something off camera. It had illustrated his incredibly handsome profile. But both had looked posed and insincere.

The last one, the one Alexandra had recommended and Jessica had gone with, had been of Grant caught in midlaugh, his eyes crinkled as he'd chatted with a group of investors at some event at his old job in California. He'd been surrounded by people of all different ages and backgrounds who were also smiling, their attention fixed on him. She'd traced a finger over his smile. It had been so long since she'd seen him smile like that.

She'd walked out of the library just as the caterers were arriving to set up and immediately departed for the Hamptons, grudgingly accepting the helicopter ride Grant had offered so she skipped traffic and had as much time as possible to work on her flowers. The afternoon had then been spent putting together the guest room arrangements and the Juliet garden roses that would be featured throughout the house. The sun had been setting as she'd finished placing red and pink zinnias into round glass bowls with tangles of ivy cascading from the rims that would take center stage during dinner on the deck that overlooked the pool and the endless expanse of ocean just beyond.

She was exhausted. And proud. This was what she had envisioned when she'd opened The Flower Bell. Long days and sometimes even longer nights full of blooms, greenery and endless opportunities to take an event from nice to extraordinary.

With a smile on her face, she closed the door to one of the four floral refrigerators Laura Jones had rented to house the flowers in the finished basement. She walked up the stairs, past the walk-in pantry that was the size of her suite upstairs and into the massive kitchen. Beyond the picture-perfect deck, infinity pool and white picket fence, the waves of the Atlantic rolled up onto the private beach.

Perhaps she would make herself a sandwich and eat it out on the deck, soak up the brief moment of aloneness before the chaos of tomorrow...

She uttered a shriek as a shadow detached itself from the wall.

"Grant!" *Damn it.* She mentally kicked herself. "Mr. Santos. You startled me."

"My apologies."

The hint of a grin lurking about his lips punched through her defenses.

Be professional. Don't give in.

"No apology needed. It's your house. I just didn't expect you until tomorrow."

Grant advanced into the kitchen, his broad frame and commanding presence filling the space.

"I wanted to be on site in case anything required my attention before the guests arrive."

"Ah."

"Still working?"

"Just finished. I'll have all the guest room flowers out by eleven, and the cocktail tables ready by five." She pulled out her phone and started to pull up the schedule. "I'd prefer to wait until as close to seven as possible to put out the dinner flowers. It's going to be warm tomorrow and—"

"I trust you, Alexandra."

Her fingers tightened around her phone. She had never expected to hear those words from his lips again. Apparently, he hadn't, either, because he looked mildly surprised at contradicting himself so quickly after telling her he wanted her to report directly to him so he could keep her in line.

Although, she realized, he had seemed...softer toward her since the attempted theft at The Flower Bell. Part of her wanted to think that maybe they were finally moving beyond the hurdles of the past. Or perhaps he just felt sorry for her. Whatever the reason, having him look at her with something akin to friendliness instead of cold derision had been a welcome change.

"Well...thank you."

"Have you eaten?"

The words had barely been spoken when her stomach let out a loud growl. Heat bloomed in her cheeks as he chuckled.

"I'll take that as a no. I didn't have time to grab dinner before I left New York City. Sara usually leaves a plate of cold cuts and fruit in the fridge if she knows I'm coming."

Alexandra had met Sara, the housekeeper, earlier. A smiling woman with a booming voice that belied her petite stature and a long brown braid that stretched past her waist, she'd oohed and aahed over the flowers to the point that Alexandra hadn't been able to resist sending her home with one of the spare bouquets she'd brought for the cocktail hour. Sara's effusive praise had been worth the little niggle of worry that something would go wrong tomorrow, and she'd regret giving away the spare.

But, she reminded herself, that was part of the business, part of what she'd worked so hard on over the past few years. Before, when things went wrong, she'd always had someone around to fix things for her to the point she'd been nearly helpless. As she'd slipped from the world of wealth and glamour to a simpler existence, she'd been confronted with how much she had taken for granted. Big things like managing a budget or little things like making her bed or scrubbing the floor in her kitchen. The first time she'd deep cleaned her studio and stepped back to survey her work, she'd felt prouder of the scarred yet shiny wood floors than she had ever felt of the trophies and medals strategically placed in her father's library from the numerous activities he'd enrolled her in.

Giving something as simple as a bouquet of flowers to someone as kind and jovial as Sara was worth a little bit of stress if it kept her tethered to the real world and reminded her of who, and what, was important.

"I met Sara earlier. She's very kind."

A frown crossed Grant's face.

"Yes, she is."

Alexandra smiled.

"You say that like it's a bad thing."

"Not a bad thing, just…" Grant rubbed the back of his neck in a gesture that almost seemed self-conscious. "I always thought of her as efficient. But she is kind."

"Efficient is a good trait, too."

"It is." He moved to the refrigerator in the kitchen, one of two set into the wall. "Would you like a glass of wine, too?"

It suddenly dawned on her what Grant was offering.

"You…you want to eat together?"

He glanced over his shoulder, one eyebrow arched.

"Was that not clear?"

"I don't think employers and employees usually eat

together, so no. I thought you were just offering for me to dig around in your fridge."

Grant grimaced as he reached in and pulled out the plate he'd mentioned. More like a platter, a silver one with curved handles and covered in berries, slices of cheese and meat, olives, artisanal crackers and several little bowls of various dips.

"I was overly harsh during our tour. My bedroom is a private space, one I hadn't intended on sharing."

His explanation both mollified and saddened her. Not only was it a private space, but he also probably didn't appreciate having an ex-lover who had ended things in such a spectacularly horrible fashion invading his sanctuary.

Yet, at one time she would have been one of the few people invited into that space. Just another reminder that staying the course and keeping things professional over the next two weeks was in both their best interests.

He set the platter on the table and pulled out two plates and a bottle of wine.

"Sara always makes enough to feed at least three people. But it gives me something to pick at for a day or two."

He poured the wine, golden liquid bubbling inside the glasses.

"Champagne?" Alexandra asked as she lifted the glass to her lips, the bubbles tickling them.

"It's a sparkling chardonnay from Rio Grande do Sol. Brazil has set itself apart as one of the top exporters of sparkling wine in recent years."

Alexandra grinned at the pride in his voice. She took a sip, her eyes widening as a light sweetness hit her tongue.

"It's delicious."

Grant's smile hit her hard. Genuine, broad and full of happiness. It transformed his face from broodingly attractive and mysterious to devastatingly handsome. It was also, she realized, the first time he had looked truly happy since they'd become reacquainted.

"My cousin's winery. She's well on her way to becoming a success."

A question jumped into her head, nearly spilling from her lips before she bit it back. She glanced down at the plate Grant had pushed toward her and popped a juicy grape into her mouth instead.

"What?"

She looked up to find him staring at her. She swallowed the grape too fast and descended into a coughing fit. Grant circled the kitchen counter and pressed her wineglass into her hand. The wine soothed her throat while giving her a pleasant burst of light-headedness that eased some of the tension in her chest.

"Nothing."

"We may not have seen each other for a long time, Alexandra, but I know when something's on your mind."

She thought about denying it, but what would be the point? One, she'd be lying, and she'd done enough lying to Grant to last a lifetime. Two, he did know her, better than anyone else.

"The photos in your room…they're from Brazil."

He nodded once. "From Carnival. An annual celebration, similar to your Mardi Gras."

"Do you miss it? Your country?"

He exhaled sharply, staring down into his wineglass before nodding again.

"Every day." He walked over to the window and looked out at the dark sea. "I've spent more of my life here in the United States than in Brazil, but it's like a piece of me is missing. My mother and father's families, my heritage…all of it is back in Fortaleza."

Had she thought her heart broken before? Because her

personal pain, caused by her own inability to stand up to her father, was nothing compared to the horrors Grant had experienced at such a young age. Horrors that continued to haunt him.

"Do you think you'll ever go back?"

He swirled the wine in his glass, held it up to the window and watched as the golden liquid circled about.

"I plan on returning later this year, after the Pearson Group launches. If the trip goes well, my mother and I will go back together next spring."

Her mouth dropped open. Fear rushed through her, momentarily robbing her of her voice.

"What?" she finally gasped. "But...you told me you and your mother could be killed."

He turned back to her, a vengeful gleam of satisfaction glinting in his tawny gaze.

"The cartel that executed my father was brutal but small, disorganized. Once I started building up my personal wealth, it wasn't hard to interfere. A delayed shipment here, police interfering there. Word got around that the man who killed my father wasn't reliable, that he might have even been working with the police. He was killed last year, and the cartel disbanded."

A shiver crept down Alexandra's spine as another question whispered through her mind.

"I didn't have him killed," he said softly, answering her unasked question.

She blinked, her lips parting.

"I... Grant, I don't—"

"You wondered. I did, too, as I accrued my wealth. Would I kill him if I got the chance?" He took a deep, long drink of his wine. "I always told myself I wanted to be rich so I could ensure my mother and I never had to go without again. We weren't wealthy in Brazil, but life was pleasant. Here, in the States, with nothing but grief and a cramped apartment…" His voice trailed off as he revisited the past in his head. "But it wasn't just for my mother. I knew if I made enough, became so rich no one could touch me, I could wipe out the cartel that killed my father."

She stared at him, confused. Bitterness coated his tone. How was taking out an organization that had caused so much pain and suffering a bad thing? He'd been a child on the verge of manhood who'd had his youth ripped from him, been torn from his home and the rest of his family that could have supported him and eased his transition into life without his father. Who wouldn't envision revenge?

"Now that you know, you probably see me as belonging in this world even less."

"What?"

Grant chuckled, the sound harsh and hollow.

"Don't deny it. I made the cartel weak. I created the situation that gave another group the nerve to kill the man who ordered my father's death. And I was glad when he died. I might wear the right clothes, drive the right cars, but underneath it all, you still see me as nothing more than common street trash."

"Don't put words in my mouth," she retorted. She set her wineglass down harder than she'd intended, the clink of glass on marble echoing in the kitchen. "Do you want to know what I'm thinking? The last time I saw my father in prison, he was vicious and nasty and cruel. I visited him every week for months like a good daughter, and the bastard never let up on all the ways I'd failed him." She circled the island, anger charging through her veins. "I walked away to him shouting at me to come back, to stop being a doormat, and all I could think was how I hoped he would die in prison." She stopped a few feet away from him, furious at the cartels that had stolen so much from Grant, at her father, at Grant himself for thinking the worst of her and, of course, at herself. Always that self-loathing lurking in the background of everything she did.

"So no, I don't think you're a monster, Grant, for wanting to avenge your father's death and make it safe for you and your mother to return to your country while stopping a drug cartel from hurting more people. Or for being happy that your father's killer is dead. I think you're a perfectly normal, rational human being who actually did something with his life, and it's about damn time you gave yourself some credit for everything you've achieved instead of doing what I imagine you've been doing for the last nine years and wondering if you're just as bad as the cartel, because you're not."

Grant set his wineglass down on the island and turned to her, his gaze impenetrable.

"Is that how you really feel, Miss Moss?"

It took a moment for his use of her preferred name to register. When it did, it cooled some of her anger and thrust her into a state of confusion.

"Yes."

He closed the distance between them until only a sliver of light separated their bodies. The heat of her anger morphed into sensual awareness that tightened her muscles into tense coils. She hated how quickly her breathing roughened, how easily he could probably perceive the effect he had on her. But there was no stopping it. He had always made her feel like this, ever since he'd smiled down at her in the gardens and made her heartbeat quicken into a thundering gallop.

"Good to know."

His lips closed over hers with a searing possessiveness that made her gasp. As soon as her lips parted, his tongue darted inside her mouth and laid claim to her body once more. She didn't waste any time in wondering whether this was a good idea or not, in questioning what was happening. Not when all she wanted was to feel him, just once more.

She flung her arms around his neck and returned the kiss with all the pent-up desire and emotion she'd suppressed the past nine years. Grant groaned her name. His hands closed around her waist, and he lifted her onto the counter. He nudged her legs apart and stepped between them. She moaned as his hips pressed into hers, the hardness of his erection setting her body on fire as she squirmed against him.

"Grant," she whispered into his mouth. "Grant, please…"

Her hands moved up to his face, her fingers settling on the curve of his jaw, the sharp cut of his cheekbones, reacquainting herself with the familiar and exploring everything she had missed as he plundered her mouth with devastating skill.

One of his hands moved to her back, his fingertips searing her skin through the thin material of her shirt. The other cupped her face as he urged her closer. Tears pricked her eyes. Even with the frantic passion building between them, the old intimacy that had drawn her to Grant, that union of souls and knowing that no one else could possibly know her and love her as he had, still burned as brightly as it had all those years ago.

Dimly, she heard a door close, followed by someone calling out Grant's name. She yanked back at the same time Grant did. They both stared at each other, chests heaving, eyes wild as they stared at each other with a mixture of lust and shock.

"Mr. Santos?"

Jessica.

Alexandra scooted off the counter, moved around Grant and ducked into the pantry seconds before she heard the telltale click of high heels on hardwood as Jessica entered the kitchen.

"Good evening."

Grant's greeting went unanswered for a moment. Alexandra scooted deeper into the pantry, her heart pounding. So much for acting like a professional. She'd just made out with her boss on his kitchen counter the night before a week that could make or break her business. And now she was hiding.

Running away, like you always do. You haven't changed.

"Good evening." A faint rustling reached Alexandra's ears. "The items you requested. I'll do an inventory before bed and meet with Miss Jones, Miss Moss and the catering team first thing in the morning."

"Thank you, Jessica."

Another pause. Alexandra glanced over her shoulder, her eyes alighting on the doorway that led to the back staircase. She moved toward the door with cautious steps.

"You're welcome, sir. Have a good night."

Was that smugness in Jessica's tone? Surely not. As much as Alexandra had enjoyed her tour with Jessica at the library and the Met on Friday, the woman didn't seem capable of deviating from her clipped monotone.

Jessica's clicking heels faded as she moved out of the kitchen. Alexandra hustled to the door and hurried up the back stairs. She didn't want to know if Grant came after her or not. His unburdening of himself in the kitchen, her unprofessional confrontation and their searingly hot make out session on the kitchen island had not been part of her evening plans.

She made it to her room and closed the door, sagging against it as she closed her eyes. It was completely foolish to give in so quickly to the desire Grant had inspired in her. Even more foolish to show him once again how much he still affected her. He trusted her to provide flowers for his events, but like he'd said at the bookstore, he didn't trust *her*, would never be able to trust her. She still doubted and questioned her motives, her abilities, her decisions. How could she possibly ask him to do more than she could do for herself?

And she would never be able to fully forgive herself for the past. Aside from the lust straining both their fortitudes, there was nothing between them except a painful history that could never be repaired.

Tomorrow. Tomorrow was an opportunity to start fresh. Tomorrow she would keep her distance, behave professionally and, above all, avoid late-night kitchen assignations with Grant Santos.

CHAPTER NINE

THE SETTING SUN lit up the sky with a dazzling display of rosy pink, vibrant orange and soft violet. Upbeat jazz pulsed through speakers strategically placed around the deck. Guests mingled among the three round tables that had been set up with the zinnia arrangements proudly on display among the white and blue china plates, elegant glassware and flickering candles.

Alexandra stood off to the side, conscious of the curious glances occasionally tossed her way. She didn't recognize anyone from her days in the Hamptons, thankfully. But she still felt unsure of herself.

And uncertain why she was here.

It had been Jessica who had insisted she stay for the dinner. It had come up that morning when they'd been doing the final walkthrough of the schedule. Mercifully, if Jessica had suspected anything last night, she'd kept it to herself.

"After dinner you'll be on the deck to welcome guests with Ms. Jones and the other Pearson Group executives—"

"Oh, no," Alexandra had cut in. "I'll just go up to my room or wander the grounds. I don't want to be in the way."

Jessica had frowned. "Both Ms. Jones and I would

feel more comfortable if you were on site, especially for the first big event. Besides, the guests were impressed by your displays at the library brunch. It would be nice for you to be available to answer questions and chat with them."

When Alexandra had opened her mouth to protest again, Jessica had speared her with an intense gaze.

"I recall in your proposal to Mr. Santos that you mentioned your flowers adding a personal touch that so many companies lacked. Surely, your attendance would reinforce that."

Alexandra had been trapped, and Jessica knew it. When Alexandra had pointed out she'd brought nothing more than a sundress, Jessica had disappeared upstairs and returned with a very large violet bag marked with the silver label of an exclusive boutique Alexandra had used to shop at in her early college days.

"What's this?"

"You mentioned during our tour this had been one of your favorite shops." Jessica had glanced down at Alexandra's T-shirt and jeans, her lips thinning. "Your standard uniform is appropriate for your shop. But I took the liberty of picking up several items in case you were needed for events like these."

Coming from almost anyone else, Alexandra would have taken the comment as an insult. Coming from Jessica, though, it wasn't meant to be rude. It was just fact.

And, Alexandra admitted as she glanced down at the dress she'd selected, after so many years of thrift store finds and secondhand items, she'd felt like a little kid at Christmas as she'd pulled out the luxury clothing. It had been a very long time since she'd worn new garments. Her favorite had been an off-the-shoulder sage-green gown with a sweetheart neckline and a long, flowing skirt. The slit over one thigh had elevated the dress from elegant to subtly sexy.

She'd set aside the dress, though, when she'd found herself wondering what Grant would think of her in it. Not a professional train of thought, nor a wise one. Day-dreaming about Grant would only lead to more confusion and, ultimately, heartache.

The dress she wore now—a white creation with wide straps, a square neck and a fitted top that flared out into a wide skirt with blue swirls that swished about her knees when she walked—had given her a renewed sense of confidence when she'd stationed herself on the deck.

Really, being out here to mingle with Grant's guests was an incredible opportunity for The Flower Bell. She'd even remembered to tuck a few business cards into the pocket of her skirt. The only drawback was that her plan to stay as far away from Grant as possible had disappeared in a puff of smoke.

Right now he stood off to the side talking with a silver-haired couple and a younger, black-haired woman with a bubbly smile. As she'd circulated around the deck, sipping on water with lemon, she'd overheard several of Grant's conversations with his guests. Unlike her father, who had reminded her of an upscale used car salesman with his too-wide smile and overly boisterous laugh, Grant was real, authentic in his communications and genuinely friendly.

His rigidness had disappeared. Now, as he talked with the couple and whom she assumed was their daughter, his smile was like the one she'd glimpsed in his biography picture at the library—genuine and warm.

Apparently, the only person who made Grant uptight and irritable was her.

Jessica walked up.

"The dress suits you."

Alexandra smiled shyly. "Thank you. I haven't worn anything like this in a very long time. I can't wait to wear the green evening gown to the Met gala. I felt like Cinderella when I held it up."

Jessica returned the smile with a tiny twitch of her lips that was most likely her version of a smile. "All you need is a pair of glass slippers."

"I once saw a pair of Christian Louboutin heels that looked like the real-life version of Cinderella's shoes."

"After your work for the Pearson Group, you could afford several pairs of Louboutins."

Jessica wasn't wrong. But there were other things that now took priority. Things like rent and hiring more staff.

"Maybe."

"There's a guest here who would like to meet you."

Jessica gestured for Alexandra to join her as she marched toward a man dressed in a navy polo shirt and tan slacks. As Alexandra passed Grant, she overheard part of his conversation.

"…not sure our fund would be the best fit in that case, Mr. Friedman. Next year might be a better time to look at your finances and whether we would be a good fit."

Alexandra nearly dropped her water glass. Never had David Waldsworth done anything but push when it came to getting his clients to invest. But then so had many other of her father's cronies. They hadn't cared about their clients' personal goals or well-being. Their only interest had been the bottom line.

Yes, Grant had changed. But the qualities she'd admired and loved about him all those years ago, especially his sense of honor and his honesty, hadn't. A frustrated sigh escaped her lips. It would be so much easier to keep her heart distant if he had turned into a monstrous ogre.

She pasted a smile on her face as she stopped next to Jessica.

"Alexandra, this is Dan Perri. He and his wife were asking about the flower arrangements."

Dan gave her a quick smile. With silver threads streaking through his dark hair, and round glasses perched on the edge of a beak-like nose, he struck her as an administrative type and not someone who noticed flowers often.

"Kimberly wanted to walk off with the arrangement at the greeting table at brunch yesterday. It was striking."

Alexandra's lips relaxed into a genuine smile. "Thank you, Mr. Perri. That's very kind."

"I haven't heard of The Flower Bell. Do you do other events like this?"

A frisson of excitement leaped inside her belly. "I do. We've been open officially for six months and are just now getting the word out."

Dan cast an appreciative eye over the tables. "This is certainly a good way to do it. Our company is looking for a new florist for the holiday season. We usually host three or four events between Halloween and New Year's. Would you be available for something like that?"

Ten minutes later she'd handed out three business cards and tentatively booked an anniversary dinner for July. Riding an emotional high, she nearly ran into a woman barreling out of the house.

"I'm sorry, I…" Alexandra's voice trailed off as she took in the woman's red-rimmed eyes and mascara-streaked cheeks.

"Are you all right?"

The woman sniffed and rubbed her nose. Dressed in a flowing blue-and-white-striped dress, she wore her brown hair wound into a chignon that could have passed for a work of art with its intricate curls and twists. She couldn't have been more than three or four years older than Alexandra.

"I will be as soon as I leave this damned house."

The woman's voice rose to a high pitch at the end. Alexandra glanced around. A couple of guests at the nearest table were watching the scene play out with undisguised curiosity. One of the investment managers Jessica had introduced her to just before the guests had arrived— Steve something—glanced at the woman with a look of petrified horror. Apparently, he could face down stock markets, but not a crying woman. Neither Laura nor Jessica were anywhere to be seen, and Grant was still talking with the Friedmans.

"How about I take you inside?" Alexandra suggested gently.

The woman took a step back.

"Who are you? I don't even know you."

The smell of alcohol hit Alexandra square in the face. Whatever had been happening the past hour, the woman had been using wine to deal with it.

"My name is Alexandra and I'm the florist for the Pearson Group." Even though the woman was glaring at her, something in her manner told Alexandra there was more going on than just a guest who had had too much to drink. "I always feel better being away from a crowd when I'm upset."

The woman blinked, her eyes sliding over Alexandra's shoulder to take in the crowded deck. Red suffused her cheeks as she ducked her head and mumbled, "Okay."

Alexandra gently but firmly grasped the woman by the elbow and led her through the kitchen. Her friend Pamela glanced up from one of the stoves and frowned. Her short brown hair had been pinned beneath her chef's cap, her hands moving with lightning speed even as she mouthed, "Are you okay?" Alexandra nodded and Pamela returned to her work, barking orders at her three chefs, their cooking and plating creating background noise that covered up the woman bursting into sobs as Alexandra maneuvered her into the breakfast nook just off the kitchen. Alexandra sat her down at the table, where she buried her face in her hands.

"I'm sorry. You must think the worst of me."

Alexandra eased into a chair across from her.

"Not really. More curious and worried."

The woman looked up and swiped her cheeks, smearing her mascara farther.

"My husband told me we were coming to the Hamptons for the week. I thought it was for our anniversary. It wasn't until we got here that I realized it was a work thing."

She spat out the word *work* with such animosity that Alexandra guessed this had been an ongoing battle between the woman and her husband.

"That had to be disappointing."

The woman sniffed. "You have no idea. I've been trying to get us into counseling for a year. All he does is focus on how much money he can make. He's become obsessed. He doesn't pay any attention to me or our son."

Alexandra stood and poured the woman a glass of water from the sideboard. She handed it to her, along with a napkin, and resisted giving the woman a hug. How many times had she heard her two stepmothers utter the same sentiment? Her father had ignored them, and he had ignored her. Too many times David hadn't bothered to show up to her piano recitals or polo matches, activities he'd pushed her to do to show off his accomplished daughter but didn't bother to see how hard she'd thrown herself into them, all in an effort to please a man who couldn't be pleased.

"What has he said about counseling?"

Beneath the harshness of the woman's laugh lurked a pain Alexandra was all too familiar with.

"Not enough time. Never enough time when there's money to be made."

Alexandra hesitated. She'd known the woman for all of five minutes. She certainly wasn't a good person to give relationship advice, and perhaps the woman wanted nothing more than to vent. But the circumstances she was describing sounded all too familiar. What if she stayed, seduced by the lifestyle her husband provided or by a futile hope that things might improve?

"Have you thought about leaving?" she finally asked.

The woman slowly shook her head. "I mean, I have. But the worst part is I love him. And he wasn't always like this."

"What changed?"

"A friend of his lost everything in an investment scam two years ago."

Alexandra looked away as nausea crawled up her throat.

"I'm sorry."

"Thank you." The woman plucked at the tablecloth. "When I say everything, I mean everything. His wife left him, he lost his job, the house. Now Harry's become obsessed at making sure we have 'enough.' Which I guess I should appreciate. I just miss my husband." She blew her nose, looked up and grimaced at the gilded mirror on the far wall. "I'm a mess, aren't I?"

Alexandra smiled reassuringly. "Nothing a splash of cold water won't fix. Your hair is stunning, by the way."

The woman laughed again, this time softer with a hint of self-deprecation.

"I thought Harry was taking me out to dinner for our anniversary. I spent two hours getting ready." She shook her head as she stood. "I don't know. Maybe I just need to accept things the way they are."

"No."

The woman looked just as shocked as Alexandra felt at her emphatic response.

"I mean…it sounds like you love him. I once gave up on something I should have fought for." Her voice dimmed as she recalled Grant's brilliant smile on the deck. A smile she would most likely never see aimed in her direction again. "I've regretted it almost every day since."

She blinked away her memories and refocused on the woman standing next to her, gripping the back of her chair like it was a lifeline.

"If you think your marriage is worth saving, don't give up."

The woman stared at her for a long moment before offering her a shy smile.

"Thank you… Alexandra?"

"Yes. Alexandra Moss."

"I'm Lucy Hill." Lucy cocked her head to one side. "You didn't used to be Alexandra Waldsworth, did you?"

The floor opened beneath her as her breath rushed out of her chest.

"Um… I…"

Lucy waved a manicured hand. "I'm sorry, that was crass. I knew your stepmother Susan back in the day, and I think I attended one of the Labor Day parties your family used to throw at the end of the summer."

At least Lucy wasn't screaming or throwing things at

her, so that was an improvement over what Alexandra had envisioned happening when she ran into someone from her past.

"I used to be, yes."

Lucy leaned down and laid a comforting hand over hers.

"You don't have to be nervous. The majority of the people who knew your father knew you and your stepbrother weren't to blame."

Alexandra's eyes widened.

"What?"

"Your father had a reputation. Most people felt sorry for you and Finley. I'm glad to see you landed on your own feet and are doing so well." She uttered another self-conscious laugh. "Well, aside from having to deal with a tipsy wife experiencing a marriage crisis. I'm going to clean up before anyone else sees me looking like a raccoon."

Lucy disappeared out into the hall before Alexandra could respond and she sat back in her chair, floored by the exchange she'd just had. Her own fears and guilt over what had happened had haunted her for years, colored so many interactions. When the agent had denied her the storefront in Greenwich Village and made it so difficult to rent a quality property, she'd accepted that her worst suspicions had been true; people blamed her for what her father had done.

But now, with Lucy's kind words lingering in the air, she didn't know what to think.

"Miss Moss?"

Alexandra looked up to see a man in his early forties with thinning blond hair and a morose expression on his narrow face standing in the door.

"Yes?"

"I'm Harry Hill."

Oh, Lord. How had she gotten sucked into the middle of a marriage mess?

"It's nice to meet you, Mr. Hill." She stood and held out her hand. "I think your wife stepped out to use the restroom."

"I heard everything." Harry shoved a hand through his hair. "I'm an idiot."

"Not an idiot," Alexandra hurried to reassure him. "Just…perhaps misguided?"

"A misguided idiot." Harry blew out a harsh breath. Even though Alexandra wanted to escape as quickly as possible—she was a florist, not a marriage counselor—she couldn't help but feel for the couple. Unlike her father and his parade of women, they seemed to truly care about each other. They just hadn't communicated in what seemed like a very long time.

"I didn't even remember that tonight's our anniversary. Not just any anniversary, but our ten-year anniversary." He grimaced. "How does someone forget something like that? I didn't even buy her flowers."

Alexandra started to smile.

"Mr. Hill, I might be able to help you. That is, if you—"

"Yes!" Harry cut her off. "Please, anything. I don't want to lose my wife."

"Follow me."

As they stepped out into the hall, a floorboard creaked. Alexandra looked over her shoulder, expecting to see Lucy coming out of the bathroom. But the hall was thankfully empty. If Lucy could stay in the bathroom for just a few more minutes, she had the perfect solution to help Harry begin the journey of earning his wife's forgiveness.

CHAPTER TEN

GRANT PAUSED IN the doorway of the kitchen, his eyes raking over Alexandra as she tucked a flower into a bouquet. Her dark hair had been pulled up into a ponytail on top of her head. The style left her face bare to his appreciative gaze. She bit down on her lower lip as she turned the flower a fraction and stepped back. To him, the arrangement looked stunning, just like everything else she'd done over the past few days. But watching her work, her attention to detail, showed him that while his initial reasons for hiring her might have been for entirely personal and vengeful purposes, he'd done the right thing. Alexandra was truly a gifted florist.

It had been seeing her talent on display inside the library's elegant Astor Hall and hearing from the guests how much they'd enjoyed the accompanying note cards explaining the meaning behind the flowers selected, complete with a handwritten note thanking them for coming, that had sent him to the Hamptons early. Like a moth to a flame, he hadn't been able to stay away. Not when he'd seen the effort she had put into helping him achieve his desires.

And then there had been her passionate defense of him last night in the kitchen, a secret he had never intended to divulge but that had nonetheless broken free from the cage he'd kept it in all these years. He'd never even told his mother his darkest desire, to use his wealth to eradicate the cartel that had ripped so much from them. Finding out a rival group had taken care of the problem once and for all had been both a relief and a regret. Relief that he wouldn't have to face a decision that would have most likely resulted in bribery, injury and perhaps even death. Regret that he hadn't been able to deliver the ultimate revenge.

Revenge.

That ugly word reared its head as he watched Alexandra circle the counter and examine the flowers from another angle. He had hired Alexandra to rub his wealth and success in her face. If she had picked up on that, she hadn't given any indication. No, she'd done something much worse; she'd poured herself into her work and made him look far better than he was.

Light from the Edison-style bulbs hanging from the ceiling cast a golden hue over her skin. Even though he had instructed Jessica to act as if the clothes she'd picked up in New York were from her, it had pleased him, to a concerning degree, when Alexandra had stepped out in the white-and-blue dress. Not only had she looked stunning, but also seeing something he had picked out on her body had made him feel like she was his.

When he'd first sent the clothing order to Jessica, he'd told himself it was because Alexandra flitting around the Hamptons house in her jeans and T-shirt wouldn't be appropriate. But there had been a part of him that had wanted to do something nice for her, something to assuage his guilt at his own desire to show her up and flaunt his success when she had repeatedly done nothing but go above and beyond in helping him wow his guests. She had always enjoyed dressing up in the past. Judging by the clothes he'd glimpsed hanging up in the little recess in her tiny apartment, not to mention her attractive but threadbare outfit she'd worn to his office when she'd come to deliver her proposal, she didn't have the money to spend on things like that anymore.

When he'd spied her running her hand over the skirt of her dress, a tiny smile playing about her lips, the jolt of satisfaction he'd experienced had bordered on the ridiculous. Unfortunately, the appreciative glances thrown her way by some of his guests had elicited a jealousy he'd managed to temper as he'd dived deeper into the various investment funds and options the Pearson Group was offering its clients.

But it had been hard. Hard to keep his attention centered on the conversations that could make or break his career instead of grabbing Alexandra, hauling her inside and finishing what they had started in the kitchen last night.

When he'd seen Lucy Hill rush out of the house, he'd been prepared for a battle. He knew through the gossip vine that wound its way through New York's upper crust that the Hills had been having marital problems. But Harry had also been funneling millions of dollars into various funds. Not inviting him would have been foolish.

Still, with Jessica inside dealing with the caterers, Grant had been prepared for the worst when he'd seen Lucy's red eyes and ruined makeup. He'd been concerned when he saw Alexandra walk Lucy back into the house, but it had taken a while to wrap up his conversation with the Friedmans without seeming rude. By the time he'd made it inside, it had taken several minutes to track the women down. He'd found them in the breakfast nook just as Alexandra had said, *I once gave up on something I should have fought for...*

He knew, deep down, that she had been talking about them. He'd wanted to burst into the nook and ask for—no, demand—an answer. But he'd hung back, partly out of respect for Lucy and her crisis, and partly because he wasn't sure he was ready to hear Alexandra's response. He'd been debating whether to go in after Lucy had gone to clean up when Harry had entered the fray so he'd hung back, just around the corner, then followed them to the pantry where Alexandra had pulled a bouquet from the spare fridge and told Harry to take Lucy out to a small restaurant up the beach.

"Open until midnight, and the seaside tables are perfect for an anniversary," she'd said with a kind smile.

That smile had slammed into his chest with a force that had almost stolen the breath from his lungs. He could acknowledge now that his so-called quest for revenge had been nothing but a cover. What he'd wanted—no, *needed*—was to understand what had happened all those years ago. How someone with a kind smile and generous heart could have such a cruel side.

Judging by the look of ecstatic happiness on Lucy Hill's face when she and Harry had come back out on the deck ten minutes later and expressed regrets that they weren't staying for the rest of the dinner, Alexandra's kindness had once again helped someone in need.

He had to ask her, he decided as he stepped into the kitchen. He had to know what truly happened, how the woman who gave up a bouquet she had worked so hard on to a man who had forgotten his anniversary and was on the verge of losing his marriage could say such vindictive and hurtful things to someone she had claimed to love.

"It's almost midnight."

Alexandra jumped, one hand flying to her chest as she whirled about.

"You have to stop doing that," she said with a smile that took the sting out of her words.

"Still working?"

She glanced back at the flowers. "Yeah, I needed one more arrangement for the guest rooms tomorrow."

"Because you gave the one you'd prepared to Harry Hill."

Her face clouded for a moment, then cleared as understanding dawned.

"You were out in the hallway, weren't you?" At Grant's nod, she grimaced. "When Jessica asked me to come to the dinner, I didn't think I would end up playing therapist to New York's elite."

"You did more than any three-hundred-dollar-an-hour counselor could have done with those two. They've been having problems for a couple years."

Alexandra looked away.

"Yeah, Lucy mentioned that."

"It wasn't your fault, you know."

Alexandra's head snapped up.

"What?"

"What your father did. It wasn't your fault."

Her throat moved as she swallowed hard.

"I don't..." She sighed and kicked off her white heels before sitting down on a stool with a heavy sigh. "It's hard not to take responsibility. For a long time I didn't pay attention to anything my father did. I just took everything he gave me."

"That's not true." Grant advanced into the kitchen and sat on the stool next to her. "I met you working in the gardens, Alexandra. You weren't just some spoiled, lazy brat. You remembered people's names and helped them out. Do you remember Louis?"

Alexandra smiled. "Yes. He was a dear."

"Do you remember when he sprained his ankle?"

Her face clouded over. "I do. My father wouldn't give the gardening staff sick time."

"And you covered for him. Every time your father wanted to know where he was, you told him Louis was off at the outdoor pool or the docks. He kept his job because of you."

Her smile returned, soft and cautious. "I'm surprised you remember that."

"I do. I remember it all." He reached out and slowly settled his hand over hers. Her sharp intake of breath sent desire bolting through his veins, but he kept his focus on the question he needed to ask. "Which is why I don't understand what happened that summer. Why it ended the way it did."

Silence thickened between them. Alexandra stared at him, hazel eyes wide and glimmering.

"I didn't have a choice, Grant."

Before he could reply, she shook her head.

"That's not true. I had a choice. And I made a choice out of fear."

A hard knot tightened his stomach.

"What are you talking about?"

She breathed in deeply and closed her eyes. The knot grew heavier. What could have possibly happened that she couldn't even look him in the eye?

"Grant..."

A tear trickled down her cheek. He reached up and brushed it away, then gave in to temptation and cupped her cheek. Her lips parted and she sighed, leaned into his touch.

Desire flooded his body as the knot in his stomach disappeared, replaced by a throbbing need. His harsh exhale echoed in the room like a gunshot. Her eyes flew open. A split second later her eyes darkened as her fingers curled beneath his on the counter.

"Grant."

This time she said his name in a voice roughened by lust. He needed answers, needed to know what had happened all those years ago.

But not now. Right now he needed Alexandra.

It was his last coherent thought as he closed the distance between them and kissed her.

CHAPTER ELEVEN

IT HAD BEEN INEVITABLE, Alexandra realized as Grant's lips pressed against hers and she tangled her fingers in his hair, that this would happen. Somewhere deep inside, no matter how much she'd reminded herself to keep her distance, a part of her had known from the moment she'd laid eyes on him in his office in New York City that they would crash into each other once again. Their love affair had been too passionate, too fiery, too all-consuming, for them to resist each other for long.

He moved with sudden, dizzying speed, lifting her off the stool and pressing her up against the wall. Knowing anyone could walk in at any moment sent a delicious, forbidden bolt of fire through her. He wanted her this badly, craved her as much as she craved him, that it didn't matter. Nothing mattered except feeling him against her again.

Grant's hands closed around her waist and he lifted her up. She followed his lead, their lips never breaking apart as she wrapped her legs around him and pressed her chest fully against his. He groaned and thrust his hips against hers. He swallowed her soft cry as the sensation of his hardness pressed against her core.

"Grant," she whimpered. "Oh, Grant, please."

He wrapped his arms around her, turned and took the

back stairs, the steps creaking beneath their combined weight. The last vestige of her rational mind listened for sounds of discovery: a horrified gasp, an exclamation from a guest.

But there was nothing. Nothing but the sound of her heartbeat pounding in her ears as they continued to kiss, to touch, as he walked up the stairs, turned and entered his room, closing the door with a kick.

She was so focused on returning his fevered kisses that it barely registered that she was falling backward until her back hit the mattress. Her eyes flew open as he released her and stepped back. She pushed up on her elbows, barely resisting reaching out to him as fear pierced through her desire.

Had he changed his mind?

"You're so damned beautiful."

The raw hunger in his voice spread through her like wildfire. Emboldened, she pushed up on her elbows and raked him with a fiery, appreciative glance of her own. It wasn't just by design; he truly was magnificent. She'd thought him handsome before but the years had chiseled him from boyish and loving into a dominant leader with a lethal, seductive charm. A charm he leveled at her as he reached down and pulled his shirt over his head in one swift movement.

Moonlight filtered in from the window behind him and backlit his incredible body with silver light. She'd been all too aware of how broad his shoulders had become. But seeing firsthand the muscles rippling across his chest, dusted with dark hair that trailed down below the waistband of his pants, made her mouth dry.

"I can't help but notice you're still fully dressed."

Her head jerked up and she met his amused gaze. The

old her would have blushed and shyly complied with the unspoken edict. But now…

"I think you should be naked first."

He blinked. "Oh, really?"

She smiled at him, savoring the rise and fall of his chest as his breathing grew harsh. Harsh because of her. Because he wanted *her*.

"Yes."

He stared at her, golden brown eyes glittering in the dark. Had she pushed too far?

His hands drifted down to his belt. Her breath caught in her chest as he undid the buckle, unzipped his pants and stepped out of them, revealing black, skintight boxers and firm, muscular legs. Despite the dim light, she could make out the thickness straining against his boxers.

And then he was removing those, too, revealing himself in all his naked glory. She stared, her lips parting. Nine years. It had been nine years since she'd seen him naked; nine years since she'd felt him inside her. Seeing him again, being reminded of the intimacy they had shared, made her so hot and wet she moved on the bed, trying to assuage the growing ache between her thighs.

"You look…" She moistened her lips with the tip of her tongue. "You're incredible, Grant."

The smug smile that crossed his face was both endearing and provoking. She scooted to the edge of the bed, sat up and reached out before her nerves could get the better of her. Her fingers closed around his hard length. His breath hissed out.

"Alexandra."

She looked up at him with a satisfied smile of her own. "I missed you, Grant."

Her admission surprised both of them. He watched her

with an enigmatic gaze that unsettled her. Did he suspect that it wasn't just physical passion spurring her on?

She pushed that disquieting possibility away and lowered her mouth to him. His guttural moan filled the room as she caressed him with her lips and tongue. Her other hand drifted up to settle on his thigh, her fingertips caressing the hardened muscle and coarse hair dusting his skin. His fingers tangled in her hair as he groaned her name.

"*Deus*, Alexandra."

His body tensed, his muscles hardening even more as she brought him to the edge. She savored the power she wielded with her touch as the scent of him, smoky cedar and rich amber, enveloped her in the seductive hold of the past. A seduction made even more potent by the intoxication of the unknown, the unexplored possibilities of the night that lay before them. No longer did the past nine years seem like a gaping wound between them. Now it was exciting, reuniting with a lover who knew her body better than anyone else while discovering new things.

Things like her newfound confidence as her fingers glided up and down his thigh in time with her caresses on the base of his hardness, the sharp inhalation as his fingers tightened even more. He never would have touched her like that before, so possessively. He'd always tried to protect her, keep her safe. At the time, she'd loved it. But now, feeling him respond to her hunger and treat her like an equal, filled her with a fervor that rose into a fever pitch and made her skin blaze with heat.

"Enough."

Grant reached down and hauled her to her feet. His mouth crushed hers in a greedy kiss, one that lasted for only a second but imprinted itself on her soul. Then he stepped back, his hands pulling her dress over her head, fingers deftly unclipping her bra before sliding down and making quick work of her underwear. Gone was the suave, controlled billionaire. In his place was a man possessed by desire, overcome by his need for her.

As his hands glided over her skin, a thought flickered through her mind.

How could I have let this go? How could I have not fought for him?

And then he stepped back even more, eyes raking over her nude body with avaricious need. Cool air whispered over her skin, a welcome balm for the fervor burning through her body.

Focus on now. Make this night worth it. For both of you.

With that commitment echoing in her mind, she raised her chin, sucked in a deep breath and stepped forward. He watched her, jaw clenched tight, arms rigid at his sides. Slowly, she brought her hands up and looped them around his neck, keeping a sliver of moonlight between their bodies as she waited, heightening the anticipation.

Then, ever so slowly, she rose onto her toes and pressed a featherlight kiss on his lips.

"I want you."

Grant stared down at Alexandra. When had she turned into such a captivating temptress? Their lovemaking before had been sweet, tender and gentle. Never had she been this bold, this daring. He'd loved her that summer, introducing her to physical pleasure and worshipping her body.

But this, this was something familiar and yet entirely new. Something he couldn't have turned away from him even if he'd wanted to. He needed not just the physical release of sex but the connection of unifying with a past lover who had known him, all of him.

An unwelcome thought infiltrated the haze of his desire. What if this bewitching side of her had developed over the years as she'd explored her sexuality with other lovers? The thought made him see red as jealousy wrapped around his heart and squeezed. Unreasonable, given that he'd had two lovers of his own since they'd parted. But he could barely stomach it. The image of another man touching her body made him want to hunt the phantom down and wrap his hands around his throat.

Dimly, he became aware of Alexandra's hold around his neck loosening. The boldness in her eyes flickered, uncertainty creeping across her face. His hands came up, fingertips gliding over her hips and grazing the sides of her breasts with a touch as light as butterfly wings. A touch that reassured her that he wanted her even as it reassured him that, no matter what had happened, Alexandra was with him now. If there was a time for revisiting the past, it would be later. Not now, not when he had her naked in his arms.

He reveled in the parting of her lips, her eyes widening, her breath quickening as his hands moved around to her back, still caressing with the barest of touches. His desire swelled, the sensitive tip grazing her stomach.

"I want you, too."

His hands grasped her about the waist. She gasped, her hands bracing on his shoulders as he lifted her up and draped her across the bed. She reached for him, but he stepped back, a slight smile on his lips to show her he wasn't going far. But given how she'd nearly made him lose control, he had to return the favor before he completely surrendered.

The moonlight lit up his bed and made Alexandra's

skin glow. Her hair lay in a thick mahogany curtain beneath her. Her breasts, so often hidden beneath those damned T-shirts, were round and fuller than they had been. She'd grown into her womanhood, her body filling out with seductive curves that begged for his hands to explore every inch. He moved to the bed, watching as her breasts rose and fell, her nipples tightening into points.

Slowly, he climbed up on the bed, caging her between his arms but keeping distance between them. He leaned down and pressed a kiss to the swell of one breast. She arched up, silently pleading for a firmer touch. He resisted the temptation to rush. He'd waited nine years for this moment. He would be damned if he didn't enjoy all of it.

He continued his kisses over her breasts, kissing and gently nipping all around her nipples. Her body shifted, hands fisting in the silk sheets as she made tiny sounds of frustration.

"Please, Grant."

He raised his head and waited for her to look at him before giving her a wolfish smile.

"Since you said please."

Before she could utter a retort, he leaned down and sucked one hardened nipple into his mouth. She cried out and arched off the bed.

"Grant!"

He made love to her breasts with his mouth, still holding himself above her, not trusting himself to press his naked body against hers until he was ready to slide into her welcoming heat. He kissed and sucked and nibbled his way down between the valley of her breasts, across the slight swell of her stomach and down to her thighs.

"Grant…"

This time her voice held a hint of doubt. He looked up and held her gaze with his.

"I won't if you don't want me to, Alexandra. But," he added as he brought one finger up and slid it along the delicate seam of her wet folds, "I hope you want me to kiss you as much as I want to taste you."

The silver moonlight revealed the delicate pink that crept over her cheeks even as she smiled, shyness tangling with that audacious new boldness. Seeing a glimpse of her old demureness reassured him. He had changed. Alexandra had changed. But there were still threads of who they used to be beneath the surface. He still didn't have the answers, would probably never know what had happened all those years ago.

But some of it had been real. And right now that was enough.

One hand came up and cupped his cheek. The soft touch traveled through him, barreling through his defenses and seizing hold of whatever emotions had been reawakened the night of her attack.

Emotions better left under lock and key if he wanted to avoid getting hurt again.

"Yes, Grant."

His hands clenched on her hips like a vise, pinning her in place as he lowered his head to her most vulnerable place. His first kiss elicited a moan that he hoped wasn't heard by the guests, although a reckless part of him didn't care if it was. Jessica and his housekeeper Sara were available if the guests needed anything, giving him the incredible opportunity of forgetting everything but the woman beneath him.

His fleeting thought of concerned guests disappeared as he was filled with the scent of her, the sweet taste of her desire for him. He trailed his lips over her most sensitive skin, used his tongue to bring her to the height of pleasure as she writhed beneath him, her fingers moving through his hair, over his face, grasping at his shoulders as she gasped and whimpered and begged.

He didn't relent, not even as her hips started to pump against his mouth, her cries growing as her thighs clenched around his head. She grabbed a pillow and pressed it over her face just as her back bowed off the bed and her body shuddered with a powerful release.

As she slowly relaxed back into the welcoming embrace of the bed, he reached into his end table and said a silent prayer of thanks when his fingers brushed against a condom packet. He ripped open the package, sheathed himself and then lowered himself onto the bed, pulling the pillow off her face as he pressed his naked body flush against hers. Her molten core cradled his thickness, her heat nearly undoing him.

"I need to be inside you."

Her eyes were glazed, her lips still parted, but as soon as she nodded, he pressed inside her slowly, savoring the sensation of her tight wetness closing around him.

At last, when he was fully sheathed inside her, he leaned down and covered her mouth with his. It was a kiss that brought him home, back to the past but also to the present, with the woman he'd never been able to fully eradicate from his heart beneath him, surrounding him, drawing him deeper into a passionate web he'd once thought himself free of.

As he began to move, slowly at first and then fiercer, deeper, capturing her cries with his lips as they both rode the rising wave of pleasure toward its peak, he wondered why he had ever wanted to be free.

She burst around him, crying out into his mouth as her nails sank into his back, her body matching his in perfect rhythm. He followed a moment later, sinking so deeply into her warm and willing body he never wanted to let go.

But he rolled off her, not wanting to crush her into the bed. When she started to inch her way toward the edge, he flung an arm around her waist and dragged her close.

"Where do you think you're going?"

She turned to look at him, her eyes surprisingly opaque. Once she'd been an open book. He could tell her every thought.

Although, he remembered as his ardor cooled, he thought he had.

"I... This was incredible."

"Yes."

Amusement flashed in her eyes and softened her face.

"Yes. I just wasn't sure... I know we're not..."

How easy it would be to use this moment, to turn the tables and reject her the way she had him. Remind her of the difference in their stations in life and thank her for a pleasant evening before asking her to leave.

The first day she had walked into his office, he might have been able to do it. But now, after everything that had transpired between them in just a couple weeks, and with the evidence mounting that there was much more to the story of their breakup, he couldn't. Couldn't deliver such cruelty and heartbreak for the sake of avenging his wounded pride.

"The choice to leave is yours."

She stared at him for a moment longer. He didn't know what he wanted more: for her to stay and for them to indulge in their rediscovered passion, or for her to leave and give him a chance to regroup before morning dawned. To prepare himself for whatever bombshell she had to drop.

The smile she gave him was forced, insincere.

"I should go."

Disappointment chased away the warmth left over from their lovemaking. But he didn't stop her as she rolled out of bed. He watched as she moved about the room, pulling on her clothes with quick movements, rushing to get away from him. The weak part of him that had felt something more as they'd made love urged him to ask her to stay. Reality and pride silenced his foolishness as his anger resurfaced. If she wanted to run away instead of giving him the answers he deserved, fine.

She was nearly at the door, her back to him, when she paused.

Stay.

The word rose to the tip of his tongue, nearly fell from his lips.

But he managed to stay silent. A moment later she turned the knob and disappeared, closing the door softly behind her.

CHAPTER TWELVE

ALEXANDRA'S GAZE FLITTED from one flower arrangement to the next, visually checking for any sign of sagging blooms or browning leaves. But everything looked perfect.

She closed the refrigerator door with a sigh. She should be satisfied, but all she could think was this left her with absolutely nothing to do on her last full day in the Hamptons. Tomorrow would end with a luncheon before everyone headed back to their respective homes. Some lived in New York City, but others had traveled from Washington, D.C., the Carolinas and even from Kansas City, in the case of one real estate tycoon. They would all return for the final event, the gala at the Met for over two hundred prospective clients and influential members of the New York financial community. Thankfully, it wasn't until next Saturday, giving her a week to decompress from what had turned out to be an emotionally trying few days.

She'd seen Grant every day since she'd fled his bedroom the night they'd made love, but aside from greeting him with a "Hello, Mr. Santos," she'd kept her distance. He hadn't approached her, either, had barely even glanced in her direction.

And why would he? She'd once again fled rather than faced up to the sins of her past. She'd wanted nothing more than to stay in his arms that night and tell him every horrible detail. Yet, she hadn't been able to move past the very real possibility that he would look at her in disgust before telling her to get out. He'd survived fleeing a drug cartel, living in a postage stamp-size apartment and working himself to the bone to provide for his mother as he'd worked toward his dream. If he had been in her shoes all those years ago, he would have found a way for them to stay together. If she did tell him the truth, how could he see her as anything but weak?

As much as it had hurt, leaving him that night had been the right thing to do. It had saved them both the anger and recriminations that would come with such a conversation. And it had allowed her to hold on to the memory of him pulling her close just after their love-making. A moment she never thought to have again, a gift worth preserving.

She moved upstairs into the kitchen where Pamela and her crew were cooking up breakfast. Part of her wanted to talk to her friend, to tell her everything and get her opinion. But if Pamela knew who she really was, knew about her past, she'd never said anything. She told herself she didn't want to burden her friend, not after Pamela had already risked her own job giving Alexandra the information she had.

But truthfully, she acknowledged as she grabbed a muffin and waved at Pamela before moving over to one of several state-of-the-art coffee machines, most of it was fear. She didn't want to confide in anyone else, to risk having someone else turn away from her because of her past.

Today had been described on the itinerary as a down day for guests with suggestions on the various sights and favored treasures of the Hamptons. Pamela and her team would keep a steady stream of snacks and light meals going throughout the day. She'd passed Jessica working in the library, Laura spending time with one of the guests in the sunroom. Most of the other guests had made use of the limos that were on standby to take them wherever they wanted to go. The other Pearson executives had flown back to New York for the day.

Leaving her with an entire day of nothing but stewing in her own thoughts.

She grabbed a cup of coffee and walked out onto the back deck. She'd been up since sunrise, putting the final touches on the arrangements for tomorrow's lunch. Most nights she'd collapsed into bed just after dusk had settled over the ocean. Between the flowers for the guest rooms and the various events Grant had hosted, plus updating her website and organizing the flurry of new orders starting to trickle in, she hadn't had time for anything but work.

She settled onto a lounge chair and pulled out her phone. No new emails. She'd blocked off orders through the gala, but a few had come in for the week after. A few taps and confirmation emails were sent. She'd scheduled social media posts through the week. And her landlord had actually come through on the electricity.

When was the last time she'd had an entire day to do nothing?

Years, she thought as she sipped her coffee. Jessica had forwarded her a copy of the guest itinerary. Maybe she could visit one of the farms or parks…

Her thoughts trailed off as movement caught her eye. She turned just in time to see Grant walk into the yard through a side gate. Her jaw dropped. A black bathing suit clung to his muscular thighs, and the white T-shirt he'd pulled on did little in the way of coverage. No, it actually did the opposite and clung to every ridge of his impressive chest. His dark hair curled in wet tangles that she wanted to reach out and brush back from his forehead.

He glanced back over his shoulder at the ocean. Perhaps he hadn't seen her yet. If she could get up fast enough and slip back inside the house, then he wouldn't catch her ogling him like a—

"Good morning."

His deep voice rumbled through her.

"Good morning, Mr. Santos."

He arched a brow as he drew closer and settled into the lounge chair next to her. She kept her gaze trained on the waves of the Atlantic.

"Don't you think *Mr. Santos* is a little formal?"

"It's what you asked me to call you. As my boss."

"That was before you were naked in my bed."

Her head whipped around to make sure no one was listening. When she looked back at Grant, it was to see him watching her with a teasing glint in his brown eyes that belied the seriousness of his expression.

"I've been calling you Mr. Santos all week," she pointed out, her hands wrapping around the coffee mug as she focused on the heat seeping from the porcelain instead of the remembered heat of their night together.

"In public, yes."

She could feel him watching her, waiting for her to say something. She kept her lips pressed firmly together.

"You've been avoiding me."

"You haven't exactly been seeking me out," she replied.

"I am now. We're going to a hydrangea farm."

Not what she had expected. Panic fluttered in her stomach even as a warm thrill shot through her veins at the prospect of spending more time with him. Part of her wondered what scheme he had up his sleeve. But she'd also never been to a hydrangea farm. The big round blooms were a fixture in many yards, but few florists used them in arrangements.

"What if I say no?"

Grant leaned in, the scent of salt mingling with his natural earthy scent.

"You won't. Because even right now you're envisioning rows upon rows of hydrangea blooms. You can't resist."

She barely stopped herself from swaying toward him. He was right. But it wasn't just the enticement of visiting the farm. No, even though she'd been avoiding him all week, suddenly she wanted nothing more than to spend the day with him. Perhaps the last day she'd have, she realized. There would be no reason for them to see each other over the next week. She would deliver the flowers to the Met on Saturday afternoon and then...

Nothing. She and Grant would part ways. He would become a part of the upper echelons of Manhattan society and she would return to her shop.

"Only because you're taking me to a flower farm."

His smile flashed white against his tan skin, an irritatingly satisfied smirk.

"Be ready in fifteen minutes out front."

Alexandra walked out the front door at fifteen minutes on the dot, wearing an indigo wrap dress that stopped just above her knee topped with a loose white shirt knotted at the waist. A straw hat with a white band shaded her face. After their evening together, and the days spent dancing around the growing tension between them, he found himself both relieved and gratified that she had once again worn one of the outfits he'd picked.

Of all the clothing he'd selected, there had been one that had stood out from the rest—an evening gown, a green creation with a full skirt that had made him think of leaves dancing in a summer breeze. He'd told himself the purchase was so she would represent the Pearson Group well at the Met gala, that his guests would see he had selected the best, and ignored the images playing on repeat in his head of sliding his fingers beneath the straps wrapped around her arms, sliding the gown down her lithe body...

An image that, if they could talk, if she would tell him what had happened in the library nine years ago, could become reality.

His chest clenched. He'd kept his distance all week, vacillating between anger and something that resembled the grief he'd experienced in the immediate aftermath of their breakup. But the more he thought of the pain he'd seen in Alexandra's face that night, the fear in her eyes, and the more he'd revisited her comments about her father, the more he'd known he needed to stop letting his own fears keep him from pursuing the truth.

Alexandra took one look at the cherry-red convertible and smiled. A big smile that made her eyes crinkle at the corners.

"You remembered."

"I did."

David had gifted her a red convertible for her nineteenth birthday. Not out of any paternal love but because it had given him the opportunity to show off his wealth that summer. He had encouraged Alexandra, if she wasn't taking the limo somewhere, to drive the convertible. Alexandra and Grant had made the most of it, driving up and down the coast at all hours of the night after he'd gotten off work, parking on the beach and listening to music as they'd lain on the hood and gazed up at the stars.

And once they'd given in to temptation, they'd made love in the backseat more times than he could count.

With the memory of Alexandra splayed across his lap, her naked body rising and falling above him as she'd ridden him to exquisite release, he started the car and drove off down the lane.

The farm was an hour's drive east of Billionaire's Lane. Soft music played as an amiable silence settled between them. Alexandra spent most of the ride gazing out at the summer homes and ocean views. He resisted the urge to push her for answers. He'd been fast-tracking so much of his life the past nine years, always focused on the goal of more money, that he'd stopped enjoying the little things like a ride along the coast.

They were five miles outside East Hampton when a wooden sign advertised the aptly named Hydrangea Farm. As Grant steered the convertible down a tree-lined gravel driveway, he watched Alexandra out of the corner of his eye.

"Oh!"

A white farmhouse with a long front porch greeted them, along with another sign with arrows pointing guests off to areas like the gift shop, coffee shop and beehives. But Alexandra wasn't looking at that. Her attention was riveted to the field off to the side.

Rows upon rows of towering hydrangea bushes covered the fields. Some of the blooms were so thick the branches bowed down to the ground, showering the green grass with petals in various shades of pinks, creams and blues. Ash trees grew here and there among the bushes, creating welcoming pockets of shade as the sun climbed higher in the sky.

"Grant," Alexandra breathed. "This is incredible."

She turned to him, her smile even wider than when she'd seen the car. For something as simple as bringing her to a flower farm. How had he ever thought her spoiled and selfish? How could he have been blind to the fact that something else had obviously been going on behind the scenes when she'd broken up with him?

They parked the car and Alexandra took off toward the fields. He quickened his pace to follow her before she disappeared among the flowering bushes.

At this hour of the morning, the farm was mostly empty, save for the gentle buzzing of bees as they flew from bloom to bloom. Alexandra mimicked them, flitting from bush to bush.

"This is a Golden Crane Hydrangea!" she cried, cupping a bunch of white flowers in her hand and closing her eyes as she inhaled. "You have to smell this. They're unlike any other hydrangea."

Grant followed her directions and lowered his head, pleasantly surprised by the jasmine-like scent.

"They should sell perfume."

Alexandra shook her head.

"It wouldn't be the same." She spread her arms wide and turned about in a circle. "This is just incredible."

He watched, entranced by the sheer happiness radiating from her smile. He'd seen her like this before, so many times over their summer together.

"What happened, Alexandra?"

The smile disappeared from her face. He wanted to make it reappear, to pretend like they could just move forward and never discuss what had happened.

But he needed to know. He had no idea what he was picturing for them or if there would even be a *them* after the gala. He did know, though, that unless they finally crossed this hurdle, whatever had started to grow between them would shrivel and die.

She turned to one of the bushes, her fingers reaching out to gently stroke the petals. He waited.

"The bonfire..." Her voice caught as her head drifted down. "Do you remember the bonfire we went to the week before?"

"Yes."

She'd wanted to go, to see her old school friends. The last thing he'd wanted had been to go to a party with a bunch of rich clowns. But it had meant something to her. She'd hardly had any close friends, so he'd said yes. Delivering a stinging put-down to the idiots who had eyeballed Alexandra like she was a piece of meat had made attending worthwhile. That and Alexandra asking if they could leave early because she wanted to spend time together just the two of them.

"Someone told their parents I was there with you, and they told my father."

The pieces that had always swirled just out of reach started to fall into place with chilling clarity.

"He confronted me the Friday before I broke things off with you." Her tone became flat, her eyes fixed on the flowers. "He told me if I didn't break up with you, and if I told you that he had talked to me, he would make sure you and your mother were sent back to Fortaleza." The tiniest shudder rippled through her. "When I told him you could die if you were sent back, he said that was the idea."

The heat from the sun bore down on him, searing his skin through his shirt.

"What you said in the library..."

"He told me to say those things. He said I had to be as cruel as possible so that you would never want anything to do with me again." A couple of petals drifted down from the bunch she clutched, and she released it as if it was on fire, crossing her arms over her stomach. "He said he could send you back anytime he wanted. That if I ever saw you again, he'd make sure you and your mother were on a plane back to Brazil within twenty-four hours."

Guilt and fury clashed in his chest. He'd known what David was capable of, had seen plenty of evidence of how horrible the man could be. He should have known something was wrong when David had sat in on their breakup with that hideous smile on his lips.

But he'd been so focused on himself, on his own hurt, and thinking that his fears of being inadequate and unequal to someone like Alexandra had been right all along, that he'd missed everything going on behind the scenes.

"That's why you suggested we run away. The night before."

She closed her eyes and nodded. "I… I should have talked to you, Grant. I should have told you what was going on." She opened her eyes and looked at him with such sorrow it nearly killed him. "I'm sorry."

Words he had wanted to hear for nine years. Words that now felt hollow and empty as he realized Alexandra hadn't been at fault, not truly. She'd been at the mercy of a wealthy, powerful man.

"That's not all."

She sucked in a deep, shuddering breath. The buzzing of the bees changed from pleasant to oppressive, the noise matching the roar building in his ears as a dozen scenarios rushed through his mind. What could possibly be worse than what her father had done?

"I…" She pulled her hat off and ran a shaky hand through her hair. "Finn and I weren't close until that fall. Until he had to take me to the hospital."

"The hospital?"

A tear slid down her cheek. "When I miscarried our child."

He'd been punched in the stomach before. The sensation was the same, the world slowing down as all the air escaped his lungs and left him adrift.

" A child?"

Alexandra nodded.

"Three months along. I had no idea. I just assumed the nausea, the exhaustion, all of it was stress. My father was out of the country. I started bleeding and Finn... He took me to the hospital. He held my hand the whole night." A feeble smile crossed her lips. "It was the one good thing that came out of that whole mess. Seeing me like that, hearing what my father did to us, changed Finn."

He would eventually be grateful for the unexpected blessing granted to Alexandra. But right now all he could see was the loss. The loss of a future with the woman he'd loved. The loss of a child he'd never even known existed. More loss, more heartbreak.

Alexandra cleared her throat.

"I should have told you, Grant, and I should have stood up to my father." Her voice cracked. "I've always been so weak—"

"Stop," Grant barked, unable to hear any more. Unable to hear how much he'd let her down. "I...there's a lot to think about."

A shutter dropped over Alexandra's face.

"Of course." She put her hat back on. "I'll just head to the gift shop."

Before he could say another word, she slipped past him and headed back toward the farmhouse.

And he didn't stop her. What could he say? That he had blamed her all these years, had hired her to rub his success in her face because he'd held on to a misplaced grudge instead of seeking her out and finding out what the hell had happened?

He wandered around the hydrangea fields, trying to figure out what he would do, what he should do. By the time he reached the farmhouse, over thirty minutes had passed. He walked into the gift shop, frowning when he didn't see Alexandra.

"Are you Grant Santos?"

Grant turned to see a white-haired woman with a wrinkled face and bright blue eyes smiling at him from behind the counter.

"I am."

"Your friend had to go back to the Hamptons house. Something about an emergency with the flowers for tomorrow's lunch? She took a taxi back and said she would see you tomorrow."

CHAPTER THIRTEEN

ALEXANDRA WALKED ALONG the beach, her toes digging into the wet sand. The sun had set long ago, but she'd waited until darkness had set in and she'd heard most of the house guests retire to their rooms to slip down the stairs and head toward the beach.

She'd been hiding in her room since she'd gotten back. She'd barely stomached the outrageous taxi bill. But it had been worth the money. At first, she'd committed to waiting for Grant to emerge from the hydrangea fields, to handling whatever mood he was in and either a very awkward silence on the ride home or a full-blown fight.

But as the minutes had ticked by with no sign of him, she hadn't been able to handle it. She'd told him everything, including that they had conceived and lost a child. And all he'd done was stare at her before asking her to stop.

Her throat tightened. She didn't know what she'd expected, but stone-cold silence had not been on her list of possible reactions.

She tilted her head back and looked up at the stars sparkling overhead. How many times had she and Grant lay on the hood of her convertible and stared up at this same sky? How many times had he spread a blanket on the sand, cradling her in his arms as he made love to her?

Part of her still felt guilty that she had allowed her father so much reign over her life. But part of her felt frustrated, too, perhaps even angry. As she'd confessed what had happened, saying it out loud had changed things for her. Yes, she'd been weak. Yes, she should have talked to Grant. But she'd done what she'd done because she had been trying to protect Grant and his mother. Could he not see that she had broken up with him because she loved him? Because loving him and not having him in her life was infinitely preferable to the dangers he would have faced if he had been sent back because she'd risked it all by dragging him to a stupid party?

She stopped at the pier jutting out of the water that marked the end of Grant's beachside property. Awareness pricked her skin. Turning, she saw a dark shape moving toward her on the beach. She knew, even in the dim light of the moon, who moved in her direction. Could tell by the way he walked, the set of his shoulders, the surety of his gait.

"You shouldn't be out here alone."

"I'm not anymore."

As he drew closer, she saw that he was wearing the same linen shirt and slacks he'd worn to the farm. Her heart ached to reach out and touch him. But she held herself in check. He'd told her to stop, unable to bear the confession he'd asked for. Who knew what he wanted now?

"You left."

"It seemed like the best option."

"No." His sigh was barely audible over the gentle roaring of the waves as they crept up the beach. "No, the best option would have been me responding to you and not acting like a self-absorbed idiot."

She stared at him, unsure of how to respond. Part of her wanted to grasp the ray of hope he offered her. But the other part of her couldn't handle another disappointment. Not after the emotional wringing out her heart had been through as she'd dredged up the past.

He held something up. A blanket, she realized.

"It's been ages since we sat on a beach."

She nodded, her throat tight this time for an entirely different reason. Every time they'd spread out a blanket on the beach in the past, it had been to lose themselves in each other's embrace.

"Would you join me?"

Her mind told her to stay strong, to not give in. Her heart was having none of it. She nodded again and watched as he spread the blanket out over the sand. He sat and reached up, holding out a hand to her. She stared at it for a long moment before slowly accepting it. His fingers closed over hers and guided her down to the blanket.

"I didn't know how to respond back at the farm. I was angry at myself. All these years I knew there was something wrong about what had happened in the library. Not just what you said, but your father being there, too. I knew something was off and I let my stupid pride tell me that you had just played me."

Her heart cracked as her own guilt reared its head. Of course he'd been convinced.

"You protested at first," she pointed out gently. "You told me you didn't believe me."

"But then I did. I gave in and did what I accused you of doing." He reached out, one hand closing over hers and enfolding her fingers in his. "I ran away. Being confronted with the reality of what happened, and then finding out that we…"

Her eyes grew hot. She had cried for days after the miscarriage. It had seemed like the cruelest twist of fate, to first lose Grant and then to lose their child.

"You didn't know, Grant."

"But I did," he said fiercely. "I did know, and I failed you. You and our...our child." Slowly, he reached out and cupped her face just like he had that night in the kitchen. "I failed you, Alexandra, and this morning I failed again. I'm sorry."

His apology lifted a heavy weight from her shoulders. Tears splashed down her cheeks as she brought her hand up to cover his.

"You don't have to apologize, Grant."

"I do. I hurt you, Alexandra. You didn't deserve any of the pain your father brought on you, and certainly none of the pain I've brought into your life."

She turned and placed a kiss in the middle of his palm. His breath hissed out. When he kissed her this time, it was a sweet kiss, tender and reminiscent of the first time he'd kissed her in the gardens. His other hand came up and he cradled her face with a tenderness that made tears prick her eyes. Their first time in his bedroom had been fiery, passionate, a fitting reunion given the years they'd been apart.

But this...this was something more. As his lips trailed over her cheek, down her neck and pressed firmly against the pulse beating in her throat, she knew what had changed, at least for her.

She had finally accepted that she was still in love with Grant Santos. A fact that at one time would have driven her into a melancholy state at not being able to let go of the past. If only she had seen sooner that loving Grant had brought out the best in her. He had been the one to challenge her, to encourage her to step outside of her comfort zone and be strong. Unlike the others in her life, he had never wanted someone to be dependent on him. He had wanted her to be free.

Her hands came up, her fingers tangling in his silky hair as she pressed a kiss to his forehead and his hands dropped to her back, pressing her closer.

I love you.

The words stayed locked in her chest, but she showed him, showed him as she undid the buttons on his shirt and kissed the warm skin of his chest. Showed him as she straddled his lap, laced her fingers behind his head and covered his lips with hers with fearless abandon.

Tonight, with the sea roaring behind them and the barest hint of silver moonlight caressing their skin as it waned, she would show him how she felt. And she would do so without fear of what tomorrow would bring.

His fingers slipped beneath the straps of her dress and eased them down over her shoulders. She smiled against his mouth. Each touch of his fingertips, each soft graze, imprinted itself on her memory. How many times had she lain in bed, remembering their passion from that summer and trying to recall the details that her subsequent heartbreak and trauma had erased? She would not make that mistake again.

Cool, salt-tinted air drifted over her breasts as Grant bared them to his gaze. He leaned forward, placed his head on her chest and breathed in deeply, as if he was inhaling the scent of her. She cradled his head in her hands, pressed him against her chest and cherished the intimate moment before he pulled back and captured one nipple in his mouth. She arched against him. He sucked her into the warm heat of his mouth, kissing and licking and nibbling with expert touches that stoked the fires building inside her body. He repeated the same process on her other breast before he pulled the dress over her head. It left her clad in nothing but her panties, legs spread across his lap as she looked down at him.

He leaned back and smirked up at her.

"What are you waiting for?"

Her answering smile was full of promise. She continued her quest to unbutton his shirt, pulling the material free of the waistband of his pants with slow, measured movements. His smirk disappeared as his eyes grew hot, watching her with an intensity that made her so wet she could barely restrain herself from freeing him from the confines of his pants and sinking down onto his hard length.

But she forced herself to go slow. The first time had been them crashing into each other, years of pain and pent-up passion and longing rolled into one incredible moment of sex.

This, though, was different. The past couple of days, overcoming their first true fight, sharing what had happened all those years ago, had made her feel as light as air. The weight of the burden she'd been carrying had been with her for so long she hadn't even realized how heavy it had become, weighing down her life, her future, everything. Without it, she felt like she could conquer the world.

Or reclaim a lost love.

Slow down.

She steadied her emotions, brought herself back under control. Tonight could be just one night, or it could be the beginning of something more. Whatever it was, she would make it last.

She reached down and grabbed his hands, guiding them to her breasts. His eyes turned molten as he cupped their full weight, his thumbs brushing the sensitive tips. She relished his touch before covering his fingers with her own and pushing them down the curves of her waist, over her hips to her thighs. As his hands settled on her, his fingertips pressing into her flesh, she slipped her hands behind his neck and leaned down. She pressed a kiss to his temple, his cheek, the curve of his ear. Her breasts grazed his chest, eliciting sharp inhales from them both as she continued to explore his face with her lips.

His hands crept up her thighs. One finger traced the sensitive skin beneath the waistband of her panties. Another gently rubbed her most sensitive flesh through the thin, lacy material, making her jump beneath his touch at the electricity that spiraled throughout her body.

"You're so wet for me, Alexandra."

His voice, rough and wondering, wound around her. With another smile she leaned down and kissed him deeply.

"Only you, Grant. Ever."

His eyes widened slightly as the meaning of her words sank in. She didn't wait to hear his reply. Instead, she placed her palms on his chest and pushed him back onto the blanket. She stood above him and slowly, teasingly, slipped her panties off, leaving her naked.

Another breeze whispered over her skin. Shyness crept in as she gazed down at her one and only lover. She loved her newfound confidence, the strength Grant had always insisted she had possessed. She hadn't fully believed him until she'd had no other choice but to be strong.

That didn't mean she was completely confident in her role of seductress, though, especially standing above him completely nude and vulnerable.

Grant pushed up off the blanket and knelt before her.

"You're beautiful, Alexandra."

With that pronouncement he placed his hands on her hips and leaned forward to kiss her between her thighs. She gasped, knees trembling, hands clutching at his shoulders as he parted her folds with his tongue.

"Grant!"

His first strokes were gentle. As the stars spun overhead and the sea rolled ever closer with each wave, his mouth firmed on her. He slid one finger inside her, pulsing in time with his lips and tongue. Pressure built inside her, intensifying and spreading throughout her body with a languid heat that suddenly escalated as he wrapped his mouth around her clitoris. One tender suck and she exploded, crying out as the pressure burst into pinpricks of light that spiraled throughout her body. She would have collapsed if Grant hadn't guided her down with his strong hands, pulling her onto the blanket and tucking her into his side.

She didn't know how long they lay there, her body trembling in the aftermath of her pleasure as Grant's fingers lovingly caressed her back.

"I was supposed to be seducing you," she finally said.

Grant's chuckle reverberated against her cheek.

"You did. I just returned the favor."

She slid one arm over his stomach and snuggled her face into the crook of his shoulder. His hand paused on her back, then slowly resumed moving over her skin.

"The last time we were like this, we were just a couple miles down the beach from here."

The warm glow evaporated. No longer did the sea air feel like a balm to the fever Grant had inspired in her. Now it felt cold and harsh as it whipped sand against her bare skin. She shivered.

"I remember that night."

Grant reached down, captured her chin in his hand and turned her to face him.

"Don't turn away from me."

The words were firm, but his voice was kind, his face gentle.

"I'm not."

"Liar."

Liar. Yes, she had lied about a great many things, but not trusting him with why she lied had been her biggest mistake. If she trusted him now, would he be able to see who she had become and allow her to atone for her past weakness?

"Why didn't you tell me that night what was going on?"

She hit pause on the panic building in her stomach and breathed in deeply. The old her would have turned away, wanting to avoid conflict. But it was a reasonable question. It was uncomfortable to revisit that moment, but he deserved an answer.

"I was scared. Scared that if I didn't break things off you and your mom would be sent back." Her voice caught. "I remembered the night you told me about finding your father's body. My heart broke for you. And then it broke for me, because the thought of you being killed…" She closed her eyes against the image that had given her the strength to deliver her performance in the library the following evening, that of Grant lying on a Brazilian street, his chest red with blood and eyes staring unseeing at the sky overhead. "I should have told you what my father had threatened. But I was worried you would confront him, and he would send you back out of spite."

She opened her eyes to see Grant staring down at her. Did he believe her? Or had the cruel words she'd hurled at him in the library, vicious sentiments that had been festering for the past nine years, done too much damage for him to ever be able to fully trust her?

"I sometimes thought about how you said we should run away. Where we would go."

A small laugh escaped her lips. "Running away. It's what I'm good at."

"Don't say that."

She blinked in surprise.

"What?"

"You rebuilt your entire life after losing everything. You could have quit at any point. You could have given up on The Flower Bell after you were turned down for a lease. You stood up to a damned thief." His arm tightened around her waist. "You have grown into an incredibly strong woman, Alexandra."

She surged forward and kissed him, her hands coming up to frame his face as she pressed her lips against his.

Grant surrendered to his need and hauled Alexandra on top of him. Her naked body seared his chest, her heat seeping through his pants. He sat up, keeping their mouths fused together as he reached between them and fumbled with his belt. Alexandra pushed him back onto the blanket and undid his belt and jeans with deft movements. He reached up, his hands cradling the full weight of her breasts, needing to touch her skin, to feel her and reassure himself that she was here, that she wasn't going to run away. He'd meant every word he said, but his damned pride and insecurities wouldn't let him completely forget.

When will you? When will you let go and free yourself?

The thought disappeared as Alexandra rolled his boxers and pants off and his erection sprang free. She settled between his thighs and ran her tongue over every inch of him. He reached down and grasped one hand in his, enfolding her fingers with his as he submitted to the lust she inspired in him.

Until, that is, he could feel his need building, threatening to undo him.

"Enough."

Before he could grab her, she moved up his body with surprising speed and straddled his hips. His breath caught as she placed the tip of his hardness against her wet heat. Knowing that he had been her first and only made the moment all the more potent as she slowly slid down, losing himself in the pleasure as she surrounded him with her silky tightness.

She rode him, then, dark hair falling over her shoulders as she moved above him, hands braced on his chest. He grabbed her hips, guided the building tempo as they thrust against each other. Her fingernails dug into his chest as her mouth rounded into an O and her head dropped back.

"Grant... I'm... Oh, God!"

He knew the moment her orgasm rolled through her, felt her clench around him as she cried out. Seeing her release, feeling her come around him, sent him over the edge with her, continuing to thrust until she collapsed onto his chest.

Unlike their first night of lovemaking, she didn't get up. Instead, she curled into his embrace and once more pressed her face into the crook of his shoulder. He reached over and grabbed the extra length of blanket, pulling it up and over. It barely covered both of them, but it provided enough coverage against the dropping temperatures.

He waited until he heard her breathing slow before he glanced down at her face. In the dim light of the moon she looked peaceful and so beautiful it made his chest ache.

It hadn't just been what sounded like genuine heartbreak in her voice that had caught his attention when she'd explained why she had followed her father's orders to break off their relationship. It had been the self-loathing when she had described herself as prone to running away. He remembered how many times she'd mentioned feeling weak and submissive during their summer together. Those first two months he'd witnessed it plenty of times himself. David Waldsworth had considered employees beneath him, mere insects compared to his greatness, so he hadn't bothered to hide his treatment of his daughter. What had it mattered if the hired help witnessed the cruel things he said? How many times had he wanted to come to Alexandra's defense as her father had lambasted her by the pool for not being friendly enough to a business associate or chastising her for not achieving a spot on the Dean's List for her spring semester?

Except as he remembered those moments, unfortunately now with stunning clarity, he was also confronted with an even harder question: Why had he dismissed all of that when Alexandra had broken things off with him? He had known how cruel David could be, seen it time and time again. He'd also seen how frantic and upset Alexandra had been the night before. Why had he let her go?

His arms tightened around the woman sleeping peacefully in his arms. He'd blamed Alexandra all these years. But what if, in the end, the person most at fault was him?

CHAPTER FOURTEEN

ALEXANDRA ADJUSTED A stalk of snapdragon before standing back to survey her work. A glass vase full of spring blooms adorned each picnic table, and the mix of lavender freesia, pale pink roses, magenta pieris and orange carnations added vivid color to the backyard, a pleasing contrast against the lush green lawn and the white beach house in the background.

Her eyes drifted up to the balcony before she yanked her gaze away and turned to face the water. Waves rolled in, crashing and tumbling onto the sand toward the grass, then smoothing out and slowly receding into the ocean.

She'd woken up in the circle of Grant's arms, snuggled deep into the warmth of his chest. They'd walked back to the mansion after the second time they'd made love. He'd carried her up the stairs, stripped her once more of her dress and tumbled her back onto his bed, where he'd worshipped her body again before they'd collapsed in each other's arms.

The perfect place to wake up and watch through the blinds as the darkness of morning gave way to the soft pastels of dawn. As she'd started to wiggle away, Grant's hold on her had tightened and he'd pulled her back against him, murmuring something in his sleep before placing a kiss to her forehead that had made her melt back into the bed.

As she'd given in to temptation and surrendered to his embrace, her head resting on his chest as the familiar, comforting rhythm of his heartbeat thudded gently against her cheek, she'd revisited her revelation from the night before.

She was in love with Grant. She might have convinced herself those first few days that she had stopped loving him, but she'd been lying to herself.

The problem now, she realized as a salty breeze came in off the water, was what happened next. She saw more and more of the old Grant: the carefree smiles, the thoughtful touches, the more relaxed approach to life. Mixed with the qualities of the new Grant, like confidence and determination. He'd become a truly incredible man.

A man on the verge of achieving something amazing with his career while she tried to save her tiny little floral shop. A barely there florist with a felon for a father living in a studio apartment she could only afford because of her stepbrother.

She'd grown so much in the past nine years. But was she good enough for the man Grant had become? Did they have a chance at starting over? She'd told him everything, bared her heart and all of her failures. She'd taken away his chance to choose all those years ago and he hadn't snapped at her or gotten angry, as he'd had every right to do.

She hadn't trusted him. She hadn't been strong enough for either of them.

But all he'd done, again, was love her. Held her through the tears, reassured her, kissed her until she hadn't been able to stand not feeling him against her, inside her, the insatiable need to touch him overriding all of her questions and doubts.

Goose bumps pebbled on her skin as she crossed her arms against the sudden chill. It wasn't just her own insecurities holding her back from confessing how she felt. No, it was the worry that her father's past would hurt Grant's future.

Could she risk telling Grant how she felt? Risk him returning her love again only to have everything crumble once someone made the connection that she was Alexandra Waldsworth, daughter of one of the greediest and cruelest investment managers in New York?

"Miss Moss!"

Alexandra whipped around, brushing her hair out of her face as she smiled at the young woman walking down the stairs. She scrambled for a moment to come up with a name.

"Good morning, Miss Friedman."

Ellen Friedman returned the smile with a sunny one of her own. She couldn't have been more than twenty-one, a tall young woman with ebony hair that seemed to defy the sea breeze and fall in a smooth curtain down to her waist.

"These flowers are stunning," she gushed as she bounced over to one of the picnic tables and leaned over to smell a carnation. "I'm used to seeing bouquets of daisies and roses, but the arrangements you come up with are so beautiful."

"Thank you, Miss Friedman."

"Call me Ellen." Her hand drifted up and she tucked a strand of hair behind her ear. "I actually had a question for you. I'm getting married this fall."

"Congratulations," Alexandra replied with genuine happiness. She'd only encountered the graduate student a couple times over the past few days, but each time the young woman had been friendly and sweet.

Ellen's smile grew.

"Thanks. We're getting married at the Rainbow Room."

Alexandra's eyebrows climbed. The skyscraper that anchored the infamous Rockefeller Plaza in Midtown offered up its sixty-fifth floor to brides with stunning views of New York City, including floor-to-ceiling windows that overlooked the Empire State Building.

"That's incredible."

"I can hardly believe it." Ellen's sculpted eyebrows drew together as she frowned. "But I just found out my florist is expecting a baby a week before, and her assistant isn't comfortable taking over." She gestured to the flowers. "I've loved everything I've seen you do this past week. I know it's a longshot, you probably book years in advance, but is there any chance you'd be free to do my wedding?"

Alexandra barely contained the cautious thrill coursing through her veins as she pulled her phone out of her pocket. Another client and another wedding. At this rate she'd be able to break her lease and find a new storefront by the winter holidays.

"When is the wedding?"

"The first weekend in October."

"I'm actually free, so I'd—"

Ellen squealed and launched herself at Alexandra, wrapping her in an enthusiastic hug.

"Oh, thank you! I actually like your flowers much better. My mother picked the first florist, and she was nice but so traditional and just not Gary and me at all. I know you're swamped with helping Mr. Santos this week, but as soon as you're free, I'd love to set up an appointment with you."

Alexandra couldn't help but laugh. Was it too much to hope for, that she'd finally paid her dues and was emerging from the shadows of the past into an incredibly happy-looking future?

Ellen chattered on about her vision for her wedding as they walked back to the house and into the kitchen. Two of Pamela's chefs hurried about, cooking pancakes and filling pitchers of orange juice. Judging by the rumbling of conversation from the dining room down the hall, many of the other guests had come down for breakfast.

"I love this house," Ellen said as she snagged a glass of juice off a passing tray. "Mr. Santos is so fortunate he got it. Dad said it was quite the bidding war."

"It is stunning."

Amazing, though, Alexandra thought as her gaze drifted down the hall toward the dining room, searching for a familiar tall, dark-haired figure, that details like the vaulted ceilings and transom windows overlooking the hedged lawn and sunken tennis court no longer mattered. None of it would matter if Grant wasn't here to transform it from an incredible mansion to a home.

Her lips curved up as confidence surged through her. No matter what, she would tell him today how she felt. It was time for her to prove to herself, and him, that she was strong enough to believe in them.

She turned back to see Ellen watching her with a glow in her brown eyes.

"So how long have you known Mr. Santos?"

Her confidence ebbed as warning slid down the back of her neck. How was she supposed to answer? She didn't want to lie, but she didn't want to risk any of Grant's past with her father coming to light.

"Not long. We met once, years ago, but we only just became reacquainted last week when he moved back to New York."

The brief sense of relief that she had successfully navigated her first test disappeared as Ellen edged closer and lowered her voice to a conspirator's whisper.

"Really? Because I could have sworn there was something between the two of you." She fanned herself. "The way he looked at you last night, it was like something out of a romance book. Gary's extremely sweet, but I thought Mr. Santos was going to burst into flames."

The warning erupted into a full-blown alarm that sounded off in her head. She and Grant had so much to discuss, from whether there was an *us* to what he wanted to share with people.

"No," she said firmly with a smile to take the sting out of the word. "Mr. Santos and I met one summer when I was in college, but that was a long time ago. He's very attractive," she agreed with a wink, "but he's just my boss."

The dejected expression on Ellen's face would have made her laugh if she hadn't felt like a cornered animal.

"Oh." Her eyes brightened. "Maybe he has a secret crush on you!"

Alexandra forced a chuckle. "I doubt it. He's not my type, and vice versa. Can you imagine Mr. Santos and me together? I don't think so."

Before Ellen could continue her relentless questioning, a silver-haired man dressed in a white shirt and matching shorts appeared at the end of the hall.

"There you are, Ellen."

"Oh, hey, Dad. I'll see you later at the picnic," she said to Alexandra. "Thank you again!"

Then she was gone, leaving Alexandra in the darkened hall. She released a sigh of relief. Hopefully, Ellen wouldn't say anything to anyone else about her romantic suspicions. She would need to talk with Grant as soon as possible and tell him what had happened.

A door creaked behind her. She jumped and whirled around.

"Grant!" Her hand flew to her chest as she smiled. "Sorry, I didn't even see the door there."

In the dim light it was hard to see his expression. But she could feel the anger rolling off him in thick, palpable waves. She reached out, then stopped herself, her hand falling back to her side. It wouldn't do to be seen touching the man she'd just sworn she had no personal interest in.

"Is everything okay?"

"Come into my office."

She quelled the sudden spurt of panic in her belly and stepped inside. Grant shut the door behind her, keeping several feet between them as he moved to a window overlooking the side yard. Silence reigned between them. The distant clink of glasses and murmur of guest voices seemed magnified tenfold.

Then, finally, "You and Ellen became acquainted fast."

"She's nice." She frowned. "Are you upset because I agreed to do her wedding?"

The look he shot over his shoulder could have frozen Hell.

"Why would I be upset?"

"I don't know. It's the only thing I can think of since I haven't seen you since..." Her words trailed off as her face heated.

"Since we had sex?"

Panic morphed into a hard ball of nauseated forbidding that lodged in her chest. The coldness in his tone, the borderline loathing as he threw out the word *sex;*

all of it set off alarm bells that something was terribly, dreadfully wrong.

"Grant, what is going on?"

He whirled around so quickly she stepped back.

"What's going on is that after the last few days, I thought things had changed between us."

Confusion swamped her.

"I… I thought so, too."

"Then why did I overhear you denying our past to Ellen? Don't lie to me." His voice was barely above a whisper, but the last four words whipped out with such ferocity she felt their sting from her head to her toes. "I heard every word. That we met once long ago? That I'm not your type?"

Her lips parted. "Grant, it's not what you think. I was worried—"

"I'm sure you were worried. Worried to be associated with the Brazilian immigrant? Worried that people like Ellen Friedman might not want to work with someone who carries on a romance with the man who used to mow her father's lawn and plant his roses?"

Her eyes burned as she reached out to him. "Grant, that's not at all how I feel about you. I told you why I said those things back then. But it wasn't how I felt."

His laugh was twisted, cruel and ugly. It shifted him from the man she loved into the icy billionaire she'd encountered in New York. Someone who was just like all the men she'd met who had made her appreciate Grant all the more that summer.

"Of course it's not. Nothing is ever how it seems with you, is it?"

"If you truly think this little of me, why did you hire me in the first place?"

He leaned down, the harsh gleam in his eye making her stomach drop.

"I hired you to show you that you were wrong. That I achieved success, worth, wealth, everything you said I wouldn't." His eyes narrowed. "And yet I failed, didn't I? Since even the lowly florist barely scraping by still sees me as less than her equal, still not someone worth the dirt on the bottom of her shoe."

The pain in her chest as her heart broke anew was almost unbearable. This wasn't her Grant, cynical and untrusting. Yet, she shared some of the blame for this transformation. If she had been stronger all those years ago, they wouldn't be standing here now, with the past coming back to rip them apart.

"Grant, this is just a misunderstanding."

Another sardonic laugh escaped his lips. "How can I believe you?"

He couldn't, she realized as she barely kept her tears in check. There was only one way for this to go.

Her fingernails bit into her palms as she curled her hands into fists, steeling herself for what needed to be done. Her heart cried out, begged her to find another way, to not let the past win.

But there was no other option. And she was tired. She was so very, very tired from running from the past.

"You can't."

The only indication of his surprise was a blink.

"Then I was right."

She shook her head at his monotone.

"No. No, you weren't right." She looked over his shoulder at the lush green grass of the lawn. "I fell in love with you nine years ago and I never stopped. But my inability to stand up to my father kept us apart then, and unfortunately, it seems like it was a mistake that has doomed us permanently."

The weight of his stare pressed on her, making it difficult to breathe. She wanted to throw herself in his arms, to beg for one more chance at a happily-ever-after. But she could never ask that of him. If she truly loved him, she needed to let him go.

"I told Ellen that we didn't have a history because I wasn't sure what you were comfortable with me telling people. I also wasn't sure if her father would continue to do business if there was any hint of you being connected to a Waldsworth."

"That was nine years ago, Alexandra."

It was her turn to laugh, all the years of pain and heartbreak twisting the sound into something wretched and bleak.

"Yes. Nine years that you've held on to your anger with me and turned into a hard man who will never trust my word again. Rightfully so," she added, holding up a hand as he opened his mouth to say something, most likely a list of reasons as to why he deserved to be furious with her. "Nine years that a woman held on to a grudge against my father and denied me a lease for a store. Nine years that I've been in love with you. Nine years is nothing when pain is involved. My father hurt a lot of people, and I will always pay the price for looking the other way."

Grant took a step toward her.

"His actions are not your fault," he growled. "I've told you that repeatedly."

"You have. But my own actions—not standing up for you and for us when I had the chance—that was all me, Grant." She sucked in a deep breath and then walked to him. His body went rigid as she reached up and laid a hand on his cheek. The heat of his skin seared her palm, made her ache to feel his embrace one last time. She would have stayed in bed just a few minutes longer this morning if she would have known it would be the last time she'd lie next to him.

"What just happened now, your real reason for hiring me…" She swallowed past the ache building in her chest, spreading throughout her body. She hadn't thought it possible to hurt any more. But knowing he hadn't hired her because she'd impressed him with her hard work, her skill, was just another stab to her shattered heart. "You'll never be able to fully trust me. I see that now. Or to believe that I love you, that I won't turn around and run away when things get tough. We've both changed. You're a chief executive officer and all the other titles you wanted so much." The smile she gave him was full of grief for what might have been. "I'm just a florist. We don't belong together. Not anymore."

He caught her wrist in an iron grasp.

"That is not—"

A knock at the door cut him off.

"What?" Grant barked.

"There's a Mr. Simon on the phone for you from the Met." Jessica's voice didn't waver. "I wouldn't interrupt, sir, if it was anyone else."

Grant looked down at Alexandra.

"Don't leave. We have a lot more to discuss."

The command saddened her even as it rankled. Exhaustion dragged her body down into a high-backed chair as Grant released her and left the office, closing the door behind him. She was so very tired. Tired of the past always catching up; tired of people telling her what to do; tired of not standing up for herself and doing the right thing.

You can do the right thing now.

She mentally ran through her list. Today's picnic was the final event before the Hamptons guests returned to the city. The flowers were set out. If Pamela would take care of packing up the flowers and delivering them to the local hospital for patients' rooms once the event was concluded, then Alexandra could leave. Pamela would want answers later, but she would do it.

Because whatever Grant had to say to her wouldn't matter. Whether he agreed that their little fling was over or, in her wildest dreams, convinced her to stay, the result was still the same. He'd never be able to truly forgive her, never be able to stop wondering if she truly loved him. They would be caught in an endless loop of incredible, passionate highs and horrifying, heartbreaking lows.

He deserved better. She did, too, despite all her faults and mistakes. Being stuck in a relationship where the past would always be lurking in the background wouldn't be full of love and joy. It would be hell.

She grabbed a notepad off his desk and jotted a quick note. As she slipped out of the office and walked up the back stairs to her room, she texted Pamela to make arrangements for the flowers. Focusing on her to-do list helped keep her mind off the fact that her patched-up heart was once more breaking into tiny pieces, pieces she would never be able to put back together again.

As she neared the top of the stairs, her focus still on her phone, she missed the last step and tripped. She stumbled forward and caught herself on the wall. She looked down and almost gave in to the sudden, hysterical urge to laugh as she looked at her bare foot and then back at the shoe lying on the floor.

Had she imagined herself as Cinderella just days ago, a princess in a fairy tale where true love conquered all? She kicked the other heel off, snatched them both off the

floor and hurried down the hall to her room. She placed
the shoes in the closet and peeled off the dress, reaching
for her jeans and T-shirt.

Fairy tales weren't real. True love certainly had no
place in her life. If she wanted to move forward, she
would have to close the door on her foolish dreams for a
happily ever after once and for all. Which, she acknowledged as she stuffed her items into her suitcase, meant
saying goodbye to Grant Santos forever.

CHAPTER FIFTEEN

GRANT GLANCED DOWN at his phone for what had to be the dozenth time in the past hour. The screen remained dark. He squelched the urge to tap out a text. It had been three days since he'd returned to an empty office and a brief note from Alexandra.

A very brief, professional note. He'd pulled it out and read it over and over again until the paper had turned soft with crinkles running through the loopy cursive.

> *Mr. Santos,*
>
> *Staff with La Meilleure will take care of flowers from the picnic. I will collaborate with Laura and Jessica on arrangements for the Met gala.*
>
> *Moving forward, a strictly professional relationship would be in both of our interests and the interests of our respective companies.*
>
> *Thank you for the opportunities you've provided me.*
>
> *Sincerely,*
> *Miss Moss*

Anger had curled through his veins, hot and furious. Miss Moss? She dared to sign "Miss Moss" when just hours before she'd dashed off that note she'd been moaning his name and raking her nails down his back as she'd arched her hips against his thrusts.

He yanked open his desk drawer, threw his phone in and slammed it shut. He'd realized almost as soon as he'd revealed his reason for hiring her that the most logical explanation was the one Alexandra had just given; that the whole situation was a misunderstanding, a misguided attempt to protect him. As he'd left to take the phone call, he'd even started to formulate an apology for jumping to the worst possible conclusion.

Except she'd left. Fled rather than stay and talk to him. Again.

He scrubbed a hand over his face as he leaned back in his chair. How could he blame her for leaving? He hadn't given her a chance to explain. He'd jumped down her throat and said horrible things. Just as she had nine years ago, except she had been trying to protect him and his mother. His words had been born out of nothing more than pride and a feeble attempt to protect his heart.

To add salt to a very deep wound, he'd walked up to her room twenty minutes later to find her gone and every piece of clothing and jewelry he'd purchased left behind.

Including the sage green gown.

Desgraçado, he cursed himself.

Why had he ignored everything screaming at him that she truly was the same kind, thoughtful woman he'd fallen for?

No, he amended. The woman Alexandra had become was even more intoxicating than the Alexandra he had fallen in love with all those years ago. Young Alexandra had been sweet, loving and passionate. The grown-up Alexandra still had those qualities, but she was more confident, self-assured. More herself.

He'd made a catastrophic error employing Alexandra

for the sake of retribution. He should have turned her away when she'd arrived at the Pearson Group with that ridiculous arrangement, never let her set foot in his office. But his own fatal fixation on revenge had backfired in spectacular fashion. Alexandra hadn't just risen to the challenge, but she'd seduced him once more with her tenacity, her thoughtfulness and, in light of her confession yesterday, her bravery and selflessness. She'd turned the tables on him and proved herself without even trying.

He stood, restless energy sending him on the prowl around his office. Once it had been a symbol of his wealth, of everything he'd accomplished. Now it felt like a cage of his own making. He'd accrued millions, and for what? For his mother to live in a small home she treasured more than any beach house or faraway villa he could buy. For people in New York he barely knew to curry his favor.

The one thing he'd accomplished, taking down the cartel, had been a victory. But it hadn't brought him the peace he sought.

The only time he'd felt truly happy during his time in the United States had been with her. And he'd ruined it.

Movement flickered on one of the security cameras. Finn walked off the elevator and crossed to Jessica's desk, a flower arrangement in his hands. Grant's eyes snapped to the elevator just as the doors swished shut on the empty car.

He watched as his event manager, Laura, came out of her office and examined the arrangement, before she gave Finn an approving nod. He flashed a friendly smile before walking back toward the elevator.

Grant was on his feet and moving to his door before he could stop himself. He walked into the lobby just as the elevator doors were opening. He followed Finn into the car, ignoring the younger man's stare as he pushed the button for the tenth floor where one of the building's numerous coffee shops resided.

He didn't want coffee. He didn't need any more frantic energy zipping through his veins. What he should do was get off the elevator, even if he looked crazy for hopping on then off.

But he couldn't. Finn was a connection to Alexandra. And right now he needed a connection to her, craved it more than anything.

The doors closed. Lilting music filtered out of the speakers, a pleasant contrast to the tense silence that thickened the air. Now that he was here, he didn't know what to say. Should he ask after Alexandra? Keep his questions strictly business and see if Finn volunteered any information? He'd gone to bat against *Fortune 500* executives, warred with international moguls... And now he couldn't even string a sentence together.

The elevator hit the fortieth floor before Finn finally broke the silence.

"I was with her when she lost the baby."

Emotion punched him hard in the gut. The only outward sign that he'd heard Finn was his sudden intake of breath. But inside he ached: for the baby he'd never known, for the pain Alexandra had faced, both physically and emotionally. The heartbreak in her voice, the anguish in her eyes when she'd told him, had stirred up the sharp feelings of regret that had always lurked in the back of his mind. Feelings he had ignored to his own, and now her, detriment.

He closed his eyes as the elevator continued its descent. He'd accused Alexandra of repeating her past behavior. But wasn't he doing the same? Letting her go when he knew, deep in his soul, that there was more to the story?

"Thank you."

He opened his eyes to see Finn staring at him with a mixture of pity and irritation, a combination that stoked his banked anger. His first inclination was to snap at Finn. He didn't need pity from a man who had once sneered and laughed at him, who had fallen from spoiled rich playboy to lowly teacher.

He tempered it, swallowed his pride and forced himself to remain calm. The Finn he'd known nine years ago had changed drastically. While he might have fallen in the social ranks, so what? It had been hardworking teachers who had taught Grant English when he and his mother had arrived in the States; a high school math teacher who had found the scholarship that changed the course of his life. He had given in to his own obsession for prestige and money, come close to the same snobbery he'd despised in people like David Waldsworth, while letting some of the best parts of himself go.

And he genuinely liked the little bit of the new Finn he'd glimpsed that night in the bookshop. He certainly liked the man who had helped Alexandra in her darkest hour and kept her secret all these years.

"She told me that night that it was like losing you all over again." A fierce glower passed over Finn's face. "Said maybe it's what she deserved."

"What?" Grant snapped. "Deserved for what?"

"For not being strong enough to stand up to David. For hurting you."

"She was trying to protect my mother and me."

As he said the words out loud, something shifted in his chest; an acceptance of what had happened. Alexandra had been all of nineteen. Yes, things might have been different if she had come to him. But David Waldsworth had still wielded significant power back then. What if he had followed through on his threat and sent Grant and his mother back to Brazil? Perhaps his successes over the past nine years wouldn't have happened without Alexandra's sacrifice.

Regret burned in his chest. He'd wasted so much time on his foolish pride. But, he resolved, no more. He loved Alexandra, loved her more than he ever thought possible. They'd lost nine years. After his knee-jerk reaction to her conversation with Ellen, his unwillingness to consider that once more Alexandra had been trying to protect him, she might not want anything to do with him.

But this time he wasn't letting her go without a fight.

Grant let out a long, slow breath.

"How is she?"

"Miserable. Almost as bad as she was the last time. I think the only thing keeping her from wallowing away in her apartment is putting together the last of the pieces for your gala."

He ached to hold her in his arms, to soothe away the stress and tell her how sorry he was.

"I love her."

"And she loves you," Finn responded without hesitation. "So what are you going to do about it?"

The elevator dinged. The doors swished open.

A smile spread across Grant's face, his first real smile in days.

"I need your help."

CHAPTER SIXTEEN

ALEXANDRA STARED DOWN at the invitation on her desk. The embossed lettering glittered up at her, a sparkling reminder of the world she was no longer a part of.

Her fingers traced the S in "Santos." It wasn't the money or name brands or fancy cars she missed. No, it was the man she had fallen in love with not once but twice.

She swallowed past the tightness in her throat. How many people went an entire lifetime without experiencing the kind of love she had? How many would give anything to feel, just for a moment, the way Grant had made her feel? And here she was, on the verge of finally finding some stability with her dream career, moping and wishing for something else.

Was she still the same selfish, spoiled girl she'd been all those years ago? The one who had been too afraid to give up what she'd known for the unknown?

Her phone dinged. She picked it up, her heart plummeting as she read the text from her stepbrother.

Hey, sis. We had an offer to see a wedding venue tonight. Any chance one of your new employees could help with the delivery? I'm sorry, I'll make it up to you!

Seriously? She hadn't told Finn what had transpired between her and Grant in the Hamptons, but when she'd asked for him and Amanda to take care of setting up the flowers at the Met, he'd looked at her like he'd understood.

She sucked in a deep breath, then another, slowly calming her racing heart. Whether she liked it or not, she hadn't told Finn. He wasn't the one to blame.

She was. She'd been so hurt that Grant had jumped to the worst possible conclusion after eavesdropping on her conversation with Ellen. But then hadn't she proven him right? Instead of staying and fighting, instead of giving him a chance to share his viewpoint, she'd run.

Her eyes drifted back down to the invitation. No longer an innocuous piece of card stock, it taunted her, challenged her to prove to herself that she had truly changed. She wasn't under her father's thumb anymore. Nine years ago, even though fear had certainly played a part in her decision to give in to David's demands, she had genuinely believed herself powerless to stop him from sending Grant and his mother back to Brazil.

She had no such excuse now. Now she was allowing fear to rule her decision making.

The silver cursive flashed in the sunlight streaming in through the front window of her shop. The shop that would only be her home for another week before she moved into a new space just a few storefronts down from The Story Keeper. Harry Hill and his wife, Lucy, had visited her store and, after Lucy had tactfully inquired whether Alexandra was happy with her location, had offered her a lease on the spot for one of their numerous properties.

The brief rekindling of her romance with Grant may have gone down in flaming glory. But at least the rest of her life finally seemed to be sliding into place. A life she had worked hard for, risked so much for.

Wasn't Grant worth one more risk?

Determination strengthened her spirit. She would conduct herself as a professional and deliver the flowers, set them up, make sure that Grant's final event went off without a hitch. And, before she left tonight, she would tell him she loved him. If his fury in the Hamptons was any indicator, he wouldn't reciprocate with loving words of his own.

But she owed them both the truth. Owed him the knowledge that he was worth more to her than her fear.

She picked up her phone before she lost her nerve and texted back.

Not a problem. I'll take care of it.

Little bubbles popped up, disappeared and then another text appeared.

Great. Tonight's your night, sis.

She bit back the urge to laugh. Yeah, tonight would be a night to remember. If things went the way they had in the Hamptons, orders would be rolling in to The Flower Bell faster than she would be able to keep up. Toss in a new location in Greenwich Village and she would be set.

It would be the thing that kept her going after she offered up her bruised and battered heart for a third and, hopefully, final rendering.

She texted back with a smiley face that mocked the ache growing inside her chest.

Yeah, maybe you're right.

Alexandra wiped her palms on her pants as she glanced nervously around the grand hall in the museum. The gala wasn't supposed to start for another hour. The setting sun's rays lit up the hall and highlighted the reds, pinks, corals and ivories of the arrangements she'd created for tonight's event. The bright colors gave a nod to the spring season, while the timeless elegance of roses and peonies reinforced the Pearson Group's image: innovative and fearless, but also trustworthy and classy. Once the lights were dimmed and the silver votives lit, the flowers would pop against the backdrop of black tablecloths.

Her gaze darted around the hall, her heart thundering in her chest. She'd expected Grant to be there, overseeing every last detail. But she'd only seen Pamela's catering staff and Jessica, who marched around in her impossible stilettos wielding a tablet like a shield and her pen like a sword.

A sigh escaped. It was better this way. Dumping something as large as an apology entwined with a confession of love right before one of the biggest events of Grant's career was poor timing at best, and selfish at worst. Perhaps she could follow up with him next week, bring him a congratulations bouquet and tell him in the privacy of his office.

Or you could be a big girl and tell him you'd just like to talk to him instead of finding an excuse.

She brushed away the pesky internal voice and started to walk away.

"Miss Moss!"

Jessica's voice cracked across the hall with the power of a lightning bolt. Alexandra turned slowly, half expecting Jessica to smack her on the back of the hand with the tablet. Truly, the woman had missed her calling as a drill sergeant.

"Yes?"

Jessica surveyed the tables with a critical eye. Had

she thought Grant was the one she needed to impress? He might make the occasional recommendation, but it was the people like Jessica, the people who ran so much of what happened behind the scenes, that could make or break a business like hers.

Jessica's head snapped back around and she stared at Alexandra for a moment. And then she did the last thing Alexandra expected.

She smiled. A true smile that softened the harsher lines of her face and transformed her statuesque beauty into jaw-dropping gorgeousness.

"This looks wonderful, Miss Moss."

"Th-thank you."

"I was skeptical when you first came to the Carlson. But you've taken these events from cold, sterile presentations to warm, inviting events. Exactly the kind of atmosphere Mr. Santos, Ms. Jones and the other executives wanted to create for his clients." She glanced down at her watch. "Ms. Jones is taking care of a small emergency with the entertainment hired for the evening, but I sent her pictures of the arrangements. She's very pleased and would like to visit with you at a later date about upcoming events for the Pearson Group."

Alexandra returned her smile even as her heart jumped at the thought of continuing to work for Grant's company. She could do it, she told herself firmly, even if it hurt like hell.

"That means a great deal coming from you, Jessica. I know your standards, and Ms. Jones's, are exceptional. Meeting them makes me feel very proud of The Flower Bell."

Jessica arched a brow. "Which is great. But you should feel proud of yourself, too."

Warmth flooded Alexandra's chest. She'd often disassociated from The Flower Bell, referring to it instead of herself, afraid of developing the kind of ego that had led her father down his dark path. But, she acknowledged as she shook Jessica's hand, she'd poured a lot into her career. She'd worked hard, and her hard work was finally paying off.

"Thank you."

One perfectly sculpted eyebrow arched. "You've been good for him, too."

Alexandra outwardly froze, her effort to keep her face neutral at odds with her heartbeat accelerating into a gallop. "What?"

"He's more relaxed. Approachable. The Pearson Group is my third startup. He's very intelligent, as you know. But I worried that his focus on achieving his version of success would deter clients. I like the Mr. Santos I've seen the past couple weeks." Jessica grimaced. "Minus the sullen, grouchy fool he's been this past week."

A reluctant smile tugged at Alexandra's lips despite the ache building into her chest. She missed him. She missed his sharp wit and intelligence, his dry humor and encouragement. He was the only person who had never discouraged her, who had always told her she could do whatever she set her mind to.

"I messed up, Jessica."

The admission slipped out before she could stop it. But it was time; time to stop hiding behind who she used to be, behind her fears and self-loathing.

"It takes two, Alexandra." Jessica surprised her again by laying a comforting hand on her shoulder. "I wouldn't write off the past just yet."

With those enigmatic words hanging in the air, Jessica turned and marched off, the clicking of her heels echoing off the soaring ceilings.

Before Alexandra could begin to dissect what Jessica's cryptic message meant, her phone dinged. She pulled it out and frowned at the unfamiliar number.

Double-check the flower arrangements in the rooftop garden.

Perhaps Jessica had given her number to one of the museum staff? Or maybe Laura Jones had shared it with a member of her team. With a resigned sigh, Alexandra headed to the elevators. She wanted nothing more than to go home, sink into her old-fashioned claw-foot tub and relax in a warm bubble bath as she talked herself through how she would contact Grant and what she would say.

But she'd already netted several new contracts, including two weddings in addition to Ellen's, a New Year's Eve party and an anniversary celebration, which would keep The Flower Bell running long into the next year. Her initial goal of boosting the shop's profile had worked. Time to follow through, even if she felt like a tornado whirled inside her chest.

The elevator swooshed up, the doors opening to the Cantor Rooftop Garden Bar. Long white tables had been set up with matching chairs decorated with delicate strands of ivy. Café lights had been strung above the tables, creating an intimate glow against the backdrop of the greenery of Central Park and the New York City skyline standing proudly against the slowly pinkening sky as the sun began its descent toward the horizon.

Pride chased away some of the chaos reeling through her body. Small glass bowls full of roses offset by tiny clusters of white blooms softened the atmosphere of the cocktail tables. They also made sure the bouquets on the dinner tables, clusters of snapdragons, freesia, scented geraniums and other blooms with Brazil's national flower, the yellow ipê flower, at the heart of the arrangement took center stage.

When the sun set, the votive candles were lit and the lights of New York sparkled in the background, it would be perfect. She'd arranged to have the photographer, who would be floating around the event, take photos she could share on social media and her website later.

A quick walk-around revealed nothing wrong with the flowers. They stood tall and proud, leaves lush, petals unfurled into full bloom.

Probably just an overeager assistant, Alexandra thought as she walked back toward the elevator.

She pushed the button. Nothing happened. With a dejected sigh, she pushed it again. Still nothing. She walked over to the door that led to the stairs. The door stayed firmly shut.

Great. She was stuck on the roof of the Met Museum in jeans and a T-shirt with less than an hour before the event of the spring kicked off with some of the wealthiest prospective clients coming up in their finest couture to party the night away.

All under the discerning eye of the man she loved and whose heart she had broken not once, but twice.

Her heartbeat kicked into overdrive as she turned and looked around for an escape. Perhaps there was a fire ladder or some other way down.

Awareness whispered across her senses and sank into her skin. She inhaled and his subtle, sensual amber scent surrounded her.

"You locked the doors."

"I did."

His deep voice rolled through her body and filled her veins with its seductive warmth. It took every ounce of willpower not to whip around and throw herself into his arms, bury her face against his neck.

"You don't need to sound so smug."

She kept her eyes on the luxurious towers that comprised Billionaires' Row at the southern end of Central Park. The blue glass panels of one of the skyscrapers glittered under the golden glow of the setting sun, lights winking on in the various windows as people continued on with their lives, oblivious to the drama playing out just a couple miles away. If she kept her attention focused on anything but the man behind her, maybe she would make it through this encounter without embarrassing herself.

"I'm anything but smug right now."

The thin thread of vulnerability in his voice, almost, but not quite masked by his gruff tone, cut her to her core and ripped her from the present into the past. Back to a library filled with expensive books that had hardly been touched aside from a daily dusting by the housekeeping staff, a diamond chandelier turned up to a blinding brightness and her father sitting in his favorite straight-backed leather chair, his hands resting on the armrests as if he was seated on a throne.

Details she had fixated on to avoid the crushing pain flickering in the eyes of her lover. Pain replaced by cold, hard contempt when she'd stood her ground and echoed what her father had told her to say.

I don't love you. I never did. You were just a fling.

The words still tasted bitter on her tongue. Uncertainty crawled beneath her skin, settling in the pit of her stomach like a coiled snake about to strike. She'd caused him so much pain over the years. Was telling him now how she felt the right thing to do? Or was she setting him up for more heartbreak?

"You ran away."

His statement held no acrimony or accusation. More an observation, a probe.

She sucked in a deep breath. She owed him so much, including the truth.

"I did run away." She swallowed hard. "I'm sorry. I…" Another deep breath, and then she summoned every ounce of strength she had as she turned to face him.

God, I miss him.

The sight of him hit her like a freight train. He looked so unbearably handsome dressed in a burgundy dress shirt, sleeves rolled up to his elbows, displaying his tanned forearms. Arms that had cradled her so tenderly, had made her feel simultaneously strong and cherished. His black tuxedo pants were fitted to his muscular legs, stylish yet sexy.

And his face… Her fingers ached to trail over the strong line of his jaw, the sharply cut cheekbones, the broad swath of his forehead and into his thick black hair, smoothing the lines that had formed at the corners of his eyes as she told him that no matter what happened between them, he had done it. He had achieved everything he'd told her he would and more. She ached for the pain he'd suffered even as pride sang through her veins at all he had overcome.

How could he not see what an incredible man he'd been over the years, from novice gardener and aspiring entrepreneur to successful business professional? Would he ever see himself the way she saw him? Or would he always see himself as he had that horrific night in the library: a failure, a reject?

She steeled herself against her body's reaction to his presence. He'd brought up the topic of their relationship. She might as well say what she'd decided to say. Let the cards fall and, when he rejected her as she'd rejected him, she could go home and comfort herself with a hot bath and a very large glass of wine.

"I have some things I need to say."

CHAPTER SEVENTEEN

GRANT DEVOURED ALEXANDRA with his gaze, his eyes seeking out every detail he'd missed since he'd last seen her. The strands of dark mahogany hair falling from her ponytail and lying gently against her neck. The small upturn to her nose that added a hint of mischief to her beautiful face. And, most of all, the determined set of her lips, an outward sign of the strength she'd developed over the years. He'd loved her that summer, fallen so deeply in love he had never stopped loving her.

But the past couple of weeks, getting to know the woman Alexandra had become, had made him fall in love with her all over again. It wasn't just her courage but her compassion, her grace, her ability to find light in darkness. That she'd remade herself without any help from her father's legacy made him love and respect her all the more.

"I have some things I need to say."

Cold fear wrapped around his heart and squeezed. She'd said similar words nine years ago. Had he imagined what was developing between them? Or had he ruined it by jumping to conclusions and lashing out from pain and shame?

"As do I. Ladies first."

She bit down on her lower lip. The sight heated his

blood as he remembered her lips closing around him, driving him to within an inch of losing control. His hands curled into fists. It was the only way he stopped himself from reaching out and pulling her against him.

"I apologized recently for being a coward all those years ago. And then I turned around and behaved cowardly again."

Her voice caught. His heart tore.

"No, Alexandra, it wasn't—"

"Don't make excuses for me." She turned away and walked to the wall of the garden, crossing her arms against a light breeze, her back ramrod straight. "When you thought I had rejected you again, I was so hurt. Even a little angry."

I know.

"But how could you not think that of me?" He could feel the doubts overtake her, saw it in the droop of her head, hear it as her voice dropped to a self-deprecating whisper. It cut through him like a knife. "After I let my father ruin what we had...after I didn't stand up for us..."

He closed the distance between them in seconds. His hands wrapped around her waist, spinning her around to face him. Her lips parted in surprise just before he cupped her face in one hand and kissed her.

He poured everything into his kiss: his love, his regret, his passion, his hope. For a moment she didn't respond and his grip on her tightened. If she turned him away, if it was too late, at least he would have this one last moment.

And then she came alive beneath his touch, her mouth opening to his caress, her arms wrapping around his neck as she pressed her body against his and moaned his name.

He wanted nothing more than to keep kissing her, to imprint his touch on her and claim her as his once and for all.

Soon.

He pulled back and rested his forehead on hers, gratified that her breath was just as harsh and fractured as his.

"Alexandra, you were nineteen. You were nineteen and innocent and under the thumb of an abusive, manipulative man." His hands slid around to her back and he pressed her close, wishing he could absorb all the pain David Waldsworth had caused her over the years. "I knew something was wrong that day. I knew you better than anyone else, and I walked away." His voice roughened as he tilted her chin up so she could look him square in the eye. "*I* walked away. I left you. Because I was hurt and embarrassed and let my damn pride keep me from seeing what was really going on. I left you, and carrying our child…" He paused, swallowed hard. "I left you both to that monster. And now, when I had a second chance at a future with you, I nearly let that same pride chase you away again."

Her hands flew up and clasped his face, tears sparkling in her eyes.

"Don't you dare take responsibility for this. I made mistakes, too."

He threw back his head and laughed.

"Are we going to stand here and argue about who is more at fault, or are you going to let me tell you that I love you?"

Her eyes widened as a cautious hope brightened their hazel depths.

"You…you love me?"

"I never stopped. Is it too much to hope that you—?"

She jumped and wrapped her legs around his waist, burying her face against his neck as she began to cry.

"Alexandra…"

"They're happy tears!" She leaned back and gave him

a smile so radiant it rivaled the lights of New York City. "I love you, Grant. I love you, and I came here tonight to tell you. I know I'm stronger and more capable, but if I couldn't take the risk of telling you how I felt, then none of what I've done the last nine years matters—"

"It matters," Grant interrupted hotly. "Alexandra, the woman you've become, all the things you've accomplished—"

"Hey, the same applies to you!" she interrupted, her brow furrowing. "How dare you question what you've built? You've done everything you ever set out to achieve. The Pearson Group is going to be a monumental success and one of the most trusted financial firms in the city."

"But also one that puts people first." He kissed the tip of her nose. "Because of you. I had become so fixated on numbers, on milestones, that I nearly became what I hated. I wanted the title of billionaire so badly while you were barely scraping by and still making donations to the victims' fund."

Alexandra ducked her head, a becoming blush stealing over her cheeks.

"How did you know?"

"Your stepbrother told me."

She frowned. "Finn? When did you talk to…?" Her voice trailed off and she muttered something under her breath. "That little toad! He was in on this whole thing, wasn't he?"

"Not the spoiled brat I used to think him. He was very amenable when I asked how best to get you here." He pressed his forehead against hers. "It's also when he told me all the incredible things you've done over the years."

Twin spots of red bloomed in her cheeks.

"Donating was the right thing to do."

"And I love that about you." He pressed another kiss

to her forehead. "It's why I made a donation to the fund and brought the total compensation up to one hundred percent yesterday."

Alexandra's mouth dropped open. "But that…that was several hundred million! What about your billion-dollar goal?"

"I'll reach it someday. This was more important than some arbitrary benchmark." His fingers slid into her hair, gently combing through the silky strands. "You make me want to be the man you fell in love with that summer, Alexandra. To be worthy of your love."

Fear flickered across her face as she unwrapped her legs and slid down his body. He sucked in a breath, willing himself to stay focused on their conversation.

"I don't feel worthy. I feel…scared."

"Scared?"

"Scared I'm going to let you down again. Or myself. Or both."

He kept one hand in her hair, the other resting gently yet possessively on the back of her neck.

"Do you love me, Alexandra?"

"With all my heart."

"And I love you. One of the mistakes I made that summer was putting you up on a pedestal, one so high you would have fallen off at some point. That was my fault, not yours," he said as she started to interrupt him. "Yes, you made mistakes, but I did, too. Yet, here we are, both willing to forgive, both still in love and, I hope, still wanting to move forward. Together."

Her lips slowly stretched into a smile.

"Together sounds very nice."

"Good." He released her and stepped back, then dropped to one knee. Her gasp filled him with pleasure as he reached into his back pocket and pulled out a small navy box. He flipped the lid to reveal a green tourmaline ring, diamonds winking up at them from silver roses carved into the band.

"Alexandra Moss, would you do me the honor of becoming my wife?"

She hesitated. "Grant, I want... Lucy Hill was so kind to me when she found out who I was. But what if there are others who aren't so forgiving? I don't want to hurt you."

"Then they're not worth a place in my life. Not if they can't see you for who you are." His voice softened. "Alexandra, you are one of the strongest people I know, if not the strongest. Don't let fear stop you now. We can do this. Together."

The last vestiges of worry eased from her body. Tears fell once more, but the smile that accompanied them made his heart nearly burst from his chest.

"Yes, Grant. I would be honored to be your—"

He surged to his feet and cut her off with a kiss that nearly burned the clothes from their bodies. His hands drifted down, cupped her rear and pressed her flush against his growing hardness.

"Grant... I want...your guests..."

"Damn." He glanced back at the closed door and then down at his watch. "Unfortunately, we don't have time to celebrate properly before they arrive. But I expect you to come home with me afterward so I can show you just how happy your answer has made me."

With a sly quirk of one eyebrow, her hand slid between their bodies and settled on his hard length, the material of his pants the only barrier between his body and her sultry caress.

"I noticed."

"Devil woman," he whispered with a playful nip at

her lips. "Since we can't leave now, you might as well open your gift."

"You're more than enough," she replied with an answering kiss.

Reluctantly, he released her and moved over to the door to the staircase, unlocking and opening it to reveal a white box tied with a red bow sitting on the top step. He set it on one of the tables.

"Open it."

Alexandra gave him a shy smile that made him resolve to buy her a gift at least once a week, just so he could see the look of excitement on her face. It could be a seashell or a flower or a book. Knowing her, just the fact that he had thought of her would be enough.

But this, he knew as he watched her lift the lid with anticipation and brush aside the tissue paper, this was something even more special.

Alexandra's mouth dropped open as she pulled the sage green gown from the box.

"Grant...it's..."

"Yours."

Her gaze flew up to his, tears making her eyes glisten. "You bought everything for me, didn't you? The dresses, the jewelry?"

"Yes." One hand came up, his fingers tracing the curve of her face. "You deserve so much, Alexandra."

She held the gown up against her body, her fingers drifting over the smooth crepe fabric in wonder.

"Jessica included something in the bottom."

"Jessica was in on this, too?" Alexandra chuckled. "I never..." Her voice trailed off as she pulled out a pair of transparent heels studded with tiny flickering diamonds. "I can't believe she remembered. I didn't even think she was really listening."

"She was. She told me she knew you would put the money you were earning back into your business instead of spending it on yourself. It was one of the many things she listed as a reason for why I needed to do whatever it took to get you back when I told her what I had planned for tonight."

He moved to her, savoring the heat that kindled in her eyes as she looked up at him.

"I would be honored if you would wear the dress, the shoes and the ring," he added as he pulled the ring from the box still clutched in his hand and slid it onto her finger, "when I announce our engagement tonight."

She started to laugh.

"Is this real? Or am I dreaming I'm in a fairy tale and I'm going to wake up?"

He pulled her close and lowered his head.

"As real as it gets. And not a day goes by that I won't remind you how lucky I am to have you in my life."

With that promise lingering in the spring air, he closed his lips over hers and claimed his runaway Cinderella with a kiss that let her know he would never let her go again.

EPILOGUE

Three years later

GRANT RAISED HIS head off the beach towel, a smile crossing his face as the soft babbles of his daughter reached his ears. Carla splashed happily in the shallow waters of the Atlantic as gentle waves lapped against the Brazilian beach. Alexandra sat next to her, scooping wet puddles of sand onto Carla's chubby thighs with one hand and adjusting their daughter's sun hat with the other.

The past three years had whipped by so quickly, sometimes Grant could hardly believe they'd happened. Their engagement had generated a surprising amount of positive press, and Jessica's quiet leaks to the media that Alexandra had been living off her own financial means and donating to the fund that had reimbursed her father's victims, along with Grant's own donation, had smoothed the majority of ruffled feathers. The few who hadn't been able to look past who Alexandra's father was had faded into the background. Grant had kept his promise; he had no interest in doing business with anyone who treated Alexandra like a second-class citizen because of the unfortunate stroke of fate that had seen her born to a man like David Waldsworth. Their intimate October wedding had been followed by the Christmas news that he was going to be a father. Seven months later Carla had entered the world with a healthy wail and beautiful green-gold eyes just like her mother.

He hadn't thought it possible to be any happier than he already was. But life with his wife and daughter had brought him more joy than he had ever experienced.

The Pearson Group had launched the night Alexandra had said yes to his proposal and quickly taken New York City by storm. Less than a year after its launch, Grant's personal net worth had soared past one billion dollars.

And he couldn't care less, he thought as he watched Alexandra pull Carla into her lap and press a salty kiss to her cheek. Alexandra had reminded him of who he used to be and what really mattered. Yes, the Pearson Group was important, but funneling money into causes they cared about, from establishing a fund for up-and-coming entrepreneurs in New York City to sending money to communities in Brazil, had become his focus. One that Alexandra, when she wasn't designing the latest wedding bouquets and centerpieces for the Big Apple's elite, helped him with.

That and making several trips throughout the year back to Brazil. Coming home, seeing his family for the first time in two decades, watching his mother blossom as she'd walked up and down the streets of her former home, had been a balm to his soul. The pain of losing his father would never fully heal. But with Alexandra by his side and the heat of a Brazilian sun warming his skin, life was better than he had ever thought possible.

Alexandra looked up, her eyes darkening as she caught Grant's gaze and gave him a saucy wink.

Thank God they had visited Brazil in the off season, when the beaches were all but empty. Otherwise, his body's uncontrolled reaction to the flirtatious smile lurking on her lips would be on display for the world to see.

"What time does your mother arrive?" Alexandra asked as she picked Carla up and bounced her on her hip.

Grant's eyes traveled over her trim frame encased in a ruby-red one-piece, her tan legs glowing under the morning sun. Legs that had been wrapped around his waist last night as he'd thrust into her, her body draped over the edge of the pool, head back as she'd tried, and failed, to keep her cries from escaping past her lips. A problem he'd been happy to solve as he'd kissed her and swallowed her moans of pleasure as he'd followed her over the top and into explosive bliss.

"Five o'clock. And Finn and Amanda and their brood arrive tomorrow. Between our little goblin and Finn's twins, my mother will be in baby heaven," Grant said with a smile as he sat up and held out his arms. His smile grew as Alexandra passed him twenty-eight pounds of wet, sandy toddler. Carla jabbered at him and wrapped her hands around one of his fingers.

"Maybe Carla would like to spend some time with her *Avó* Jordana tonight and we could go out for dinner."

He arched a suggestive eyebrow at her. "Is that code for something?"

Alexandra playfully swatted at his thigh as she sat down on a towel next to him. "No. I was just thinking we should take advantage while we can. It'll be a lot harder to go out when there are two kids."

"I can…"

His voice trailed off as her words sank in. His head whipped around, his chest expanding as he took in her radiant smile.

"You're…" His eyes drifted down to her stomach, then back to her face. "Really?"

"Probably close to seven weeks."

He reached over, snaked an arm around her waist, pulled her across the sand onto his towel and kissed her long and hard.

"I kiss Daddy!"

Grant pulled back just as Carla threw her arms around his neck and planted a sandy kiss on his cheek. Grant threw back his head and laughed as Alexandra snuggled into his side.

"I was wrong," he said as he kissed first the top of his daughter's head and then his wife's.

"Oh?"

"I think we're living in a fairy tale."

* * * * *

COMING SOON!

We really hope you enjoyed reading this book.
If you're looking for more romance, be sure to
head to the shops when new books are
available on

Thursday 2nd February

MILLS & BOON®

Coming next month

THE HOUSEKEEPER'S INVITATION TO ITALY
Cathy Williams

"I'm not following you. Where is he going to move to? London? Leonard has always told me how much he hates London."

"Not that he's actually been there more than a handful of times," Alessio returned drily. "But no. London wasn't what I had in mind."

"Then where?"

"I have a place at Lake Garda in northern Italy. It's close enough to get there on my private jet in a matter of hours so the trip shouldn't be too taxing for him."

"Oh, right. Okay."

"If we plan on leaving in roughly a week's time, it will give me sufficient time to get the ball rolling with the company so that I can install some of my own people to tie up all the loose ends. I'll also have enough time for my PA to source the best crew available to get this job done here and of course, there will have to be time spent packing away anything valuable that needs to be protected. I suggest several of the more robust rooms in the West Wing would be suitable for that."

"Wait, hang on just a minute! We...?"

Continue reading
THE HOUSEKEEPER'S INVITATION TO ITALY
Cathy Williams

Available next month
www.millsandboon.co.uk

MILLS & BOON

THE HEART OF ROMANCE

A ROMANCE FOR EVERY READER

MODERN

Prepare to be swept off your feet by sophisticated, sexy and seductive heroes, in some of the world's most glamourous and romantic locations, where power and passion collide.

HISTORICAL

Escape with historical heroes from time gone by. Whether your passion is for wicked Regency Rakes, muscled Vikings or rugged Highlanders, awaken the romance of the past.

MEDICAL

Set your pulse racing with dedicated, delectable doctors in the high-pressure world of medicine, where emotions run high and passion, comfort and love are the best medicine.

True Love

Celebrate true love with tender stories of heartfelt romance, from the rush of falling in love to the joy a new baby can bring, and a focus on the emotional heart of a relationship.

Desire

Indulge in secrets and scandal, intense drama and plenty of sizzling hot action with powerful and passionate heroes who have it all: wealth, status, good looks…everything but the right woman.

HEROES

Experience all the excitement of a gripping thriller, with an intense romance at its heart. Resourceful, true-to-life women and strong, fearless men face danger and desire - a killer combination!

To see which titles are coming soon, please visit

millsandboon.co.uk/nextmonth

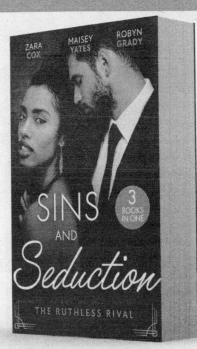

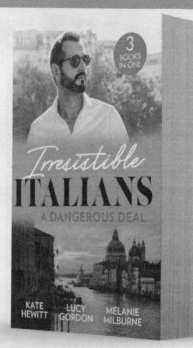